Formerly a video and radi̶ now spends her time writing provocative, passionate, seductive romance. When she's not writing, she can be found enjoying life with her husband and three children, walking for pleasure, and researching other people's deepest secrets and desires.

Author of more than one hundred novels, **Gina Wilkins** loves exploring complex interpersonal relationships and the universal search for 'a safe place to call home.' Her books have appeared on numerous bestseller lists, and she was a nominee for a lifetime achievement award from *RT* magazine. A lifelong resident of Arkansas, she credits her writing career to a nagging imagination, a book-loving mother, an encouraging husband and three 'extraordinary' offspring.

Shirley Hailstock likes to explore new worlds and visit exotic places. As an author, she can visit those places, and be the heroine of her own stories. The author of over thirty novels and novellas, Shirley has received numerous awards. Her books have appeared on *BlackBoard*, *Essence*, and *Library Journal* bestseller lists. She is a past president of Romance Writers of America.

Fake Dating:

Home for Christmas

CHRISTY McKELLEN

GINA WILKINS

SHIRLEY HAILSTOCK

MILLS & BOON

First Published in Great Britain 2023
by Mills & Boon, an imprint of HarperCollins*Publishers* Ltd,
1 London Bridge Street, London, SE1 9GF

www.harpercollins.co.uk

HarperCollins*Publishers*
Macken House, 39/40 Mayor Street Upper,
Dublin 1, D01 C9W8, Ireland

Fake Dating: Home for Christmas © 2023 Harlequin Enterprises ULC.

A Countess for Christmas © 2016 Harlequin Enterprises ULC.
The Boss's Marriage Plan © 2015 Gina Wilkins
Someone Like You © 2014 Shirley Hailstock

Special thanks and acknowledgement are given to Christy McKellen for her contribution to the *Maids Under the Mistletoe* series.

ISBN: 978-0-263-32040-4

This book is produced from independently certified FSC™ paper
to ensure responsible forest management.

For more information visit: www.harpercollins.co.uk/green

Printed and Bound in the UK using 100% Renewable Electricity
at CPI Group (UK) Ltd, Croydon, CR0 4YY

A COUNTESS FOR CHRISTMAS

CHRISTY McKELLEN

This one's for all my wonderful friends, especially Alice, Karen and Sophie, my best buddies since our school days, and for the fabulous ladies writing this continuity with me, Kandy, Scarlet, and Jessica, who I'm also privileged to call my friends.

CHAPTER ONE

THIS HAD TO be the most challenging party that Emma Carmichael had ever worked at.

As fabulous as the setting was—a grand Chelsea town house that had been interior designed to within an inch of its life, presiding over the genteel glamour of Sloane Square—the party itself felt stilted and lifeless.

The trouble was, Emma mused as she glided inconspicuously through the throng, handing out drinks to the primped and polished partygoers, it was full of people who attended parties for a living rather than for pleasure, in an attempt to rub shoulders with London's great and good.

She knew all about that type of party after being invited to a glut of them in her late teens, either with her parents or with friends from her private girls' school in Cambridge. But she'd been a very different person then, pampered and carefree. Those privileged days were long gone now though, along with her darling late father's reputation and all their family's money.

As if her thoughts had conjured up the demons that had plagued her for the six years following his death, her phone vibrated in her pocket and she discreetly slipped it out and glanced at it, only to see it was another text message from her last remaining creditor reminding her she was late with her final repayment. Stomach sinking, she shoved the phone back into her pocket and desperately tried to reinstate the cheerful smile that her boss, Jolyon Fitzherbert, expected his staff to wear at all times.

'Emma, a word! Over here!' came the peremptory tones of the man himself from the other side of the room.

Darn. Busted.

Turning, she met her boss's narrowed eyes and swallowed hard as he beckoned her over to where he stood holding court to a small group of guests with one elbow propped jauntily against the vulgar marble fireplace.

Emma had encountered the bunch of reprobates he was with a number of times since she'd begun working for Jolyon two months ago so she was well used to their contemptuous gazes that slid over her face as she approached now. They didn't believe in fraternising with the hired help.

If only Jolyon felt the same.

It was becoming harder and harder to avoid his wandering hands and suggestive gaze, especially when she found herself alone with him. So far she'd been politely cool and it seemed to have held him at bay, but as soon as he got a couple of drinks into him dodging his advances became a whole lot harder.

Fighting down her apprehension, she gave Jolyon a respectful nod and smile as she came to a halt in front of him.

'Can I be of service?'

Jolyon's eyes seemed to bulge with menace in his flushed face. 'I do hope I didn't just see you playing with your mobile phone when you're supposed to be serving these good people, Emma, because that would be rude and unprofessional, would it not?' he drawled.

Emma's stomach rolled with unease. 'Er—yes. I mean no, I wasn't—' She could feel heat creeping up her neck as the whole group stared at her with ill-disguised disdain. 'I was just checking—'

'I'm sure you think you're too good to be serving drinks to the likes of us—' Jolyon said loudly over the top of her, layering his voice with haughty sarcasm.

'No, of course not—'

The expression on his face was now half leer, half snarl. '—but since I'm paying you to be here, I expect to have your full attention.'

'Yes, of course, Jolyon. You absolutely have it,' Emma said, somehow managing to dredge up a smile, despite the sickening pull of humiliation dragging her spirits down towards the floor.

He eyed her with an unnerving twinkle of malice in his expression, as if he was getting a thrill out of embarrassing her. 'In that case I'll have a large whisky.'

Emma opened her mouth to ask whether anyone else in the group required anything, but before the words could emerge Jolyon flapped a dismissive hand in her face and barked, 'Go on, fetch!'

Stumbling backwards, stupefied by his rudeness, she gave him a jerky nod and turned away, mortification flooding her whole body with unwelcome heat.

Twisting the chain she always wore around her neck to remind her of better times—before everything in her life had gone to hell in a hand basket—

she took a deep, calming breath as she walked stiffly over to where Jolyon kept his whisky decanter in an antique burr walnut drinks cabinet. Pouring his regular measure of two fingers of the dark amber liquid into a cut-glass tumbler with a shaking hand, she managed to slosh a little over the rim and had to surreptitiously wipe it off the wood with her apron so she didn't get shouted at for not treating his furniture with due respect.

That was the most frustrating thing about working for Jolyon; he treated *her* with less respect than an inanimate object and all she could do was bite her lip and get on with it.

Clio Caldwell, who ran the high-end agency Maids in Chelsea that had found her this housekeeping position, had warned her that Jolyon was a difficult character when she'd offered her the job, but since he also paid extremely well Emma had decided she was prepared to handle his irascible outbursts and overly tactile ways if she was well remunerated for it. If she could just stick it out here for a little while longer she'd be in the position to pay off the last of her father's debts and be able to put this whole sordid business to bed, then she could finally move on with her life.

What a relief that would be.

Out of nowhere the old familiar grief hit her hard in the chest.

Some days she missed her father so much her heart throbbed with pain. What she wouldn't give to have him back again, enveloping her in a great big bear hug and telling her that everything was going to be okay, that she was loved and that he wouldn't let anything hurt her.

But she knew she was being naïve. All the years he'd been telling her that, he'd actually been racking up astronomical debts. The life that she'd once believed was real and safe had evaporated into thin air the moment she'd lost him to a sudden heart attack and her mother had promptly fallen apart, leaving her to deal with a world of grief and uncertainty on her own.

Gripping the tumbler so hard her knuckles cracked, she returned to where her boss stood. 'Here you go, Jolyon,' she said calmly.

He didn't even look at her, just took the glass from her outstretched hand and turned his back on her, murmuring something to the man next to him, who let out a low guffaw and gave Emma the most fleeting of glances.

It reminded her all too keenly of the time right after her father's funeral when she couldn't go anywhere without being gossiped about and stared at with a mixture of pity and condescension.

Forcing herself to ignore the old familiar sting of angry defensiveness, she plastered a nonchalant smile onto her face and dashed back to the kitchen, and sanctuary.

Stumbling in through the door, she let out a sigh of relief, taking a moment to survey the scene and to centre herself, feeling her heart rate begin to slow down now that she was back in friendly company.

She didn't want anyone in here to see how shaken up she was, not when she was supposed to be the one in charge of running the party. After years of handling difficult situations on her own she was damned if she was going to fall apart now.

Fortunately, Clio at the agency had come up trumps

with the additional waiting staff for the party today. Two of the girls, Sophie and Grace, had become firm friends of hers after they'd all found themselves working at a lot of the same events throughout the last year. Before meeting these two it had been a long time since Emma had had friends that she could laugh with so easily. The very public scandal surrounding her father's enormous debts had put paid to a lot of what she'd thought were solid friendships in the past—owing someone's family an obscene amount of money would do that to a relationship, it seemed, especially within the censorious societal set in which she used to circulate.

Sophie, a bubbly blonde with a generous smile and a quick wit, had brought along an old school friend of hers tonight too, a cute-as-a-button Australian who was visiting England for a few months called Ashleigh, whose glossy mane of chestnut-red hair shone so radiantly under the glaring kitchen lights it was impossible to look away from her.

During short breaks in serving the partygoers that evening, the four of them had bonded while having a good giggle at some of the entitled behaviour they'd witnessed.

Emma's mirth had been somewhat tainted though, by the memory of how she'd acted much the same way when she was younger and how ashamed she felt now about taking her formerly privileged life so much for granted.

'Hey, lovely ladies,' she said, joining them at the kitchen counter where they were all busying about, filling fresh glasses with pink champagne and mojitos for the demanding guests.

'Hey, Emma, I was just telling Ashleigh how much fun it was, working at the Snowflake Ball last New Year's Eve,' Sophie said, making her eyebrows dance with delight. 'Are you working there again this year? Please say yes!'

'I hope so, as long as Jolyon agrees to give me the time off. He's supposed to be going skiing in Banff, so I should be free for it,' Emma said, shooting her friend a hopeful smile.

The annual New Year's Snowflake Ball was a glittering and awe-inspiring event that the whole of Chelsea society turned out for. Last year she and the girls had enjoyed themselves immensely from the wings after serving the guests with the most delectable— and eye-wateringly expensive—food and drink that London had to offer. Caught up in the romance of it all, Emma had even allowed herself to fantasise along with the others about how perhaps they'd end up attending as guests one day, instead of as waiting staff.

Not that there was a snowflake's chance in hell of that happening any time soon, not with her finances in their current state.

'Are you ladies working there too?' Emma asked, bouncing her gaze from Sophie to Grace, then on to Ashleigh.

Grace, a willowy, strikingly pretty woman who wore a perpetual air of no-nonsense purpose like a warm but practical coat, flashed her a grin. 'Wouldn't miss it for the world. You should definitely let Clio know if you're interested, Ashleigh.' She turned to give the bright-eyed redhead an earnest look. 'I know she's looking for smart, dedicated people to work at that event. She'd snap you up in a second.'

'Yeah, I might. I'm supposed to be going back to Australia to spend Christmas with my folks, but I don't know if I can face it,' Ashleigh said, self-consciously smoothing a strand of hair behind her ear. 'It's not going to be much of a celebratory atmosphere if I'm constantly trying to avoid being in the same room as my ex-fiancé the whole time.'

'He's going to be at your parents' house for Christmas?' Grace asked, aghast. 'Wow. Awkward.'

'Yeah, just a bit,' Ashleigh said, shuffling on the spot. 'If I do stay here I'm going to have to find another place to live though. I'm only booked into the B and B until the beginning of December, which means I've got less than a month to find new digs.' She glanced at them all, her eyes wide with hope. 'Anyone looking for a roomie by any chance? I'll take a floor, a sofa, whatever you've got!'

'Sorry, sweetheart,' Sophie said, shaking her head so her long sleek hair swished across her shoulders. 'As you know, my tiny bedroom's barely big enough for the single mattress I have in it and with my living area doubling as my dressmaking studio I can't even see the sofa under all the boxes of cloth and sewing materials.' She smiled grimly. 'And even if I could, it's on its last legs and not exactly comfortable.'

The other girls shook their heads too.

'I can't help either, Ashleigh, I'm afraid,' Emma said. 'My mother's staying with me on and off at the minute while her place in France is being damp proofed and redecorated and I don't think her nerves would take having someone she doesn't know kipping on the sofa. She's a little highly strung like that.'

'No worries,' Ashleigh said, batting a hand even

though her shoulders remained tense, 'I'm sure something will turn up.'

One of the other waitresses came banging into the kitchen then, looking harassed.

'Emma, the guests are starting to complain about running out of drinks out there.'

'On it,' Emma said, picking up a tray filled with the drinks that Grace had been diligently pouring throughout their conversation and backing out through the swinging kitchen door with it.

'Later, babes.'

Turning round to face the party, readying herself to put on her best and most professional smile again, her gaze alighted on a tall male figure that she'd not noticed before on the other side of the room. There was an intense familiarity about him that shot an unsettling feeling straight to her stomach.

It was something about the breadth of his back and the way his hair curled a little at his nape that set her senses on high alert. The perfect triangle of his body, which led her gaze down to long, long legs, was her idea of the perfect male body shape.

A shape she knew as well as her own and a body she'd once loved very, very much.

Blood began to pump wildly through her veins.

The shape and body of Jack Westwood, Earl of Redminster.

The man in question turned to speak to someone next to him, revealing his profile and confirming her instincts.

It was him.

Prickly heat cascaded over her skin as she stared

with a mixture of shock and nervous excitement at the man she'd not set eyes on for six years.

Ever since her life had fallen apart around her.

Taking a step backwards, she looked wildly around her for some kind of cover to give her a moment to pull herself together, but other than dashing back to the kitchen, which she couldn't do without drawing attention to herself, there wasn't any.

What was he doing here? He was supposed to be living in the States heading up the billion-dollar global electronics empire he'd left England to set up six years ago.

At the age of twenty-one he'd been dead set on making a name for himself outside the aristocratic life he'd been born into and had been determined not to trade on the family name but to make a success of himself through hard work and being the best in his field. From what she'd read in the press it seemed he'd been very successful at it too. But then she'd always known he would be. The man positively exuded power and intelligence from every pore.

After reading in the papers that his grandfather had died recently she'd wondered whether he'd come back to England.

It looked as if she had her answer.

He was surrounded, as ever, by a gaggle of beautiful women, all looking at him as if he was the most desirable man on earth. It had always been that way with him; he drew women to him like bees to a honeypot. The first time she'd ever laid eyes on him, at the tender age of twelve, he'd been surrounded by girls desperate for his attention. His sister, Clare—her best friend from her exclusive day school—had laughed and rolled her eyes about it, but Emma knew she loved her brother deeply and was in awe of his charisma.

Emma, on the other hand, had spent years feeling rattled and annoyed by his unjustified judgemental sniping at her and for a long time she'd thought he truly disliked her. Her greatest frustration at that point in her life was not being able to work out why.

As she watched, still frozen to the spot, one of the women in his group leaned towards him, laying a possessive hand on his arm as she murmured something into his ear, and Emma's heart gave an extra-hard squeeze.

Was he with her?

The thought made her stomach roll with nausea.

Feeling as though she'd stepped into the middle of one of her nightmares, she took a tentative pace sideways, hoping to goodness he wouldn't choose that exact moment to turn around and see her standing there wearing her Maids in Chelsea apron, holding a tray of drinks.

'Hey, you, don't just stand there gawping, missy, bring me one of those drinks. I'm parched!' one of Jolyon's most obstreperous acquaintances shouted over to her.

Face flaming, Emma sidestepped towards him, keeping Jack's broad back in her peripheral vision, hoping, *praying*, he wouldn't spot her.

Unfortunately, because she wasn't paying full attention to where she was stepping, she managed to stand on the toe of the woman talking with Mr Shouty, who then gave out a loud squeal of protest, flinging her arms out and catching the underside of the tray Emma was holding. Before she had a chance to save it, the entire tray filled with fine crystal glasses and their lurid contents flipped up into the air, then rained down onto the beige carpet that Jolyon had had laid only the week before.

Gaudy-coloured alcohol splattered the legs of the man standing nearby and a deathly silence fell, swiftly followed by a wave of amused chatter and tittering in its wake.

Emma dropped to her knees, desperately trying to save the fine crystal glasses from being trampled underfoot, feeling the sticky drinks that now coated the carpet soak into her skirt and tights.

All she needed now was for Jolyon to start shouting at her in front of Jack and her humiliation would be complete.

Glancing up through the sea of legs, desperate to catch the eye of a friendly face so she could escape quickly, her stomach flipped as her gaze connected with a pair of the most striking eyes she'd ever known.

Jack Westwood was staring at her, his brow creased into a deep frown and the expression on his face as shocked as she suspected hers had been to see him only moments ago.

Heart thumping, she tore her gaze away from his, somehow managing to pile the glasses haphazardly back onto the tray with shaking hands, then stand up and push her way through the agitated crowd, back to the safety of the kitchen.

'Sorry! Sorry!' she muttered as she shuffled past people. 'I'll be back in a moment to clean up the mess. Please mind your feet in case there's any broken glass.'

Her voice shook so much she wouldn't have been surprised if nobody had understood a word she'd said.

Please let him think he just imagined it was me. Please, please!

As she stumbled into the kitchen the first person she saw was Grace.

'Oh, my goodness, Emma! What happened?'

Her friend darted towards her, relieving her of the drinks tray with its precariously balanced glasses.

Grabbing the worktop for support, Emma took a couple of deep breaths before turning to face her friend's worried expression.

'Emma? Are you okay? You're as white as a sheet,' Sophie gasped, also alerted by her dramatic entrance. 'Did someone say something to you? Did they hurt you?' From the mixture of fear and anger on Sophie's face, Emma suspected her friend had some experience in that domain.

'No, no, it's nothing like that.' She swallowed hard, desperately grasping for some semblance of cool, but all her carefully crafted control seemed to have deserted her the moment she'd spotted Jack.

'There's someone here—someone I haven't seen for a very long time,' she said, her voice wobbling with emotion.

He'd always had this effect on her, turning her brain to jelly and her heart to goo, and after six long years without hearing the deep rumble of his voice or catching sight of his breathtaking smile or breathing in his heady, utterly beguiling scent her body seemed to have gone into a frenzy of longing for him.

'I wasn't expecting to see him, that's all. It took me by surprise,' she finished, forcing a smile onto her face.

The girls didn't look convinced by her attempt at

upbeat nonchalance, which wasn't surprising considering she was still visibly trembling.

'So when you say "him",' Ashleigh said, with a shrewd look in her eye, 'I'm guessing we're talking about an ex here?'

Emma nodded and looked away, not wanting to be drawn into giving them the painful details about what had happened between her and Jack. She needed to be able to do her job here tonight, or risk being fired, and if she talked about him now there was a good chance she'd lose her grip on her very last thread of calm.

'It's okay, I can handle it, but I managed to drop a whole tray of drinks out there. The carpet's absolutely covered in booze right by the camel-coloured sofa and I managed to spray the legs of a partygoer as well. He didn't seem entirely pleased to be showered in pink champagne.' She let out a shaky laugh.

'Don't worry, Emma, we'll cover it,' Grace said, putting a reassuring hand on her arm. 'Sophie, find a cloth to mop up as much of the liquid as possible, will you?'

'Will do,' Sophie said, swivelling on the spot and heading over to the broom cupboard where all the cleaning materials were kept.

'Ashleigh—'

'I'll get another tray of drinks out there right now and go and flirt with the guy you splattered with booze,' Ashleigh cut in with a smile, first at Emma, then at Grace.

'Great,' Grace said, grinning back. 'Emma, go and sit down with your head between your knees until your colour returns.'

'But—' Emma started to protest, but Grace put her

hands on her shoulders and gently pushed her back towards one of the kitchen chairs.

Emma sat down gratefully, relieved that everything was being taken care of but experiencing a rush of embarrassment at causing so much trouble for her friends.

After a moment of sitting quietly, her heart rate had almost returned to normal and the feeling that she was about to pass out had receded.

She was just about to stand up and get back out there, determined not to shy away from this, but to deal with Jack's reappearance head-on, when Sophie came striding back into the kitchen.

'You look better,' she said, giving Emma an assessing once-over.

'Yeah, I'm okay now. Ready to get back out there.'

'You know, you could stay in the kitchen and orchestrate things from here if you want. We can handle keeping all the guests happy out there.'

Emma sighed, grateful to her friend for the offer, but knowing that hiding wasn't an option.

'Thanks, but I can't stay in here all evening. Jolyon expects me to be out there charming his guests and keeping a general eye on things.' Rubbing a hand over her forehead, she gave her friend a smile, which she hoped came across with more confidence than she felt.

'Okay, well, let's fix your hair a bit, then,' Sophie said, moving towards her with her hands outstretched. 'We'll get it out of that restricting band and you can use it to shield your face if you need to hide for a second.'

Grateful for her friend's concern, Emma let Sophie gently pull out the band that was holding her up-do neatly away from her face so that her long sheet of hair swung down to cover each side of her face.

'It's such a beautiful colour—baby blonde,' Sophie said appreciatively, her gaze sweeping from one side of Emma's face to the other. 'Is it natural?'

Emma nodded, feeling gratified warmth flood her cheeks. 'Yes, thank goodness. I'd never be able to afford the hairdressing bills.' Her thoughts flew back to how much money she used to waste on expensive haircuts in her pampered youth and she cringed as she considered what she could do with that money now—things like putting it towards the cost of more night classes and studying materials.

The kitchen door banged open, making them both jump, and Emma's gaze zeroed in on the puce-coloured face of Jolyon Fitzherbert as he advanced towards her.

'Emma! What's going on? Why are you skulking in here when you should be out there making sure my party's running smoothly? And what the hell was that, throwing a tray of drinks all over my new carpet?'

She put up a placating hand, realising her mistake when his scowl only deepened. Jolyon hated it when people tried to soothe him.

'I was just checking on the stores of alcohol in here. I'm going back out there right now,' she said, plastering a benevolent smile onto her face.

Jolyon's eyes narrowed. 'Come with me,' he ground out, turning clumsily on the spot and giving away just how drunk he was.

Sophie put a hand on Emma's arm, but she brushed her off gently. 'It's okay, I can handle him. You make sure everything runs smoothly here while I'm dealing with this, okay?' She gave her friend a beseeching look, pleading for her support, and was rewarded with a firm nod.

'No problem.'

Running to catch up with Jolyon, Emma saw him unlocking the door to his study and the lump in her throat thickened. This couldn't be good. She was only ever summoned to his study when he felt something had gone badly wrong. He liked to sit behind his big oak desk in his puffy leather armchair as if he were lord of the manor and she were his serving wench being given a severe dressing-down.

Deciding to pre-empt his lecture, she put out both hands in a gesture of apology. 'Jolyon, I'm very sorry about dropping those drinks. It was a genuine accident and I promise it won't ever happen again.'

Stopping before he reached the desk, he turned to regard her through red-rimmed eyes, his gaze a little unfocussed due to the enormous amount of whisky he'd drunk throughout the evening.

'What are you going to do to make it up to me?' he asked.

She didn't like the expression in his eyes. Not one little bit.

'I'll pay to have the carpet professionally cleaned. None of the glasses broke, so it's just the stain that needs taking care of.'

He shook his head slowly. 'I don't think that's apology enough. You ruined my party!'

Despite knowing it would be unwise to push him when he was in this kind of mood, she couldn't help but fold her arms and tilt up her chin in defiance. She might have made a bit of a mess, but, if anything, her little accident had livened the party up.

'Jolyon, everyone's having a great time. You've thrown a wonderful party here today,' she said carefully. What she actually wanted to do was suggest where he could shove his job, but she bit her lip, mentally picturing the meagre numbers in her bank balance rapidly ticking down if she let her anger get the better of her.

As she'd predicted, her boldness only seemed to exacerbate his determination to have his pound of flesh and he took a deliberate step towards her and, lifting his hand, he slid it roughly under her jaw and into her hair. His grip was decisive and strong and she acknowledged a twinge of unease in the pit of her stomach as she realised how alone they were in here, away from the rest of the party.

He began to stroke his thumb along her jaw, grazing the bottom of her lip. Waves of revulsion flooded through her at his touch, but she didn't move. She needed to brazen this out. She knew exactly what he was like—if you showed any sign of weakness that was it, you were fired on the spot.

'Well, you ruined it for me,' he growled, moving even closer so she could smell the sharp tang of whisky on his breath. 'But perhaps we can figure out a satisfactory way for you to make it up to me,' he said, his gaze roving lasciviously over her face and halting on her mouth.

She clamped her lips together, racking her brains for a way out of this without making the situation worse.

'Jolyon, let go of me,' she said, forcing as much authority into her voice as she could summon, which wasn't a lot. 'I need to get back to the party and serve your guests and they'll be missing you, wondering where you are,' she said, grasping for something—anything—to aid her getaway. Appealing to his ego had worked well before, but she could tell from the look in his eyes that it wasn't going to fly this time. He wanted much more than a verbal apology from her.

The thought made her shudder.

Taking a sudden step backwards, she managed to break his hold on her. 'I need to get back. Let's talk about this tomorrow, shall we?' Before he could react, she turned and walked swiftly out of the door and back towards the noisy hubbub of the party, her heart thumping hard against her ribcage and the erratic pulse of her blood spurring her on.

She heard him come after her, his breath rasping in his throat as his movements picked up into a drunken jog. She'd just made it to the living-room doorway when he caught up with her, grabbing hold of her arm and spinning her around to face him.

'Jolyon, please—' she gasped, then froze in horror as his lips came crashing down onto hers, his arms wrapping around her like a vice. She couldn't breathe, couldn't move, her heart hammering hard in her ears as she struggled to get away from him—

Then suddenly he seemed to let go of her—or was he being dragged away? The loud *ooof!* sound he made in the back of his throat made her think that perhaps he *had* been and she spun around only to come face to face with Jack.

His mesmerising eyes bore into hers, blazing with anger as a muscle ticced in his clenched jaw, and her stomach did a slow somersault. His gaze swept over her face for the merest of seconds before moving to lock onto Jolyon instead, who was now leaning against the doorjamb, gasping as if he'd been winded.

'What do you want, Westwood?' Jolyon snapped at Jack, flashing him a look of fear-tinged contempt.

Jack glared back, his whole body radiating tension as if he was having to physically restrain himself from landing a punch right on Jolyon's pudgy jaw.

He took a purposeful step towards the cowering man and leaned one strong arm on the jamb above Jolyon's head, forming a formidable six-foot-three enclosure of angry, powerful man around him.

'I want you to keep your hands off my wife!'

CHAPTER TWO

JACK WESTWOOD KNEW he'd made a monumental mistake the moment he heard the collective gasp of the crowd in the room behind him.

What the hell had he just done?

It wasn't like him to lose his head, in fact he was famous in the business circles in which he presided for being a cool customer and impossible to intimidate, but seeing Emma again like this had shaken him to his very soul.

It occurred to him with a sick twist of irony that the last time he'd acted so rashly was when he'd asked her to marry him. She'd always had this effect on him, messing with his head and undermining his control until he didn't know which way was up.

Logically he knew he should have stayed away from her tonight, just until he was mentally prepared to see her again, but after finding he couldn't concentrate on a word anyone had said to him after he'd spotted her earlier his instinct had been to search her out, then jump in to defend her when he'd seen Fitzherbert trying to kiss her.

She was still his wife after all, even if they hadn't had any contact for the last few years—that was what had prompted him to do it. That and the fact he hated any kind of violence towards women.

The searing anger he'd felt at seeing this idiot being so rough with her still buzzed through his veins. Who did he think he was, forcing himself on a woman who clearly wasn't interested in him? And it was obvious that Emma wasn't. He knew her too well not to be able to read her body language and interpret her facial expressions, even when she was trying to hide her true feelings.

'Emma, are you okay?' he asked, turning to check her face for bruises. But it seemed all that was bruised was her pride. At least that was what the flash of discomfiture in her eyes led him to believe.

'I'm fine, thank you, Jack. I can handle this,' she said, laying a gentle hand on his arm and giving him a supplicatory smile.

Unnerved by the prickle of sensation that rushed across his skin where she touched him, he shook the feeling off, putting it down to his shock at seeing her again mixed in with the tension of the situation. Nodding, he took a couple of steps backwards, allowing Jolyon to push himself upright, and watched with bitter distaste as the man brushed himself down with shaking hands and rolled back his portly shoulders.

'I'd like you both to leave,' Fitzherbert said, his voice firm, even if it did resonate with a top note of panic.

Jack turned to see Emma looking at Fitzherbert with a pleading expression, making him think that leaving was the last thing she wanted to do. Why on earth would she want to stay? Unless they were together as a couple?

The thought of that made him shudder. Surely she couldn't have stooped so low as to have attached herself to a playboy like Fitzherbert. He knew she'd been brought up living the high life, was used to being taken care of by other people, but this was beyond the pale.

'Jolyon, please, this is just a misunderstanding. Can we talk about it—?'

Fitzherbert held up a hand to halt her speech and shook his head slowly, his piggy eyes squinty and mean.

'I don't want to hear it, Emma. I want you to leave. Right now. The other girls can cover for you. From what I've seen tonight that's already been happening anyway. Whenever I've looked for you, you've been skulking in the kitchen.'

'I've been orchestrating the party from there, Jolyon—'

He held up his hand higher, his palm only inches away from her face.

Jack experienced a low throb of anger at the condescension of the act, but he kept his mouth shut. He didn't think Emma would appreciate him butting in right now. He'd let her handle this.

For now.

'Didn't you hear me, Emma? You're fired!' There was no mistaking Fitzherbert's tone now. Even though he was drunk, his conviction was clear.

Fired? So she was working for him? Jack found this revelation even more shocking than the idea that they'd been a couple.

She went to argue, but Fitzherbert shouted over her.

'I specifically requested the agency find me a

housekeeper that wasn't married so there wouldn't be any difficulties with priorities. I need someone who can work late into the evening or on short notice without having to check with a partner first. I've been burned by problems like that before.'

He glanced at Jack now, his expression full of reproach. 'A *decent* chap doesn't want his *wife* working for a bachelor such as myself.'

By that, Jack assumed what Fitzherbert actually meant was that he'd wanted the option to pursue more than just housekeeping duties with his employees without the fear of a husband turning up to spoil his fun, or, worse, send him to the hospital.

A prickle of pure disgust shot up his spine at the thought.

'You said in your application that you were unmarried,' Fitzherbert went on, apparently choosing to ignore Jack's balled fists and tense stance now.

'You lied. So I'm terminating our contract forthwith. I don't want a liar as well as the daughter of a wastrel working in my house.'

Shock clouded Emma's face at this low jibe and Fitzherbert smiled and leaned closer to her, clearly relishing the fact that he'd hit a nerve. 'Yes, that's right, I know all about your father's reputation for spending other people's money. I make sure to look up everyone I employ in order to protect myself.'

He jabbed a finger at her. 'I gave you the benefit of the doubt because you're a hard worker and easy on the eye...' his snarl increased '...but who knows what could have gone missing in the time you've been here?'

That did it.

'Don't you dare speak to her like that!' Jack ground out.

Emma turned to him with frustration in her eyes and held up a hand. 'Jack, I said I can handle this. Please keep out of it!'

'No wonder you've kept your marriage to her a secret if that's the way she speaks to you,' Fitzherbert muttered, slanting Jack a sly glance.

'Oh, go to hell, Jolyon,' Emma shot back, with a vehemence that both surprised and impressed Jack. 'You know what, you can keep your measly job. I was going to leave at the end of the month anyway. Your wandering hands had got a bit too adventurous for my liking.'

And with that, she pulled an apron that Jack had not noticed she was wearing before from around her middle and dropped it on the floor at Fitzherbert's feet, then spun on her heel and strode towards the front door.

Glancing back into the room, Jack saw that a large crowd of partygoers had gathered to watch their tawdry little show and every one of them was now staring at him in curious anticipation.

It suddenly occurred to him that they were waiting for him to chase after his *wife*.

Damn it.

Now the secret was out, he was going to have to find a way to handle this situation without causing more problems for himself. The last thing he needed was to catch the attention of the gutter press when he was just finding his feet again here in England. Knowing Emma as he did, he was aware that it would be down to him to handle the fallout from this, which was fine, he was used to dealing with complex situations in his role as CEO so this shouldn't be much of a stretch, but he could really do without an added complication like this right now.

Throwing Fitzherbert one last disgusted glance, Jack turned his back on the man then went to grab his overcoat from the peg by the door. Following Emma out, he caught her up as she exited into the cold mid-November night air.

She didn't turn round as she hopped down the marble steps of the town house and out into the square.

'Emma, wait!' Jack shouted, worried she might jump into a cab and he'd lose her before he had a chance to figure out what he was going to do about all this.

'Why did you have to get involved, Jack?' she asked, swinging round to face him, her cheeks pink and her eyes wild with a mixture of embarrassment and anxiety.

The sight of it stopped him in his tracks. Even in his state of agitation he was acutely aware that she was still a heart-stoppingly beautiful woman. If anything she was even more beautiful now than when he'd last seen her six years ago, with those full wide lips that used to haunt his dreams and those bright, intelligent green eyes that had always glowed with spirit and an innate joy of life.

Not that she looked particularly joyful right now.

Shaking off the unwelcome rush of feelings this brought, he folded his arms and raised an eyebrow at her.

'I wasn't going to just stand by and watch Fitzherbert manhandle you like that,' he said, aiming for a cool, reasonable tone. There was no way he was going to have a public row in the middle of Sloane Square with her. What if there were paparazzi lurking behind one of the trees nearby?

He shifted on the spot. 'I would have done the same for any woman in that position.'

There was a flash of hurt in her eyes. 'Well, for future reference, I can take care of myself, thanks. It wasn't your place to get involved, Jack.'

The muscles in his shoulders tensed instinctively. 'I'm your husband. Of course it was my place.'

She sighed, kicking awkwardly at the ground. 'Technically, maybe, but nobody knew that. I certainly haven't told anyone.'

He was annoyed by how riled he felt by her saying that, as if he was a dirty secret she'd been keeping.

It was on the tip of his tongue to start demanding answers of her—about what had happened in the intervening years to make it necessary for her to work for a man like Fitzherbert and why she hadn't contacted him once in the six years they'd been estranged, even just to let him know that she was okay.

But he didn't, because this wasn't the time or place to discuss things like that.

'Why did you shout about us being married in front of all those people?' she asked, her voice wobbling a little now.

He took a deep breath, rubbing a hand over his forehead in agitation. 'I reacted without thinking in the heat of the moment.'

That had always been his problem when she was around. For some reason she shook him up, made him lose control, like no one else in the world could.

To his surprise the corner of her mouth quirked

into a reluctant smile. 'Well, it's going to be round Chelsea society like wildfire now. That crowd loves a bit of salacious gossip.'

Sighing, he batted a hand at her. 'Don't worry, people will talk for a while, then it'll become old news. I'll handle it.'

She looked at him for a moment, her eyes searching his face as if checking for reassurance.

Jack stared back at her, trying not to let a sudden feeling of edginess get to him. As much as he'd love to be able to brush the problem of them still being married under the carpet he knew it would be a foolish thing to do. There was no point in letting it drag on any more now he was back. It needed to be faced head-on so they could resolve it quickly and with as little pain as possible.

Because, inevitably, it would still be painful for them, even after all this time.

Emma tore her gaze away from him, frowning down at the pavement now and letting out a growl of frustration. 'I could have done with keeping that job. It paid really well,' she muttered. 'And who knows what the knock-on effect of embarrassing Jolyon like that is going to be?'

He balled his fists, trying to keep a resurgence of temper under control at the memory of Fitzherbert's treatment of her. 'He won't do anything—the man's a coward.'

'Jolyon's an influential man around here,' she pointed out, biting her lip. 'He has the ear of a lot of powerful people.'

She stared off into the distance, her breath coming rapidly now, streaking the dark night air with clouds of white. 'Hopefully Clio at the agency will believe my side of the story and still put me forward for other jobs, but people might not want to take me on if Jolyon gets to them first.'

'Surely you don't need a job that badly?' he asked, completely bemused by her anxiety about not being able to land another waitressing role. What had happened to her plans to go to university? She couldn't have been working in the service industry all this time, could she?

The rueful smile she flashed him made something twang in his chest.

'Unfortunately I do, Jack. We can't all be CEO of our own company,' she said with a teasing glint in her eye now.

He huffed out a mirthless laugh and shook his head, recalling how it had been through Emma's encouragement that he'd accepted the prodigious offer for a highly sought-after job at an electronics company in the States right after graduating from university, which had enabled him to chase his dream of setting up his own company.

It had been an incredible opportunity and one he'd been required to act on quickly. Emma had understood how important it had been to him to become financially independent on his own merits, rather than trading on his family name as his father had, and had urged him to go. In a burst of youthful optimism, he'd asked her to marry him so she could go with him. She'd been all he could think about when he was twenty-one. He'd been obsessed with her— every second away from her had felt empty—and the mere suggestion of leaving her behind in England had filled him with dismay.

In retrospect it had been ridiculous for them to tie the knot so young; with him only just graduated from Cambridge University and she only eighteen years old.

They'd practically been children then: closeted and naïve.

She coughed and took an awkward step backwards and he realised with a start that he'd been scowling at her while these unsettling memories had flitted through his mind.

'It's good to see you again, Jack, despite the less than ideal circumstances,' she said softly, her expression guarded and her voice holding a slight tremor now, 'but I guess I should get going.'

She seemed to fold in on herself and he realised with a jolt that she was shivering.

'Where's your coat?' he asked, perhaps a little more sharply than was necessary.

'It's back in the house, along with my handbag,' she muttered. 'I can't go back in there for them now though. I'll give one of the girls a ring when I get home and ask her to drop them over to me tomorrow.' She paused as a sheepish look crossed her face. 'I don't suppose you could lend me a couple of pounds for my bus fare, could you?'

The tension in her voice touched something deep inside him, making him suddenly conscious of what a rough night she was having.

'Yes, of course.' Taking off his overcoat, he wrapped it around her shoulders. 'Here, take my coat. There's money in the pocket.'

She looked up at him with wide, grateful eyes. 'Are you sure?'

'Yes,' he clipped out, a little unnerved by how his body was responding to the way she was looking at him.

He cleared his throat. 'Will you be able to get into your—er—flat?' he asked. He wasn't sure where she was living now. He'd heard that she'd moved to London after they'd sold the family home in Cambridge, but other than that his information about her was a black hole. He'd deliberately kept it that way, needing to emotionally distance himself from her after what had happened between them.

He'd told himself he'd find out where she was once he'd had time to get settled in London but he'd had a lot on his plate up till now. His business back in the States still needed a close eye kept on it until the chap he'd chosen to take over the CEO role in his absence was up to speed and he was keenly aware of his new familial duties here.

'My mother's staying with me at the moment so she'll be able to let me in,' Emma replied with a smile that didn't quite reach her eyes.

He nodded slowly, his brain whirring now. It occurred to him with a jolt of unease that he couldn't let her just skip off home. If she disappeared on him he'd end up looking a fool if the press came to call and he said something about their relationship that she contradicted later when they caught up with her. Which they would eventually.

And after not having seen her for nearly six years he had a thousand and one questions he wanted to ask her, which would continue to haunt him if she vanished on him again.

No, he couldn't let her leave.

'Look, why don't we go back to my house to talk? It's only a couple of streets away,' he said, wishing he hadn't dismissed his driver for the night. He hadn't intended to go out this evening but had been chivvied along at the last minute by an old friend from his university days who was a business acquaintance of Fitzherbert's.

'We need to figure out what we're going to do about this,' he said, registering her slight hesitation. 'You know what the gutter press are like in this country. We need to be able to give them a plausible answer if they come calling. If they think there's any kind of mystery about it they'll hound us for ever. I don't know about you, but I'm not prepared to have the red tops digging into my past.'

That seemed to get through to her and he saw a chink of acceptance in her expression. And trepidation.

He moved closer to her, then regretted it when he caught the sweet, intoxicating scent of her in the air. 'All I'm asking is that you come back to my house for an hour so we can talk. It's been a long time. I want to know how you are, Em.'

She looked at him steadily, her expression closed now, giving nothing away. He recognised it as a look she'd perfected after the news of her father's sudden death. He'd been a victim of it before, right after the tragedy had struck, and then repeatedly in the time that had followed—the longest and most painful days of his life.

'Okay,' she said finally, letting out a rush of breath.

Nodding stiffly, he pointed in the direction they needed to go. 'It's this way,' he said, steeling himself to endure the tense walk home with his wife at his side for the first time in six years.

CHAPTER THREE

IT WAS A blessing that Jack's house was only two streets away because Emma didn't think she'd be able to cope with wearing his heavy wool coat so close to her skin for much longer, having to breathe in the poignantly familiar scent of him and feel the residual warmth of his body against her own.

It had been a huge struggle to maintain her act of upbeat nonchalance in front of him outside Jolyon's house and she knew she'd lost her fight the moment she'd seen the look in his eyes when he'd realised how cold she was. It was the same look he used to give her when they were younger—a kind of intense concern for her well-being, which reached right into the heart of her and twisted her insides into knots.

Gesturing for her to follow him, Jack led her up the stone steps of the elegant town house and in through a tall black front door that was so shiny she could see her reflection in it.

The house was incredible, of course, but with a dated, rather rundown interior, overfilled with old-fashioned antique furniture in looming, dark mahogany and with a dull, oppressively dark colour scheme covering the walls and floors.

Jack's family had a huge amount of wealth behind them and owned a number of houses around the country, including the Cambridge town house overlooking Jesus Green and the River Cam that Jack and his sister, Clare, had grown up in. She'd never been to this property before though. They'd not been together long enough for her to see inside the entire portfolio of his life.

'What a—er—lovely place,' she said, cringing at the insincerity in her voice.

'Thank you,' he replied coolly, ignoring her accidental rudeness and walking straight through to the sitting room.

She followed him in, noticing that the décor was just as unpleasantly depressing in here.

'Was this place your grandfather's?'

'Yes,' he said. There was tension in his face, and a flash of sorrow. 'He left me this house and Clare the one in Edinburgh.'

Emma recalled how Jack had loved spending time with his grandfather, a shrewd businessman and a greatly respected peer of the realm. He'd always had an easy smile and kind word for her—unlike Jack's parents—and she'd got on well with him the few times she'd met him. Jack had notably inherited the man's good looks, as well as his business acumen.

'I was sorry to read about him passing, Jack,' she said, wanting to try and soothe the glimmer of pain she saw there, but knowing there wasn't any way to do that without overstepping the mark. He'd been very careful up until this point not to touch her and, judging by his tense body language, would probably reject any attempt she made to reach out to him.

She needed to keep her head here. This wasn't going to be an easy ride for either of them, so rising above the emotion of it was probably the best thing they could do. In fact they really ought to treat this whole mess like a business transaction, nothing more, if they were going to get through it with their hearts intact.

The mere thought of what they had ahead of them made her spirits plummet and she dropped into the nearest heavily brocaded sofa, sinking back against the comforting softness of the cushions and pulling her legs up under her.

'Have you seen Clare recently?' she asked, for want of a topic to move them on from the tense atmosphere that now stretched between them.

'Not since Grandfather's funeral,' he replied, his brow drawn into a frown. 'She's doing well though—settled in Edinburgh and happy.' He looked at her directly now, locking his gaze with hers. 'She misses you, you know.'

Sadness sank through her, right down to her toes. 'I miss her too. It's been a long time since we talked. I've been busy—'

She stopped herself from saying any more, embarrassed by how pathetic that weak justification sounded.

In truth, she'd deliberately let her friendship with Clare slip away from her.

A couple of months after Emma's father had passed away, Clare had gone off to university in Edinburgh and Emma had stayed at home, giving up her own place in an Art course there, which had made it easier to disassociate herself from her friend. Not that Clare hadn't put up a fight about being routinely ignored and pushed away, sounding more and more hurt and bewildered every time Emma made a lame excuse about why she couldn't go up to Scotland and visit her.

There had been a good reason for letting their friendship lapse as she had though. Clare hadn't known about her and Jack's whirlwind relationship. Emma hadn't known quite how to tell her friend about it at the time—in her youthful innocence she hadn't even known how to feel about it all herself—and she'd been sure Clare wouldn't have responded well to hearing how she'd snuck around with her brother behind her back, then how much she'd hurt Jack by walking away from their marriage.

Emma couldn't have borne being around her friend, whose smile struck such an unnerving resemblance to Jack's own it had caused Emma physical pain to see it, and not being able to talk about him to her. It would have been lying by omission. So instead she'd cut her friend out of her life.

The thought of it now made her hot with shame.

'How's your mother?' Jack asked stiffly, breaking into her thoughts.

She realised she was worrying at her nail, a habit she'd picked up after her father had died, and forced herself to lay her hands back in her lap.

'She's fine, thanks,' she said, deciding not to go into how fragile her mother had become after losing her wealth, good standing and her husband in one fell swoop. She liked to pretend none of it had happened now and had banned Emma from talking about it. 'She's living in France with her new husband, except for this week—she's staying with me while Philippe's away and the house is being damp proofed and re-decorated.'

Jack let out a sudden huff of agitation, apparently frustrated with their diversion into small talk. 'Do you want a drink?' Jack asked brusquely.

Clearly *he* did.

'Er, yes. Thanks. I'll have a whisky if you have it, neat.' A strong shot of alcohol would be most welcome right now. It was supposed to be good for shock, wasn't it?

Jack got up and moved restlessly around the room, gathering glasses and splashing large measures of whisky into them.

The low-level tension in the pit of her stomach intensified. She'd thought she'd be able to cope with being around him here, but his cool distantness towards her was making her nerves twang.

'So how's the electronics business in the good old US of A?' she asked, wiggling her eyebrows at him in an attempt to lighten the atmosphere.

'Profitable,' was all he said, striding over to her and handing her a heavy cut-glass tumbler with a good two fingers of whisky in it.

'Are you trying to get me drunk?' she asked, shooting him a wry smile.

He didn't smile back, just turned away and paced towards the window to stare out at the dark evening.

Her heart sank. Where had the impassioned, playful Jack she'd once known gone? He'd been replaced with this tightly controlled automaton of a man. There was no longer any sign of the wit and charm she'd loved him so much for.

Knocking back a good gulp of whisky, she turned

in her seat to face him, determined not to let her discouragement get to her. 'So you decided to come back and take on your social responsibilities as an earl, then?' She rolled the glass between her hands, feeling the pattern of the cut glass press into her palms.

He turned his head to look at her, his gaze unnervingly piercing in the gloomy room.

'Yes, well, after being responsible for running my own company for the last five years it's made me realise how important it is to uphold a legacy,' he said, folding his arms and leaning back against the window sill. 'How much blood, sweat and tears goes into building a heritage. My ancestors put a lot of hard work into maintaining the estate they'd inherited and it'd be arrogant and short-sighted of me to turn my back on everything they strove so hard to preserve.'

She was surprised to hear him saying this. She'd expected him to be reluctant to return to take on his aristocratic responsibilities after working so hard to achieve such a powerful position in his industry.

But then for Jack it had always been about doing things on his own terms. From the sounds of it *he'd* made the decision to come back here; no one had forced him to do it.

She gave an involuntary shiver as a draught of cool air from somewhere blew across her skin.

Frowning, Jack left his vantage point at the window and paced over to the other side of the room, bending down and grabbing a pack of matches by the fireplace to light the tinder in the grate.

'So you're going to be living in England now?' she asked, her voice trembling as she realised what that would mean. There was a very good chance they'd see each other again, especially as Jack would be frater-nising with the type of people they'd just left at the party. The worst of it was that she'd probably find her-self serving him drinks and nibbles as a waitress at the society events he was bound to be invited to now.

'Yes, I'll be based in England from now on.' He sat back on his heels and watched the tinder catch alight, before reaching for a couple of logs from a basket next to him and laying them carefully over the growing flames.

Turning back to face her, he fixed her with a seri-ous stare. 'So I guess we should talk about what we're going to do about still being married.'

Divorce.

That was what he meant by that.

She knew it was high time they got around to offi-cially ending their marriage, but the thought of it still chafed. Dealing with getting divorced from Jack was never going to be easy, that was why she'd not made any effort to get in contact with him over the years, but the mere thought of it now made her stomach turn.

They'd been so happy once, so in love and full of excitement for the future.

She wanted to cry for what they'd lost.

'Yes. I suppose we should start talking to lawyers about drawing up the paperwork,' she said, desper-ately trying to keep her voice even so he wouldn't see how much the subject upset her. 'If that's what you want?'

He didn't say anything, just looked at her with hooded eyes.

'Are you—' she could barely form the words '—getting married again?'

To her relief he shook his head. 'No, but it's time to get my affairs straight now I'm back in England.'

'Before the press interest in you becomes even more intense, you mean?'

She saw him swallow. 'Speaking of which, we need to work out what we're prepared to say to reporters about our relationship if they come calling.' He stood up and came to sit on the sofa opposite her. He was suddenly all business now, his back straight and his expression blank.

She took a shaky breath. 'Should we tell them we were married but we got divorced and we're just friends now?' The uncertainty in her voice gave away the fact that she knew deep down that that would never work.

He shook his head. 'They'll go and look for the decree absolute and see that we're lying. It'll only make things worse.'

Sighing, she pushed her hair away from her face. 'So what do we say? That our marriage broke down six years ago after you moved to the States, but we're only just getting round to finalising a divorce?'

'They'll want to know why you didn't go to America with me,' he pointed out.

'We could just say that I needed to stay here for family reasons,' she suggested, feeling a rush of uncomfortable heat swamp her as it occurred to her that they might go after her mother too.

'Well, at least that would be pretty close to the truth and it's better to keep things simple,' Jack said, seeming not to notice her sudden panic.

'It doesn't sound great though, does it?' she said, aware of her heart thumping hard against her chest.

'In fact it's probably going to pique their interest even more. They'll want to know what was so important here to make me stay and that'll mean dragging up my father's debts all over again.'

And if they did that Jack would find out she'd been keeping the true extent of them a secret from him for all these years.

After he'd left for the States she'd become increasingly overwhelmed by what she'd had to deal with and had eventually become so buried by it all she'd ended up shutting out everything except for dealing with her new responsibilities in order to just get through the day. Which meant, to her shame, that she'd shut Jack out too.

She'd been so young when it had happened though, only eighteen, and incredibly naïve about the way the world worked and how people's cruelty and selfishness kicked in when it came to protecting their wealth.

Not that there was any point in trying to explain all that to him now. Jack liked to feel he was in control of everything all the time and he'd probably only get angry with her for having kept him in the dark.

And anyway, there was no point getting into it if they were going to get a divorce.

She sighed heavily and put her head in her hands, massaging her throbbing temples. 'I don't know if I could bear having the press camped out on my doorstep, documenting my every move. And I know my mother certainly can't.'

'That might not happen,' Jack said softly. 'They may not even get wind of this. It depends on who overheard us at that party. But if they do find out about us I'll deal with it. If the question is asked we'll just say we got married on a whim when we were young and it didn't work out, but that we've always been on friendly terms and have decided to get a divorce now I'm back in England.'

She nodded her acceptance, feeling a great surge of sadness at how such a happy event could now be causing such problems for them.

Fatigue, chased on by the heavyweight alcohol, suddenly overwhelmed her and she hid a large yawn behind her hand, thinking wistfully of her bed.

The problem was, she was a long way from home and would need to take two different buses to get there. The thought of facing her mother's inquisitive gaze when she walked in made her stomach sink. She'd know immediately that something was wrong; the woman was particularly sensitive to changes in moods now after suffering with depression for years after her first husband's death.

Jack must have seen the worry in her face because he frowned and got up and came to sit down next to her.

'You're exhausted,' he said, the unexpected concern in his voice making the hairs stand up on her arms.

She shrugged, trying to make light of it. She didn't want him to think he had to mollycoddle her; she was perfectly capable of looking after herself. 'That's what happens when you work for a man like Jolyon Fitzherbert. He expects perfection from his employees. I've been up since five a.m. preparing for that party.'

Jack continued to look at her, his gaze searching her face.

Her stomach jumped with nerves as she forced herself to maintain eye contact with him, not wanting him to know just how fragile she was right now. He could probably blow her into dust if he breathed on her hard enough.

'Where do you live?' he asked.

She shifted in her seat. 'Tottenham.'

Not her first choice of places to live, but it was cheap.

'How were you planning on getting home?'

'We mere mortals take the bus.'

He ignored her wry joke. 'You can't take a bus all the way to Tottenham now. Stay here tonight, then we can talk again in the morning when we've both had a good rest and a chance to get over the shock of seeing each other again.'

She hesitated, on the brink of refusing his suggestion, but also keenly aware that if she left now she'd only have to psych herself up to see him again anyway, and probably somewhere much less convivial than here. Despite the terrible décor the house had the comforting atmosphere of a family home.

She realised with a shock that she'd missed the feeling of belonging somewhere, having lost her own family home and all the happy memories that went along with it when they'd been forced to sell it to pay off some of the debts.

So many memories had been tarnished by finding out the truth about her father.

She shook the sadness off, not wanting to dwell on it right now.

'Okay, thank you. I'll stay tonight and leave first thing in the morning,' she said.

He nodded, standing up. 'Good. The first bedroom

you come to at the top of the stairs is made up for guests. Feel free to make yourself at home there.'

Make yourself at home. That wasn't something that was ever going to happen here, Emma reflected with another swell of sadness.

It was such a shame too. This house had the potential to be amazing if only someone showed it some love.

Not that she should be thinking things like that right now.

Pushing the rogue thought away, she stood up and brushed self-consciously at her skirt, trying to smooth out the still-sticky wrinkles. She must look such a mess, especially compared to Jack in his pristine designer shirt and trousers.

'Thank you,' she said stiffly. 'Could I use your phone? I'll need to let my mother know I won't be home tonight or she'll worry.'

'The landline's in the hall,' Jack said.

She gave him a stilted nod—how had things become so formal between them? They were acting like strangers with each other now—and made her way out to the hallway to find the phone.

It was telling that he hadn't lent her his mobile. Perhaps he didn't want her scrolling through his contacts or messages, nosing into his life. Was he trying to hide something from her? Or someone?

She didn't want to consider that eventuality right now; it would only increase the painful tightness she was experiencing in her chest and she needed all her composure if she was going to sound normal on the phone and not worry her mother.

It was telling a few rings before the line at home was

picked up. From the sounds of her mother's voice she'd woken her up, so Emma quickly reeled off a story about Jolyon wanting her to work late and told her she was going to stay with a friend because she'd finish too late to get the last bus home.

At one point during the conversation, she heard Jack come out of the living room and mount the stairs, presumably going up to his room, and a layer of tension peeled away, making it easier to breathe.

From the tone of her mother's voice she could tell she wasn't convinced by the lie, but seemed to think Emma was ensconced in some clandestine affair instead. Which ironically wasn't far from the truth.

What would her mother say once she knew the truth? She'd be hurt, of course, that Emma hadn't felt she could confide in her, but the last thing she'd wanted to do right after her father's shocking death was add more stress to the situation by admitting to getting married to Jack without her mother's knowledge. And then when things had calmed down a little there had been no point in saying anything about it because things had fallen apart with Jack by then and she hadn't been able to see any way to fix them.

So she'd kept mum. In every sense of the word.

After saying goodbye to her mother, she made her way wearily up the stairs, turning onto the landing to find Jack standing outside the door of the bedroom she was meant to be staying in.

She came to a stop and stared at him in confusion. Why was he waiting for her here?

Unless…

'Were you listening to my phone call?' she asked, unable to keep the reproachful tone out of her voice.

'I was waiting to show you which room was yours,' he said, but she could tell from a slight falter in his voice that he was lying.

'You were checking that I wasn't calling a boyfriend, weren't you?' she said, narrowing her eyes.

He raised an eyebrow, refusing to be intimidated by her pointed accusation. 'I am still your husband, Emma.'

She folded her arms. 'Well, don't worry, you don't need to set the dogs on anyone. I haven't had a boyfriend since you left.'

There was a heavy pause where he looked at her with a muscle flicking in his clenched jaw. 'Since you decided not to follow me, you mean,' he corrected.

She sighed, feeling the weight of his resentment pressing in on her. 'I really don't want to argue with you right now, Jack. Can we discuss my failings tomorrow? It's been a very long day.' She forced herself to smile at him and went to walk past him, but he put an arm out, barring her way.

'Have you really not had another partner since we split up?'

Taking a breath, she turned to face him, feeling a small shiver run up her spine at the dark intensity she saw in his gaze. 'Well, my mother needed me for a long time after my father died and I've been working all the hours of the day to fit in both full-time work and night classes since then. So no. There hasn't been a lot of space for romance in my life.' She was aware of the bitter bite to her voice now and couldn't stop herself from adding, 'From what I've read in the press, it hasn't been the same for you though.'

When she'd first seen the articles about the high-profile relationship he'd had with the daughter of a famous hotelier six months after he'd moved to the States she'd had to rush to the toilet to be sick. She suspected it had been a deliberate move on his part to let her know that he'd moved on and that she hadn't broken his heart.

Even though she knew she had.

She'd heard the pain in his voice the last time they'd spoken to each other. The desperation, the frustration. But she'd had to harden herself to it.

They were never meant to be. The universe had made that very clear to her when it had killed her father.

Jack's eyes flashed with anger. 'Our relationship was over by then, Emma. You'd made that perfectly clear when you decided to stay in England with your mother instead of joining me, your *husband*, in the States.'

She took a calming breath, knowing that now wasn't the time to have a conversation about this when they were both stressed and still in shock from seeing each other again. 'I never meant to hurt you, Jack. Please believe that.'

He leant in towards her, his expression hard. 'I waited for you, Emma, like a fool, thinking you'd finally put us first once you'd had time to grieve for your father, but you never did.'

His gaze burnt into hers, his eyes dark with frustration.

'I know you took it all very personally, Jack, and I can't blame you for that, but I promise you it wasn't because I didn't love you. It was just the wrong time for us.'

He didn't respond to that, just kept looking at her with that unsettling, intense gaze of his.

'Goodnight, Jack,' she forced herself to say, moderating her tone so he wouldn't hear the pain this was causing her in her voice, and without waiting for his response she walked past him and shut the door.

Staggering into the room, her legs suddenly weak and shaky, she flopped down onto the large four-poster bed, its heavy mahogany frame squeaking with the movement, and curled into a ball, taking deep, calming breaths through her nose to stop herself from crying.

She understood why he was still upset with her. In his eyes she'd betrayed him, and Jack was not a man to easily forgive people who had hurt him. And she really couldn't blame him for so publicly cutting off their association at the knees, instead of letting it limp on painfully when there had been nowhere left for it to go.

Uncurling herself, she turned onto her back and stared up at the dark burgundy canopy above her.

Seeing him again, after all these years apart, made her heart heavy with a sorrowful nostalgia for the past. She'd grieved for Jack the same way she'd mourned her father at the time, only it had been a different kind of pain—with a sharp edge that constantly sliced into her well-being, reminding her that it had been her decision to end things with him and that there could be no going back from it. The damage had been done.

It had left a residual raw ache deep inside her that she'd never been able to shake.

Too tired now to even get undressed, she crawled

beneath the sheets and let her mind run over the events of the evening. Her heart beat forcefully in her chest as she finally accepted that Jack was back in her life, although for how long she had no idea. He was obviously keen to get their 'situation' resolved so he could cut her completely out of his life and become available to marry someone more fitting of his position when the need arose.

She lay there with her thoughts spinning, suddenly wide awake.

In the first year after they'd parted she'd regularly tossed and turned in her bed like this, feeling so painfully alone that she'd given in to the tears, physically aching for Jack to be there with her, to hold her and whisper that everything would be okay, that she was doing a good job of dealing with the fallout from her father's death and that he was proud of her.

That he was there for her.

But he hadn't been.

Because she hadn't let him be.

A while after they'd split she'd considered moving on from him, finding someone new to love, but what with her intense working schedule and the mental rigor of taking care of her emotionally delicate mother there hadn't been room for anyone else in her life.

So she'd been on her own since Jack left for the States, and perhaps that had been for the best. She hadn't wanted to rely on someone else for emotional support after her father had let her down so badly, because that would have left her exposed and vulnerable again, something she'd been careful to put up walls against over the last few years.

At least on her own she felt some semblance of control. She was the one who would make things better.

She turned over in bed and snuggled down further into the covers, hoping that fatigue would pull her under soon.

She'd find a way to deal with having Jack back in her life again. It would all be okay.

Or so she thought.

Waking early the next morning, her head fuzzy from a night of broken sleep and disturbingly intense dreams, Emma heaved herself groggily out of bed, wrinkling her nose at the smell of old booze on her crumpled clothes, and went to the window to see what sort of weather they had in store for them today, hoping for a bit of late autumn sunshine to give her the boost of optimism she needed before facing Jack again.

But it seemed that bad weather was to be the least of her problems.

Peering down at the street below her window, Emma realised with a sickening lurch that the pavement in front of Jack's house was swarming with people, some of whom were gazing up at the window she was looking out of as if waiting to see something. When they spotted her, almost as one, they raised a bank of long-lens cameras to point right at her. Even from this distance she could see the press of their fingers on the shutter buttons and practically hear the ominous clicking of hundreds of pictures being taken of her standing at Jack's window looking as if she'd just climbed out of his bed.

Leaping away from the window, she hastily yanked the curtains together again.

Someone at the party must have blabbed about what they saw and heard last night.

The press had found out about them.

CHAPTER FOUR

JACK HAD WOKEN EARLY, feeling uneasy about what he'd said to Emma the night before. He was annoyed with himself for losing his temper as he had, but hearing her practically accusing him of cheating on her had caused something to snap inside him.

He'd waited for *months* after moving to the States for word from her to let him know she was finally going to join him there, months of loneliness and uncertainty, only to finally be told, in the most painful conversation of his life, that she wasn't coming after all.

She'd given up on their marriage before it had even started.

He'd understood in theory that he'd been asking too much of her, expecting her to walk away from her life in England at such a difficult time, but he'd also been left with a niggling feeing that she'd chosen her mother over him and that she hadn't loved him enough to put him first.

After taking a quick shower and pulling on some clothes he strode down to the kitchen to set the coffee maker up, waiting impatiently for the liquid to filter through.

He was determined to stay in control today. There was no point in rehashing the past. It was time to move on.

Lifting a mug out of the cupboard, he banged it down on the counter. What was he thinking? He *had* moved on. Years ago.

But seeing Emma again had apparently brought back those feelings of frustration and inadequacy that had haunted him after he'd finally accepted she wasn't interested in being married to him any longer.

Sighing, he rubbed a hand over his face. He needed to get a grip on himself if he was going to get through this unscathed. The last thing he needed right now was Emma's reappearance in his life messing with his carefully constructed plan for the future.

He'd just sat down at the kitchen table with a mug of very strong coffee when she came hurrying into the kitchen, her eyes wide with worry and her hair dishevelled.

'What's wrong?' he asked, standing up on instinct, his heart racing in response to the sense of panic she brought in with her.

'The press—they must have found out about you being married because they're swarming around outside like a pack of locusts trying to get pictures.' She frowned and shook her head vigorously, as if trying to shake out the words she needed. 'They just got one of me peering out of my bedroom window at them—make that *your* bedroom window. I don't know whether they'll be able to tell exactly who I am, but their lenses were about a foot long, so they'll probably be pretty sharp images.'

He watched her start to pace the floor, adrenaline humming through his veins as he took in her distress.

Damn it! This was his fault for announcing their marriage to the whole of Fitzherbert's party last night. He'd been a fool to think they might get away with hiding from it. There was always going to be someone in a crowd like that that could be trusted to go to the papers for a bit of a backhander or the promise of future positive exposure for themselves.

'Okay. Don't panic, it might not be as bad as we think,' he said, reaching for his laptop, which he'd left on the table. Opening it up, he typed a web address into the browser and brought up the biggest of the English gossip sites.

He stared at the headline two down from the top of the list, feeling his spirits plummet.

The Earl of Redminster's Secret Waitress Wife! the link shouted back at him from the page.

He scanned the article, but there was no mention of Emma's name. 'Well, it can't have been Fitzherbert who tipped them off because they don't seem to know who you are. I guess he's kept his mouth shut out of embarrassment about the way he acted last night. Despite his drunken bluster, he won't want to get on the wrong side of the Westwood family in the cold light of day.'

He shut the laptop with a decisive *click*. 'Still, it looks like neither of us are going anywhere today. We can't risk going out there and having more photos taken of us until we've spoken to our parents and briefed them about what to say if any reporters contact them.'

She flopped into the chair opposite and raised a

teasing eyebrow. 'What exactly do you intend to tell them, Jack? Funny story, Mum and Dad. You know how you thought your son was the most eligible bachelor in England? Well, guess what…?'

He tried and failed to stop his lips from twitching, gratified to see she wasn't going to let this beat her. Even so, he needed to keep this conversation on a practical level because this was a serious business they were dealing with.

'We can't hide from this, Emma, it'll only make things worse.'

She frowned at his admonishing tone. 'You think I don't know that? It took years for the papers to stop rehashing the story about my father's debts. Any time high society or bankruptcy was mentioned in a story, they always seemed to find a way to drag his name and his "misdemeanours" into it.'

She sighed and ran a hand through her rumpled hair, wincing as her fingers caught in the tangles.

He stared at her in shock. 'Really? I had no idea they'd gone after your family like that,' he said, guilt tugging at his conscience. 'I didn't keep up with news in the UK once I'd moved to the States.'

What he didn't add was that after leaving England he'd shut himself off from anything that would remind him of her and embraced his new life in America instead. It seemed that by doing that he'd missed quite a lot more than he'd realised.

'Look, why don't you take a shower and I'll go and find you some fresh clothes to put on,' he suggested in an attempt to relieve the self-reproach now sinking through him. 'I'm pretty sure Clare keeps a couple of outfits here for when she visits London—

they'll fit you, right? You were always a similar shape and height.'

The grateful smile she gave him made his stomach twist. 'That would be great. Yes, I'm sure Clare's stuff would fit me fine. Don't tell her I've borrowed it though, will you? She always hated me stealing her stuff.' Her eyes glazed over as she seemed to recall something from the past. 'I really do miss her, you know. I was an idiot to let our friendship fizzle out.' She paused and took a breath. 'But she reminded me too much of you,' she blurted, her eyes glinting with tears.

The painful honesty of her statement broke through the tension in his chest and he leant forward, making sure he had her full attention before he spoke. 'You should tell her that yourself. I'm sure she'd love to hear from you, even after all this time.'

Emma's gaze flicked away and she nodded down at the table, clearly embarrassed that he'd seen her flash of weakness. 'Yeah, maybe I'll do that.'

Standing up quickly, she clapped her hands together as if using the momentum to move herself. 'Right. A shower.'

He felt a sudden urge to do something to cheer her up. There was no need for them to be at each other's throats after all—what was done was done. In fact, thinking about it practically, it would make the divorce proceedings easier to handle if they were on amicable terms.

'When you come back down I'll make you some breakfast. Bacon and eggs okay with you?'

'You cook now?' Her expression was so incredulous he couldn't help but smile.

'I've been known to dabble in the culinary arts.'

She grinned back and he felt something lift a little in his chest.

'Well, in that case, I'd love some artistic bacon and eggs.'

'Great,' he said, watching her walk away, exuding her usual elegance, despite her crumpled clothes.

Out of nowhere, an acute awareness that she was still the most beautiful woman he'd ever known—even with her hair a mess and a face clean of make-up—hit him right in the solar plexus, stealing his breath away.

He thumped the table in frustration. How did she do this to him? Shake him up and make him lose his cool? No one else could, not even the bullying business people he'd battled with on a daily basis for the last few years.

Ever since the day he'd met her she'd been able to addle his brain like this, by simply smiling in his direction. As a teenager he'd been angry with her for it at first and to his enduring shame he'd treated her appallingly, picking at her life choices, her manners, the boyfriends she chose. Particularly her boyfriends.

The way she used to glide through life had bothered him on a visceral level. She was poised and prepossessing, and, according to his sister, the girl most likely to be voted the winner of any popularity contest at the eminent private girls' school they'd both attended in Cambridge. She'd seemed to him at the time to accept her charmed position in life as if it was her God-given right. He, on the other hand, had always prided himself on being subversive, bucking the trends and eschewing the norm and the fact she epitomised what others considered to be the perfect woman frustrated him. He hadn't wanted to be attracted to her. But he had been. Intensely and without reprieve.

What would it be like to hold her in his arms again, he wondered now, to feel her soft, pliant body pressed up against his just one more time, to kiss those sultry lips and taste that distinctive sweetness he remembered so well?

He pushed the thoughts from his mind.

The last thing they both needed now was to slip back into their old ways.

It could only end in disaster.

Even after a bracingly cool shower, Emma still felt prickly and hot with nervous tension.

Being here, in such close proximity to Jack, was playing havoc with her composure.

She knew it was necessary and practical to stay here today, but she had no idea how she was going to get through the day without doing or saying something she might regret—just as she had a few minutes ago in the kitchen when she'd blurted out why she'd deliberately cut contact with his sister.

Not wanting to dwell on that misstep right now, she dried herself and put on the clothes Jack had found for her and left out on her bed while she was in the en-suite bathroom.

The thought of him being in her room while she was naked next door gave her a twinge of nerves. He could so easily have come in when she was in there. Walked into the shower and joined her. If he'd wanted.

But clearly he didn't. And that was for the best.

It would be ridiculous to even contemplate the idea of anything developing between them again.

They'd be fools to think they could breach the chasm that had grown between them over the years. They were different people now. Wiser, older—harder, perhaps. More set in their ways. Certainly not young and carefree and full of excitement for the future as they had been right before they got married.

Twisting the necklace that had her wedding ring looped through it—something she'd never taken off, not in all the years they'd been apart—she gave it a sharp tug, feeling it digging into the back of her neck, reminding herself that any connection they'd once had was lost now and that she'd do well to remember that.

They would get a divorce and that would be the end of it. Then they could move on with their lives.

Trying to ignore the tension in her chest that this thought triggered, she turned on her heel and went downstairs to eat the breakfast Jack had promised her.

Passing through the hallway, she noticed that the handset had been left off the phone and it occurred to her that the press must have started calling by now to try and find out who she was and to hound them for details about their clandestine marriage.

It seemed Jack's plan was to ignore them for as long as possible.

Just as she thought this, the doorbell rang and continued to ring as if someone was leaning on it, determined not to stop until someone answered the door.

Damn press. They'd been the same way right after her father's death, hounding her and her mother for weeks, trying to get titillating sound bites or pictures that they could use in their repellent articles.

Hurrying out of the hall, she went straight to the kitchen to find Jack standing at the large range cooker, frying delicious-smelling bacon in a cast-iron pan.

It was such an anachronistic scene it made her tummy flip.

This was not how she'd pictured Jack whenever she'd allowed herself to think about him over the years.

Not that she'd allowed herself to do that too often.

When they'd been young and in love she'd thought of nothing but him: how it felt to be held in his arms, to be loved and worshipped by him. Then how it would be to live with him. Laugh with him every day. Grow old with him.

He was just as handsome now as he'd been when they'd got married, more so if anything. He'd grown into his looks, his face more angular, showing off that amazing bone structure of his, and his body harder and leaner than it had been in his youth.

She guessed he must have done regular power-gyming along with his power-businessing in the States. Wasn't that what all executives did now? Strong body, strong mind and all that.

'Something smells wonderful,' she said, walking over to where he was busy cracking eggs into the pan.

'It's my natural scent. I call it Eau de Charisma,' he said with a quirked brow as she came level with where he was standing.

She was so surprised that he'd made a joke, she instinctively slapped him gently on the arm in jest and just like that she was transported back in time, into a memory of Jack making her laugh like this the morning before they'd skipped off to the register office.

She'd been trying to fix his tie and their fake squabbling had almost escalated into a rough and lustful lovemaking session on the kitchen table.

The memory of it hit her hard, chasing the breath from her body so that she had to back away from him quickly and sit down at the table, her legs suddenly shaky and weak.

What was wrong with her?

Couldn't she even eat breakfast without going to pieces?

Jack didn't seem to notice though and, after tipping their food onto bone-china plates, each one probably worth more than her entire stock of crockery at home, he brought them over to the table, placing hers in front of her without a word and sitting down opposite.

'Thank you,' she managed to murmur, and he nodded back, immediately tucking into his food.

Her appetite had totally deserted her, but she couldn't leave the food he'd so generously made for her, so she struggled through it, taking a lot of sips of tea to wash it past the large lump that had formed in her throat.

Neither of them spoke until their plates were clean.

Jack leant back in his chair and studied her, only making the jitters in her stomach worse.

Clearing her throat hard, she looked down and concentrated on straightening her knife and fork on the table until she'd got the feeling under control.

'Let's go and sit in the living room where it's more comfortable,' he suggested, and she nodded and got up gratefully, feeling a twang of nerves playing deep inside her.

* * *

Jack took the armchair near the fireplace and watched Emma as she fussed around the sofa she'd chosen to sit on, fluffing cushions and straightening the covers.

He felt stressed just watching her.

'Emma, why don't you sit down? I don't think that cushion's going to get any fluffier.'

Giving the offending article one last pat, she plonked herself onto the sofa opposite him and let out a low groan.

'I'm so full! There's a good chance I won't be able to move off this sofa now I've sat down, which is a worry because the view from here is giving me a headache.' She flashed him a speculative smile.

'Who decorated this place anyway? Please tell me it wasn't you,' she said with a glint in her eye. 'I really can't be associated with a man that thinks that aubergine and mustard yellow are good colour choices for what's meant to be a relaxing environment.'

He snorted in amusement. 'It was chosen by my grandfather's assistant—who he was not so secretly bedding—and I haven't had time to change it since I've been back in England.'

She tipped her head to one side and studied him. 'I bet your place in the States was all cool chrome and marble without a speck of colour to be seen.'

He shrugged, a little stung by her pointed attack on his taste. 'I like my surroundings to feel clean and calming.' Despite his attempt not to sound defensive he could see from her expression that he hadn't managed it.

'Sterile, you mean.' She wrinkled her nose.

'Okay, Miss I-Have-Better-Taste-Than-You, what would you do to improve this place?'

'All sorts of things.' She got up again and walked around the room, peering around at the décor. 'Get rid of the awful dark wood furniture for a start. Put some warm heritage colours in here and some furniture to reflect the era in which the house was built, but with a modern twist.'

'A *modern twist*?'

She folded her arms and raised a brow. 'Yes. What's wrong with that?'

He grinned, amused by her pseudo outrage. 'Nothing. Nothing at all. I'm just not sure what a *modern twist* is. Do you mean you want to fill it with chrome and plastic?'

'No!' She slanted him a wry glance. 'Well, maybe a little of both, but only as accents.'

'Right,' he said, 'accents. Uh-huh.'

He realised with a shock that his earlier joke in the kitchen had brokered an unspoken truce between them and he was actually enjoying teasing her like this. It had been such a long time since they'd had a conversation that didn't end in one or both of them getting overly emotional, and it was comfortingly familiar to have a sparky back and forth with her again. He'd forgotten how fun it was to banter with her.

How? How had he forgotten so much? The gulf between them had been more than just a physical ocean, he realised; it had been a metaphorical minefield too, filled with piranhas. And quicksand. At least a galaxy wide.

They were both quiet for a minute, each seemingly lost in their thoughts.

Emma walked over to the mantelpiece and straightened the ugly carriage clock in the centre. 'Sorry,' she said when he glanced at her with an eyebrow raised. 'This is what stress does to me. It makes me want to tidy and clean things.'

'I know. I remember Clare telling me that you'd blitzed your whole house from top to bottom, including the attic, during your exams when you were seventeen.'

That had been about the time he was most struggling with his feelings for her. He'd been half relieved, half frantic when she'd failed to come over to their house to see Clare for two weeks during that time. It had made him realise just how strong his feelings for her were, which had only made him step up his condescension of her when she'd finally turned up again, looking fresh faced and so exquisitely beautiful it had taken his breath away. He also remembered the look of abject hurt on her face when he'd snapped at her for something totally inconsequential. And then what had happened as a direct result of it.

He was suddenly aware that he'd been staring at her while she stood there with a puzzled smile playing around her lips. 'You look awfully serious all of a sudden. What are you thinking about?' she asked, her voice soft and a little husky as if she'd read his thoughts.

He cleared his throat, which suddenly felt a little strained. 'Actually I was thinking about what happened after you came back to our house after going AWOL for those two weeks after your exams.'

She visibly swallowed as she seemed to grasp what he was talking about.

'You mean when you laid into me about how I'd supposedly flirted with the guy that was painting your parents' house and I decided to finally confront you about why you hated me so much?'

'Yes,' he said, remembering how she'd stormed up to his room after him and hammered on the door until he'd been forced to let her in. How she'd shoved him hard in the chest in her anger, the force of it pushing him against the wall, and how something inside him had snapped and he'd grabbed her and kissed her hard, sliding his hands into her silky hair and plundering her mouth, wanting to show her what she did to him and how much he hated it.

That was what he'd *actually* hated: his inability to control his feelings for her.

But instead of pushing him away, she'd let out a deep breathy moan that he'd felt all the way down to his toes and kissed him back, just as fiercely.

It had been as if a dam had broken. They couldn't get enough of each other's touch. He'd thought in those seconds that he'd go crazy from the feel of her cool hands on him. He'd wanted her so much, he'd ached for her. Desperate to get closer, he'd tugged at the thin T-shirt she'd been wearing, yanking it over her head until they were skin to skin. It had electrified him. He'd never felt anything like it before. Or since.

Getting up from the armchair, he went over to the fireplace to prod at a piece of charred wood that had fallen out of the grate, feeling adrenaline buzz through his veins from the intense mix of emotions the memories had conjured up.

'Jack? Are you okay?' She looked worried now and he mentally shook himself, angry for letting himself think about the past, something he'd been fighting not to do. For so, so long now.

'I'm fine,' he said tersely.

She recoiled a little at his sharp tone, looking at him with an expression of such hurt and confusion he had a crazy urge to drag her into his arms and soothe her worries away.

Fighting past the inappropriate instinct, he went over to the window to peer through a crack in the drawn curtains at the world outside to try and distract himself. The press were still milling around the front of the house, chatting and smoking and laughing as if they didn't have a care in the world.

Vultures.

'You know it won't be long until they find out who I am,' Emma said behind him. She'd walked over to where he was standing and as he turned to face her the sweet, familiar scent of her overwhelmed him, making his senses reel.

He struggled past it, taking a couple of paces away from her and folding his arms.

Obviously a little stung by his withdrawal, she frowned and mirrored his stance, crossing her own arms in front of her.

'You're right. We should go to see our parents right away. I don't want to do it all over the phone—it's too delicate a situation. I'll call the car and we'll go to Cambridgeshire to see my parents this afternoon, then we can both go and see your mother together when we get back to London. We owe them that consideration at least.'

As if the mere mention of them had conjured them

up, Jack's mobile rang and he glanced at the screen to see his parents' home phone number flash up.

A heavy feeling sank through his gut. This didn't bode well. His parents rarely contacted him unless they needed something from him.

He pressed to receive the call. 'Father.'

'Jack? What the hell's going on? Apparently the press have got it into their heads that you're married to some down-and-out waitress! I've had a number of them already call the house this morning asking us to comment on it. Please tell me this ludicrous bit of gossip is unfounded!'

Judging by the strain in his voice, Jack could tell his father was not a happy man. This was the epitome of a disaster as far as Charles Westwood was concerned.

Jack took a steadying breath before answering. 'I am married. To Emma Carmichael. You remember her, she's Clare's best friend from school.'

There was a shocked silence on the other end of the line.

'Is this a joke?'

'No joke, Father. We got married six years ago, just before I moved to the States. We didn't tell anyone at the time because we thought both you and Emma's parents might try to stop us, thinking we were too young to know what we wanted.'

He actually heard his father swallow.

'Well, if she's Duncan Carmichael's offspring that makes total sense. That family was always good at wheedling what they needed out of people.'

Jack felt rage begin to build from the pit of his

stomach. 'Emma can't be held responsible for her father's actions.'

His father let out a grunt of disdainful laughter. 'I'm surprised at you, Jack. I thought you were more savvy than to be taken in by a gold-digger.'

'I'll thank you not to speak like that about my wife,' Jack ground out.

'I'll speak any way I choose when it comes to the reputation of my family name,' his father said, his voice full of angry bluster. 'You need to come to the house *today* and explain yourself.'

'We were already planning on doing that,' Jack said coldly, barely hanging onto the last thread of his cool. 'We'll be with you just after lunchtime.'

'Good. I hope for everyone's sake you're not letting this woman manipulate you. She could take a large part of your fortune if she decides to divorce you and we can't have our family's name brought into disrepute by having it dragged through the courts!' Before Jack could answer there was a click on the line as his father cut the call.

Jack stuffed his phone back in his pocket and turned to face Emma, who was staring at him with dismay on her face.

'They're expecting us,' he said unnecessarily. Clearly she'd heard the whole conversation judging by her expression.

'He thinks I married you for your money and that I'm going to take you for every penny you've got in the divorce,' she whispered, her voice raw with dismay.

Instinctively, he put a steadying hand on her arm, feeling the heat of her skin warm his palm. 'It'll be fine. I'll deal with him and my mother. They're just in shock at the moment and don't know how to handle what little they've been told.'

She blinked and gave her head a little shake as if trying to pull herself together.

'Okay,' she said on a breathy exhalation, lifting her hands to smooth her already perfect hair down against her head. 'Well, I guess we'd better get ready to leave pretty soon if we're going to make it over there for after lunch. I'll call my friend Sophie now and ask her to bring my bag and coat here, then.'

Once again he found himself impressed with her cool handling of the situation. He hadn't expected her to be so composed about it all.

'Okay, you do that. I'll see you back down here in an hour and we'll hit the road.'

She gave him one last assertive nod and turned away.

He watched her go. Despite her fortitude he was unable to shake the feeling that exposing Emma to his parents was tantamount to taking a lamb to the slaughter.

CHAPTER FIVE

THE THOUGHT OF seeing Jack's parents again fired adrenaline through Emma's veins as she walked out of the room to get herself ready to face them.

It had been years since she'd had any contact with the marquess and marchioness. They'd been quick to cut ties with her family the moment the news of her father's debts had broken, not even sending a card of condolence at his passing, and a little part of her hated them for that.

They'd known her quite well when she was a child, after all. She'd spent a lot of time at their house visiting Clare, but as soon as there was a hint of scandal attached to her she'd become persona non grata in their eyes.

And she was absolutely certain their opinion of her wasn't going to change any time soon.

Not that she particularly cared what they thought about her any more.

Unfortunately though, their interference still had the potential to make things very difficult for her if they decided she was a threat to them and their family's assets.

She was going to have to watch her back around them.

Shaking off the twinge of worry, she took a deep breath and went over to the phone in the hallway. She wouldn't worry about that now. There were more important things to give headspace to before they left for Cambridge.

The first thing she needed to do was call her boss, Clio, and let her know what had happened last night at Jolyon's house.

Clio picked up after a couple of rings and before she had a chance to say much, Emma launched into an abbreviated story of last night's debacle, quickly filling her boss in on the state of her and Jack's relationship and the complicated situation she found herself in now.

There was a pause on the line as Clio took a moment to digest all that Emma had told her before she spoke.

'It sounds like you had quite a night, Emma. Are you okay?'

Her boss's concern for her well-being above all else reminded Emma of why she loved working for her so much.

Even though she hadn't expected Clio to be angry with her it was still a relief to actually hear that she wasn't.

'I'm okay. Sort of. I'm not quite sure how this is all going to play out, but there's a good chance I won't be available to work for at least a week or two.'

'Don't worry about that,' Clio reassured her in soothing tones. 'I'll be able to find another job for you as soon as you're ready, Emma. You're one of my best girls; all the other clients you've worked for have sung your praises to me.'

Emma let out an involuntary sigh of relief. 'That's good to hear, Clio. Thank you.'

There was a pause on the line before her boss spoke again. 'You know, Emma, if you ever need to talk you give me a ring, okay? I'm always here if you need a listening ear.' She paused again. 'I had a similar experience myself a few years ago so I understand what you're going through.'

'Really?'

Emma was shocked to hear this. Her boss seemed so together, so focussed on her business. It was comforting to hear that someone she respected and looked up to so much wasn't infallible either.

'Are you secretly married too?' she asked tentatively.

Clio made a wryly amused sound in the back of her throat. 'Unfortunately it's not as straight forward as that.'

'When are relationships ever straight forward?' Emma said with a sigh.

'A good point,' Clio agreed.

There was a short pause. 'Listen, Emma,' Clio said carefully, 'for what it's worth, my advice is to keep in mind that just because the marriage wasn't right for you then, it doesn't mean it isn't right for you now. Both of you have had a lot of time to grow and learn things about yourself since then. That's worth considering.'

Emma's first reaction was one of scepticism that Jack would be at all interested in a reconciliation based on his angry outburst last night, but maybe Clio had a point. Sure, they'd grown apart over the years, each finding their own way forwards, but neither of them had gone so far as to ask the other for a divorce. And surely he never would have lost his cool with Jolyon if he didn't still care about her, at least in some small way?

Her heartbeat picked up as she cautiously entertained the idea of it. Even though he'd been standoffish around her since then, she couldn't help but wonder whether the more time they spent together, the more chance there was she'd spot a chink in his armour.

That there might still be hope for them.

But she'd be a fool to get too excited about the idea of it. There was probably too much water under the bridge now for them to turn things around.

Wasn't there?

'Anyway,' Clio said, breaking into her racing thoughts, 'like I said, don't worry about anything. Just let me know when you're in a position to take on another job and I'll make sure to find you something. In the meantime you take care of yourself, okay?'

'I will, Clio. And thanks. I really appreciate the support.'

She became aware of an achy tension building at the back of her throat and she concluded the call quickly so that her boss wouldn't hear the emotion in her voice.

She felt so confused all of a sudden.

After putting down the phone to Clio she took a moment to compose herself before calling Sophie, whose number she'd memorised because they'd worked so frequently together for the agency.

After giving her the same quick summary that she'd given Clio, she asked her friend to drop her missing bag and coat over to Jack's house, as she couldn't risk picking them up in person in case the press took more photos of her leaving.

Sophie's mixture of earnest concern and soothing support nearly set Emma's tears off again, but she managed to hold it together until they'd arranged how to get the missing items back to her.

Twenty minutes after she'd put the phone down to her friend there was a discreet knock at the back door where they'd agreed to rendezvous. Emma opened it to find Sophie waiting there with a look of worried anticipation on her face.

'One handbag, one coat,' Sophie said, holding the items up for her to grab as she dashed inside before any press noticed that she'd vaulted over the back wall and snuck through Jack's garden to gain entry.

'You're a lifesaver,' Emma said, giving her a tight hug.

'Are you okay?' Sophie asked, her voice muffled by Emma's hair.

It took Emma a moment before she was able to let go of her friend—the comfort of the hug seemed to be releasing some of the straining tension in her—and they drew away from each other.

Emma nodded, tried to smile, failed, then shook her head. 'Not really.'

'You poor thing. What a mess,' Sophie cooed.

'I know, and it's all of my own making. I should have contacted Jack before now...' she sighed and tugged a hand through her hair '...but I never seemed to find the strength to do it.'

'It must be a horrible thing to have to deal with. I don't blame you one little bit for letting it slide.'

'Well, there's no sliding out of it now. We're leaving to see his parents at their massive stately pile in Cambridgeshire in about ten minutes. I'll certainly be facing the firing squad there. They're very uptight about how their family is portrayed in the media and I'm not exactly the daughter-in-law they were hoping for.'

'Emma, how can they not love you? You're an amazing woman, kind, compassionate, smart. They'd be lucky to have you as part of their family.'

Emma managed to dredge up a droll smile. 'Try telling Jack that.'

Sophie gave her a discerning look. 'You still have feelings for him, don't you?'

Emma sighed and rubbed a hand across her aching forehead. 'To be honest I don't know how I feel about him right now. He can be the most frustrating man in the world, but he does something to me on a visceral level, you know?'

'I do,' Sophie said, watching her with a worried frown. 'You can't help who you fall in love with.'

'No.'

They were both silent for a moment, each of them lost in their own personal reverie.

'Hey, do you have something knockout to wear to meet his parents?' Sophie asked, breaking Emma out of her thoughts about how she was going to deal with spending more up-close-and-personal time with Jack when she was feeling so mixed up about him.

She glanced up at her friend. 'Jack's sister left some of her clothes here, which I can wear. They're a bit casual for a meeting with a marquess and marchioness, but they'll have to do. I haven't got time to go home now. Not that I've got anything suitable there either.'

'Okay, well in that case I'm glad I brought these with me.' Sophie slipped the strap of a suit carrier off her shoulder and held it out towards her.

'They're dresses I've just finished sewing for a charity catwalk show. You're so lovely and slim I think they'll fit you perfectly.'

The kindness of the act brought tears straight to Emma's eyes and she blinked hard, knowing that if she let as much as one of them fall she was a goner.

'That's so sweet of you, thanks,' she said, pulling Sophie in for another hug and holding onto her tightly until she'd got herself under control.

After disentangling herself, Sophie smoothed down her hair and gave her a warm smile. 'You're welcome. Knock their socks off, Emma! And call me as soon as you can to let me know that you're okay, all right. The girls and I were really worried about you when you disappeared like you did last night and they'll want to know you're in good hands.'

'I will. And thanks again, you're a good friend.'

'My pleasure, sweetheart.'

Blowing her one final kiss, Sophie nipped out of the door and hared back off across the garden before the paps got a chance to get a good look at her.

Shutting the door firmly behind her friend, Emma smiled and took a deep fortifying breath, thanking her lucky stars for such good friends.

It was so good to know that she wasn't completely on her own with this.

Jack was pacing the hall when Emma walked down the stairs to meet him looking a little pale, though still her poised, beautiful self. She was wearing a stunning dress, the structured soft grey material framing her curves in a way that made it impossible for him to drag his eyes away from her. There was something sharply stylish about the cut of it, even though the design was simple, giving the impression of confidence and effortless style. He had to hand it to her, she was a class act, even in the face of such a challenging situation.

In fact after what he'd witnessed in the last twenty-four hours it seemed he'd done her a disservice by assuming he'd have to handle the fallout from this all by himself. Instead of shying away from it, she'd stepped right up when it had become clear he needed her in this with him, and without one murmur of protest.

'My friend Sophie loaned it to me,' she said, following his gaze and fluttering her hands across the front of the dress. The strap of the handbag she was wearing over her shoulder slipped down her arm at the movement and dropped to the floor before she could catch it. As she bent down to pick it up something slipped out of the neck of her dress and flashed in the light as it twisted and swung around. He stared at the slim sliver chain. And the ring that was looped through it.

With a lurch of astonishment he realised he recognised it.

Her wedding ring.

She still wore it. Close to her heart.

Following his gaze, Emma looked down to see what he was staring at and when she realised what it was, she tried to stuff the necklace hastily back inside her dress again.

'You still have it,' he said, the words sounding broken and raw as he forced them past his throat.

'Of course.' She was frowning now and wouldn't meet his eye.

'Why—?' He walked to where she was standing with her hand gripping her handbag so hard her knuckles were white.

'I'm not very good at letting go of the past,' she said, shrugging and tilting up her chin to look him straight in the eye, as if to dare him to challenge her about it. 'I don't have a lot left from my old life and I couldn't bear to get rid of this ring. It reminds me of a happier time in my life. A simpler time, which I don't want to forget about.'

She blinked hard and clenched her jaw together and it suddenly occurred to him that she was struggling with being around him as much as he was with her.

The atmosphere hung heavy and tense between them, with only the sound of their breathing breaking the silence.

His throat felt tight with tension and his pulse had picked up so he felt the heavy beat of it in his chest.

Why was it so important to him that she hadn't completely eschewed their past?

He didn't know, but it was.

Taking a step towards her, he slid his fingers under the thin silver chain around her neck, feeling the heat of her soft skin as he brushed the backs of his fingers over it, and drew the ring out of her dress again to look at it.

He remembered picking this out with her. They'd been so happy then, so full of excitement and love for each other.

He heard her ragged intake of breath as the chain slid against the back of her neck and looked up to see confusion in her eyes, and something else. Regret, perhaps, or sorrow for what they'd lost.

Something seemed to be tugging hard inside him, drawing him closer to her.

Her lips parted and he found he couldn't drag his gaze away from her mouth. That beautiful, sensual mouth that used to haunt his dreams all those years ago.

A lifetime ago.

'Jack?' she murmured and he frowned and shut his eyes, taking a step away from her, letting go of the chain so that the ring thumped back against her chest, breaking the strange sensuous connection between them. This was crazy; he shouldn't be giving in to his body's primal urges, not with her. Not now.

It was too late for them. They were different people now. There was no point trying to rehash the past.

'We should go,' he said, giving her a reassuring smile, which faltered when he caught the look of pained confusion on her face. 'We don't want to be late.'

Jack had arranged for his driver to pull up right outside the house and he and Emma—who had hidden her face behind a pair of Clare's old sunglasses and the brim of a baseball cap—practically sprinted to the car and flung themselves inside, determinedly ignoring the questions that were hurled at them from all sides.

Once safely in the back seat, Jack shouted for his driver to hit the gas and they left the pack of journalists behind them, scrambling for their own transport. Luckily his driver was able to shake them all off by taking a convoluted route through some back streets and when Jack checked behind them ten minutes later, there still wasn't anyone obviously tailing them.

They sat quietly, not speaking for the first part of the journey, and Jack took the opportunity to check work emails and calls. After he'd satisfied himself that everything was running smoothly without him, he sat back and looked out of the window, finally allowing his mind to dwell on the situation with Emma again, his thoughts whirring relentlessly.

Something had been bothering him since the phone call with his father, and it suddenly struck him what it was.

They'd be fools to think that trying to get divorced quickly would make all their problems go away. The press would be far more interested in them if they suddenly announced they were splitting up after their marriage had only just become news. His father would be sure to drag Emma's troubled past into the spotlight again, especially if he thought it would add weight to the Westwood's side of the claim in the divorce settlement. The man was capable of doing whatever it took to protect the family's estate.

He hated the idea of Emma having to go through the torture of being hounded by photographers again, having them hiding in her bushes and jumping out at the most inopportune moments. It would be incredibly stressful, especially if she had to cope with it on her own. At least when she was with him he could protect her from the majority of it, using the vast resources he had to hand.

The more he thought about it, the more an idea began to take shape in his mind. What if they stayed married, at least for the time being, and made out to the world that they were happy together? The press would soon grow bored with that—there wouldn't be any conflict in the story to get excited about. His father would be forced to leave her alone too if she retained the Westwood name.

Surely they could deal with being around each other for a while longer, just until the interest in them had died down.

'Emma?'

'Hmm?' She turned to look at him with an unfocussed gaze as if she too had been deep in thought.

'What if we stayed married?'

Her gaze sharpened up pretty quickly at that.

'What do you mean?'

'I mean what if we pretend our marriage is solid? To everyone. Including our parents. That would give them time to get used to it and for the press interest in us to die down, then we could get divorced quietly and without anyone noticing in a few months' time.'

'A few months?' she repeated, as if she couldn't believe what she'd just heard and was a little unnerved by it.

'We'd only have to project a happy marriage in public—in private we could completely ignore each other if you like.' He knew he sounded defensive, but her sceptical response had rattled him.

Surely they could get past any awkwardness about being around each other again if it meant they'd be left alone to deal with this mess in a private and dignified manner. On their terms.

She seemed to be mulling the idea over now that she'd got over the initial shock of his suggestion, and she turned to face him again with a small pinch in her brow.

'You mean we'd live together in the same house?'

He took a breath. 'Yes, I guess that would make sense. To make it seem plausible that we're a happy couple, madly in love.' He was aware of tension building in his throat as he talked. 'You could move into my house. Just for those months. You'd be able to hide out there more easily than your flat and use my driver to get where you wanted to go.'

Turning away, she stared out of the window, her shoulders slightly hunched and her hands clasped in her lap.

'Okay,' she said so quietly he wasn't sure if he'd heard her correctly.

'Did you say okay?'

'Yes.' She swivelled to face him. 'I said okay. It makes sense to do that.' She paused to swallow, the look in her eyes a little circumspect. 'Just to be clear, you are talking about just being housemates, nothing more?'

He clamped his jaw together and nodded. 'Yes, that's what I meant.'

They'd be fools not to keep things strictly platonic between them; it would only complicate things if they didn't.

Sex hadn't even been on his mind when he'd made the suggestion. He'd been more concerned with protecting her from the press and keeping his own family out of the limelight.

He was thinking about sex now though.

That dress she was wearing was doing something unnerving to his senses. It accentuated her body in all the right places, making his blood race and his skin prickle as an urge to run his hands down it and trace her soft curves with his fingertips tugged at him.

Giving a small cough to clear the sudden tension in his throat, he gripped the handle of the door more tightly.

'I'm sure we can outwardly project the image that we're madly in love if we try hard enough,' she said quietly.

He twisted to look at her again, but she was staring out of the window again, her face turned away from him.

Sighing, he sat back in his seat and watched the countryside whizzing past, wondering exactly what they were letting themselves in for here.

The Westwood ducal estate was one of the most impressive in the country. Emma had heard that whenever the family opened their doors to the public, which wasn't often, they were so inundated with eager visitors there was gridlock in the roads around the estate for miles.

She would have been excited to have been invited to visit here under less stressful conditions, but as it was her stomach rolled with nerves as Jack's driver drove the car up the oak-tree-lined road to the front of the formidable-looking gothic stately home, with its geometric towers interspersed with harsh spires of grey stone, and came to halt in front of the grand entrance.

Jack's suggestion that they live together for the next couple of months had both terrified and electrified her.

The tense standoff at the bottom of the stairs earlier when he'd discovered that she wore her wedding ring around her neck seemed to have changed something between them. In that moment when he'd lifted it from around her neck she'd thought for a second he was going to kiss her. Her whole body had responded on a primitive level, her blood rushing through her veins and heating her skin in anticipation of the feel of his mouth on hers again after all this time.

The scary thing was, she'd wanted him to. So much.

Because then she'd know once and for all whether there was any way they could rekindle what they'd once had.

But he'd pulled away from her and the moment had disintegrated around them, taking any hope she might have had with it.

Until he'd just made the suggestion that they stay married, at least for a little while longer.

She could see that he was coming at it from a practical point of view, but, even so, she didn't think he would have suggested it if he didn't still care about her, at least a little bit.

Jack got out of the car and walked round to her side, opening her door and holding out his hand to her.

'Shall we?' Jack asked, his voice tinged with tension. Hearing that he wasn't entirely comfortable with being here either gave her that little bit of determination she needed to swing her legs out of the car, put her hand into his and stand up with a grace and dignity that she summoned from the depths of her soul.

They were in this together now.

He squeezed her fingers gently, as if hearing her thoughts, sending goose bumps rushing up her arm from where his warm skin made contact with hers.

'Okay. Are you ready?' he asked.

'As I'll ever be,' she said, dredging up a tense smile for him.

'Good. Remember, we're the ones in control here, not them.'

She let out a nervous laugh. 'If you say so.'

He nodded, his mouth twisting into a grim smile, and tugged gently on her hand, asking her to walk with him.

They'd barely made it halfway up the wide stone steps when the door was flung open and Jack's mother appeared on the doorstep, her perfectly coiffed chignon wobbling a little in her haste to get to them.

'Jack! Darling!' She tripped nimbly down the steps to meet them, the pearls around her neck swinging merrily from side to side. 'I'm so glad you're here.' Taking his face in her hands, she drew him towards her for a kiss on each cheek, then turned to Emma, giving her an assessing glance. 'It's good to see you again, Emma, dear.' The wary expression in the marchioness's eyes made Emma think she wasn't being entirely truthful about the 'good' part.

'Come on in, we're all in the drawing room.'

All? Emma mouthed at Jack with a worried frown as his mother walked regally back up the steps, leaving them to follow in her wake.

Jack just shrugged, looking as confused as she felt.

Emma had never been in this house before. It had

belonged to Jack and Clare's grandfather when she'd known them and she'd never been invited here. It was a breathtakingly impressive seat, with wide corridors filled with ancient paintings and artwork, leaning heavily on gold and marble to propagate the ridiculous wealth of the family.

'We're just through here,' the marchioness called over her shoulder, her voice sounding a little more strained now they were about to walk into what was bound to be the close equivalent of the Spanish Inquisition.

The room they walked into, with their hands still tightly entwined and their postures stiff, was positively cavernous, with a soaring ceiling painted with gaudy frescos of angels frolicking in the clouds. Emma held her breath, her eyes scanning the room quickly to take it all in before she was forced to concentrate solely on the people that sat stiffly on the sofas positioned around the grand gothic fireplace in the centre of the room.

Which was why it took her a good few seconds to realise that there was at least one other friendly face in the room.

'Clare!' she gasped, dropping Jack's hand in her shock at seeing the woman she'd considered to be her best friend for most of the formative years of her life.

Clare stood up and walked towards them, her face breaking into a huge smile, a smile that flipped Emma's stomach with the warm familiarity of it.

'What are you doing here?'

'I happened to be visiting the olds and thought I'd stick around to greet my new sister-in-law. Or apparently not so new,' her friend said, her lips twisting into a wry, quizzical smile.

'It's so good to see you,' Emma said, burying her face in her friend's curly auburn hair and breathing in the comfortingly floral scent of her. 'I've missed you,' she whispered fiercely into Clare's ear, pulling back to look into her face so her friend could see just how sincerely she meant that.

'I've missed you too, Em,' Clare said, her eyes glinting with tears.

'Well, Jack,' Clare said, turning to give her brother the same perplexed smile, 'you've pulled some crazy stunts in your life, but I never thought getting secretly married to my best friend would be one of them.'

Jack smiled at her with a pinch in his brow as if trying to figure out how best to frame his answer.

'How—? I mean, when—?' Clare shook her head and took a breath. 'I mean *how* did I not know about this? I'm beginning to worry I've been abducted by aliens and had six years' worth of memories erased or something.'

A lead weight of guilt dropped into Emma's stomach.

Jack advanced towards his sister and pulled her into a tight hug before releasing her to look her in the eye.

'I'm sorry we didn't tell you, Clare. I feel terrible about keeping you in the dark all this time.'

Emma put her hand on Clare's other shoulder. 'I'm sorry too, sweetie. I should have told you when it happened, but I—' She looked down at the floor and shook her head. 'I guess I got a bit carried away with the romance of it all and I had no idea how to explain my feelings for Jack to you. To be honest, I was terrified you'd hate me for falling for your brother. The last thing I meant to do was hurt you.'

'Yes, yes, this is all very touching, but I'd like to hear how this all came about,' said a deep, penetrating voice from the corner of the room.

Emma turned to see Jack's father, Charles Westwood, Marquess of Harmiston, advancing towards her.

'Emma,' he said, giving her a curt nod.

She wondered for a second whether he expected her to drop into a curtsey.

Well, he could expect all he wanted, there was no way she was going to pander to him.

'My Lord,' she said, keeping her chin up and her back straight. 'Thank you for welcoming me here today. I can imagine how upsetting it must have been for you to hear about Jack and I being married the way you did, and I apologise for that.'

Something flickered in the man's eyes, but his expression remained impassive.

'Are you going to tell us why it's been kept such a secret for all this time?' he asked, his tone strident now.

Before she could speak, Jack stepped up next to her to address his father.

'As I mentioned on the phone, we started a relationship when Emma was seventeen and I was twenty, but we decided to keep it quiet at the time because we wanted time to explore it without our families sticking their noses into our business.'

Jack let that hang in the air for a moment before continuing.

'Then when I got the offer from the States to go and work out there I decided I wanted Emma to go with me and the easiest way to make that happen was for us to get married.'

His father raised a censorious eyebrow and looked as though he was about to say something, but Jack ignored him and carried on speaking.

'Unfortunately Emma's father passed away right after the wedding ceremony so it became impossible for her to follow me out there and I'm sad to say our relationship drifted after that. In retrospect we realise we weren't emotionally mature enough at the time to make it work then.'

She felt his arm slide around her shoulders and forced herself to relax into his hold, as a woman who felt loved would, despite the awareness that Jack must be struggling not to add that he actually believed she'd abandoned him.

'We've stayed in contact over the years and since I've been back in England we've decided to reconcile our marriage,' Jack continued, still not looking at her. Even though he looked outwardly relaxed she would swear she could feel the underlying tension in his hold on her.

To her surprise, Clare moved quickly towards them and wrapped her arms around her and Jack, dragging them all into an awkward group hug.

'Well, I couldn't be happier for you both. Honestly. I always thought you'd make a great couple. You were always so sparky together. And now there's definitive proof that I'm *always right*,' Clare said, grinning at them both.

Emma forced herself to grin back, her scalp feeling hot and tight as her friend's misplaced enthusiasm caused a stream of discomfort to trickle through her.

She pushed the feeling away. Now wasn't the time to feel guilty about what they were doing.

'Well, now that's all straightened out I suppose we can relax a little,' the marchioness said in a rather brusque voice.

Clearly she didn't share Clare's joy at the news that she now had a waitress with a tarnished reputation for a daughter-in-law for the foreseeable future.

Jack's father didn't say anything, just looked at them with a disconcerting smile playing about his lips, as if he suspected there was more to it than they were telling him.

Shrewd man.

And a dangerous one. Emma could see now why Jack had wanted them to show a united front. Judging by the look of cold distrust in the marquess's eyes, Emma imagined the man would happily feed her to the wolves, given half a chance.

Well, at least it was over with now and they could go back to London without the fear of Jack's parents interfering in their relationship.

A loud ring of the doorbell made them all start in surprise.

'Ah, that will be Perdita,' the marchioness said, rising from her chair.

A moment later a deathly pale woman with a shock of white-blonde hair and the palest eyes Emma had ever seen was shown into the room by a butler, followed by a man with a camera slung around his neck.

'Perdita is our good friend and a journalist from *Babbler* magazine,' Jack's mother announced to them all with a cool smile. 'She's going to do a lovely feature for us showing how invested we all are in your marriage and how excited we are about welcoming you into your place in our family, Emma.'

CHAPTER SIX

'WHAT THE HELL is this?' Emma heard Jack growl under his breath to his father as his mother tripped over to greet her friend with an exaggerated air kiss.

Emma knew exactly why he was so angry. The more fuss they made about being a happily married couple, the harder it would be to let the relationship dissolve without a lot more press attention.

'Surely you don't mind having people know how happy you are to be married to each other?' his father said loudly with a glint of devilry in his eyes.

He had them trapped. There was no way they could refuse to do this without it looking suspect. Clearly Jack knew that too because he gave her an extra hard squeeze as if asking her to play along.

She turned to smile at him. 'Of course we don't mind, do we, darling?' she said, hoping her expression relayed her understanding of the situation to him and her acceptance of it.

A whole conversation passed between them in that look and Jack finally nodded curtly and turned to the new additions to their group and said, 'What exactly did you have in mind?'

'We only have time for a couple of photos today

if we're going to squeeze you into the next issue, but I'll come over to your house in a week or so and do a more in-depth interview for an *"At home with the Earl and Countess of Redminster"* feature,' Perdita said in a gush of fawning enthusiasm. 'For starters I'd like to get some lovely shots of the happy family together.'

Reluctantly, they allowed themselves to be herded into a tight group in front of the looming marble fireplace in the centre of the room and Emma found herself standing between the marquess and marchioness, pressed up tightly to Jack, with her back flat against his broad chest and his arms wrapped around her waist.

'Love's young dream!' Perdita gushed, giving them an insipid smile that made Emma squirm inside.

Heat rushed through her as she felt Jack shift behind her, his arms tightening infinitesimally to press a little harder into her pelvis, only increasing the heavy pounding of her heart. The fresh, exotic scent of his aftershave mixed with his own unique scent enveloped her, making her head swim.

He'd always smelled good. More than good. In fact in her younger days after being with him she used to hold the clothes she'd been wearing up to her nose and breathe in his lingering scent. She'd not been able to get enough of it.

She still had one of his old sweaters at home that he'd loaned to her one day when they'd gone on a cold walk together, just days before they were married, which she'd deliberately not given back so she could sniff it at home like some kind of Jack junkie.

She remembered with a twang of nostalgia how full of hope she'd been that day, how excited about their future together. The intensity of her love for him had taken her breath away, robbed her of all common sense, made her dopey with happiness.

The day she'd married him had been the best day of her life—and the worst.

She could still remember the feeling of absolute horror and helplessness when she'd arrived home after their clandestine marriage—her one and only rebellion in a life of respectful rule-following—ready to tell her parents that she was going to move to America to build a life with Jack there, only to find her mother prostrate on the sofa, her face a sickly white and her eyes wild with grief. She'd rushed to her, panicked by the look on her face, and her mother had told her in a broken voice filled with tears that her father was dead.

She'd spent the next few hours desperately trying to hold herself together for the sake of her mother, who had totally fallen apart by then, as if Emma's appearance had released her from the responsibilities of dealing with her husband's death.

In her state of shock she'd ignored the calls on her mobile from Jack, who had been waiting impatiently for her to meet him in the hotel room they'd booked, where they had been going to celebrate their wedding night together.

Eventually she'd called him, finding him in a state of frantic worry, and explained what had happened, feeling as though she was looking down at herself from above. Jack had wanted to come over and be with her, to help in some way, but she'd told him no, that it would only distress her mother more to have him in the house and that she didn't want to have to explain his presence there. She wasn't going to tell her they were married, it wasn't the right time.

That moment was the point at which their relationship had begun to unravel. She recognised it now, in a flash of clarity. She'd pushed him away, rejecting his love and support, and it had hurt him more deeply than she'd realised at the time.

So it was absolute torture, standing there enfolded in his arms once again, but this time having to fake their love for the camera so that strangers could gawp at their lives as if it was entertainment.

If only her father hadn't died, maybe they would have still been blissfully happy together today.

If only…

But there was no point in wishing she could change the past. It was futile and a waste of energy. Instead she needed to look to the future with positivity and have faith that she'd find happiness again there.

'Ooh, that's a lovely one,' Perdita purred from the other side of the room as her photographer snapped another shot and it appeared on the screen of a laptop Emma had seen him toying with earlier.

'Let's just have one of the happy couple on their own now, shall we?' Perdita said with a cajoling lilt to her voice. Emma thought she and Jack had been doing a convincing job of looking comfortable with each other, but there was a strange gleam in the journalist's eye that she didn't like the look of. Did she suspect all wasn't quite as it seemed? Probably. It was her job to see past people's façades and get to the heart of a story, after all.

Emma swallowed hard, but managed to keep her smile in place.

The rest of Jack's family moved away from the stiff tableau they'd formed for the photo and went to perch on the nearby sofas to watch the rest of the show.

'When will the next issue of the magazine come out, Perdie?' Jack's mother asked, her eyes glued to the way Jack's arms were still wrapped around Emma's middle as if she was looking for something to criticise.

'In a couple of days. We'll just be able to squeak them into the next issue along with some upbeat captions about them renewing their vows.'

Jack's arms tightened around her and her heart jumped in her chest in response.

'What makes you think we're going to renew our vows?' he snapped.

'I told Perdita that's what was going to happen, dear,' Jack's mother broke in. 'It's such a *prudent* course of action, what with being so suddenly reconciled after all this time. And it means all your friends and family will be able to celebrate your union with you this time.' Despite the cajoling note in her voice Emma clearly heard the undertone of steel in her mother-in-law's words.

Jack didn't say anything more, but she could practically feel the waves of frustration rolling off him.

'The full interview will be in the next issue because there just isn't room for it in this one and we'll want to do a nice big spread,' Perdita went on gaily, apparently enjoying the drama that was unfolding in front of her. Emma guessed she could see a whole career's worth of titillating stories in the offing.

'I had a fight on my hands finding some room for these pictures, to be honest,' Perdita went on. 'We had to bump a spread on Fenella Fenwicke's third wedding.'

Tripping over to where she and Jack stood shifting uncomfortably on their feet, she put a cool hand onto Emma's wrist.

Emma had to work hard not to whip her arm away from the clingy covetousness of the woman's grip.

'Now then. Shall we have one of the two of you looking adoringly into each other's eyes? That should play well with our readers.'

Emma's heart sank. She was going to have to look into Jack's eyes with the same insipid expression she'd been struggling to maintain for the past twenty minutes and still hold it together.

What if he saw past her nonchalant façade and noticed how she was desperately trying to hide how much she still cared for him? And what if he didn't actually care about her any more and she saw it there clearly in his face? How would she cope when all these people were watching them?

Taking a breath, she steeled herself against her trepidation and turned around to look at him.

Jack looked back at her, his green-flecked hazel eyes filled with an unnerving intensity behind his long dark lashes.

Emma's heart thumped hard against her chest as she forced herself not to break eye contact with him.

He was so outrageously handsome it dragged the breath from her lungs.

But handsome didn't keep her warm at night, she reminded herself. It didn't make her feel secure and loved, wanted and treasured.

Safe.

Falling in love was a precarious business, full of hidden dangers and potential heartbreak, and she didn't know if she could bear the idea of being that vulnerable again. Not when she'd already experienced how quickly and catastrophically things could go wrong.

After a few more seconds of torture, Jack and Emma holding the same pseudo loving pose for the camera, Perdita finally clapped her hands together and gave a tinkling little laugh.

'That's it! Perfect. I think we have all we need for now.' She turned to Jack's mother. 'I'll let you know when the issue with the pictures is out, Miranda.'

'Thank you, Perdie. You're a good friend.'

And a shrewd businesswoman, Emma thought with a twinge of distaste. Those pictures would probably be worth a fortune if she leaked them to the papers, not to mention the career-enhancing glory of getting the scoop for her magazine.

'I'll call you about setting up that *at home* interview in a couple of days,' she shouted across to Jack and Emma as she bustled about, gathering up her bag and laptop.

After another minute of fussing and gushing pleasantries with the marquess and marchioness, Perdita finally left in a flurry of kisses and a blast of expensive perfume and the atmosphere in the room settled into an unnerving hum of prickly discontent.

Jack had had enough of his parents' intrusion into his affairs.

'Right, well, now this circus is over we'll be leaving,' he said to them.

'Wait, Jack, why don't you stay a little longer so we can get to know our new daughter-in-law a bit better?' his mother said in an appeasing tone, bustling over to where he and Emma stood.

He didn't like the glint of mischief in her eyes. No doubt she would spend the time grilling Emma in the hope of getting her to admit to something they could use against her later.

There was no way he was letting that happen.

'You got what you wanted. We put on a good show for the sake of your image as invested parents-in-law, so now you can leave us alone,' he snapped.

'Jack, we just want what's best for the family—' his father began.

'No, you don't,' Jack broke in angrily, 'you want what's best for you. Well, I'm doing what's best for *us* and that means getting the hell away from this toxic atmosphere. Come on, Emma.' He held out his hand to her.

She took it, wrapping her fingers tightly around his, and he was alarmed to feel how much she was trembling.

She'd projected such an outwardly cool exterior throughout the whole debacle he was surprised to discover she seemed to be suffering just as much as he was.

'I'm sorry to leave so suddenly, Clare,' he said, turning to his sister.

He was grateful that she'd stuck around to be here today. It had been good to have another ally for Emma in a strained situation like this.

And he was glad for the opportunity to see his sister again; he'd missed her open smile and levelheaded, easy company while he'd been living away in the States.

Clare gave them both an understanding smile. 'You must both come up to Edinburgh soon,' she said, her expression telling him there was no way she was letting them get away without seeing her for that long again.

He just nodded at her, uncomfortably aware that he and Emma might not be together for very much longer so there was no point in trying to arrange anything with his sister for the future.

He'd work out how to handle all that later though.

Right now he wanted to get Emma out of there and as far away from his parents as possible.

They left without another word, Jack aware of his parents' disgruntled gazes on his back but not giving a fig how they felt about him laying down the law to them. No way was he going to let them try to run his life.

Back outside he opened the passenger door for Emma and watched her slide into the car, as graceful as ever—struck by how even in the most difficult situations she still managed to maintain her poise—then went round to the other side of the car and got in next to her.

They drove away in silence, Emma watching out of the window as the car made its way down the long driveway, glancing back to look at the house as if concerned that his parents might come out and hotfoot it after them.

She caught his eye and he gave her a tight smile, which she returned.

'Are you okay?' he asked her, half expecting her

to shout at him now for putting her through that. 'I'm sorry about them landing a journalist on us like that. I know how you must hate them after what they did to your family when your father died.'

'It wasn't your fault, Jack. It's fine,' she said, but he was sure he saw a glimmer of reproach in her eyes.

For some reason her controlled restraint bothered him. He realised he actually wanted her to rage at him, so he could rage back at her. To get all the pain and anger out in the open, instead of all this polite pussy-footing around they were doing.

Instead, he took a deep breath and told himself to calm down. His parents' meddling was no fault of hers. Or his.

But as he stared out of the window the memory of having to stand in full view of his family and look lovingly into Emma's eyes came back to haunt him, crushing the air from his lungs. He could have sworn he'd seen something in her gaze, something that made his heart beat faster and his blood soar through his veins.

It had made him nervous.

He still felt twitchy and wound up from it now and a sudden urge to get out of the confines of the car and walk around for a minute to get rid of his restless energy overwhelmed him.

'We should stop and get a drink somewhere before we head back to London,' he muttered, and before Emma could protest he leant forwards and asked John to stop at the country pub that was coming up on their left.

Once they'd pulled into the car park he said, 'Let's

take a quick break here,' getting out before she had chance to answer him.

The temperature was cool, but the sun was out and Jack felt it warm the skin of his face as they walked towards the pub. It was a relief to be outside again. Despite the impressive dimensions of the rooms in his parents' house he'd felt claustrophobic there and had been hugely relieved to leave its austere atmosphere.

The exterior of the pub had already been decorated for Christmas and strings of fairy lights winked merrily at them as they walked up to the front of the building.

'Let's sit out in the beer garden,' he suggested as they came to a halt at the front door. He could already imagine how the dark cosy interior would press in on him. He needed air right now.

'Sure, okay,' Emma said, slanting him a quizzical glance.

'I just need to be outside for a while.'

She nodded. 'Okay, I understand. I'll go and get the drinks. What would you like?'

He frowned. 'No, I'll get them.'

Putting up a hand, she fixed him with a determined stare. 'Jack, I can stretch to buying us a couple of drinks. Let me get them.'

Knowing how stubborn she could be when she put her mind to it, he conceded defeat. 'Okay, thanks. I'll have an orange and soda,' he said, aware he needed to keep his wits about him, despite an almost overwhelming craving for a large shot of whisky to calm his frazzled nerves.

'Okay, you go and find us a good table in the sun.

I'll see you out there,' she said, already heading into the pub.

He found a bench right by a small brook in the garden and sat down to wait for her to return, watching the fairy lights twinkling in the distance. Barely a minute later he spotted her striding over the grass to join him, a drink in each hand. It looked as though she'd gone for the soft option as well.

He was surprised. He'd expected her to come back with something much stronger after having to deal with the nonsense his parents had subjected her to.

A sudden and savage anger rose from somewhere deep inside him—at his parents, at her, at the world for the twisted carnage it had thrown at them both.

She put the drinks carefully down on the table like the good little server she'd become.

It burned him that she hadn't done anything worthwhile with her life when there had been so much potential for her to do great things with it.

Instead she'd given up her life with him in the States for what? To become a *waitress*. At this last thought his temper finally snapped.

'Why the hell are you wasting your time working in the service industry? I thought your plan was to go to university to study art and design,' he said roughly, no longer able to hold back from asking the question that had been burning a hole in his brain since he'd first seen her again.

Her initial shock at his abrasive tone quickly flipped to indignation.

'Because I've had to work to pay off my father's debts, Jack,' she blurted, sitting down heavily opposite him, clearly regretting her loss of control as soon as the words were out.

He stared at her in shock. *'What?'*

She swallowed visibly but didn't break eye contact. 'They were rather more substantial than I told you they were, but I was finally on track to pay off the last of them—until I lost my job yesterday.'

Guilt-fuelled horror hit him hard in the chest. 'Why didn't you tell me? You said the money from the sale of your family house had taken care of the debts your father left.'

Frustration burned through him. If she'd told him she needed money he would have offered to help. Not that she would have taken it from him at that point, he was sure. After her father's death she'd sunk into herself, pushing everyone she'd loved away from her. Including him.

'It wasn't just the banks he owed money to,' she said with a sigh. 'He'd taken loans from friends and relatives too, who all came out of the woodwork to call the debts in as soon as they'd heard he'd passed away.'

Jack frowned and shook his head in frustration. 'Emma, your father's debts weren't yours to reconcile all by yourself.'

She shrugged and took a sip of her drink before responding. 'I didn't want to be known for ever as the poor little rich girl whose daddy had to borrow money from his friends in order to keep her in the lifestyle to which she'd become accustomed, who then ran to her rich husband to sort out her problems.'

The pain in her eyes made his stomach burn. He went to put a reassuring hand on her arm but stopped himself. He couldn't touch her again. It might undo something in him that he was hanging onto by a mere thread.

'I didn't want you to have to deal with being hounded by the press too,' she added in a small voice. 'You had enough on your plate what with starting at your new job.'

He thought again about how he'd avoided seeking out any news from the UK after moving to the States. The cruel irony of it was, if he hadn't done that he'd have been more aware of how her father's name had been dragged through the press and what she'd been put through after he'd left. And ultimately that would have helped him understand why she'd shut him out of her life once he'd moved away.

'I'm sorry I didn't tell you the whole truth, Jack, but I was overwhelmed by it all at the time. I guess I was too young and naïve to deal with it properly. It felt easier just to shut you out of it,' she said suddenly, shocking him out of his torment.

He felt a sting of conscience as he remembered his angry rant at her the other night.

'I know I promised I'd put us first once things had settled down but sorting out the carnage that my father had left us to deal with took up my every waking second, my every ounce of energy. I felt adrift and panicky most of the time, lost and alone, and I couldn't see past it. There didn't ever seem to be an end in sight.'

She took another sip of her drink but her hand was shaking so much some of the liquid sloshed over the edge of the glass and onto the table.

'Every day after you'd gone I told myself that I'd

call you tomorrow, that once things had settled down I'd get on a plane and go and find you, but they never did.'

She mopped absently at the spillage with a tissue that she'd pulled out of her bag.

'Months bled into each other until suddenly a whole year had passed and by that time it felt too late. I'm sorry I let things drag on the way I did, but I didn't want to have to face the reality that there couldn't be any *us* any more. That my life with you was over. You were everything I'd ever wanted but I had to let you go. I didn't feel I had any choice.'

She rubbed a hand across her forehead and blew out a calming sigh. 'The other problem was that my mother wasn't well after my father died. She became very depressed and couldn't get out of bed for a long time. I needed to be there for her twenty-four hours a day. To check she wasn't going to do anything—' She paused, clearly reliving the terror that she might come back home to find herself an orphan if she left her mother alone for too long.

Jack nodded and closed his eyes, trying to make it clear he understood what she was telling him without her needing to spell it out.

Dragging in a breath, she gave him a sad smile. 'So it was left to me to organise the funeral, arrange the quick sale of the home I'd lived in since I was a little girl and face the angry creditors on my own while my mother lay in bed staring at the wall.'

'I could have helped you, Emma, if you'd let me,' he broke in, feeling angry frustration flare in his chest.

'I didn't want you involved, Jack. I was hollowed

out, a ghost of my former self, and I didn't want you to see me like that. You would have hated it. I wanted to be sparkling and bright for you but my father's death drained it all away.' She sighed. 'Anyway, it was my family's mess, not yours.'

He leaned in towards her. 'I was your family too, Emma. Not by blood, but in every other way. But you pushed me away.'

She took a shaky-sounding breath. 'I know my decision to stay in England hurt you terribly at the time, but my mother needed me more than you did. She would have had no one left if I'd slunk off to America and there was no way I could just leave her. There was no one else to look after her. All her friends—and I use the word in the loosest of terms—abandoned her so they didn't find themselves tainted by our scandal.'

Her voice was wobbling now with the effort not to cry. 'I know that my father would have expected me to look after my mother. He would have expected us to stick together. I didn't want to dishonour his memory by running away from our family as if I was ashamed to be a part of it.'

She held up a hand, palm facing him. 'I accept that he made mistakes, borrowing all that money, but I believe he did it in order to make his family happy. So I've spent the last six years working hard to pay off his debts. To finally clear our name—'

Her voice caught on the last word and Jack shifted in his seat, distraught to hear how much she'd suffered in silence, but he didn't speak, letting her keep the floor, sensing how much she needed to let it all out now.

'I didn't want you to be dragged down by the mistakes my father made too. It wouldn't have been fair on you when you were so excited about taking that amazing job offer in America. I knew it was a once in a lifetime opportunity, and how determined you were to shun the unfair advantage of your family name and do something great with your life on your own merits. It would have been cruel of me to take that chance away from you, Jack.'

'There would have been other opportunities though, Emma. I was more concerned about the two of us making a new life for ourselves *together*,' he broke in, before he could stop himself.

She sighed and rubbed at her brow. 'I wasn't the same flighty, naïve girl you'd fallen in love with by then though. My father's death changed me. The girl you knew died the moment he did. The last thing you needed was an emotionally crippled wife pulling at your attention while you were trying to build a successful future for us. You would have only resented me for it.' She frowned. 'And I loved you too much at the time to put you through all that.'

At the time.

Those three words said it all. She *had* loved him, but apparently she didn't feel the same way any more.

His chest felt hollow with sadness, the desolation of it spreading out from the centre of him, eating away at his insides.

Her voice had become increasingly shaky as she'd gone on with her speech and she stood up now and brushed a tear away from under her eye.

'Will you excuse me? I'm just going to visit the bathroom before we get back into the car,' she said, giving him a wobbly smile.

'Yes, of course,' he said, grateful for a break from the intense atmosphere so he could mull over everything she'd just told him.

He sat staring into space after she'd walked away, acutely aware of the bizarre normality of the sounds in the garden all around them while he desperately tried to make sense of the heavy weight of emotion pressing in on him.

Emma's painful confession had pierced him to the core.

He was in awe of her courage and her strength in the face of such a humbling experience, but he still couldn't shake the painful awareness that she'd chosen her mother over him.

Frustration bit at him. If she'd only let him know what was going on at the time, how bad things had got for her, he could have helped her. But she'd chosen to shut him out and handle it all without him. She hadn't trusted him or his love for her enough to let him be the husband he'd wanted to be.

Though, to be fair to her, he had to give her credit for showing such strength of character in stepping up and taking on her responsibilities, even though it had meant giving up a life with him—an easy, wrapped-in-cotton-wool existence.

If she'd been a more fragile person she could have asked him to pay off her family's debts and saddled him with a reputation for having a gold-digging wife, but she hadn't wanted that for him. Or for herself.

She had more integrity than that.

She returned a minute later and he stood up to meet her, frustration, hurt and sorrow for what they'd lost still warring in his mind.

Just as she reached the table her phone rang and she plucked it out of her bag, giving him an apologetic smile at the interruption and muttering, 'It's my mother, I'd better get this,' before answering the call.

She sounded worried at first, which made his heart thump with concern that there was more bad news to deal with, but then her voice softened into a soothing coo as she listened to a tale of woe that her mother had called to impart to her. From what he could glean from Emma's responses it sounded as if her mother's new husband, Philippe, had broken something while skiing off-piste with friends and her mother was going to have to rush back to France to see him. Emma assured her that that was fine and that she'd fly over very soon to see them both.

After cutting the call she confirmed the news, assuring him that it was better if her mother didn't hear about what was going on with them right now as she was already upset and worried about Philippe.

He wanted to say something to her about how it wasn't right for her to feel she still had to protect her mother and that it should be the other way around, but he didn't. Because it wasn't really any of his business.

For some reason that simple truth filled him with despair.

Sliding her phone back into her bag, she gave him a grateful nod for waiting and started walking back to the car. He stood rooted to the spot for a moment, watching her go, and as she reached the edge of the garden he had an overwhelming urge to try and reassure her that everything would be okay.

'Emma.'

She stopped under a large tree strung with twinkling fairy lights and turned back to face him, her expression one of open interest.

He walked quickly up to where she stood. 'I wanted to say thank you,' he said, taking another step towards her, closing more of the gap between them.

'What for?' Her brow crinkled in confusion.

'For being so honest with me just now. It's obviously still hard for you to talk about.'

She glanced away, then back at him with a small smile of gratitude.

He took another step towards her, standing so close now he could smell the intoxicating, floral scent of her.

She looked up at him, her eyes wide and bright with unshed tears.

'I also wanted to say thank you for what you did today, standing up in front of my parents like that,' he said, putting a hand on her arm, his breath hitching as he felt her tremble under his touch. 'It was brave of you.'

Glancing up, he realised there was a sprig of mistletoe hanging from a branch above them, tied in amongst the glimmering lights.

Without thinking about what he was doing, he lifted his hand and slid his fingers along her jaw, cupping her face and rubbing his thumb across the flawless skin of her cheek.

Her eyes flickered closed for a second and she drew in a small, sharp breath as if his touch had burnt her.

'Emma?' he murmured, dropping his gaze to her beautiful, Cupid's-bow-shaped mouth. A mouth that he had a sudden mad urge to kiss.

His insides felt tangled, as if she'd reached inside him and twisted them in her hands.

He wanted to do something to take away the pain and uncertainty he saw in her eyes, but intellectually he knew that kissing her now would only make things more complicated between them.

Clearly she was feeling vulnerable and there was no way he was going to consciously make that worse.

So he dropped his hand to his side and took a step away from her. Then another.

'We should get back on the road so we miss the rush-hour traffic,' he said gruffly, concerned at how wild the look in her eyes was and how flushed her cheeks were.

The stress of their situation must be getting to her too.

'Okay,' she said roughly, nodding and glancing away towards where John, their driver, stood leaning against the car, his face turned towards the late autumn sunshine.

When she looked back her eyes seemed to have taken on a glazed look.

Perhaps she was just tired.

Giving her a nod and a smile, which he hoped would go some way towards reassuring her that he was with her in this, he gestured for her to lead the way.

He watched her walk back towards the car, stumbling a little on the uneven gravel.

If they were going to get through this without getting hurt again he was going to have to be very strict with himself about how close he let himself get to her again. From this point on he would do everything in his power to make her life easier and make sure that she was as secure and happy as she deserved to be.

But he'd be doing it from a distance.

CHAPTER SEVEN

WHEN EMMA WOKE up the next morning she felt as if she hadn't slept a wink.

The memory of the way Jack had looked at her with such warmth and understanding yesterday, after she'd opened up about what she'd gone through after her father died, had haunted her dreams.

Standing under that mistletoe outside the pub, she'd thought for one heart-stopping moment that he was going to kiss her. It had actually scared her how much she'd wanted him to, but judging by his swift withdrawal apparently she'd been crazy to imagine that he'd wanted it too.

But she could have sworn…

Ugh! This was all so confusing.

She was better off on her own anyway—at least that way she could keep full control over her life and keep her heart in one piece.

Rolling out of bed, she went over to the window and peered out at the street below, this time making sure to keep well hidden behind the curtain. There were still a few photographers lurking down on the street, but the majority of journalists seemed to have gone.

They must have grown bored with trying to get information about her. That was a relief.

After taking a quick shower and pulling on another one of the beautiful dresses that Sophie had brought over for her, this time in a flattering, draped soft green fabric that swished around her legs and clung gently to her torso, she clomped downstairs, steeling herself to face Jack again.

She had absolutely no idea what to expect from him today. What she did know was that she sure as heck wasn't going to hide from whatever was going on between them.

Walking into the kitchen, she spotted him sitting at the table with his broad back to her looking at something on his laptop.

The worry about how they were going to be with each other this morning evaporated the moment he looked round and she saw the flash of panic on his face.

'Emma, I didn't hear you come in.'

'What are you looking at?' she asked, already knowing she wasn't going to like the answer.

Snapping the laptop shut, he gave what she suspected was meant to be a diffident shrug. 'Nothing of any consequence.'

Folding her arms, she gave him a hard stare. 'Jack, there's no point in trying to hide anything from me. I'll see it sooner or later.'

He swallowed, then nodded towards the computer in front of him. 'The press found out who you are,' he said, rubbing a hand over his eyes.

Sitting down next to him, she slid the laptop towards her and opened it up to look at what he'd been reading.

All the blood seemed to drain from her head as she saw numerous links on the screen, all with her family name slashed across them with a variation on the theme of her family's money scandal and their exile from high society as well as Jack's name and title.

Gold-digger seemed to be the most commonly used term.

It was inevitable, she supposed. Once the press had that photo of her there must have been a race on to discover as much as they could about her in order to get their stories filed for this morning's news. The public seemed to be captivated by the lives of the upper-class gentry and apparently theirs were no exception.

Feeling sick, she leant back against the chair and covered her face with her hands, letting out a long low breath and concentrating hard on getting her raging heartbeat back under control.

'Are you okay?' Jack asked gently.

'I'm fine,' she said, dismissing his concern with the flip of her hand. She wasn't going to fall apart in front of him now. She still had her pride.

Getting up from the table, she smoothed her hands down her dress. 'Well, I guess if I'm going to be living here for a while I'll need to go to my flat to pick up some of my things,' she managed to say, amazed at how calm she sounded when her heart was thumping so hard she thought it might explode in her chest.

Jack looked surprised for a moment, then smiled and nodded. 'Take the car. In fact, I'll give you John's number now, then you can call him whenever you need to go somewhere.'

She frowned in surprise. 'Won't you need him?'

'I have another driver I can use.'

She must have still looked a little uncertain because he said, 'It's fine, Emma, and it's only until the press get bored and leave us alone. It'll be much less stressful for both of us.'

'Well, okay. If it's not going to cause any trouble.'

'No trouble,' he said, giving her a reassuring smile, which made something flip in her tummy.

His phone rang then, and he turned away to answer it with a curt, 'Westwood.'

She could tell from the look on his face that it wasn't someone he was keen to speak to.

He confirmed this by mouthing, 'It's Perdita,' and putting the phone on speaker so they could both hear the conversation.

'I'm calling to set up a good time to come and do that *"At home with the Earl and Countess of Redminster"* piece for the magazine,' came the journalist's crooning tones down the line.

Emma's heart sank. She'd hoped the woman would leave them alone for a little while, at least until they'd had a bit more time to practise playing the happily married couple, but apparently it was not to be.

'I was thinking a week on Friday,' Perdita continued, not giving either of them the chance to even draw breath, let alone answer. 'I'll pop over at about nine in the morning, which should mean we have plenty of light to get everything shot. Now the nights are drawing in, we have to start our days that bit earlier. Okay?' she finished finally, the uplift in her voice making the word sound more like a command than a question.

'Yes, fine,' Jack bit out. 'We'll see you then, Perdita.'

'Lovely!' Perdita breathed, then cut the call.

Jack scowled at his phone, looking as though he'd quite like to fling it across the room.

When he turned to look at her with a raised brow she matched his frustrated expression. 'So she's set on doing that interview, then,' she said, keenly aware of the tension in her voice.

'Sounds like it. We ought to do it though, just to keep my parents off our back.'

'I agree.'

He nodded. 'Thank you for understanding, Em.'

'No problem,' she said, forcing herself to smile back, feeling a little panicky about what exactly they were going to say to Perdita that would satisfy her curiosity about their relationship. They didn't even know what the state of it was themselves, for goodness' sake.

She got up from the table and went into the living room to peek out at the photographers still milling about outside.

Jack had followed her in and he flopped onto one of the sagging armchairs near the fireplace, wincing as it gave a groan of protest.

She walked over to where he sat and perched on the edge of the arm. 'You know, Perdita might think it's strange that we're living in a house like this,' she said, sweeping her hand around to encompass the nineteen seventies throwback décor. 'She'll never buy that a young couple plan to live here, and the readers certainly won't.'

He frowned. 'Good point.'

'Can you get it updated in time?' she asked hesitantly.

He ran a hand through his hair, messing up the neat

waves and making her long to smooth it back down for him. 'I don't have time to arrange it right now. I'm snowed under at work.'

'I can do it,' she said before she could check herself. 'If you like,' she added less forcefully, pulling her arms tightly across her middle. 'I can't work at the moment anyway, so I may as well make myself useful.'

He looked up at her with a smile of relief. 'That would be great, if you wouldn't mind. Spend whatever you think necessary—'

She gave an involuntary grimace at that and he frowned as if realising what a tactless thing that was to say to her.

'I'll transfer some money to you to get started and if you need any more, just let me know.'

'Okay. Should I give you my account details now?' she asked, feeling incredibly awkward about discussing money with him, especially with the word *gold-digger* still floating around her mind.

'Sure. Go ahead,' he said, opening up an app on his phone and tapping in the numbers she gave him. 'I'll do a transfer as soon as I get to my desk. 'I've got a meeting in Belgravia now so I'll get out of your way.'

Emma was frustrated that they were dancing so politely around each other like this, with neither of them making any mention of their moment under the mistletoe yesterday. But then what was there to say? Nothing had actually happened.

They'd not talked at all on the journey back from Cambridge because Jack had been on the phone to his colleagues in America the whole time dealing with a crisis that had arisen, then he'd excused himself the moment they'd walked into the house, citing the need to do more work. She suspected he'd actually been avoiding having to talk about what was hanging in the air between them.

She followed him into the hallway, where Jack grabbed his coat from the cloakroom.

It can't have meant as much to him as it had to her, she decided with a sting of sadness.

It had probably just been a moment of camaraderie to him after a long and stressful day. But that was all. It hadn't meant anything more than that.

Disappointment was doing something funny to her insides, but she squashed the feeling quickly.

'Have a good day. I'll see you later,' Jack said, sliding his arms into his overcoat and giving her a tight smile.

She nodded solemnly, not wanting to give away how disconcerted she felt about being left alone with the press still hanging around the front of the building. Not that she'd ever admit that to Jack. She didn't want him thinking he had to mollycoddle her.

'Are you sure you trust me to redecorate your house?' she blurted in a moment of nervousness, belatedly adding a twinkle of mirth to her expression so he'd see she was only joking. The idea of being let loose on this place—to have such a fun project to get immersed in—filled her with utter joy.

Flashing her a wry smile back, he leant his arm against the wall next to her and regarded her with a mock stern stare. 'If I find you've kitted the whole house out in rubber and woodchip I will not be pleased. Other than that, go for your life. I'll be interested to see what you do with the place. It's crying out for a make over and you've always had great taste.'

'You think so?' she said, surprised by the out-of-left-field compliment.

He shot her a grin. 'You married me, didn't you?'

She couldn't stop her mouth from twisting with amusement. 'You just can't help yourself, can you?'

'I never could with you, my darling.' He leaned in a bit closer to her, capturing her gaze, and the mood changed in a second, the air seeming to crackle between them, the quiet in the hallway suddenly sounding too loud, the colours around them too bright.

Clearing his throat with a rough cough, Jack stepped back, snapping the mood, and Emma found she was digging her nails into her palms.

'I'll see you later,' he said, turning on the spot and striding away to pull the door open, then slamming it shut behind him.

The sound of him leaving reverberated around the hallway, making her suddenly feel very, very alone in the big empty house.

It took Emma a good twenty minutes to come down from her jittery high after Jack left.

Crikey, it was going to be hard, living here with him and having to get through those moments when they both became uncomfortably aware of how happy they'd once been together, but how much had come between them since.

Despite her body telling her she wanted him, more desperately than she could believe, she knew deep down that hoping things would get physical between them was foolish when their feelings about each other were so tangled. It would only make living together more problematic than it already was.

Sighing, she made her way to the kitchen to put the kettle on for a much-needed cup of tea.

At least throwing herself into redecorating the house would give her something to distract herself from thinking about him all the time.

Her thoughts were interrupted by the sound of her phone ringing in her back pocket. Plucking it out, she was pleased to see Grace's name flash up on the screen.

'Hello, you, how's it going?'

'I was going to ask you the same thing. I hope you don't mind, but Sophie filled me in on what happened after Jolyon's party and I read about the rest of it in the papers. Nice photo of you and your husband on the *Babbler* website by the way.'

'Er—thanks.' Was the picture out already? She hadn't expected it to appear for another few days. Thank goodness her mother never looked at the internet and was unlikely to see any of the news articles over in France.

'Are you okay, Emma? You must be having a rough time with the press camped out on your doorstep,' Grace asked in her usual no-nonsense manner.

There was a long pause where Emma tried to form a coherent sentence about how she felt about it all.

Where to begin?

'Yes, I'm fine. It all feels like a dream, to be honest, but we're handling it.'

'So you really are married to an earl?' There was a note of gleeful fascination in her friend's voice now.

'I am.' She swallowed, feeling her earlier nervousness returning. 'Although for how much longer I don't know,' she blurted.

There was a pause on the line. 'Really? Are things difficult between you?'

Emma sighed, annoyed with herself for losing her cool like that. She didn't want Grace to worry about her; her friend had enough on her plate. 'No, no, it's fine, ignore me. I'm just a bit stressed at the minute. I'm supposed to be interior designing the downstairs of the house we're living in for a photo shoot a week on Friday and I have absolutely no idea where to start.'

There was another small pause on the line before Grace spoke again. 'You know, I worked in a lovely boutique hotel in Chelsea called Daphne's a while ago. It has every bedroom decorated in a style from a different time period and the communal rooms are done out in a really cool and quirky way. It would be a great place to get some inspiration.'

'Ooh, I think I know it,' Emma said, feeling excitement begin to bubble in her stomach. 'I read an article about it a while ago. I've been meaning to go and have a peek at it. It looked like a fascinating place.'

'You should,' Grace said. 'I'm sure the manager would jump at the chance to show you around if you suggested that you were thinking about hiring the place for your vow-renewal ceremony.'

Emma tried to ignore the twist of unease that the mention of renewing their vows provoked.

'It would be great publicity for them if they could boast about having the famous Earl and Countess of Redminster as patrons,' Grace added with a smile in her voice.

'That's a fantastic idea,' Emma said, feeling a real buzz of excitement now. It was exactly what she needed today: a chance to escape from the house and take her mind off Jack for a while.

'I don't suppose you're free today to come with me, are you?' she asked her friend. 'We could go for a coffee afterwards.'

It would be lovely to spend some time in Grace's easy company. She desperately needed to do something *normal* feeling after the craziness of the last couple of days.

'I'd love to,' Grace said. 'I've just finished work so I can meet you there in half an hour.'

'Fantastic,' Emma said with a grateful sigh. 'I'll see you there.'

They spent a happy half-hour looking around the hotel, with Emma making copious notes on things that inspired her, then chatting it all over with Grace over large mugs of cream-topped hot chocolate in a nearby café afterwards, sitting next to a large Scandinavian-style Christmas tree hung with silvery white snowflakes, quirky wooden reindeer and red felt hearts.

It was lovely spending time with just Grace on her own for once and they discovered to their delight just how much their tastes aligned. It turned out Grace wasn't a fan of the pure white and chrome interior look that Emma had teased Jack about either.

'That must be tough,' she said, as her friend finished a diatribe about the hotel where she was currently working, which felt so clinical she was continually transported back to the months she'd spent visiting her grandmother in hospital before cancer finally took her from her.

'Your house is going to look wonderful when you're

finished,' Grace said, changing the subject and shaking off the air of sadness that had fallen over her at the mention of her beloved grandmother—the woman, Emma knew, who had been more like a mother to Grace.

She was perpetually impressed by the strength and tenacity that Grace showed to the world, despite having had such a tough start in life.

'What a fantastic opportunity to showcase your skills as a designer too,' her friend said. 'Hey, do you think it's something you'd be interested in pursuing as a career?'

Giving Grace a smile, she shrugged non-committally, but felt a tug of something akin to excitement deep in her belly. She'd always loved art and design at school and had done both a graphic design and business night class recently in the hope she'd be able to apply her artistic bent to a job in the future. Fortuitously, the classes had given her a set of skills to be able to make up mood boards on a computer, put together cost sheets and even do some technical drawing, which would no doubt prove very useful for this project.

While she'd been paying off her father's debts she hadn't allowed herself to think about what else she could be doing with her life, but now she was getting so close to reconciling them it really was time to think about the next steps. As much as she loved working for Clio at the Maids in Chelsea agency, she'd be very happy for her long-term career to take another direction. One that didn't involve toadying to people who made an art form of peering down their noses at the hired help. She'd probably have to go to college and get proper qualifications if she wanted to pursue something like interior design, which she'd need to save up for, but it was a worthy goal to aim for.

It would be a good way to safeguard a more settled future for herself.

After losing everything she had once already, she never wanted to be in a position where she was at risk of that happening again. No way was she going to rely on someone else to keep her afloat.

Pushing away a concern about how this fed into her muddled feelings regarding her relationship with Jack, she turned her attention back to her friend.

'Thanks so much for today, Grace, it's been really useful. Now all I have to do is get out there and make it happen.'

CHAPTER EIGHT

To HER DISAPPOINTMENT, Emma didn't see much of Jack over the next ten days. For the first couple of them his work took him into his office in the City at a totally unreasonable hour in the morning and kept him there until well after Emma had dragged herself to bed in the evenings. Though to be fair, she *was* crashing out early after long, intense days of researching and planning the new design scheme for the downstairs of the house.

On the odd occasion when she did see him their conversations were stilted and tended to focus on the practicalities of living together, with him excusing himself before she had chance to ask him anything of a personal nature.

Seeing the place in total disarray on Friday night when he returned from work, Jack had then suddenly announced he was flying off to Italy for a few days to meet with a business acquaintance, though she suspected he was deliberately making himself scarce— partly to avoid having to live in what felt very much like a building site, but mostly to avoid having to be around her all weekend.

This thought made her stomach twist with a mixture of sadness and dejection. She'd really hoped that her confession in the pub garden would bring them closer, but instead it seemed to have driven even more of a wedge between them, crushing any hope she'd once had of a reconciliation.

So it was actually a relief in a way to have this huge project to take her mind off things.

With the contacts that she and her friends from the agency had managed to scrape together between them, she'd hired a talented, hard-working team and less than two weeks on she barely recognised the place. Luckily it had only needed cosmetic changes—though old, the house had been kept in good condition—and they'd been achieved with the minimum of fuss.

She'd not had so much fun at work in a very long time.

The new furniture was sourced from a couple of funky little independent shops on Columbia Road, which suited the brighter, more contemporary palette of colours she'd chosen for the walls and flooring. While it wasn't up to Daphne's standards of wow factor, she was delighted with the end result.

It was a much more relaxing, comfortable place to hang out in now.

When Jack returned a couple of days before they were due to do the interview with Perdita she stood nervously in the living room with him, crossing her fingers as he stared around him with an expression of pure amazement on his face.

'Well, Em, I think you've found your calling. This is fantastic!' he said finally, turning to give her a wide, genuine smile.

Her heart lurched at the sight of his pleasure, the tension in her shoulders fading away.

'Not a woodchip to be seen,' she joked, feeling her tummy flip when he grinned back at her.

'You've done an amazing job, thank you,' he said, walking over to where she stood.

Seeing him here again, with his hair dishevelled and dark smudges under his eyes, had sent her senses into overdrive and she was having a hard time keeping her nerves under wraps.

'I'm glad you like it. I had a real blast working on it,' she said, having to force herself to maintain eye contact so he wouldn't see how jittery she was feeling in his charismatic presence.

'I can tell. It shows,' he said, looking at her with a strange expression now. Was that pride she could see in his eyes?

Prickly heat rushed over her skin as they both stared at each other for a long, tension-filled moment.

Jack broke the atmosphere by clearing his throat. 'Well, I'm going to go and check in with the US office then head off to bed,' he said, running a hand over his tousled hair. He looked so exhausted she had a mad urge to spring into full-on wife mode and start fussing around him, telling him not to bother with work, but to go straight to bed and get some rest.

She didn't though.

Because she knew that it wasn't her place to do that. She was only his wife in name after all.

Sadness swamped her as she accepted the painful reality that she'd forfeited the right to have a say in how he lived his life six years ago.

He wasn't hers to care for any more.

* * *

The next morning, just one day before Perdita and her crew were due to sweep in and dissect their lives for the entertainment of the general public like some kind of twisted anthropology project, she was surprised to see Jack striding into the kitchen at nine o'clock in the morning.

She was in the process of stuffing her mouth with a croissant she'd rewarded herself with for all her hard work over the last few days, so it took her a moment to comment on his remarkable appearance.

'What are you doing here?' she muttered through a mouthful of buttery pastry, her heart racing at the sight of him looking all fresh and clean from the shower and, oh, so strikingly handsome in a dark grey, sharply tailored Italian suit.

'I happen to live here,' he replied, with one eyebrow raised.

'I know that. I'm just surprised to see you here so late in the day. You've always been up and out with the lark before now.'

'Some of us don't have the good fortune of having regular lie-ins,' he said, the twinkle in his eye letting her know he was only teasing her.

She turned back to her plate and chewed the last of the croissant hard, feeling heat rise to her cheeks. She hadn't even brushed her hair this morning and was still in her scruffy old brushed-cotton pyjamas, assuming he'd already left for the office when she'd got up to a quiet house.

Hearing the kettle begin to boil, she turned to look towards where he now stood, dropping a teabag into a mug. The ends of his hair were curling around the collar of his pristine white shirt and without thinking she said, 'You need a haircut.'

Swivelling to face her, he shot her an amused grin. 'Are you nagging me, wife?'

The heat in her cheeks increased. 'No!' She cleared her throat, distracted by the sudden lump she found there. 'I don't know why I said that. I just noticed, that's all.'

Turning back to her croissant again, she tried to ignore his rueful chuckle and the clinking and clanking noises as he made his breakfast. Grace and economy of movement had never been his more dominant traits.

He sat down opposite her, bringing with him his fresh, clean scent, and her stomach did a little dance.

Trying to smooth out some of the tangles in her hair, she gave him a sheepish smile.

Not that she should worry about what Jack thought of her looking such a mess. He'd always liked seeing her in disarray and had often commented on how sexy he found it after they'd made love in the good old days.

The rogue memory of it only made her face flame even hotter.

'How come you're not in the office already?' she asked, concentrating on brushing her fingers together to knock off the remaining flaky crumbs so she didn't have to look him in the eye.

'I have a meeting in Chelsea at nine-thirty so I'm having a slow start to the morning for once.' He shifted in his chair so he could pick up his mug of tea and take a swig from it, peering at her from over the top of the rim.

'And I have a favour to ask of you,' he said, once he'd had a good swallow of tea.

She looked at him in surprise. 'A favour?'

'Yes.'

'What is it?'

He shifted in his chair again, only this time looking a little discomfited.

'We've been invited to a party tonight, by a business acquaintance of mine. I could do with turning up and doing some schmoozing. The guy might be interested in having me buy out his company and I wanted to work on him in a more relaxed environment.'

'Okay,' she said slowly, her pulse picking up at the thought of spending the evening at his side. 'This is tonight, did you say?'

'Yes. It's in a house a couple of streets away.'

'And you want me to go with you as your *wife*?' Saying the words made her ache a little inside.

'You've got it in one.' He flashed her a grin, which she struggled to return.

Splaying his hands on the table, he looked her directly in the eye now. 'Look, I know it's probably the last thing you feel like doing, what with our lives and relationship being so complicated at the moment, but I wouldn't ask if it wasn't really important.'

She glanced down at the table where his hands still lay spread on the solid oak top, her eyes snagging on the second finger of his left hand as she noticed something glinting there.

He was wearing his wedding ring.

Her blood began to pound through her veins. Even though she knew it was all for show, the sight of the gold ring that she'd touched with such wonder and awe after she'd slid it onto his finger at their simple wedding ceremony, back there on his finger, made her body buzz with elation.

'Yes, okay, I'll go,' she blurted, buoyed by the fact that he'd asked for her help. She would happily do whatever it took to make things easier between them. She owed him that. And she'd missed him while he'd been away and liked the idea of spending time with him this evening.

His look of gratified surprise made her think he'd been expecting her to refuse.

'Thank you, Emma, I really appreciate it.'

'You're welcome.'

His full mouth widened into a smile, the lines at the corners of his eyes deepening, reviving the look of boyish charm that had swept her off her feet all those years ago, stealing her breath away.

She loved his face, especially when he let down that façade of cool that he wore for the rest of the world. It had taken a long time for him to trust her enough to let her see the real him, but when he had it had blown her away.

Was this the Jack she used to know finally peering out at her?

They stared at each other for another long, painful moment, where her traitorous brain decided to give her a Technicolor recap of the most blissful moments from their past, until she finally managed to tear her gaze away from his and stand up.

'What time do we need to get there?' she asked, making a big show of pushing her chair neatly under the table so she didn't have to look at him again in case her apprehension was written all over her face.

She needed to remember that this was just a business arrangement to him, not a date.

'We'll leave here at eight-thirty. It's a formal do, so if you have a little black dress or something it would be great if you could wear it.'

His voice sounded strained now and she wondered wistfully whether she'd somehow infected him with her own feelings of poignant nostalgia.

'No problem,' she said, turning and walking away from him before she blurted out something she might regret later.

The party was in full swing when they arrived and Emma was surprised, but delighted, when Jack kept hold of her arm after helping her climb the smooth slate steps up to the house in her sky-high heels. He'd been very complimentary about how she looked this evening, and she'd had to forcefully remind herself that his noticing how she looked probably didn't mean the same thing to him as it did to her.

After greeting their hosts, they walked into the living room to mingle with the rest of the partygoers and he turned to give her a reassuring smile as she tightened her grip on him, feeling a little overawed at being a guest at a party like this again.

'Just relax, it's a friendly crowd,' he told her.

But unfortunately he couldn't have been more wrong.

'Oh, no!' she whispered, coming to a halt in the middle of the room as a horrible thump of recognition hit her in the chest at the sight of a group of people standing next to the large picture window.

Angry resentment rattled through her as she relived the whispered taunts and cruel asides she'd been the victim to from this very group of people after the scandalous news about her father came out.

'Vultures,' she whispered to Jack, 'who used to call themselves friends of my family, until they called in their loans and sold us out to the press.'

Looking up into his handsome face, she was a little afraid of what she might see there. Would he be sorry now that he'd brought her here tonight?

But instead of showing concern, his eyes darkened with anger. 'No one here will dare say a word to you, I promise you that,' he growled, putting her in mind of a wild animal defending its territory. 'If anyone so much as smirks in your general direction I'll make sure they regret it.'

Her heart leapt at his show of protectiveness, but she knew she couldn't really expect him to step in for her; this was her problem to deal with, not his. 'As heartening as this display of macho chest-beating is, I can't expect you to hang around by my side all night, ready to jump in and defend my honour,' she joked, trying to lighten the atmosphere. She didn't want this to have any kind of impact on his business deal.

'Yes, you can, Em. You're my wife and I'm staying right here next to you.'

The resolve in his eyes gave her goose bumps. She knew he meant every word he said—could feel it in the crackling atmosphere around him. He would look after her tonight, if she needed him to.

'Emma, look at me,' he said quietly, cupping her jaw in his hands and drawing her closer to him so she was forced to look him in the eye, her pulse playing a merry beat in her throat.

'You're the bravest person I know,' he said. 'You didn't slink away and give up when everything went to hell for you and I know you won't give these idiots the satisfaction of breaking you tonight either. This is an opportunity for you to show them just how incredibly strong you are and how much you've achieved despite the cards being stacked against you. You should be proud of yourself. I'm proud of you. Proud to call you my wife.'

The air beat a pulse between them, as she rolled his pep talk around in her mind. He was proud of her? Proud to be her husband? Hearing those words suddenly made her anger at the people here fade into the background. She could handle anything they said to her if she truly had Jack on her side. There wasn't anything they could do to hurt her any more.

Buoyed by that uplifting insight, she gave Jack a grateful nod and a smile.

'It means a lot to me to hear you say that, Jack.' She turned and took his arm again, wrapping her fingers tightly around his biceps, feeling him pull her more tightly against his body.

To her surprise, Jack then marched them straight up to the group, who were staring at them with a kind of cynical fascination.

'Do you have something you'd like to say to my wife?' Jack growled at them and she was both astonished and amused to see them all take a small step backwards and shake their heads as one.

'We were just saying what an impressive couple you make,' a red-faced man who used to go out shooting with her father said in a faltering voice. 'And that you're a very lucky man to have such a beautiful wife, Westwood.'

The whole group nodded in agreement, but Jack didn't move away from them, giving every last one of them that unnerving weighted stare that Emma knew from first-hand experience he was so good at employing.

'And that we're sorry we weren't more supportive about your situation after your father died, Emma,' a tall, moustached man with a slight stoop said hurriedly. 'It's good to see that you're happy and settled now though,' he added.

Emma coolly nodded her thanks, knowing he didn't mean a word of it.

Not that she cared one jot.

'It's all water under the bridge,' she said, smiling serenely to show them just how little they meant to her now.

After that, they strode confidently around the room, arm in arm in a show of solidarity, with Jack loudly and proudly introducing her to everyone as his wife, and her floating around on a cloud of happy contentment.

Jack's gaze followed Emma as she walked back towards him after getting her glass refilled at the makeshift bar that Rob, a prospective business partner, had set up in the corner of his grand living room.

She really was breathtaking to behold. Her head was held high and her body language confident, showcasing the natural elegance and poise he admired so much in her.

Emma had been brilliant with Rob, laughing at his

jokes and showing interest in his tales of his children and their schooling. She'd asked him intelligent questions and had clearly listened to the answers because she was able to comment on them with thoughtful insight. Even Rob's wife was charmed by her, which was an unexpected bonus. The woman was known for being standoffish with the wives of her husband's business acquaintances, but Emma had managed to break through her wall of cool and engage her in a conversation about interior design and the woman had even gone so far as to give Emma a quick tour of their newly decorated bedrooms.

He'd been intrigued to see how genuinely interested Emma was in talking about the redecoration she'd done to his house. Considering how little time she'd had to get it done, he was hugely impressed by what she'd achieved. And she really seemed to have enjoyed it too, judging by the gleam in her eye and the flush in her cheeks when they'd looked over the improvements together.

It seemed she was a natural.

And far too talented to be wasting her time serving drinks at parties.

He ran a hand over his hair, watching with a growing sense of impatience as she stopped to talk to a woman who pointed at the dress she was wearing and gave her a complimentary smile.

Even though he'd been flat out with work, he'd not been able to keep his mind off the knowledge that she'd be there in his house when he got home each evening—and, even more frustratingly, that he wouldn't be returning to one of her beguiling smiles and her soothing embrace.

After having time away from her for the last week or so, which had given him more of a chance to ruminate on what she'd revealed after they'd visited his parents' house, he realised that her heartfelt admission seemed to have broken the evil spell his pride had held over him since they'd parted ways.

He ached to be on friendlier terms with her, rather than having to step so carefully around her as he had been doing.

Hopefully the plan he'd put in place for when they were finally able to escape this party would set him on a path towards that.

'Did you manage to speak to Rob alone? Is it a done deal?' Emma murmured into his ear as she finally made it back to where he stood.

The soft caress of her breath on his skin chased shivers up his spine.

Taking a steadying breath, he turned to look her in the eye; hyperaware of his pulse beating an erratic rhythm through his veins as he looked into her beautiful face and saw only genuine interest and concern for him there.

Was there still something there between them? And could there be something again, even after all this time?

He pushed the thought away, knowing he was playing with fire even considering the idea.

'Yes, I'm all done here. It's time to go,' he told her, detecting a flash of relief on her face.

He made a mental note to pay her back tenfold for putting herself out for him like this. Her willingness to help him proved she was still the same big-hearted, generous person she'd always been. This travesty with her father hadn't broken her—in fact, like the age-old adage, it had only made her stronger.

Taking her hand, he gently led her towards the door, where their hosts were standing, chatting to a group of new people that had just arrived.

'Rob, we're going to make a move. Thanks for a good party,' he said to his future associate, shaking the man's hand.

'Glad the two of you could make it,' Rob said, returning the firm handshake and giving Emma a courteous nod. 'It was lovely to meet you, Emma. I hope we get to spend more time with you soon.'

He meant it too; Jack could tell by the conviction in the man's voice. It was one of the things that had him excited about amalgamating their companies. Rob was well known for his straight-talking attitude and ability to cut through the bull. They seemed to be very similar in the way they conducted business and he was going to be a most useful ally.

'Thank you for your kind hospitality,' Emma said graciously, returning Rob's smile and accepting a kiss on both cheeks from his apparently rather lovestruck wife, who was gazing at Emma with something akin to adoration in her eyes.

Not that he was surprised; she was such a genuine, warm person it was impossible not to fall under her spell.

The air was mercifully cool on his overheated skin as they walked carefully down the smooth slate steps of the Chelsea town house, making allowances for Emma's high heels.

His body twitched with nerves as he ran over what he had planned for them this evening. It had taken some doing—calling in favours from here, there and everywhere—but he was pleased with what he'd been able to pull together at the last second.

The idea had struck him earlier as he'd watched her walk away from the kitchen table looking adorably dishevelled in her baggy old pyjamas that had done absolutely nothing to dampen his body's desire for her.

She was the kind of woman that would look sexy in a hessian sack.

After the years of hard work she'd put into clearing her father's name, denying herself the kind of life that she ought to have been living as a young, driven and intelligent woman, it was time she was allowed to have some fun for once.

As they reached the pavement, right on cue his driver pulled up next to them in the car.

Emma turned to frown at him. 'You ordered the car to pick us up to drive us the two streets home? I know my heels are a bit high, but I think that's what you'd call overkill, Jack. I can make it a hundred yards in them without falling flat on my face, you know.'

He shot her a grin. 'I'm sure you can, but do you really want to take the chance? Especially if we have to make a run for it into the house.'

Shaking her long, sleek hair back over her shoulder, she gave an indifferent shrug. 'I've been managing fine all evening and I'm getting quite good at putting on a blithely bored face for any journos that cross my path now.'

He smiled as she treated him to a demonstration of the facial expression she'd just described.

'Actually, we're not going home,' he told her.

'Where are we going, then? We have the interview

with Perdita in the morning, remember, and I don't think she'll be too impressed to have to change her article's name to *"At home with two hungover zombies"*. It's not that kind of magazine.'

Flashing her a grin of wry amusement, he motioned for her to get into the car, holding the door open for her and raising a playful eyebrow when she frowned at him in confusion.

'Don't worry, Cinderella, I'll have you back before midnight. Well, maybe a *little* after midnight.'

'From *where*?' she asked pointedly.

'You'll see. It's a surprise. Trust me,' he added when she gave him the side-eye.

Muttering under her breath, she finally relented and slid into the back seat of the car, swinging her long legs in last so he was rewarded with a flash of her slender, creamy-skinned thighs before shutting the door for her.

The evocative image remained stubbornly planted in his mind until he managed to shake it out by determinedly replacing it with a vision of his plan for the evening.

The car drove them slowly out of Chelsea then along the tree-lined Embankment that ran next to the majestic expanse of the river Thames, the newly hung sparkling Christmas lights running parallel with their route. Taking a right, they travelled across Vauxhall Bridge then past the vibrant greenery of Lambeth Palace Gardens until their final destination was in sight.

Emma didn't utter a word throughout their whole journey, but repeatedly gave him searching looks as famous landmarks passed them by, which he gently rebuffed each time with a secretive smile.

By the time John pulled the car up a short walking distance from the South Bank promenade her brow was so crinkled and her eyes so wide with bafflement he couldn't help but laugh.

'We're here,' he said, and, not waiting for her reply, he got out to walk round the back of the car and open her door for her. 'I wanted to do something to say thank you for all the work you've put into making the house look so spectacular,' he said as he took her hand and helped her out of the car, holding onto her until she'd centred her balance on those preposterously high heels of hers.

Her fingers felt cool and fragile in his grip and he had a mad urge to wrap his arms around her and hold her close, to let her know he was there for her now and she didn't need to do it on her own any more.

He didn't though, afraid that he might wind up with both a sore shin and a profoundly bruised ego.

Not that he didn't deserve that.

'Are we going to see a film?' she asked with a hint of disappointment in her voice.

'Nope,' he said, looping his arm through hers and letting out a secret breath of relief when she didn't pull away from him.

Her body radiated heat next to him as they walked along the mercifully deserted riverside towards their destination, arm in arm, the culmination of his plan for the evening looming over them in all its grand spherical glory.

She stumbled a little and he tightened his grip to keep her upright.

'Okay, you're going to have to tell me where we're going so I know how far I have to make it in these *not made for hiking along the South Bank* heels,' she grumbled.

He smiled at her frustration, which of course only made her scowl back at him.

'Okay, we're here,' he said as they reached the entrance to the London Eye where a young woman was standing at the end of a plush red carpet, snuggled into a jacket branded with the attraction's logo.

Emma stared at him in surprise. 'The Eye? But I thought they closed it at night.'

'Not for us. They've made a special exception.'

She blinked twice. 'Why?'

'Because when I told them how much you deserved a chance to finally have something you wanted they had no choice but to say yes.'

She looked at him as if she couldn't quite believe this was happening, her nose adorably wrinkled.

'Let's get on,' he said, tugging gently on her arm.

She looked up at him and he smiled at the expression of awe on her face.

'I hope you're ready for the ride of your life, Em.'

CHAPTER NINE

EMMA SMILED IN stunned wonder at the woman who greeted them warmly by name and invited them to board one of the luxurious glass-domed pods that gradually travelled upwards to give the rider an un-surpassed view of the London skyline.

Tightening his grip on her arm, as if sensing she needed a little persuading to believe this was actu-ally real, Jack guided her along the carpet and into the dimly lit interior of the pod, where the doors im-mediately swished closed behind them.

It hit her then exactly what this meant.

Jack had remembered how she'd once talked about wanting to commandeer the whole wheel for her own personal ride one day, so she could look down on the sprawling metropolis at midnight—how it was on her whimsical bucket list to gaze down at the city that had always held such excitement for her in her youth and feel like a goddess of all she surveyed.

He'd remembered that and gone out of his way to make it happen for her.

Her heart did a somersault in her chest at the thought.

In fact the only thing missing from her fantasy was—

'Champagne!'

Swivelling to face him, she was totally unable to keep the astonished grin off her face. 'You arranged for a bottle of champagne on ice for us to drink up there?'

'I did.' The look of deep gratification in his eyes at her excited response sent shivers down her spine.

Deftly popping the cork out of the bottle, he filled two flutes and handed one to her.

She took it with a trembling hand, first clinking it against his then taking a long sip in the hope the alcohol would help calm her raging pulse.

'Cheers,' he murmured, taking a sip from his own glass but keeping his gaze fixed firmly on hers.

Unable to maintain eye contact for fear of giving away her nervous excitement at what he'd done for her and what it could mean, she moved away from him, taking a long, low breath in an attempt to pull herself together. She shouldn't read too much into this. After all, he'd made sure to tell her it was a reward for helping him out, nothing more.

Walking further into the pod and taking another large gulp of fizz, she noticed that the large wooden bench in the middle had been covered in soft red velvet cushions for them to sit on.

'You know, for the want of a camping stove and some basic provisions I could probably live in here for the rest of my life,' she joked nervously, walking over to look out of the floor-to-ceiling glass windows as the pod continued its breathtaking ascent.

The hairs stood up on the back of her neck as she felt him come to stand behind her, so close that she could feel his warm breath tickling the skin of her cheek.

'Beautiful,' he murmured, and she wasn't sure whether he was talking about her or the view.

She was trembling all over now, unable to keep her nerves at being here alone with him from visibly showing. It *terrified* her how much she craved to feel his arms around her, holding her tightly as they enjoyed this experience together.

Taking another big gulp of champagne, she was surprised to find she'd finished the glassful.

'Here, let me refill that for you,' Jack said, taking the flute gently out of her fingers.

She stared sightlessly out at the view, her senses entirely diverted by the man moving purposefully around behind her.

He returned a moment later and she took the refilled glass gratefully from him, recognising a desperate need to maintain the bolstering buzz of courage that the alcohol gave her as it warmed her chest.

'Em? Are you okay?' she heard him murmur behind her, the power of his presence overwhelming her senses and making her head spin.

'I'm fine, Jack.'

He put a hand on her arm, urging her to turn and face him.

Swivelling reluctantly on the spot, she looked up into his captivating eyes.

'You were amazing tonight, you know,' he said, pushing a strand of hair away from her face and tucking it behind her ear, sending a rush of goose bumps across her skin where he touched her. 'You conducted yourself with such integrity, a quality a lot of the people there tonight would never be able to claim for themselves.'

'Thank you.' Her words came out sounding stilted and coarse due to a sudden constriction in her chest. 'Well, I'm glad I didn't let you down as your—' she swallowed '—wife.'

He snorted gently and glanced down, frowning. 'You've never let me down, Em.' When he looked back at her his eyes were full of regret. 'It was me that expected too much from you too fast after your father died, then gave up on you too quickly. I've been selfish and short-sighted.'

She blinked, shocked by his sudden confession and not sure how to respond to it.

He sighed, his shoulders slumping. Moving to stand next to her now at the floor-to-ceiling window, he rested his forehead against the glass and stared out across the vast, night-lit city. They were a good way up in the air now, much higher than any of the buildings that surrounded them.

Together, but alone, at the top of the world.

'I hate myself for the way I treated you back then. I don't know what made me think it was okay to expect you to jump, just because I asked you to. I was an arrogant, naïve fool who had no idea how a marriage really worked.'

Pushing away from the window, he turned to face her again, his expression fierce.

'I miss what we had, Emma.'

He took a small step towards her and her heart rate accelerated.

'I remember everything from our time together as if it was yesterday,' he murmured, his gaze sweeping her face. 'How beautiful you look when you wake up all tousled in the mornings, the way your laugh never fails to send a shiver down my spine, how kind and non-judgemental you are towards every single person you meet.' His gaze rested on her mouth, which tingled in response to his avid attention.

'You're a good person through and through, Emma Westwood.'

Adrenaline was making her heart leap about in her chest now and the pod, which had felt so spacious for two people only minutes ago, suddenly felt too small.

His dark gaze moved up to fix on hers. 'I've been punishing you for rejecting me—' he took a ragged breath '—because you broke my heart, Em.' His voice cracked on the words and on instinct she reached out to lay a hand against his chest, over his heart, as if she could somehow undo the damage she'd done to it.

He glanced down at where her hand lay before looking up to recapture her gaze with his. 'The way I responded was totally unfair. I know that now. And I'm sorry. Truly sorry, Emma.'

Her breath caught in her throat as she saw tears well in his eyes.

He was hurting as badly as she was.

This revelation finally broke through her restraint and an overwhelming urge to soothe him compelled her to close the gap between them. Wrapping her arms around him, she pressed her lips to his and immediately felt him respond by pulling her hard against his body and kissing her back with an intensity that took her breath away.

Opening her mouth to drag in a gasp of pleasure, she felt his tongue slide between her parted lips and skim against her own, bringing with it the heady familiar taste of him. She'd missed kissing him, so profoundly it made her physically ache with relief to finally be able to revel in its glorious return.

They moved against each other in an exquisitely sensual dance, their hands pushing under clothing, sliding over skin, reading each other's bodies with their fingertips.

Stumbling together, they moved to the centre of the pod and Jack carefully laid her down on the soft velvet cushions, not letting her go for a second, and she let him take control, forcing herself not to ruin this by questioning the wisdom of what they were doing—because she needed this right now, needed to blot out all the complications and responsibilities in her life and just sink into the safe familiarity of his strength.

To feel desired and happy and free again.

The sex was fast and desperate, as if they couldn't stop themselves even if they'd wanted to. Their hands and mouths were everywhere, their touch wild and unrestrained.

Alone, but together, at the top of the world.

Afterwards, after they'd come back down to earth and stumbled out of the pod, rumpled and high on champagne and emotion, they returned home and made love again, this time taking the opportunity to explore each other's bodies properly, relearning what they used to know and finding comfort and joy in the fact that being together again was as wonderful as they remembered—maybe even more so—until they finally fell asleep in each other's arms, both mentally and physically replete after their long-awaited wedding night.

* * *

Jack woke the next morning with a deep sense of satisfaction warming his body.

Memories of having Emma in his arms last night swam across his vision and he allowed himself to exult in them for a while before opening his eyes.

He hadn't intended to make love to her last night, the trip on the London Eye was meant to be an apology for the awful, cold way he'd been acting towards her, but she'd looked so wary to be there alone with him he'd known if he wanted to gain her trust again he was going to have to be totally honest with her about how he was feeling.

It had been incredibly hard saying those things to her after years of burying his feelings so deeply inside him, but he was intensely relieved that they were finally out in the open.

He knew now with agonising certainty that he'd never felt like this with anyone but her. The women he'd dated in the years they'd been apart had all been pale imitations of her. Mere tracing paper versions. Without substance. None of them had her grace and finesse, or her smart, sharp wit. Or her beauty.

After Emma had left him, he'd shut himself off from romantic emotion, not wanting to deal with the torment he'd been put through, but as soon as she'd reappeared in his life all those feelings had come rushing back. But it had been too painful to bear at first, like emotional pins and needles. So he'd numbed himself against her.

Until it wasn't possible to any more.

From the way she'd kept herself gently aloof from him since they'd met again he'd been afraid that she wasn't interested in renewing their connection—that she'd moved on from him—but judging by the passionate fervour of her lovemaking last night, it seemed she did still care about him after all.

Which led him to believe that there might be hope for them yet.

Excitement buzzed through his veins and he turned to look for the woman who had made him an intensely happy man last night, only to be disappointed when he found the space where she'd lain in bed next to him empty and cold.

Frowning, he grabbed his phone, glancing at the screen to see it was already eight-thirty. It wasn't like him to sleep in late, but after the intensity of the night before he guessed it wasn't entirely surprising.

At least he'd taken today off work to be available for the *Babbler* interview, so he and Emma would be able to spend the day in each other's company— hopefully most of it in bed.

Heart feeling lighter than it had in years, he got up and took a quick shower, then pulled on some fresh clothes.

It was a shame there wasn't time to lure her back to bed now. That damn interview! It was the very last thing he wanted to do today.

Still, perhaps once Perdita had cleared off he could take Emma out for a slap-up meal to apologise for forcing her to take part in his father's media circus, then drag her back to the house for a lot more personal attention and a chance for them to talk about their future together.

Taking the stairs two at a time, he went straight to

the kitchen to seek out Emma so they could start their life together again as soon as possible.

Emma had woken up in the dark to find Jack's arm lying heavily across her chest and his leg hooked over hers, trapping her within the cage of his body.

Her first thought was, *What have I done?*

She'd let her crazy romantic notions get the better of her, that was what.

She was suddenly terrified that she'd made a terrible mistake.

Heart pounding, she'd wriggled out of his covetous embrace and dashed into the en-suite bathroom, her forehead damp with sweat and her limbs twitchy with adrenaline.

After splashing some water on her face and feeling her heart rate begin to return to normal, she'd crept back out to the bedroom and stood looking at Jack as he slept. He'd looked so peaceful, lying there on his side, with his arm still outstretched as if he were holding onto the ghost of her presence.

Unable to bear the idea of getting back into bed with him when her feelings were in such chaos, she went to her own room to get dressed, then headed downstairs to make herself a soothing cup of tea. She sat with it at the table, staring into space and thinking, thinking, thinking...

Half an hour later, she was still sitting there with a cold cup of tea in front of her, her thoughts a blur of conflicting emotions.

She was so confused, so twisted into knots. In her haze of lust and alcohol last night she'd thought she'd be able to remain in control and keep her feelings safe.

What an idiot she'd been.

It hadn't taken much for him to break through the barriers she'd so carefully constructed over the last six years to keep her safe from any more emotional upheaval.

Just the thought of it made her go cold with fear.

What had she been thinking, imagining reconciliation with Jack was what she wanted? It was crazy to try and reinstate what they'd once had. Impossible! They couldn't just pick up where they'd left off and she couldn't put herself through the torment of wondering when it was all going to be ripped away from her again.

Because it would be.

She didn't get to keep the people she loved.

Anyway, he was still probably clinging on to a vision of her from when she was eighteen, all bright-eyed and full of naïve optimism. The Emma she'd been then was the perfect match for someone of his standing—a billionaire businessman and earl of the realm—but the Emma she was now was all wrong to be the wife of someone like that. Especially as his family put such store in appearances. They'd humoured the match up till now, but surely it would cause all sorts of friction for Jack in the future. It could tear his family apart, and, after having her own torn asunder, that was the last thing she'd wish on him.

He'd only end up hating her for it.

After already suffering through the turmoil of losing him once; she couldn't bear the thought of going through it again. It would break her in two.

She jumped in surprise as Jack came striding into

the kitchen looking all rumpled and sexy, with a wide smile on his face.

Her stomach did an almighty flip at the sight of him, but she dug her fingernails into the table top, reminding herself of all the reasons why it would be a bad idea to take things any further with him.

Striding over to where she sat, he bent down to kiss her and she steeled herself, flinching a little as his mouth made contact with hers.

As he pulled away she could tell from the look of wounded surprise in his eyes that he'd noticed her withdrawal.

'Emma? What's wrong?' he asked, his tone confirming his apprehension.

But before she could answer there was a long ring on the doorbell.

'That'll be Perdita,' Jack said, annoyance tingeing his voice. 'She's early.'

Jack paced the floor of the living room with a feeling of dread lying heavily in his gut while Emma went to let Perdita and the photographer in.

He didn't understand why she was suddenly acting so coldly towards him after what they'd shared last night. The way she'd flinched away from his kiss had completely rattled him.

A moment later she reappeared with Perdita hot on her heels, the journalist bringing with her a cloud of the same cloying perfume she'd worn the last time they'd seen her.

Jack's stomach rolled as it twisted up his nose.

'Jack, darling! How lovely to see you again!' Perdita shot him a quick smile before striding around the room, glancing around at the décor that Emma had so painstakingly instated.

'What a wonderful room! The lighting is perfect for taking some photos of the two of you in here. What do you think, David?'

David, the photographer, nodded his agreement, then carelessly dumped his camera bag and laptop onto the polished cherry-wood coffee table.

Jack saw Emma wince in his peripheral vision, but she didn't utter a word of reproach. Perhaps she thought she had no right to because this wasn't her house. The thought frustrated him, making his limbs twitchy and his head throb.

'It's good for me,' David said, nodding at a light metre he was now holding up. 'I'll get set up while you do the interview, Perdie.'

'Okey-dokey,' Perdita trilled, turning to Jack with a simpering smile, then looking towards where Emma still stood in the doorway. 'Let's get started, shall we?'

They all sat down, he and Emma on the sofa next to each other and Perdita in the armchair opposite.

As Jack sat back his leg pressed up against Emma's and he bristled as she shifted away from his touch. Perdita was never going to believe they were a happily married couple if it looked as if she couldn't even stand to sit next to him.

What was going on? Had he done or said something last night that had upset her? If he had, he had no idea what it could have been.

He took a breath and slung his arm around her shoulders. She tensed a little under his touch, but at least she didn't move away this time.

Looking over at Perdita, he steeled himself for

spending the next half an hour—that was all he was going to give her—fielding her impertinent questions about his and Emma's life together, while also trying to make their relationship sound real and exciting enough to titillate the readers of *Babbler* magazine.

'So, how are the plans for the renewal of your wedding vows going?' Perdita purred, after she'd set up her phone to record their conversation.

'Er…well, we're still talking about when and how we're going to do it—' Emma said quickly, her smile looking fixed and her eyes overly bright when he glanced round at her.

'Uh-huh,' Perdita intoned, looking between the two of them with a quizzical little pinch in her forehead.

'We're hoping it'll be some time in the new year. We'll let you know when we've made some firm plans,' Jack said brusquely, in an attempt to close that line of questioning down as quickly as possible. Emma shuffled in her seat beside him.

Luckily Perdita didn't press them on it.

'So are you planning on spending Christmas here? I see you already have your decorations up,' Perdita said brightly, sweeping her hands around to gesture at the strings of silver baubles that Emma had hung from the picture rails and the spicy scented Douglas fir she'd covered with tasteful vintage Victorian ornaments.

'Yes, I think we'll be here for Christmas this year,' Jack replied, glancing around him at the decorations. They lent the room such a cosy festive air, so much so he found he was actually enjoying sitting in his living room for once, despite having to answer Perdita's inane questions.

'It must be so lovely to have a family home again to spend Christmas Day in, Emma. I understand you had to sell the house you grew up in after your poor father passed on,' Perdita cooed, raising her brow in a shocking show of pseudo sympathy.

'That's right, Perdita, we did,' Emma answered, keeping her chin up and her gaze locked with the woman's though Jack was aware of her shoulders tensing ever so slightly. 'And yes, it'll be a lovely house to spend Christmas in.'

He was desperate to call a halt to this ridiculous debacle, but he didn't want to give the woman the satisfaction of seeing him riled.

'You know, Perdita, Emma did all the interior design in the house,' he said, leaning in to draw the journalist's unscrupulous attention away from his wife.

Perdita glanced around at him, quickly hiding a flash of irritation that he'd foiled her underhand pursuit of some juicy gossip with which to titillate her readers. 'Is that right?'

'Yes. She has a real talent for it, my wife. I'm incredibly proud of her. In fact, why don't you mention to your readers that she's available for consultation if they're looking for an interior designer? I can give them a personal guarantee that they'll be delighted with Emma's talent for making a house into a home.'

He picked up Emma's hand from her lap, giving it a reassuring squeeze. After a second's pause she gave him a squeeze back.

There was definitely something very wrong here. Was she feeling ill? Too tired from their night of passion to think straight? Just sick to death of being hounded for answers to questions that brought up painful memories from her past?

Perdita continued to fire tricky questions at them: about how they fell in love, how they came to be reconciled, what their plans were for their future together and even though Emma fielded the questions well with vague but upbeat answers he imagined he could feel her slipping further and further away from him with every second that passed.

By the time the interview finally concluded he was desperate to get Perdita out of the house so that he and Emma could talk again in private.

But unfortunately the journalist had other ideas.

'Well, I've got everything I need for the article. We just need to get some lovely snaps of the two of you together in this beautiful living room. You've done such a wonderful job on the décor, Emma. It'll make a lovely backdrop.'

She stood up from the armchair that she'd been perched on and Jack and Emma stood up awkwardly too.

Judging by the look on Emma's face, Jack was pretty sure she was as desperate for this to be over as he was.

'Are you ready for us, David?' Perdita called out to her photographer.

'As I'll ever be, Perdie,' David replied, shooting them all a wink.

They allowed Perdita to manhandle them into a 'loving' clinch on the sofa by the window, and Jack's spirits sank even lower as he felt Emma tense as he wrapped his arms around her.

'Okay, let's have a lovely kiss now, shall we?' Perdita purred, giving them a lascivious smile.

To his horror, he realised Emma was actually vibrating with tension now and when he turned his head to look at her, his gut twisted as he saw only a cool remoteness in her eyes.

Leaning forwards, he pressed his lips to hers, hoping he could somehow wake the Emma from last night, to remind her how good it had been between them, and how good it could be again, if only she'd let him back in.

Her mouth was cool and pliant beneath his, but he could feel the reluctance in her, taste it on her lips, sense it in the raggedness of her breathing—as if she was only tolerating his touch until she could get away from him without looking bad in front of Perdita.

The rejection tugged hard at him, causing pain in his chest as if she'd torn something loose inside him.

'Wonderful!' Perdita said, as they drew apart.

'Is that it?' Jack asked gruffly, at the very end of his patience with the woman now. He wanted her and her nauseating presence out of his house so he could be on his own with Emma again and finally be able to find out what was going on with her.

'We're done,' Perdita said, all businesslike now as David gathered up his equipment behind her.

'I'll let your mother know when to expect to see the article,' she said.

As soon as he shut the door on Perdita's designer-suited back, Jack returned to the living room to find Emma perched on the arm of the sofa, staring out of the window.

'Thank you for doing that,' he said, walking towards her. 'I'm sorry to put you through it.'

She shrugged, but didn't look at him.

'I guess it'll satisfy your parents. At least for a while.' She took a deep shaky-sounding breath. 'I'm going to go now, Jack,' she said quietly, still not turning around.

His heart turned over at her words. 'What are you talking about?'

She turned to face him, her expression shuttered. 'I need to get out of here.'

Emma took a deep breath, trying not to let Jack's incredulous glare stop her from saying what needed to be said.

'I don't need to stay here now the journalists have stopped prowling around the house and Perdita's got her pound of flesh from us,' she said, keeping her voice steady and emotionless, even though it nearly killed her to do it.

Jack stared at her in shock. 'But you don't need to go, Em. You should stay. I want you to.'

She shook her head. 'I can't stay here now, Jack, not now we've crossed an irreversible line by sleeping together, something we agreed not to do.'

Couldn't he see that they shouldn't risk putting themselves in a position where it might happen again, that it would only make things harder and more complicated later when they started the inevitable divorce proceedings?

'I thought it's what you wanted too,' he ground out, his troubled gaze boring into hers. 'It certainly seemed like it last night.'

She folded her arms across her chest, hugging them around her. 'You didn't really think that one night together would fix what's wrong with our relationship, did you?'

His steady gaze continued to bore into hers, his eyes dark with intent. Sitting down opposite her, he put his elbows on his knees and leaned forwards, his eyes not leaving hers. 'Emma, I want us to try and make this marriage work.'

Her mouth was suddenly so dry she found it hard to swallow and she was aware of a low level of panic beginning to grow in the pit of her stomach.

'We've been apart for too long, Jack. How can we expect to make a relationship work now?' Her voice shook with the effort of keeping her emotions at bay.

'But it does work, Emma, we proved that last night.'

'You didn't really think we could just pick up from where we left off, did you?'

He blinked at her in surprise, then opened his mouth as if to answer.

But she couldn't let him try and persuade her otherwise; this was hard enough as it was. She really couldn't bring herself to trust that it could all be okay with them this time. What guarantees did they have that it wouldn't all fall apart again?

'We shouldn't have let last night happen. Sex always messes things up,' she said, her voice wobbling with tension.

He cleared his throat uncomfortably. 'Are you telling me you regret what happened now?' A muscle was twitching in his jaw and his brow pinched into a disbelieving frown.

She was hurting him; she could see it in his eyes and it was tearing her apart.

'I—can't do this again, Jack.' But her voice held no conviction. She could see that he thought so too by the way he was looking at her.

As if he knew how very close she was to giving in.

He was still looking at her that way as he got up and walked towards her. Still looking as he pushed his hand gently into her hair and tilted her face towards him. Still looking as he brushed his lips against hers with a feather-light kiss that made her insides melt and fizz.

'Don't, Jack...' she murmured against his mouth, her willpower a frail and insubstantial thing that she was having trouble holding onto.

To her surprise he drew back, giving her the space she needed.

Finally acting as though he was *listening* to her.

Sliding his hand out of her hair, he took a deliberate step backwards, but didn't stop looking at her.

She felt the loss of his touch so keenly her body gave a throb of anguish.

'I want us to have another try at our marriage.' He took a breath. 'I need you.'

The passion and the absolute certainty she heard in his voice sent her heart into a slow dive, but she fought the feeling, still too afraid to believe what he was saying was true. 'You don't *need* me, Jack.'

'Yes, I do! There's this big hole in my life without you that I've never been able to fill. It's like part of me is hollow. A wound that just won't heal.'

'You're comparing me to a wound now? How romantic.' But despite her jibe she was aware of a warm glow of longing pulsing deep in her chest now.

She pushed it away, telling herself not to be a fool. It was dangerous to hope for this to work out after last time. Too much time and pain and heartache had come between them since those happier days. He was being naïve to think they could get back what they once had.

He locked his gaze with hers, his expression sincere. 'I'm going to be here for you this time, Em, every step of the way. I'll look after you, I promise.'

'Promises aren't enough, Jack.'

He ran a hand over his face, suddenly looking tired. 'Then what do you want from me? Tell me, Emma!'

'A divorce! Like we'd planned!' she shouted back in frustration.

He stared at her in shock. 'You want to get a divorce after what happened between us last night?'

'It was just sex, Jack. We were both a little tipsy and feeling lonely. It was inevitable, I suppose, after all the time we've been spending together. But it didn't mean anything to me.' She swallowed hard, forcing back a lash of anguish as he stared at her with pain in his eyes.

'Don't tell me last night didn't mean anything to you because I won't believe you, Emma. You're not that good an actress,' he shot at her.

She recoiled at the fury in his voice, resentment suddenly rising from the pit of her belly at the unfairness of it all. 'You want to bet?' she retorted in anger. 'I've had years to perfect my mask. Years of smiling and looking serene in the face of some very taxing situations.'

'Is that what our marriage is to you? A *taxing situation*?'

'It hasn't been a marriage for years, Jack, just an inconvenience,' she shouted in utter frustration, feeling a jab of shame at how cruel that sounded.

Unable to bear the look of hurt on his face any longer, she strode away from him, banging her shin hard on the coffee table in her haste. But she didn't stop to soothe the pain away. She had to get out of there. Away from his befuddling presence. He was making her crazy—bringing back all these feelings she didn't want to have again.

'Where are you going?' he said, trying to block her path with his body, but she pushed past him, dodging away from his outstretched hand.

'Emma, can we please talk some more about this?'

'It's not what I want, Jack. I've already explained that. There's no point trying to hold onto the past. We can never get back what we once had. Everything's different now.'

'It doesn't have to be, Em. Fundamentally we're still the same people. We can make this marriage work.'

Shaking her head, she backed away from him. 'No, I'm sorry, Jack.' She took a deep shaky breath and dug her nails into her palms. 'I don't want to be married to you any more.'

Jack felt as though his heart were being crushed in his chest.

'Don't leave, Emma. Please. Stay and we'll talk some more about it.' He put a hand on her arm, aware that he was vibrating with fear now. *'Please.'*

Shaking her head, she pulled away from his touch and stumbled backwards. 'I can't, Jack.'

Her gaze met his and all he saw there was a wild determination to get away from him.

Chest tight with sorrow, he tried one last time to get through to her. 'Emma, I love you, please don't leave me again.'

Putting up a hand as if to block his words, she took another step away, reinforcing the barrier between them, rebuffing his pleas.

'I have to go,' she said, her voice rough and broken. 'I can't be here any more. Don't follow me. I don't want you to.'

And with that, she turned on her heel and strode away from him.

Frozen with frustration, he remained standing where she'd left him, listening to her mount the stairs and a minute later come back down, hoping—praying—that she'd pause on her way out, to stop and look at him one last time. If she did that, he'd go to her. Hold and comfort her. Tell her she could trust him and he'd make everything okay.

If she did that, he'd know there was still a chance for them.

But she didn't.

Instead he saw a flash of colour as she walked quickly past the doorway to the living room, and a few seconds later he heard the front door open, then close with the resounding sound of her leaving.

Silence echoed around the room, taunting him, widening the hollow cavity that she'd punched into his chest with her words.

Picking up a vase that Emma had bought as part

of the house redecoration project, he hurled it against the wall with all his strength, drawing a crude satisfaction from seeing it smash into tiny little pieces and litter the floor.

He knew then that this was why he hadn't been back to see her in the six years since he moved to America. His heart had been so eviscerated the first time he hadn't wanted to risk damaging it again.

But the moment he'd seen her again at Fitzherbert's party he'd known in the deepest darkest recesses of his brain that he had to have her back. She was the only woman he'd ever loved and making himself vulnerable again for her would be worth the risk.

But it had all been for nothing.

Six years after she'd first broken his heart she'd done it to him all over again.

CHAPTER TEN

EMMA GOT OFF the plane in Bergerac, head-weary and heart-sore.

The very moment she saw her mother's anxious face in the crowd of people waiting to pick up the new arrivals at the airport, the swell of emotion that she'd been keeping firmly tamped down throughout the journey finally broke through. Tears flowed freely down her face as she ran into her mother's arms and held onto her tightly, burying her face in the soft wool of her jumper and breathing in her comforting scent.

'Darling, darling! What's wrong? I was so worried when I picked up your message. Is everything okay?' her mother muttered into her hair.

It took the whole of the thirty-minute journey to her mother's house in the tiny village of Sainte-Alvère for Emma to explain—in a halting monologue broken with tears—about the marriage and aborted elopement and all that had happened to her since Jack had made his shocking reappearance.

Her mother listened in silence. Only once Emma had finished did she reach out her hand to cover her daughter's in a show of understanding and solidarity.

It was such a relief to finally talk to her mother

about it all. She apologised profusely for keeping her in the dark for all this time, but, in a surprising show of self-awareness, her mother seemed more concerned with apologising to Emma for not being there to support her through such tough times.

A little while later they were ensconced on her mother's plant-pot-filled terrace sitting under thick woollen blankets, looking out over the fields behind the house with steaming cups of coffee cradled in their hands.

Philippe, her stepfather, had taken one look at her tear-stained face and promptly left the house so that she and her mother could talk on their own.

'Poor, Philippe, I hope he doesn't feel like I've chased him out of his own home,' Emma said, grimacing at her mother. 'He must still be in pain with his leg.'

'Don't be silly,' her mother said, flapping a hand. 'It's good for him to get out after being stuck here with just me for company for the last few days. He'll be much happier at the bar with Jean.'

Emma stared into the distance, watching the birds wheel in dizzying circles over a copse of trees as dusk fell, bathing the autumnal landscape in a soft, hazy glow.

'You know, I keep asking myself why Jack would want to be with a lowly waitress when he's a billionaire earl,' she said quietly, turning to flash her mother a crooked smile.

Her mother frowned and swatted her hand dismissively. 'He won't be with a *waitress*, he'll be with *you*,' she said fiercely. 'What you do for a living has no bearing whatsoever on you as a person. I'm sure he'll tell you the same.'

Emma sighed and pulled the blanket tighter around her. 'Yeah, I know that really. It's just—' She paused, then said in a rush, 'What if it all went wrong again?'

Her mother smiled sadly. 'That's the chance you take when you fall in love. It's terrifying to make yourself vulnerable like that, but you know what? I was more afraid of what would happen to me if I didn't allow myself to have a relationship with Philippe. It was a good instinct to trust in his love because he brought me alive again.'

She watched her mother smooth her hands over the blanket on her lap.

'I still had to take a leap of faith when he asked me to marry him though,' her mother said, glancing at her with a small frown.

Emma tried to smile, but the muscles around her mouth refused to work, so she stared down at her hands in her lap instead, trying to get herself under control.

'Imagine the alternative, Emma,' her mother said, obviously noticing her distress. 'Imagine what you'll lose if you turn him away because you've given in to your fear. Imagine how that will make you feel. It'll eat away at you, darling—the "What if?"'

When she looked up she was surprised to see tears in her mother's eyes.

'This is all my fault. I should have been stronger for you when your father passed away, Emma. You were too young to take on all that responsibility by yourself—you were just a baby.'

Emma frowned. 'You weren't well, Mum. It wasn't your fault.'

Her mother shook her head, her bottom lip trembling. Lifting a hand, she touched her fingers softly to Emma's cheek. 'You lost your youth and innocence too early and look what it's done to you. You can't even let yourself be loved by a man who's perfect for you. You should. Give him a chance to prove himself to you, Emma. You owe him that much at least. You owe it to yourself to be happy.'

The memory of the hurt on Jack's face suddenly flashed across her vision, causing the hollow ache in her chest to throb and intensify.

Poor Jack.

He'd opened his heart to her and she'd pushed him away.

Again.

It had to have been just as hard for him to let himself fall in love with her again after the way she'd let him down, but he'd trusted his heart to her anyway, making the ultimate sacrifice.

Could she really not do the same for him?

Taking a long, deep breath, she felt determination start to course through her veins.

After everything she'd been through, was she really going to deny herself the chance to carve out a happy and rewarding life for herself?

In that moment she knew deep down that she wanted to be with Jack, she loved him and it was worth risking her heart if it meant she got the chance to be with him again.

But would Jack still want her after all she'd put him through?

There was only one way to find out.

She was going to have to go home and ask him.

His house, which had come alive with the addition of Emma's vibrant presence, felt still and vacant without her.

Lying awake until the early hours, tossing and turning in his empty bed, Jack relived the way Emma had rebuffed his affection with such vehement dismissal over and over again.

His stomach ached with misery as he finally gave up on sleep and made his way to his office at three in the morning.

He spent the rest of the early hours working on a project that had taken second place in his attention ever since Emma had reappeared in his life. Keeping busy had helped him the last time she'd left him, for a while at least, but it didn't seem to hold the same restorative powers any more.

Where was his wife?

He pictured her sleeping on one of her friends' sofas, getting on with her life without him. Going back to work for some idiot like Fitzherbert again. Keeping him well and truly out of the picture, only to turn up one day with divorce papers in her hands.

Finally, giving up on the hope of concentrating on anything else, he went to lie on the sofa and put the television on, staring at the news channel with unseeing eyes until exhaustion finally overtook him and dragged him into a restless sleep.

He woke a few hours later with a start, blearily checking his phone to realise with a shock that it was lunchtime.

Pulling himself into a sitting position, he was just about to haul himself up and go and make some strong coffee in the kitchen when a movement in the corner of his eye made him start in surprise.

Jumping to his feet, he turned to see Emma standing in the doorway, looking at him with a hesitant smile.

'You came back,' was all he could utter past the huge lump in his throat, the unexpected sight of her standing there in front of him making him stupid with relief.

She walked tentatively into the room towards him, as if she wasn't sure what sort of reaction to expect. 'I'm so sorry I left, Jack.' She visibly swallowed. 'I was scared. Terrified to let myself love you again.' Breaking eye contact, she turned to glance out of the window, and let out a low laugh. 'Not that I ever really stopped.'

He stared at her, not sure whether to believe what he was hearing in case his addled brain was playing cruel tricks on him.

'Are you okay?' she asked shakily, turning back, her nose wrinkled with worry.

He continued to stare at her, only becoming aware that he was frowning when he noticed the anxiety in her expression.

Finally managing to pull himself together, he walked to meet her in the middle of the room and raised his hand to touch her soft cheek with his fingertips.

'Are you really here?' he murmured.

She laughed quietly and he saw relief in her face.

'It looks like I woke you. Did you sleep on the sofa all night?' she asked, her eyes clouding with concern.

He glanced back towards the rumpled cushions. 'Er…no. I couldn't sleep so I got up and worked, then I dozed off in here this morning.' He shook his head, trying to clear it. 'Where did you go?'

'To France. To see my mother.'

He nodded. 'Did you tell her about us?'

She smiled sheepishly. 'I did. She was really supportive. She basically told me to stop being such an idiot and to come back to the man I love.'

Emma couldn't help but smile at the almost comical look of relief on Jack's face.

'I guess I owe you an explanation about what got me so spooked,' she said, waiting until he'd nodded before continuing.

She played with a loose thread on the sleeve of her jumper, summoning the courage to speak.

'I think losing you and my father in such quick succession must have damaged me on a fundamental level.'

She rubbed a hand over her face, letting out a low sigh.

'Ever since then I've been terrified of putting myself in a position where I have to trust my heart to someone again.'

He looked down at her with a small pinch between his brows. 'I understand that, Emma. It makes total sense after everything you've been through.'

'When it looked like it might be possible to have you again I panicked,' she said with a sad smile. 'I wanted you so much it scared me. I think I was afraid to be happy in case it was all whipped away from me again.'

She took a deep shaky breath.

'You know, the day we got married I couldn't quite believe I could be so lucky as to have you. You were everything I'd ever wanted and when I looked at you I could see a bright shiny future shimmering in front of me. And then when it was whisked away from under my nose I sincerely wondered whether I was being punished for something. Up till then I'd led such a charmed life and just taken and taken without appreciating how much I had. Perhaps I was being penalised for my selfishness?'

'You weren't being selfish, you were living the life you'd been dealt and what happened was just really bad luck. It wasn't your fault. None of it was your fault.'

He sighed and frowned down at the floor, then looked up at her again with one eyebrow cocked.

'Pretending we were happily reconciled to everyone was a ridiculous thing to put ourselves through,' he said with a sigh. 'We should have been braver and talked about how we really felt, honestly and openly, instead of hiding and pretending there wasn't anything between us any more.'

He ran a hand through his hair, then scrubbed it across his face.

'I don't know what I was thinking, imagining I could have you living here, so close, without it driving me crazy with longing for you.'

Reaching out for her, he slid his hands around her waist and drew her nearer to him.

'Let's make a pact to deal with anything that comes

at us *together* from this point on. We can take things as slowly as you like—take time to get to know each other properly again. I'm more than prepared to do that, Em. I just want you back in my life.'

There was a heavy beat of silence where they stared into each other's eyes.

'I love you, Emma,' Jack murmured.

She smiled as joy flooded through her. 'You really still love me after what I've just put you through?'

'Are you kidding? I've never *not* loved you.'

He gave her a squeeze. 'I'm in awe of you and what you've achieved on your own—what you must have gone through to pay off those debts and what you've given up to do that. A lesser person would have thrown in the towel a long time ago. But you didn't and I have the utmost respect for you for that.'

She cupped his jaw in her hands, feeling his un-shaven bristles tickling her palms. 'Thank you for saying that. It means a lot.'

She felt his chin slide beneath her touch as he turned his head until his lips came into contact with her palm. He kissed her there lightly, before turning back to look at her again.

'You know I'll support you in whatever you want to do, don't you?'

She flashed him a smile, excitement making her heart race. 'Actually, I've been wondering about train-ing to be an interior designer. I'd have to go to college and become qualified for it, but I think it's something I'd love to do for a living.'

He nodded. 'If that's what you want I'll support you one hundred per cent with it. You can practise on this place if you like. As you've seen, it needs a lot more tender loving care upstairs, so perhaps you could fix the rest of it up as a practice project.'

'I would love that,' she said, a surge of joy lifting her onto her toes to kiss him.

His mouth was warm and firm and she sighed with relief as she felt his lips open under hers. And then he was kissing her fiercely, as if he never wanted to stop.

It felt so right, so absolutely *right* that it dragged all the breath from her lungs and the blood from her head, sending her dizzy with happiness. She knew with absolute certainty now that this was exactly where she was meant to be—in Jack's arms.

Finally, he drew away from her and she almost complained bitterly about the loss of his mouth on hers, until he pulled her tightly against his chest and held her there, safe in his embrace while they swayed gently together on the spot.

They stayed like that for a long time, feeling the beat of each other's hearts under their palms and listening to the gentle exhalation of their breath.

She knew then that she was never going to walk away from this man ever again.

On a sigh of satisfaction, Jack finally drew back and brought both hands up to cup her chin, gazing down into her eyes. 'I love you, Emma Westwood.'

Looking up into his handsome face, a face she knew as well as her own, she smiled at him with everything she had. 'I love you too.'

This admission seemed to galvanise something in him. Releasing his hold on her, he got down on one knee and looked up at her with resolution in his eyes.

'Well, in that case, will you renew your marriage vows with me?'

She looked down at the man she loved—had always loved—and knew in her heart that remaining married to him, fighting any battles she might encounter in the future with him there at her side, would make her the happiest woman on earth.

'I will!'

A wide smile of relief broke over Jack's face and he stood up and lifted her off the ground, hugging her fiercely to him.

'It looks like we've got another job to do, then—planning our vow renewal ceremony, which apparently is happening some time in the new year,' he said, pulling back to grin at her. 'Do you know anyone that can help us out with that?'

Emma smiled, imagining the looks of delight on Sophie, Grace and Ashleigh's faces when she asked for their assistance.

'I know exactly the right people to ask,' she said, bouncing up and down on the spot in her excitement. 'I can't wait to tell the girls our news. They're going to be thrilled!'

Jack smiled at her, his face alive with happiness, then drew her towards him, pressing his mouth to hers and sealing their future with a kiss to end all kisses.

* * * * *

THE BOSS'S
MARRIAGE PLAN

GINA WILKINS

As always, for the family that gives me strength and my reason for living, my husband of more than thirty years and our amazing son, two daughters, son-in-law, and precious grandson.

Chapter One

Tess Miller stood quietly nearby as her older sister, Nina Miller Wheatley, made a minute adjustment to an impeccably set Thanksgiving dinner table. Nina's formal dining room glowed not only with the light from a crystal chandelier but from multiple candles on the table and antique sideboard. Fall flowers spilled over crystal vases onto Pilgrim figurines and pumpkins nestled beside them. Calligraphy place cards rested in little turkey-shaped holders beside the brown-and-orange plaid place mats. Tess didn't know why they needed place cards when the entire dinner party consisted of Nina, her husband, their three kids and herself, but her overachieving sister never did anything halfway.

There was enough food for another six people, at a minimum. Turkey and dressing, several side dishes, salads and four choices of desserts crowded the serving tables. Tess had brought a casserole and a cake, both of which Nina had proclaimed "very nice" and had then set at the back of the buffet.

Nina wore a rust silk blouse and dark brown slacks that showed off her gym-toned body. Not a salon-tinted blond hair was out of place in her stylish do, and her makeup was perfect despite the hours she'd spent in the kitchen. She'd given a critical once-over to Tess's black wrap top and slim charcoal pants, but her only comment had been that maybe Tess should consider adding more red highlights to her hair, just to "spice up" her shoulder-length auburn bob. Tess was perfectly content for now with the color nature had given her, but she hadn't wasted breath arguing.

The sisters didn't look much alike. Tess's brown eyes had a more golden tint than Nina's, her face was more oval and she'd inherited their father's shallow chin cleft. At five-four, she was two inches shorter than her sister, though she'd always wondered if being taller would have made any difference in Nina's still treating her like a child.

"Everything looks beautiful, Nina," she said, knowing just what to say to make her sister happy. "I can tell you've worked very hard."

Nina heaved a long-suffering sigh. "You have no idea. All the chopping and mixing, cooking and baking, not to mention keeping up with all the kids' extra-curricular activities and volunteering at two different schools. I'm utterly exhausted, but of course it's all worth it for my family."

Through her mental sigh, Tess heard a football game playing in the den. She knew her brother-in-law, Ken, and her nephews, thirteen-year-old Cameron and nine-year-old Austin, were parked in front of it, though both boys were probably engrossed in handheld video games. Almost fifteen-year-old Olivia was in her room, likely risking carpal tunnel syndrome with marathon texting to her bazillion friends. None of them had offered assistance to their mother, though Nina wouldn't have accepted if they had. She loved being a martyr to her overly indulged family.

Nina shook off her air of selfless weariness to replace it with a sympathetic smile toward her much younger sibling. "You wouldn't understand, of course, not having a husband and children of your own to take care of."

She didn't add the uniquely Southern, artfully patronizing "bless your heart," but Tess heard it anyway. Ever since Tess turned twenty-one eight years ago, Nina rarely missed an opportunity to voice her concern that her sister would remain single and childless. It didn't help that her only semiserious relationship during those years had crashed and burned.

While Tess wanted a family of her own, she was increasingly resentful of her sister's condescension, making every holiday gathering progressively more uncomfortable. That was a shame, because she and her sister were the only surviving members of their immediate family. Their parents, who'd been in their midforties when Tess was born thirteen years after Nina, had both died within the past six years. Now Nina always made a big show of including Tess at every holiday table because as she said, "Tess has no one else to share the special days with."

Tess drew a deep breath before asking, "Would you like me to call everyone to the table?"

"In a moment. First I want to ask if you'd allow me to

give your number to Cameron's orthodontist, Dr. Mike. He's really quite nice, if a bit socially awkward. He's been divorced for almost a year. He seemed interested when I showed him your photo on my phone, but after that little fit you threw last time, I knew better than to give him your number without asking." Nina rolled her eyes, as if making it clear she thought it unreasonable that Tess objected to Nina handing out her number to just any single stranger.

"Seriously, Nina, stop trying to fix me up," Tess said with a firm shake of her head. She didn't mind her friends arranging the occasional blind date, but she'd rather her meddlesome sister stay out of her love life, such as it was. The thought of her photo being shown to random men made her very uncomfortable. "I don't need you to arrange dates for me."

"Well, someone should. I don't see how you're going to find anyone sitting in that office working for your taskmaster of a boss. I mean, sure, you meet construction workers and architects and suppliers, but you're too professional to flirt with them on the job and you're never *not* on the job, so where does that leave you, hmm? Needing a little help meeting someone, that's where. And because I'm actually out in the community mingling with nice, successful people, who better to direct a lead or two your way?"

"If I want your help, I'll let you know, all right?"

Nina didn't quite growl her frustration, but she seemed to be making an effort to restrain herself. "You haven't forgotten about Dana's party the second Saturday in December, have you? You have to be there. Everyone's expecting you. You can come alone, of course, but you know how snooty some of our cousins would be if they think you can't find a date. Perhaps that would be a good time for you to spend an evening getting to know Dr. Mike?"

"I'll find my own date, thank you." Tess wasn't sure where or how, but she'd bring a date if she had to hire someone!

Maybe she shouldn't let Nina get to her this way. Maybe she should go to the family gathering alone as she usually did, with her head high and her shoulders squared. Confident, composed and contentedly independent. But then she'd have to endure everyone trying to set her up with their dentists, accountants and gynecologists.

Before her sister could demand details, Tess turned toward the dining room doorway, which was decorated with a garland of autumn leaves and just-too-cute little gourds. "I'll call everyone in to eat. It would be a shame to let this delicious food get cold."

It was probably the only threat that could have derailed Nina's attention from Tess's personal life. At least for now.

Tess must not have known anyone else was in the office at 6:00 p.m. on the Saturday after Thanksgiving. No other reason she'd be chatting on her cell phone with her office door open, so her words drifted out very clearly to Scott Prince in the lobby. He didn't mean to eavesdrop, really. It was simply that while he hesitated, trying to decide if it would be rude to interrupt her, he heard a bit more than he intended.

He'd just quietly entered the reception area of Prince Construction Company, Inc., the Little Rock enterprise into which he'd invested all his time, sweat, money and dreams for the past nine years. It had been a struggling little local-only construction company when he'd purchased it from the retiring owner, with whom Scott had interned while he'd obtained a master's degree in construction management. His family and friends had been concerned to see him take such a major financial risk, considering him too young and inexperienced at twenty-seven to successfully run a complicated business. It had taken almost a decade of personal sacrifice and unwavering determination to prove their doubts unfounded, but he was now owner and CEO of a successful, multistate enterprise specializing in small to medium commercial construction projects.

Tess had started working for him as a clerk over six years ago and had become his office manager and valued administrative assistant. No one got to him except through her. Some people said he was gifted when it came to surrounding himself with the right people. Tess was a prime example of that. He admitted freely that the whole operation would fall apart without her to oversee the office.

But this was Thanksgiving weekend, not an official workday. Shouldn't she be spending it with family or friends—at least unless he needed her for some crisis or another, as he confessed he so often did?

"It was the usual painful family meal," he heard her say from the other room, almost as if in answer to his silent question. "My sister tried to fix me up with every single male she's ever met, because she says I'm incapable of finding eligible men on my own. My brother-in-law finally told her to lay off because as he said, 'Some women are just meant to be single.'"

Scott grimaced, knowing now why Tess had chosen to work on the long weekend rather than to spend more time with family. He almost spoke up then to let her know he was there, but she started talking again.

"So, anyway, Nina nagged me about bringing her son's orthodontist to Dana's big Christmas bash, but I told her I'd find my own date, thank you very much. No, I don't know who it will be. You know my lousy luck with the online dating sites I've tried lately. Maybe I'll just take Glenn. Yes, I know you keep telling me he's boring, but maybe we've been too critical of him. He's a nice enough guy. Makes no secret that he's ready to settle down and start a family. Maybe I've just been too—"

Scott opened and closed the front door. More loudly this time. He'd suddenly realized that he'd been standing in one place for too long, hearing more than Tess would surely want him to know.

He heard her mutter something quickly, followed by the thud of her phone, then the squeak of her chair. Moments later she appeared in the open doorway looking slightly flustered, though she almost instantly assumed her usual calm and collected expression. She was dressed more casually than on weekdays in a blue-and-black patterned tunic with black leggings tucked into flat boots. She'd left her hair down rather than in the neat twist she usually wore for work. He'd seen her weekend look many times before, of course—but he thought she looked particularly pretty today. The slight flush that lingered on her cheeks was definitely becoming.

"Scott? What are you doing here? I thought you and your dad and brothers were driving to Missouri for the Razorbacks game today."

"We were. But Eli had to be on call because one of

his partners broke an arm in a Thanksgiving biking accident. Then Jake's son came down with a virus and our plans all fell apart. We gave our tickets to Mom and Dad's neighbors and their kids. They were happy to get them."

"I'm sorry your plans were canceled. You really needed a break from work."

He felt his mouth quirk into a half smile. "Are you saying I've been surly lately?"

"Not surly, just… Okay, maybe a little surly," she said with a quiet laugh.

He could count on Tess to be honest with him, sometimes brutally so. Somehow she always managed to do so without crossing boundaries of the employee-employer relationship, even when she was annoyed with him. And she had been annoyed with him on several occasions.

He cleared his throat. "Sorry about that. You have to admit, the past few months have been challenging." They'd dealt with a couple of big, complicated jobs, a burglary at a job site that had cost them several expensive tools, even a break-in here at the office earlier in the year. Speaking of which…

He frowned. "Why was the security system turned off? You shouldn't be here alone on a weekend, especially after dark, without that alarm activated. As I've just proved, anyone could have walked in."

She lifted an eyebrow. "Didn't you have to use your key?"

He was still surprised she hadn't heard him enter the first time, which only illustrated how focused she'd been on her conversation. "Well, yes, but still…"

Relenting, she smiled. "I've had the security system

on almost the whole time I've been here. I turned it off when I ran out to my car for something I'd forgotten and I was going to turn it back on after I finished a phone call in my office."

He kept his expression as unrevealing as he could manage. He knew she'd be embarrassed if she thought he'd overheard too much of that call. "I want you to be safe when you're here alone. Keep the blasted thing turned on."

Sending a salute toward him that was just short of impertinent, she said, "Yes, sir. I'll do that."

He sighed and shook his head. "Insubordination. Remind me again why I keep you around?"

She laughed easily, slipping back into the comfortable relationship they'd forged during their years of working side by side. "Because you know this entire enterprise would collapse without me."

He chuckled after she pretty much echoed his thoughts from earlier. He had to concede her point.

She'd made her mark on every aspect of his business, from the state of the reception area to the total of the bottom line.

Speaking of the reception area... He suddenly noticed decorations that hadn't been there a few days earlier. A Christmas tree sat in the front corner, decorated with gold-and-white ornaments and tiny white lights. A strand of garland wound with gold ribbon draped the front of the reception desk, matching the wreath on the door. On the tables sat frosted glass holders with fat white candles. All very subtle and tasteful—very Tess, he thought with a faint smile. She could have assigned one or two of the clerical workers she now supervised to decorate, but she'd no doubt taken care of it herself, as she had every Christmas since she'd started working for him.

"You came in today just to decorate?"

"I thought I'd get the decorations up while I had a quiet afternoon to work on them. I'm almost finished."

"Looks nice. Is there anything I can do to help?"

"I've got it, thanks. There are only a few more things I want to do."

Nodding, he moved toward the closed door of his own larger office to the right side of hers. "Let me know if you need anything. I'm going to review the paperwork for that Springdale job we start Monday, just to make sure everything is lined up."

"I left a couple of contracts on your desk for you to look over and sign. They could have waited until Monday, but since you're here…"

"I'm on it."

He glanced over his shoulder as he opened the door with his name engraved on a brass plaque. Tess stood half-turned away from him, frowning in concentration at the Christmas tree, which looked perfect already to him. She really did look pretty today. He thought fleetingly about telling her so, but something held him back.

He made a cup of coffee with the pod brewer on his credenza. "Would you like a hot drink?" he asked through the open doorway as the enticing aroma filled his office. The rack beside the pot always included a variety of herbal teas that he knew Tess liked. They often shared drinks at his desk as they discussed business.

"No, thank you," she called back without making an appearance. He told himself he wasn't disappointed that she was too busy for a cozy chat, which meant he had no excuse to procrastinate any longer with the work he'd come in to see to.

Taking a seat at his desk, he tried to concentrate on paperwork for the next twenty minutes. Despite his resistance, his thoughts kept returning to the one-sided conversation he'd accidentally overheard, and the glimpse of insight it had provided into Tess's personal life. Of course, he couldn't have worked so closely with her for six years without knowing some things about her.

Through night classes and online courses, she'd completed her business degree and had earned postgraduate hours since she'd started working with him. He knew she took pride in those accomplishments. During that same time, he'd seen her deal with the illness and loss of both her parents. He'd gotten the impression the majority of the caregiving had been on her shoulders because her sister had been so busy with her young children. Yet he'd never once heard Tess complain. Whatever she dealt with in her off-hours, she'd always reported to work with her usual serene efficiency.

Serene. He repeated the word in his head, thinking how well it suited his assistant. Throughout several major work upheavals, when he'd been edgy and bad-tempered amid the confusion and mayhem, Tess had remained…well, Tess. She came in every morning with a smile, an encouraging word and a roll-up-her-sleeves attitude that let her tackle each day's tasks with single-minded focus.

One would think someone so agreeable would be a bit of a doormat, easily intimidated, perhaps. Not Tess. He'd witnessed her hold her own with even the most belligerent, disgruntled employees and clients. One of his job foremen had confided to Scott that Tess reminded him of a nun who'd taught his junior high math classes. "Nice lady most of the time," he'd clarified. "But get out of line, and you'd get a ruler across the knuckles before you could spit."

Scott could imagine Tess wielding a mean ruler if necessary. But he'd never thought of her as a nun—had he?

He cleared his throat and reached hastily for his quickly cooling coffee, almost knocking over the cup in his clumsiness. He salvaged the papers on his desk at the last moment and with a muttered curse.

"Everything okay in there?" Tess called from the other room.

"Yes, fine, thanks."

Maybe he hadn't thought of Tess as a nun, but before that overheard conversation, he'd had no idea she'd tried online dating, or that she'd been actively looking for a match. Meeting strange men online was dangerous, he thought in disapproval. Sure, people did it all the time these days, but it just didn't seem right for Tess.

He knew she'd been in a relationship about three years back that hadn't worked out. That was about the same time he'd been briefly engaged to a stunning but capricious woman who'd understandably—and angrily—chosen to pursue a career in modeling over marriage to an often-neglectful workaholic. He still winced when he remembered the scene Sharon had caused when she'd broken up with him in a crowded restaurant, and all because he'd been a few minutes late meeting her there. Okay, twenty minutes late, but he'd texted to let her know he'd been held up—again—by yet another work crisis. She'd known going into the relationship that his business required a great deal of his time, but like others he'd dated before her, she'd expected more from him than he'd been able to give. She'd stormed off furiously when she'd finally concluded that his construction company meant more to him than their relationship. The split hadn't been amicable, but then for some reason, his breakups never were.

He wondered if Tess had remained on good terms with her former flames. He wouldn't be surprised if she had. Unlike the volatile Sharon, Tess was the practical, pragmatic type. In the years she had worked for him, he'd never heard her carry on about romance and unrealistic fantasies.

Of course, he rarely allowed himself to think of Tess as a vibrant, available single woman. After all, she worked for him, and he'd never even considered overstepping their professional boundaries and risking their comfortable work relationship. She had just turned twenty-three when she'd applied for the clerical job with him. He'd been a couple months shy of thirty-one, and had already owned the business for over three years. Perhaps that was why he'd thought of her all this time as much too young for him, though the actual gap was only seven years. She would soon turn thirty, he mused, surprised by how quickly time had passed. He supposed it was only natural that she would now be considering marriage and children. After all, he'd given quite a lot of deliberation to those things lately, too.

She strolled in through his open doorway. "I thought I'd put this candle on your table. I know you don't like a lot of froufrou in your office, but this isn't too much, is it?" She held a hurricane glass candleholder with a little garland around the base. "You've got a few meetings scheduled in here during the next couple of weeks."

He often eschewed the main conference room in favor of the cherry table in his office. Everything he needed was available to him in here—a projector and screen, whiteboard and display easels and blackout shades to hide the distracting views of the Arkansas River and the distant rolling hills. He loved his office. It was exactly what he'd envisioned back when he'd first started building his own business.

"I don't mind a candle on the table," he assured Tess, making her smile.

"How was your Thanksgiving?" she asked as she fussed with the garland.

"Nice. Noisy. The kids were wound up from all the attention."

Both his brothers were happily married fathers. His older brother, Eli, a family practice physician, had twin girls, Madison and Miranda. Cute as little bunnies, they were almost five years old and full of energy. He was their "uncle Scotty," and he adored them, just as he did his little nephew, too. Six-month-old Henry was his younger brother, Jake's, kid. Both his brothers had been lucky enough to find their soul mates—Eli and Libby had started dating when both were in medical school, while Jake, an attorney, had met psychologist Christina at a cocktail party a couple years ago.

As much as he'd enjoyed the gathering, Scott had been painfully aware that he was no closer to having a family of his own than he'd been during the last solo holiday season. None of his relatives was actually nagging him to marry—after all, the next generation of Princes was already well established—but he couldn't help wondering if they thought something must be lacking in him. Increasingly, he wondered the same thing about himself.

Without arrogance, he could admit he'd accomplished a great deal in his almost thirty-seven years. Valedictorian in high school. Summa cum laude college graduate. A master's degree. His own business. He had a nice home he'd remodeled himself, with a couple of empty bedrooms he hoped to fill someday. All his life he'd heard about biological clocks, but he'd never quite understood the term until he found himself only a few years from forty without any immediate prospect of a wife and kids. During these past twelve months, he had attended cocktail parties and professional mixers—more than he would have liked, actually. He'd gone on blind dates, been to clubs and bars and charity fundraisers. He'd met a lot of nice women, had some good times, made a few friends…but he'd yet to find anyone he thought would be a lifelong partner.

After his brief engagement to Sharon had ended so disastrously, he'd wondered privately if he was destined to remain a workaholic bachelor. He was accustomed to success, to achieving the high-reaching goals he set for himself. His only experiences with failure had been in the romantic area of his life. He really hated failure.

Tess stepped back to critically study the centerpiece she'd created. Apparently deciding it would suffice, she turned to the door, asking over her shoulder on the way out, "Have you signed those contracts?"

He reached hastily for the stack he'd yet to touch. "On it."

He wondered half seriously what she'd have said if he shared that he'd been fretting about how to find a mate.

Knowing Tess, she'd set her mind to solving that issue for him. He'd probably come in on Monday to find a line of qualified applicants standing outside his office door. Having trouble in her own quest wouldn't stop her from setting to work on his if he asked.

His smile faded as it occurred to him that maybe he was on to something here. Oh, not the part about asking Tess to find candidates for him, but the idea that he'd been going about this all wrong. Perhaps he should approach this endeavor with the same attitude he'd used in establishing his successful business. Practicality and analysis were his strengths. Romance obviously was not. There had to be nice women out there who didn't require all the fancy trappings of courtship, but simply wanted to marry an upstanding, decent guy and start a family. Surely a union based on common goals and values, preferably even friendship, would appeal to someone besides himself. Maybe if he spelled out from the start what he had to offer—and what he didn't—there would be no artificial expectations that could only lead to another disappointing failure.

When he'd drawn up his original business plan, he'd made lots of lists. Where he needed to focus his efforts, how he wanted to solicit clients, specific steps for growing the business in a sensible, feasible manner and at a reasonable, sustainable pace. Perhaps he should approach his marriage plan in a similar vein.

He visualized a mental list of the type of woman he thought would suit him best. It should be someone organized and efficient, much like himself. Practical—the kind of woman who would understand he was never going to be a smooth-talking Romeo, but that he would be loyal, generous, committed, dependable. That was the type of husband and father his dad was, and that his brothers had become. Maybe they had married for more emotional reasons, but that didn't mean he couldn't make his own future partnership just as successful. Middle kid that he was, he'd always had his own way of doing things, as his mother had pointed out on many occasions. His way had turned out well for him in business, so why not in marriage?

His wife didn't have to be model beautiful, as his ex-fiancée had been, but it would be best, of course, if he was attracted to her. He'd always been drawn to kind eyes and a warm smile, and he had an admitted weakness for dimples...

He heard Tess moving around in the other room. She had nice eyes, he thought, along with a generous smile with occasional flashes of dimples in the corners. She never wore much makeup, but he'd noted some time ago—just in passing—that her skin was creamy and flawless without it. He supposed she would be considered girl-next-door attractive rather than strikingly beautiful—but then again, there was nothing he'd have changed about her appearance. On more than one occasion, especially during the past year or so, he'd found himself admiring her attributes in a manner that had made him immediately redirect his thoughts, chiding himself that it was inappropriate to even notice those things.

A muffled thud and a disgruntled mutter drifted in from the lobby. Curious, he stood and walked around his desk to stand in the open doorway. "What are you doing?"

Tess was on the floor beneath the big artificial tree, propped on one arm as she stretched to reach something he couldn't see. "I knocked off an ornament when I was trying to straighten a branch. Oh, here it is."

Holding a sparkling gold orb in her hand, she swiveled so that she was sitting cross-legged on the floor looking thoughtfully up at the tree. After a moment, she leaned forward and hooked the ornament to a branch, then leaned back on her hands to gaze upward. Tiny white lights glittered among the thick green branches, their reflection gleaming in the dark red highlights in her hair.

"How does that look?" she asked.

"Looks good," he murmured slowly, his eyes on her. "Really good."

She pushed herself to her feet and brushed absently at her slacks. "Do you think a candle in a snowflake-shaped holder on the reception desk would be too much?"

He cleared his throat. "I'm sorry. What?"

When she realized he was staring at her, she cocked her head to eye him with a frown. "Scott? Are you okay?"

"Yeah, fine. Just…absorbed with a dilemma."

"You'll figure it out," she said encouragingly. "You always do."

Her steadfast confidence in him had bolstered him through some of his most challenging periods during the past six years. Her absolute dedication to the company had been instrumental in its success. She understood why it was so important to him in a way that perhaps no one else did, because it seemed almost equally valuable to her. In some ways, he thought she knew him better than anyone outside his immediate family. Even some of his longtime friends were unable to read him as well as Tess. She was more than an employee, more than a professional associate. Not exactly a personal friend—but whose fault was that? His or hers? Both?

Tess had often teased him about being "blessed with strokes of inspiration," in her words. Solutions to thorny problems tended to occur to him in sudden, compelling flashes, and he had learned to respect his own instincts. They had let him down only on very rare occasions.

He had just been staggered by another one of those brilliant moments of insight. In a near-blinding flash of awareness, he'd realized suddenly that the woman he'd mentally described as his perfect mate had just been sitting under the Christmas tree.

Chapter Two

Tess wasn't particularly concerned about Scott's sudden distraction. This was an expression she knew very well, the way he always looked when he'd been struck with a possibly brilliant solution to a troublesome dilemma. She would wait patiently for him to share what he was thinking—or not. Sometimes he had to mull over details for days before he enlightened anyone else about his latest inspired idea.

Glancing around the reception area, she decided she'd finished decorating. The offices looked festive and welcoming but not over the top. "I'm calling it done," she said, more to herself than Scott, who probably wasn't listening anyway. "Any more would be too much."

He gave a little start in response to her voice—honestly, had he forgotten she was even there?—then cleared his throat. "Um, Tess?"

Picking up an empty ornament box to stow away in a supply closet, she responded absently, "Yes?"

When he didn't immediately reply, she glanced around to find him studying her with a frown. The way he was staring took her aback. Did she have something on her face? Glitter in her hair? She thought he might look just this way at finding a stranger in his reception room.

"Scott?"

He blinked, then glanced quickly around them. "Not here," he muttered, apparently to himself, then addressed her again. "Have you eaten?"

"I was going to stop for takeout on my way home."

"Want to share a pizza at Giulia's? There's something I'd like to discuss with you."

It wasn't unusual for them to share a meal after working late, and the nearby casual Italian place was one of their customary destinations. Because she had no other plans for the evening, she nodded. "Sure. I'll just grab a notebook."

"You won't need to take notes. We're just going to talk."

That was odd, too. They'd worked through shared meals but never just talked.

He was still acting peculiarly when they were seated in a back booth in the restaurant.

Sipping her soda while waiting for their pizza, Tess studied Scott over the rim of the glass. He was visibly preoccupied, but she knew occasionally it was possible to sidetrack him from his musings, at least briefly. She gave it a try. "Tell me a funny story about your nieces," she suggested, leaning back in her seat. "I could use a good laugh this evening."

He blinked a couple of times before focusing on her from across the table. Candlelight gleamed in his dark blue eyes. His hair, the color of strong, rich coffee and a bit mussed from the winter evening breeze, was brushed back casually from a shallow widow's peak. A few strands of premature silver glittered in the dark depths. There was no denying that her boss was a fine-looking man, trim and tanned with a firm, square jaw, nicely chiseled features and a smile that could melt glaciers when he turned on the charm.

Sometimes she still thought of the first time she'd met him. She'd been struck almost dumb by her first sight of the great-looking, intensely focused man sitting behind a cheap, cluttered desk in his first office. She still cringed a little when she thought of how incoherent she'd been during that awkward interview. She wasn't sure what he'd seen in her to take a chance on hiring her, but she was so glad he had. She loved her job and took great pride in the success of the business.

Scott thought for a moment before complying with her impulsive request. "During breakfast Thanksgiving morning, Madison reached for the butter and knocked over an entire glass of cold milk directly into Eli's lap. Eli jumped and knocked over his cereal bowl, which landed on their shih tzu. The dog went tearing through the house scattering milk and Cheerios all over the floors while the girls chased after it, smashing the cereal underfoot. Eli was laughing when he told us the story over Thanksgiving dinner, but his wife was not amused."

Tess laughed. "That sounds like a scene from a TV sitcom."

"Right? Eli said it's pretty much life as expected with energetic almost-five-year-old twins."

"I can imagine. It must be exhausting."

He smiled up at the server who set their pizza in front of them, then continued the conversation as Tess reached for a slice. "Eli and Libby put on the long-suffering act, but they love every minute with those girls."

She'd met all the members of Scott's family, most recently in September, at the annual PCCI picnic at sprawling Burns Park in North Little Rock.

She doubted he got the same kind of grief from his family that she did from hers just because he hadn't yet found his own life mate. From what she knew of them, she thought perhaps they'd tease him a little, but probably not in the insultingly patronizing tone her sister used toward her. With Thanksgiving behind them, the holiday season was now well under way. Parties, traditions, family gatherings loomed ahead. She wished she could feel a little more enthusiastic about what was to come in the next month.

"You like children, don't you, Tess?" Scott asked unexpectedly.

"I love children." She hoped her quick smile hid the wistfulness that underlaid her reply.

"Yeah, me, too."

Looking down at his plate, Scott toyed with his food, seemingly lost in his thoughts again. With silence reigning, she took another bite of her veggie pizza.

He cleared his throat and she glanced up. Her eyebrows rose in response to his expression. "What?"

"You remember when I had that unexpected appendectomy last year and you had to come to my house to work the next day because we had that big deadline?"

She was rather surprised he'd mentioned that incident. He'd seemed to try very hard to forget that day since. "Of course I remember."

Hypersensitive to the painkillers, Scott had spent a few hours rambling somewhat disjointedly until the effects wore off. He hadn't said anything too far out of line, but he'd been amusingly whimsical and had continually heaped praise on her, telling her how important she was to him and how he couldn't get by without her. Even knowing his effusiveness was fueled by medication, she'd taken the compliments to heart.

The only seriously awkward moment had come as she'd prepared to leave. Though Scott wasn't a "hugger," he'd hauled her into his arms for a somewhat clumsy embrace, thanking her too heartily for her help. She'd convinced herself afterward that he had surely intended to kiss her cheek, but he'd missed. His lips had landed squarely on her mouth.

It had lasted only seconds. Hardly long enough to be called a kiss. Even under the influence of the medicines, he'd been aware enough to jump back immediately, stammering apologies, flustered, his face uncharacteristically flushed. Tess had laughed it off, attempting to mask her own reactions behind indulgent humor. Despite her assurances the next day that he'd said nothing untoward, Scott had been embarrassed by his lack of control and obviously concerned that he'd crossed professional lines. They had implicitly agreed to put the incident behind them and never refer to it again. To be honest, though, there'd been times when she'd found herself reliving that almost kiss and wondering what it might have been like had it been real.

Scott cleared his throat, bringing her abruptly back

to the present. "So, the thing is, I'd like to handle this conversation the same way we did that incident. Though I am completely clearheaded and unaffected by any outside influences tonight, feel free to forget anything I'm about to say, if you want, and to pretend it never happened next time we see each other. That's why I wanted to talk here, away from the office."

Lifting her eyebrows in confusion, she looked at the tall, thin glass in his hand. "You've only had a few sips of your beer, so that's probably not the reason you aren't making any sense."

Setting the glass aside, he shook his head. "As I said, I'm not under the influence of anything. Just not quite sure how to begin this conversation."

Swallowing a bit nervously, she touched her napkin to her lips, then lowered her hands to her lap to toy with the checkered tablecloth. Since when had Scott ever had trouble talking with her? This couldn't be good. "Just say it, Scott."

He nodded. "Your job means a lot to you, right? I mean, it matters to you that the company is successful. Reputable."

Her chest tightened. A cold, hard knot formed in her throat, forcing her to clear it before she could ask, "Have I done something wrong? Have I messed up somehow? Is that what you're trying to tell me?"

He shook his head quickly. "Of course not. Just the opposite, in fact. You've gone above and beyond this past year. I'm not exaggerating when I say I don't know what I'd do without you."

Relief flooded her. Her hand felt just a little unsteady when she tucked a strand of hair behind her ear. "Then, what…?"

"I overheard some of a phone conversation you had earlier," he blurted. "You were talking about the upcoming holiday parties, and about problems you've been having with online dating."

She felt warmth spread across her face. He'd heard her conversation with her friend Stevie? How humiliating!

"So anyway," he continued before she could speak, "I've got a bunch of holiday events coming up, too, and no one to attend them with me. Which made me wonder why we couldn't go to some of those parties together."

Of all the things he could have said, this was the least expected. Surely he wasn't suggesting...

"You mean...as coworkers?" she asked in a tentative attempt at clarification.

"No, nothing to do with work. I guess you could say I'm asking you out."

She stared at him, her mind going completely blank with shock. "Oh. Ah."

"I've been thinking about how you and I get along so well and always have," he said, cutting into her stunned stammering. "About how much more comfortable it could be if we attend these things together rather than going alone or trying to deal with early-dating drama with other people during the holidays. So, what do you think?"

She moved his glass firmly to the other side of the table, symbolically out of his reach. "I think you had too much of this on an empty stomach. It must have gone straight to your head."

He made a sound that was half amusement, half exasperation. "I've had maybe three sips of the beer. I'm not intoxicated. I had this inspiration at the office and

I've been trying to figure out how to bring it up to you. I guess I'm not doing a very good job of it. I'm really bad at this sort of thing."

"After hearing me complain about online dating, you decided we should attend holiday parties together?" She still wasn't sure she entirely understood where he was going with this. "And you're not just talking about business-related events?"

"No. There are several events coming up very soon that I'll be expected to attend with a plus one. I'll admit I've been putting off thinking about them until the last minute because I didn't know who to ask, but I suddenly realized there's no one I'd rather go with than you. And wouldn't you rather attend your parties with me than with some guy you think is boring?"

So he'd heard her talk about Glenn. She resisted an impulse to hide her face in her hands as she understood exactly how much of her conversation he'd unintentionally overheard. She wasn't angry with him for his eavesdropping; after all, her door had been open and she'd made no effort to speak quietly. But that was because she'd thought herself alone in the office. Remembering the way he'd announced his arrival with excessive noise, she figured he must have been uncomfortable with what he'd overheard. But that hadn't stopped him from mulling it over afterward, had it?

After clearing her throat, she said, "The holidays can be difficult for singles. Trust me, I know. My older sister is a champ when it comes to dropping patronizing hints and comments, especially since one of my two best friends just got married and the other is in a steady relationship. Even though I'm mostly okay with going to parties and other events on my own, sometimes I think it would be nice to have someone to accompany me. Someone I like and enjoy spending time with. But—"

"You don't feel that way about me?"

"Of course I do. But—"

"You like me. You're certainly comfortable with me. You seem to enjoy spending time with me."

"Well, yes, but—"

"So what's the problem? You attend a few things with me. I'll go to your gigs. It'll take a lot of pressure off both of us."

He was on a roll now, a mode she'd seen him in many times. He'd had what he considered a brilliant idea and he was running with it. True, his "aha" moments had served him well in the past, earning him a reputation as a business genius. But he'd really gone off the rails this time.

"May I speak now?"

He grimaced. "Oh. Sorry. Go ahead."

"As I was trying to say, I understand what prompted your suggestion and it makes sense in some ways. But," she said quickly when he started to speak again, "I don't think you've considered all the ramifications. Showing up together for professional gatherings wouldn't raise eyebrows because we're usually together in that capacity. But in social functions, with families and friends... Everyone's going to wonder if there's something going on between us other than the construction business."

"Would that be such a bad thing?"

Maybe he'd misunderstood what she was trying to say. "To have people speculating about us? It's not that I care so much about gossip, personally—well, not too much—but I'm not sure how good it would be for the company."

He shook his head. "I wasn't talking about the gossip. I meant the part about our relationship being more than a professional one."

She stared at him across the table, trying to read his face. Was he joking? It wasn't his usual style of humor, but surely he wasn't suggesting that they should start... dating?

"Okay, maybe I'm getting a little ahead of myself," he said quickly, probably in response to her stunned expression. "But think about it, Tess. We make a hell of a team. Everyone says so. How many times have we been teased about being so in sync that we're accused of communicating telepathically?"

She could hardly count the number of times during meetings when she and Scott had exchanged thoughts with little more than a glance and a nod, to the bemusement of their associates. "Well, sure, but—"

"We both love children," he reminded her. "We want families of our own. We share many of the same values. I always respected the way you took care of your parents, even though it meant a great deal of sacrifice for yourself. That's the same kind of family loyalty my own parents instilled in me and my brothers."

Children? He was talking about kids now? "I've, um, always admired how close you are with your family. But—"

"I'm pretty sure we've both tried all the conventional dating methods. We've had relationships we hoped would lead somewhere, only to end up single again. It occurred to me that maybe we've both been going about the process all wrong, ignoring the obvious solution right in front of us. We've been successful partners for more than six years, longer than any other relationship I've ever had."

She bit her lip. He was doing it again. Enthusiastically barreling along without giving her much chance to respond. She knew how to break in, how to get his attention and make her point. Even if he didn't agree, he always listened and respected her opinion—but she didn't for the life of her know what she'd say if she stopped him just then. She was literally struck speechless.

After a moment, Scott grimaced and made a little sound that seemed self-chiding. "You're completely gobsmacked by all this, aren't you?"

"That's one way to phrase it," she managed to say fairly steadily, though her pulse rate was still fluttering like crazy.

He reached across the table to lay his hand over hers. "Sorry, Tess. You know how I get when I'm inspired by an idea."

She knew exactly how he got. Which was why she was suddenly so nervous.

He squeezed her fingers. "It's just something to think about. You have to admit it makes sense, but I won't take offense if you decide you don't want to try it. Nothing will change between us, if that's what you prefer."

Her attention was drawn to their joined hands. His was strong, tanned and very warm. She'd always admired his hands, secretly studying them as his capable fingers had flown over the keyboard or tablet screen. Her own felt suddenly small and soft beneath his, feminine to his masculine. She found herself mesmerized by the contrasts, the sensations, the intimacy of that contact.

What on earth was wrong with her? Though that

medicine-fueled embrace had been a definite glitch, it wasn't as if Scott never touched her. He was in the habit of patting her shoulder when he was particularly pleased with her or high-fiving her when a job was completed satisfactorily. But now, with just this casual hand-holding, she was suddenly transported back to inarticulate appreciation of just what an attractive and compelling man he was. The thought had always been present at the back of her mind, but she'd kept it firmly locked behind professional boundaries she had never expected to cross.

Maybe they had both lost their minds.

"Why don't you think about it for a couple of days?" Scott suggested after another moment of silence. "We could start slow, attend a party or two together, see how it feels. We'd figure out what to say to anyone who questions us. Whatever happens, nothing has to change at work. This would be a totally separate experiment."

Experiment. The word cut through the daze that had temporarily engulfed her. She drew her hand from beneath his and picked up her soda again, holding the cool glass in a firm grip to control a slight tremor. "I'll think about it," she said evenly, "but I'm not sure it's a good idea to mix business with personal pursuits. From my observances, it's rarely successful."

"Maybe for people like us it's exactly the right way to go about this. Thoughtfully, practically, logically. As adults who share common goals and common interests, not starry-eyed kids too caught up in fantasy to give serious consideration to the future."

People like us. This could be the least romantic discussion of dating and potential marriage she'd ever had, she thought, frowning down at the now unappetizing food that remained on her plate. Not that she'd ever expected romance from her prosaic employer. Okay, maybe she'd let herself daydream a time or two, especially in those early years, but she'd long since convinced herself she was completely happy with her comfortable friendship with Scott. Now he was suggesting changing the parameters of their relationship, carrying the success of their business collaboration into a personal partnership. And while she was utterly—well, gobsmacked by the proposition, she had to admit that a part of her recognized the unassailable logic of his idea.

She'd tried romance. She'd crashed and burned. Scott had been engaged. It hadn't ended well. So maybe he was right that a union based on common goals and interests was much more fitting for, as he'd said, people like them.

He gave her one of the quick, crooked smiles that almost always made her melt inside, even when she'd been annoyed with him. "Or you could always go to your parties with boring, no-chemistry Glenn."

She pointed a finger at him. "It's not wise to tease me about something you overheard while eavesdropping on a private conversation."

He held up both hands in a gesture of surrender. "You're right and I apologize. But will you think about what I suggested?'

"I'll think about it," she agreed after a moment.

Looking satisfied that she hadn't shot down the idea out of hand, he nodded and pushed away his plate. "Great. Just let me know what you decide."

As far as he was concerned, apparently, the new business at this impromptu meeting was concluded.

She had no doubt that if she presented good reasons

why she thought it best to decline, he would accept her answer graciously and they would go on with their professional lives exactly as they had before. But maybe she needed to give his suggestion a bit more thought before she reached that conclusion.

Declining dessert, she gave the excuse that she had things to do that evening. The silence wasn't quite as comfortable during the short drive back to the office in Scott's car. She suspected that was why he turned on the radio to a station already playing nonstop holiday music.

"I left my tablet inside," she said after he parked next to her car. "I'll just run in and get it."

"I need to collect a few things, too. I'll walk you in."

She'd left the Christmas lights on when they'd gone out, so they were greeted by the cheery glow of the tiny white bulbs on the tree and garlands, an unnecessary reminder of the upcoming festivities. She glanced at Scott. It was all too easy to imagine herself walking into her cousin's party with him at her side. Her sister, especially, would be stunned to see Tess with her handsome, socially prominent boss.

Was that really a good enough reason to risk upsetting the solid working relationship they'd built between them during the past six years?

Needing a distraction, she glanced around the reception area and noticed a strand of garland had slipped from the light fixture behind the desk. She rose on tiptoes to fix it, but Scott stepped up to help her, reaching over her head to secure the end into the cluster of greenery and glitter.

"Thanks," she said, smiling automatically up at him.

Her smile faded when their gazes met and she realized just how close he stood to her. So close she could almost feel the warmth and energy radiating from him. So close she could see the sudden heat reflected in his dark blue eyes. It was a look she'd never seen there before during all the times they'd been alone in the office together, all the late nights and long weekends and holidays when they'd given up personal time to work toward the mutual goal of making the business successful and profitable.

He took a half step nearer, so that they were almost but not quite touching. His voice sounded deeper than usual when he said, "We've agreed that come Monday this conversation never happened, if that's the way you want to play it. With that caveat in mind, there's one more experiment I think we should try to help you make up your mind."

That was the only warning of his intention as he dipped his head down to hers. He stopped with his lips only a whisper away from hers. "Say the word and I'll back away now," he murmured, his warm breath brushing her skin. "Or we can satisfy our curiosity and give you just a little more to think about while you make your decision about my proposition."

She couldn't even argue about that "our curiosity" comment. He'd know she was fibbing if she denied that she'd ever wondered what it might be like to kiss him—a real kiss, this time, not an accidental brush of lips.

"This never happened?" she asked in a husky whisper, letting her hands rest against his broad chest.

His lips curved into a smile. "Totally your call."

The temptation was too great. A chance to find out what it would be like to share a kiss with Scott without worrying about the consequences? Maybe it wouldn't be quite as easy as he made it sound, but for once in her safe, responsible life, she gave in to a reckless impulse. It took only a shift of her weight to bring their lips together.

Chapter Three

Maybe Scott had intended for it to be a quick meeting of lips, merely a sample taste of what could be—but it turned quickly into a kiss that made her knees go weak. He wrapped his arms around her and drew her more firmly into his embrace. Gripping his shirt, Tess tilted her head to provide better access for both of them, her lips parting and softening beneath his. Heat coursed between them, surging through her veins to sizzle in her pounding heart. She felt her toes curl in her shoes, the kiss affecting her literally from head to heel.

Her pulse raced frantically by the time they broke apart. For a moment Scott looked as disoriented as she felt, blinking as if to bring their surroundings into focus. It seemed that he, too, had been surprised by just how good the kiss had been.

Maybe they shouldn't have conducted that particular

experiment here at the office, she thought with belated qualms. She might never again stand in this particular spot without remembering how it felt to be held against that hard, strong body, their mouths fused, their hearts pounding together.

Maybe once all the Christmas decorations were put away, once the place looked normal and completely businesslike again, it would be easier to wave this off as a holiday anomaly.

Maybe.

Scott tugged at the unbuttoned collar of his shirt as if to loosen it, then glanced up at the garland they'd just straightened. With a slightly lopsided smile, he asked, "Did you tuck a sprig of mistletoe into that thing, by any chance?"

Clearing her throat, she tried to speak in the same light tone he'd used. "No mistletoe. Just a little fake balsam and holly."

"The whole place looks great. You did a nice job decorating." He scooted backward as he spoke, looking around the office as if suddenly fascinated by the holiday touches. Did he regret the kiss, or was he giving them both time to mentally process what had just happened between them? She couldn't tell from his profile, and he wasn't meeting her eyes.

She pushed back her hair and took a steadying breath. "I'd better go now. I have some things to do at home."

After a moment, he turned to face her, his expression still inscrutable. "We're okay?"

"We're okay," she assured him, touched by the hint of anxiety she thought she detected in his voice, though it didn't show on his face.

"And you'll think about the things I said?"

"Of course I will." As if she'd have any other choice.

"You have to admit, we make a hell of a team, Tess. We always have."

She couldn't argue with that. There'd been a connection between them from that very first day. But was their professional bond strong enough to sustain a more personal relationship?

Making a hasty escape from the office that was as much her home as her own apartment, she decided to call an emergency meeting of her two best friends. She very much needed Stevie and Jenny to let her know if she was insane. Because she was suddenly thinking that maybe Scott's surprising proposition wasn't completely crazy.

"Wow."

Tess nodded ruefully in response to her friend Stevie's succinct response to being told about Scott's out-of-the-blue proposition. "I know. I'm still trying to wrap my head around it myself."

Sitting in the living room of Tess's place Sunday afternoon with cups of tea in hand, her friends Stevie McLane and Jenny Baer Locke stared at her with almost identical thunderstruck expressions. Tess figured her own face must have looked much like that when Scott had sprung his suggestion on her that they should try dating. Especially when he'd made it clear that he was looking beyond merely attending events together to potentially building a future as a couple.

"He really hinted you could have children together?" Jenny asked, her dark eyes wide.

"Indirectly. At least, I think he did." Tess held up

her free hand in a gesture of bewilderment. "The whole conversation was a little hard to follow."

"What did you say?" Stevie demanded with avid curiosity.

"I told him I'd think about it."

"Wow." This time it was Jenny who expressed the sentiment. "You must have been stunned."

"That's an understatement." *Gobsmacked* still seemed a more accurate description.

Stevie set down her teacup to study Tess intently. "This could make things awkward, to say the least, when you report to work on Monday."

"Scott assured me there would be no awkwardness. He said when we're at work, we can pretend the conversation never took place."

"Can you do that?" Stevie sounded skeptical. "Really?"

After only a momentary hesitation, Tess nodded. "I think so. Scott and I have never had trouble being completely professional on the job, no matter what was going on in our personal lives. We just focus on business."

Which didn't mean there wouldn't be complicated emotions swirling inside her next time she was with her employer, she acknowledged privately. She only hoped she would do as good a job of hiding them as she had in the past.

Stevie shook her head, making her blond curls bob around her pretty face. "I have to admit I wasn't expecting to hear this when you invited us here this afternoon. I thought you'd tell us about the latest aggravating thing your sister did to you. Hey, you don't suppose she somehow put Scott up to this, do you? She is determined to marry you off after all."

With a wry smile, Tess said confidently, "No, Nina wasn't involved. This was totally one of Scott's brain flashes. Apparently, something he overheard me say to you triggered it."

Jenny nodded thoughtfully. "That sort of makes sense. You said you were complaining about your bad experiences with online dating and wishing you had a companion for some upcoming events. If he's been thinking along the same lines lately for himself, I can see how he might make this leap."

Successful business owner Jenny always looked at all the angles. Until six months ago, Tess had thought Jenny the most practical of all her friends. It had turned out, however, that Jenny had a romantic and slightly reckless side she'd been suppressing for quite a long time, a side that had emerged when she'd been reunited unexpectedly with her college boyfriend after a decade apart. Jenny had been considering an offer of marriage from a wealthy, socially connected attorney most people had considered a perfect match for her. Yet only a couple weeks after a chance reunion with Gavin Locke, she'd surprised everyone by breaking off her relationship with Thad. Barely two months later, she'd married her police officer first love in a sweet, simple little ceremony that had been a far cry from the lavish, very public wedding she would surely have had with Thad.

Stevie swiveled in her seat to frown at Jenny. Both daughters of single mothers, Stevie and Jenny had become friends in high school. They'd attended the same college and had remained close since. Tess had met them two years ago in a yoga class, and she'd fit right in with them, so that they were now a tight trio. Each brought her own strengths to the alliance. Jenny was the friend who offered shrewd advice and blunt candor. Stevie was the embodiment of generosity and thoughtfulness, the one who'd do anything for a pal—to her own detriment, at times. As for Tess... Well, she'd been told she was the encourager, the one who always supported and bolstered the confidence of her friends. She could use a little of that encouragement herself as she faced this potentially life-changing decision.

"Surely you of all people aren't suggesting Tess should actually consider marrying His Highness?" Stevie demanded of Jenny, employing the nickname she often used when referring to Scott. Tess was actually surprised Stevie seemed so perturbed. Perpetually upbeat and positive, Stevie was an unapologetic romantic, and Tess would have thought her friend would be more intrigued than troubled by this development.

"I'm not saying she should start booking bands or ordering flowers," Jenny shot back with a shake of her head. "Just that maybe it's not such a crazy idea. I can understand why Scott thinks it's worth examining more closely. Assuming he and Tess really are able to compartmentalize their work and personal lives so it wouldn't affect their professional relationship, what could it hurt to go to a few parties together?"

"I don't think anyone's that good at compartmentalizing. I mean, seriously, could you work with Thad now after dumping him for Gavin? You don't think that would be awkward?"

While Tess swallowed hard at the images Stevie's question invoked, Jenny squirmed a bit in her chair. "I didn't dump Thad," she muttered, obviously uncomfortable with the blunt term. "When I told him Gavin and I had found each other again and realized we were still in love, Thad graciously bowed out."

"Okay, that's not dumping at all," Stevie said, her tone fondly mocking.

Jenny sighed. "Still, point taken. I've crossed paths with Thad a couple times in the past six months and we've been perfectly civil, but I can't deny it was awkward. I can't imagine spending eight hours a day with him now that I'm happily married to Gavin."

Jenny wasn't just happily married, she was blissfully married, Tess thought with a touch of wistfulness. Jenny would always fret about the dangers in Gavin's job, just as he occasionally became frustrated with the long hours her popular fashion boutiques required of her, but they were crazy in love.

"So even though you turned down a practical business-based marriage in favor of true love for yourself, you think this would be a good idea for Tess?" Stevie challenged.

Jenny tossed back her layered dark hair and lifted her chin in a familiar pose of obstinacy. "All I said was that maybe she should at least consider the possibility. And it wouldn't be such a bad idea for Tess to examine her feelings for Scott. It's not as if you and I haven't wondered—"

Stevie cleared her throat loudly, but not before Tess figured out exactly where that statement had been headed. "The two of you have talked about my feelings for Scott?"

With a chiding look at Jenny, Stevie sighed. "Okay, maybe it's crossed our minds that your total devotion to Scott isn't entirely due to employee loyalty. But we both know you'd never overstep any professional lines," she said hastily. "You've risen in the ranks of his company because you're damned good at your job—irreplaceable, really—and everyone knows it. You've always insisted you had no romantic feelings for Scott, but I couldn't help thinking sometimes you were denying those feelings even to yourself.

"It's not like I've made a secret of my suspicions," she added with a touch of defensiveness. "I've asked you several times if you've been so picky about the men you've dated lately because you've compared them to His Highness and they've all come up short. I just don't want you to get hurt if it should turn out his feelings aren't the same as yours."

Tess felt her cheeks warm. She had to concede Stevie had quizzed her about Scott on more than one occasion, and each time she'd laughed and brushed off the questions. "I wasn't comparing other men to Scott."

"Not consciously, maybe, but subconsciously?"

"We are not getting into amateur psychoanalysis hour," Tess grumbled into her teacup.

Jenny crossed her ankles and settled more comfortably into her chair. "You have to admit Scott has quite a few qualities you would naturally look for in a mate. Let's face it, if you didn't work for him and you met him online, you'd think he was exactly what you're looking for."

Tess looped a strand of her hair idly around one finger. "A workaholic confirmed bachelor with a noted weakness for busty blondes? Really?"

Jenny shrugged. "Obviously he's not that confirmed a bachelor if he's actively contemplating marriage and children. And he's never married any of the busty blondes he dated, so maybe it's not such a weakness after all."

"He did propose to one." With a slight scowl, Tess pictured the stunningly beautiful almost Mrs. Prince. Sharon had always been perfectly civil to Tess, though she'd had a subtle way of making it clear that as valuable as Tess might be to Scott in the office, he belonged to her after hours. Tess had never wanted to believe she'd thrown herself into an ill-fated romance of her own at about that same time as a reaction to Scott's engagement—but there had been times in the past couple years when she'd wondered...

Jenny made a face. "And his engagement lasted all of—what?—five months?"

"Four." Her own failed romance hadn't even made it that long before it crashed and burned, a year or so before she'd met Jenny and Stevie. James had accused her of always putting her job ahead of him, and he'd been jealous of her relationship with Scott, though she'd assured him repeatedly that there had never been anything personal between her and her employer.

Jenny gave a hint of a righteous smile. "So there you go. After realizing said busty blonde was the wrong match for him, he started thinking about a right match... and maybe he finally realized she'd been right in front of him for a long time. Is that so hard to believe?"

"What is easier to believe is that my newlywed friend is seeing everything through romance-tinted filters these days," Tess replied indulgently to Jenny. "It's very sweet, but..."

"*Was* there any romance to Scott's proposition?" Stevie cut in to ask.

"Not an iota," Tess answered, and though she'd tried

for wry humor, she was aware her tone came across more as grumpy. "Unless you consider 'we make a hell of a team' a passionate declaration."

"Not so much," Stevie said with a sigh. "Not even a kiss, huh?"

Tess took a too-hasty sip of her tea that made her cough. By the time she caught her breath again, both her friends were studying her much too closely.

Stevie leaned forward. "There *was* a kiss?"

"Well, yes. Sort of...coincidentally."

Jenny's cup hit the side table with an eager little *thump.* "Oh, this I have to hear. How did he coincidentally kiss you?"

"He, um, thought I'd hung some mistletoe in the office."

Neither of her friends bought that explanation for a moment, as their expressions clearly informed her.

She sighed. "Okay, we knew what we were doing. I guess it was an impulse. Curiosity. Scott called it an experiment. I'm not sure I can explain it completely."

Stevie waved a hand dismissively. "Forget explanations. We want details. How was it?"

"It was nice."

Her friends groaned in unison at the guarded reply.

Stevie cocked her head skeptically. "You're telling me that after six years of being pretty much joined at the hip with that undeniably great-looking guy, you finally kiss him and it's just...nice?"

Jenny tsked her tongue. "I don't believe it. Scott hasn't spent time with all those busty blondes without picking up a few tricks."

The image of Scott picking up kissing tricks from a series of blondes made Tess scowl when she realized just how intensely she disliked the idea. It was difficult to keep believing she wasn't harboring secret feelings for Scott when just the thought of him kissing another woman caused a knot to form in her stomach.

"Well?" Jenny teased. "Was it good?"

"It was better than good," she conceded with a sigh. "The man knows how to kiss. No surprise, I guess, since he's so successful at everything he does."

"Except finding a bride," Stevie added pointedly.

"That remains to be seen," Jenny murmured.

Tess made a sound like a strangled growl. "Can someone remind me why I thought it was a good idea to consult with you two about this?"

"Because we're your best friends and we love you," Stevie replied immediately. "Even if Jen and I don't necessarily agree on everything, we absolutely want what's best for you."

Tess could hardly continue to pout after that. "That is why I called you. I just needed to talk this through while I decide how to answer him."

"You didn't mention any of this to your sister?" Jenny looked as though she already knew the answer, but asked just for confirmation.

"I wish Nina and I had the kind of relationship that would make me feel comfortable discussing this sort of thing with her, but we just don't. I don't know if it's because of the age gap or her preoccupation with her family and her schedule, or maybe we're just too different to fully understand each other, but I don't think she'd be of any help at all with this."

Nina would probably tell her to stop waffling and latch on to this eligible bachelor before he got away, perhaps adding that it wasn't as if Tess could count on any other offers. Tess bit her lip as she could almost hear the words in her sister's blunt voice—or was that her own insecurity whispering at the back of her mind?

"It really is a shame you and Nina aren't closer. I always wanted a sister, myself," Jenny mused with regret. "I thought I'd missed out on something, being an only child. I was lucky enough to meet Stevie in high school, and she filled a big gap for me."

"That goes both ways," Stevie assured her. "I love my brother, but I certainly can't talk to him about relationship issues."

"And I'm lucky to have you both in my life now," Tess assured them, then quickly waved a hand. "That's enough of the sappy talk or we'll all end up sniffling. So I'm ready for advice. Stevie?"

Uncharacteristically somber, Stevie took her time deliberating her response. "I'd be wary," she said after a moment. "You and Scott work together so well, and you love your job so much. I'd hate for what could turn out to be an impulsive mistake to change everything for you."

"Jenny?"

Jenny shrugged. "As I've already said, I think it could be worth considering. You and Scott are mature adults with a great deal in common. You both know the personal and professional risks you'd be taking, so maybe you could take steps to minimize repercussions if it doesn't work out. Yes, it's a gamble, but isn't every relationship, in some way?"

Any other time, Tess might have been amused at the role reversal from her friends. Reckless Stevie advising prudence, practical Jenny encouraging a romantic gamble. Tess couldn't help wondering if the turnaround could be attributed to the state of her friends' own relationships—Jenny was so happy in her new marriage, whereas Stevie had been involved for some time with a moody musician who'd been spending increasingly more time with his moderately successful local band than with her. Tess and Jenny had worried lately that Joe was growing restless, perhaps even beginning to stray. Both suspected Stevie secretly echoed their concerns. Tess had never truly believed Stevie and Joe shared the kind of commitment that would last a lifetime, but Stevie always gave everything she had to making her relationships work, even when it became obvious to others that her efforts would ultimately fail. She was always so optimistic—which made Tess even more nervous that Stevie was the one urging caution.

"So what are you going to tell Scott?" Stevie asked.

Tess spread her hands in confusion. "I have no idea."

"And we haven't helped much, have we?" Jenny asked ruefully. "With our completely opposite advice."

"You've helped tremendously. You've listened without judgment while I expressed my concerns. I'll think about everything you've both said while I make up my mind."

"If you need to talk any more, you know where to find us," Stevie offered.

"I know. Thanks. And now, how about if we table this topic for a while and maybe order take-out?"

"I'd love to, but I can't stay," Jenny said with a glance at her watch. "Gavin has the night off and we're having a date night. We might even see a movie. In a theater. With popcorn and everything."

Knowing how rare a free evening was for them, Tess smiled. "Good for you. Stevie?"

"Sorry. I'm out, too. I promised Joe I'd drive him and his band mates to the airport this evening. They're catching a late flight to Austin for a gig there."

Tess and Jenny exchanged quick glances. Stevie spent a lot of time as an unpaid assistant for her boyfriend's alternative rock band, Eleven Twenty-Five. As busy as she was with her own kitchen design business, she still spent hours making calls for the band, dealing with printers and club owners, hauling supplies in her SUV, making flight arrangements. Tess wasn't entirely sure what Stevie received in return. But because it was none of her business and Stevie hadn't asked for advice, she kept her mouth shut. "Another time, then."

"Soon," Stevie promised. She jumped to her feet, tossed back her curls and carried her teacup toward the kitchen, looking suddenly restless. "I'd better get going. I promised Cole I'd feed his cat while he's out of town."

Cole McKellar was Stevie's next-door neighbor, a quiet widower who sometimes helped Stevie with home maintenance in exchange for occasional cat-sitting. Tess hadn't met him, but Stevie always spoke fondly of him. It was part of Stevie's charm, as well as her weakness, that she liked almost everyone, and she had a near compulsive desire to take care of her friends. She stopped to give Tess a quick hug on her way out. "Seriously, call if you want to talk more. I'm always available as a sounding board."

"Same here," Jenny seconded as she prepared to follow Stevie out. "We're here for you, pal."

Smiling broadly, Tess locked the door behind them. Her smile faded as it occurred to her that an entire Sunday evening of solitude stretched in front of her now that her friends had rushed off to be with their significant others. Maybe she'd do a little Christmas decorating of her own place.

Not much was going on this last day of the long holiday weekend. Her sister had invited her for dinner, but she'd begged off, having endured enough nagging this week. Usually Tess enjoyed an evening to herself with nothing to do but lose herself in a good book or catch up on TV shows she'd recorded. Tonight she felt too antsy to relax, too aware of the silence in her condo. There were too few distractions from her convoluted thoughts, and she was no closer to a decision now than she'd been before her friends had arrived.

As she retrieved her small artificial Christmas tree from the storage room attached to her condo's little balcony, she had to face the fact that neither Jenny nor Stevie could really help her with her personal problem. Sure, they could offer suggestions, advice—even differing opinions, as it turned out. Yet she was the one who was going to have to decide whether to take Scott up on his offer to explore new possibilities in their relationship or remain on the same safe, comfortable path they'd walked for the past six-plus years.

She'd never been a risk taker. The dutiful, responsible younger daughter—she'd always been so cautious, so careful. How could she possibly foresee all the potential pitfalls this time, when it affected every aspect of her future—her social life, her career…and maybe even her so-far-unbroken heart?

After the long weekend, the Monday workday hit the floor running. Phones were already ringing when Tess walked into the office, and the buzzing, beeping and bustling continued for hours. Before two o'clock she'd dealt with one panicky client, two surly vendors, three frantic contractors and a clerical job applicant who could barely articulate around the wad of gum in her mouth. Mentally marking that name off the list of potential employees, she sat back and drew a long breath. It felt almost like the first chance she'd had to breathe since she'd arrived almost six hours earlier.

At least she hadn't had to worry about what to say to Scott. He'd been in meetings and phone conferences all day, and she'd seen him only for a brief consultation about a business issue. There'd been no time for personal conversation, nor even for awkward pauses. Today had been all about work, catching up and looking ahead. As she'd assured her friends, compartmentalizing wasn't really that difficult for her and Scott. When they were in the office, nothing was more important to them than taking care of business.

As if in response to her thoughts, he stuck his head in the open doorway to her office. "What's Art Connolly's wife's name?"

"Debbie. And their son is Art Jr., but they call him Buzz."

"Debbie. Buzz. Got it. Heading out for the meeting. Shoot me a text if you need anything."

"Okay. Have a good—" But he was gone before she could finish the sentiment.

Her mouth twisted in a wry smile. If nothing else had demonstrated how efficiently Scott could put their Saturday-evening conversation out of his mind, that little exchange would have done the trick. There had been nothing at all personal in his tone or expression, no meeting of eyes, no more warmth in his voice than she heard when he spoke with the receptionist on his way

out. She couldn't imagine any observer would even suspect that less than forty-eight hours earlier, Scott had all
but asked her outright to consider having his children.

Had their conversation even crossed his mind this
morning? Despite how busy she'd been, it had hovered
constantly at the back of hers. Did that mean they were
already unevenly invested in this looming decision?
Was it really of little import to him if she accepted his
offer or politely declined? Was he less concerned about
the repercussions—maybe because he didn't believe he
would be as deeply affected in the long run? Had he
changed his mind, had later misgivings about his impulsive suggestions, or was he really too wrapped up in
business today to give anything else a second thought?

"Um, Tess?"

Blinking, she glanced toward the doorway to find a
heavily pregnant young woman standing there studying
her with a slight frown. She got the distinct impression
it wasn't the first time her name had been spoken. "I'm
sorry, Heather, I was distracted. What can I do for you?"

"The next applicant for my job is here for her interview. And I wanted to remind you I'm leaving a little
early today for a doctor's appointment."

Tess nodded. "I remember. I hope it goes well."

At almost eight months along, Heather had recently
given notice that she would not be returning after her
delivery. Now Tess was hiring a replacement.

"The applicant's name is Sofia Vasquez. She seems
very nice—and she's not chewing gum," Heather added
with a wink.

Tess laughed. "Good to hear."

"I'll send her in. And unless you need anything more
from me, I'll see you tomorrow."

Tess couldn't help smiling as she watched Heather retreat in her pregnancy waddle. Which reminded her, she needed to pick up a gift for the office baby shower scheduled for tomorrow afternoon. She should have taken care of that already, but she'd been so busy lately.

Putting thoughts of tiny sleepers and pastel blankets out of her mind, she stood with a professional smile to greet the job applicant entering her doorway.

As was so often the case, Tess was the last person remaining in the offices that evening, well after darkness had fallen. She'd just completed the hiring of Sofia Vasquez, and sat back in her chair with a weary sigh. It had been a long day, with only a twenty-minute respite for a quick salad in the break room, and she was tired to her toes.

She cleared her desk and pulled out her phone, doing a quick check of her personal email before calling it a day. She frowned when she saw an evite to her cousin's holiday party. It was addressed to "Tess and guest," and she was expected to RSVP. She would deal with that later, she decided. It was after six, and she was ready to hole up at home with pj's and tea. Slinging the strap of her bag over her shoulder, she grabbed her coat and headed for the break room to retrieve her salad container.

Now, of course, she was reminded again about Scott's offer to accompany her to her holiday affairs. There certainly hadn't been time during the past couple of hours to think about his proposition—not much anyway. Scott wasn't the only one who could compartmentalize, she thought in satisfaction. And if he'd changed his mind, fine. They could agree to pretend the conversation had never taken place. After a few days, she probably wouldn't give it another thought.

"Yeah, right," she muttered, thinking she'd never convince her concerned friends if she couldn't even believe it herself.

Impatient with her own dithering, she collected her plastic salad container from the drying rack next to the sink. With big windows looking out over the now-dark river, the break room had been decorated by the office staff. Normally, Tess's spirits would have been lifted by the sight of the silly stuffed reindeer grinning from the top of the microwave, but she had too much on her mind this evening. Gripping her salad dish, she turned toward the door. She jerked to a stop when she saw someone standing there.

"Scott," she said when she caught her breath again. "I didn't hear you come in."

Leaning casually against the doorway, he smiled. "Seems as if that's becoming a pattern. And do I have to point out again that the security system isn't on?"

"Give me a break, everyone just left. I'm on the way out myself."

"Crazy day, huh?"

"Very." She filled him in on the new hire.

Scott nodded. For the past couple of years he'd given her free rein for hiring and supervising the office staff. She often joked that her official title should have several "slashes" in it—office manager/human resources director/customer service representative/personal assistant to the boss. While she enjoyed the variety of her duties, the challenge was doing them all well, a feat she thought she managed most days.

"I'm sure you made the right choice," he said. "Oh, and we got the Kilgo job today."

"Congratulations. I know you and Andy put a lot of hours into that bid." Andy Staples was one of the project managers, an architect who'd been with the firm from the beginning. If Tess thought of herself as Scott's right-hand woman within the home office, Andy was definitely Scott's second in command everywhere else.

"Yeah. We're both excited about the project. So you were about to leave for the day?"

Because she was wearing her coat and holding her purse and empty lunch dish, the answer seemed obvious, but she nodded. "Yes. Do you need anything before I go?"

"Want to have an early dinner somewhere? Talk awhile?"

His smile and the gleam in his navy eyes took her aback. That quickly, he'd transformed from work associate to would-be suitor. Was he really able to separate the professional from the personal that easily, or was he just that much better at masking his thoughts and feelings when he was in work mode?

"I, um—" It took her a bit longer to make the switch. "I have to stop by a baby-supplies store. We're having Heather's shower tomorrow afternoon and I haven't had a chance to get anything for her. So maybe we should—"

"Stop by there together," he finished for her. "I haven't gotten anything for her, either."

She blinked. "You want to go baby shower shopping together?"

"Well, there are things I'd rather do," he replied candidly. "But you need a gift and so do I, so it makes sense for us to go together, right?"

She bit her lip. She wasn't sure she knew what made sense anymore.

The phone in her hand beeped and she glanced down at the screen. Her sister had sent a text unnecessarily alerting her that cousin Dana's party invitations had gone out. Nina had also felt the need to remind her that Awkward Orthodontist was still available as a potential escort—though not in those exact words, of course.

Tess sighed, then glanced up at the doorway where her good-looking employer stood smiling at her. "Okay, fine. Let's go buy something cute and fuzzy," she said more gruffly than she'd intended.

His eyebrows rose and his smile turned a bit quizzical, but he merely nodded and moved out of the doorway, motioning for her to precede him.

Chapter Four

Had they done this even a week earlier, Tess thought it wouldn't have felt at all odd to walk into the baby store with Scott to find gifts for their coworker. Well, not very odd anyway. But now the comfortably established camaraderie that had previous existed between them had changed. Permanently? That remained to be seen.

She and Scott paused in the baby furniture aisle, their heads close together as she scrolled through the baby registry on her smartphone, showing him the check marks that indicated items already purchased by others.

"There's not a lot left," she said with a self-censuring frown. "I should have taken care of this sooner."

Scott glanced up from the phone screen to study her face. "That's not like you. You're usually ahead of schedule on stuff like this."

She gave a little shrug. "I guess it was Freudian," she

said lightly. "As happy as I am for Heather, I hate the thought of her leaving us. I'll miss her."

She didn't want to think there'd been an even deeper emotional reason she had been reluctant to peruse catalogs of baby supplies.

Before Scott could respond, a young man in a store uniform paused near them. "Can I help you find anything?" he asked cheerily. "Do you need help setting up a registry?"

"Oh, no, we're not—" Tess stopped her automatic and completely unnecessarily explanation with a slight grimace. "I mean, we don't need help right now. Thank you."

The young man moved on and Tess focused more intently on the list, avoiding Scott's eyes. "There are still a few nice things left. I'm sure we can each find something."

"Maybe we could go in together on a gift?"

Picturing someone reading aloud a card that said, "From Tess and Scott," she cleared her throat. "Maybe we'll just each buy our own."

She heard the amusement in Scott's voice when he said, "Or that. What should I get?"

She pointed to the screen. "No one's bought this fancy baby monitor set yet. That's about what you usually spend for this sort of thing."

"And no one would know that better than you," he murmured with a smile. "Okay, so I'll get the monitor. That was easy enough. What are you getting?"

"I don't know yet." She scooted past a giddy young couple who appeared to be choosing items for their own registry, so absorbed in the colorful displays that they didn't realize they were blocking an aisle. Tess couldn't really be annoyed with them; they looked so excited and eager, and they apologized sheepishly when they realized they were in her way.

She moved down an aisle, idly touching one cute little item after another, looking for something that spoke to her of Heather. Heather and her husband had chosen a nautical theme in navy, red and taupe. According to the registry, the bedding items had all been purchased, but the coordinating laundry hamper and changing table cover were still available. She chewed her lower lip as she debated between the two.

"Not exactly an exciting choice, is it?" Scott asked as he eyed the options. "A laundry hamper?"

"They're things Heather wants. That's all that matters. I'll get the hamper. But I'm going to get a nice little outfit to go with it," she added with a decisive nod. "Something not on the list for a surprise."

"Excuse me?"

In response to the voice, Tess glanced around to find an older, silver-haired woman eying Scott with an oddly assessing expression.

Scott smiled at the woman. "Yes, ma'am?" he asked, instinctively displaying the manners his Southern mother had drilled into him.

"Do you mind if I ask how tall you are?"

With a quick, amused glance toward Tess, Scott replied politely to the diminutive senior citizen. "I'm six-one. Do you need help reaching something?"

"No. I need you to stand right here by these strollers and tell me which one would be more comfortable for you to push. My grandson is about your height, and his wife's expecting. I'm here to buy them a stroller, but

I want to make sure the handle is high enough for my grandson to push comfortably."

"I think most of them are adjustable," he explained, reminding Tess of his familiarity with his young nieces and nephew. "There's usually a button to push to raise or lower the handle."

The woman still wanted him to pose with a couple of strollers, just so she could "get a mental picture" of her grandson with her ultimate choice. Obliging, Scott took down the display models the woman indicated, then stood behind each one. His mouth quirked into a wry smile, he waited patiently while she studied him from all angles. She narrowed her choices down to two, had him stand behind each for another look, then pointed. "I think I like that one best."

"That's the one I'd have picked, too," Scott assured her as he hoisted the display model back onto its shelf. Having enjoyed the entire encounter from close by, Tess couldn't help but admire his gracefully strong movements.

"Really?" His new friend beamed in pleasure. "Is that the same stroller you two are buying for your little one?"

Tess's smile faded. "We're shopping for a friend's baby shower," she blurted.

"Oh. Well, I'm sure you'll choose something nice. Thank you, young man," she said over her shoulder as she bustled toward the customer service desk. "I appreciate your help."

"You're very welcome," Scott called after her before turning back to Tess. "Well, that was interesting."

Ready to get out of this baby-obsessed place, Tess grabbed the hamper, then marched over to the clothing section with Scott behind her. Flipping through the outfits, she selected a three-piece set consisting of a red snap-bottom shirt, navy pull-on knit pants and a navy-and-white-striped hoodie with an embroidered sailboat. It was cute and looked comfortable, and it worked well with the nautical theme. "This will do. I'm ready to check out now."

They paid at separate registers for their purchases, then headed for the door almost at the same time. Still, she was a good three steps ahead of Scott when they reached their cars, which were parked side by side in the lot.

"Were we racing?" he asked ironically when he caught up. "If so, you win."

"Sorry," she muttered. A night breeze blew steadily against her face, but didn't seem to cool her overly warm cheeks. She couldn't have explained why she felt so uncharacteristically awkward and foolish all of a sudden. She hated this feeling of being not quite in control.

He took a step closer to her. The parking lot was well lit with tall security lamps decorated with holiday wreaths, but his eyes were shadowed from the light behind him. She couldn't quite read his expression. Still, she could see he wasn't smiling now.

He touched her arm. Even through the fabric of her coat and clothing she was intensely aware of that point of contact between them. She hoped he attributed her shiver to the weather.

"Tess, you've been tense and jumpy ever since I came back to the office. I'm guessing you're trying to figure out how to tell me you aren't interested in the suggestion I made the other night. I don't know if you're afraid of hurting my feelings or worried that I'll be upset with you or what, but really, you can relax. I promised I wouldn't let your answer affect our working relationship—or our friendship—and I'm standing by that promise."

A brisk gust of cold wind whipped a strand of hair out of her loose updo and into her eyes. She reached up to push it back. Were they truly going to have this conversation in a parking lot?

"We can get past this, right?" he asked quietly, the question barely audible over the drone of passing cars and the voices of shoppers milling in the lot around them. "We'll be okay?"

She moistened her chilled, dry lips. "Actually, you've completed misinterpreted why I'm so nervous tonight," she said. "I'm not trying to figure out how to turn you down, Scott. I'm trying to find the courage to tell you I'm willing to give it a try."

It wasn't often she saw Scott startled into immobility. She thought maybe she was viewing it now, as he went very still, his hand unmoving on her arm. After a moment, he said, "So it's a yes?"

She took a leap of faith and nodded. "Yes."

A car cruised past them in search of a parking space, bone-vibrating bass booming from the interior as the passengers gambled deafness in favor of volume. Roused into recognition of their surroundings, Scott glanced around with a grimace. "So...dinner?"

She nodded again. It was too late to bolt in panic now, she reminded herself, though she had to admit the thought occurred to her.

They dined at a barbecue restaurant within view of the baby store. First pizza and then barbecue, Scott thought after they were seated in the casual, noisy dining room. He made a mental note to take her someplace nice soon, now that they were dating…or whatever it was they were doing. For now he was aware of a deep sense of satisfaction that she'd decided his brainstorm wasn't so crazy after all.

Because it seemed to calm her, he kept the dinner conversation light and primarily centered on work. They discussed the new employee she'd hired, and he shared his enthusiasm for the apartment complex project he'd contracted that day. Though a bit quiet at first, Tess was soon chatting easily enough, helping him plan ahead for the holidays that always played havoc with schedules. Every year it seemed they ran into delays and shortages between the first of December and New Year's Day, whether because of vacations or weather or a half dozen other seasonal issues.

This was their strength, he reminded himself. Their common ground. He didn't have to try to woo her or put on a calculatedly romantic facade for her. He could simply be himself, which only confirmed his belief that they were uniquely suited as a match. Pushing his luck a bit, he took advantage of her more relaxed mood to say, "There's that thing Thursday night. The Holiday Open Home party."

He knew he didn't have to be more specific. His company had participated in the Holiday Open Home fund-raiser for the past five years. Each year, one of the area's most luxurious homes was lavishly outfitted for the holidays with donations from local builders and decorators. Tours were conducted during the first three weekends of December, with all the receipts given to a local women's shelter. In return for a monetary donation, Scott's company was listed in the publicity material. The event's organizers always hosted a cocktail party for donors on Thursday evening before the tours began on the first Friday. The gathering was covered by the media and attended by the professionals who considered the event part of their annual advertising and charitable budget.

The parties were usually rather dull, but Scott figured it was good to be seen at them, so he tried to make a regular appearance. Because Tess was in charge of the firm's charitable donations, she was always invited to the cocktail party by the organizers. It occurred to him only then that though she'd probably been invited to bring a guest, as he was, she'd always attended on her own. He wasn't sure why, unless she'd considered the event strictly business.

She toyed with a forkful of coleslaw. "Yes, I remember."

"Why don't I pick you up and we can go together?" It seemed like a good opportunity to make their debut as a couple. Their business associates could become accustomed to seeing them together outside the office so that it wouldn't cause quite such a stir when they made it clear their relationship had moved beyond professional.

"We won't be making any announcements about our personal plans or anything like that," he assured her when she didn't immediately respond. "Just attending together. You know, sort of kicking off the season."

She nodded. "All right. We'll go together."

He chuckled drily. "It's a party, Tess, not a tax audit."

A quick, rueful laugh lit her eyes and curved her lips. She had such a very nice mouth. Full and soft, perfectly shaped. He found himself transfixed by her lips now, remembering the feel of them against his. The taste of them.

"I was somewhat less than gracious, wasn't I?" she acknowledged apologetically. "I'm sorry, it isn't that I don't want to go with you. I'm probably just overthinking things. You know how I get."

"Having second thoughts?"

"No." Her answer was immediate and steady. "I've considered everything you said and it makes sense to me. We do make a good team."

"We always have," he agreed with a surge of satisfaction.

"And it will be nice to have you with me at some of the events I have to attend in the next few weeks. I can't wait to see my sister's face when she sees you at the parties with me," she added, almost as if to herself. "I dare her to find anything to criticize about you."

He was a bit taken aback by the glint in her amber eyes. Maybe she'd intended that as a compliment? But he wasn't sure he wanted to be used as a pawn in some sort of battle of wills between Tess and her sister. He was trying to decide how to broach the subject when someone called his name from nearby. "Hey, Scott, thought that was you. How's it going?"

He glanced up to nod warmly at the couple who paused beside him. An old friend of Eli's, Bryan Crawford, held a towheaded toddler on one hip while his wife, Jessica, held the little boy's golden-blond older sister by one hand. "Hi, Bryan. Jessica. Nice to see you both."

"This is a coincidence," Bryan said with a broad grin spread over his ruddy face. "We just saw Eli and Libby an hour ago. We were all attending an open house at the girls' preschool. Your nieces are growing fast, aren't they?"

"They are. It's been a while since I've seen you, Bryan."

The other man chuckled and ruffled the hair of the drowsy boy he held. "Yeah, I haven't had much time for pickup basketball games lately. You know how it is once you have kids, always something on their schedule."

Jessica rolled her eyes with a weary bark of a laugh. "Now, how would Scott know about that, honey? He's the carefree bachelor in the Prince family, remember? Libby says he's too busy running that company of his to settle down and chase after a couple of kids." As if on cue, their daughter, who was the same age as Scott's nieces, whined and tugged impatiently at her mother's hand.

"Yeah, lucky guy," Bryan said with a grin, but the way he patted his son's back made it clear he wouldn't change places with the "carefree bachelor."

His smile feeling a bit strained, Scott motioned toward Tess, who was sitting very quietly watching the exchange. "Bryan and Jessica Crawford, this is my friend, Tess Miller."

He very deliberately neglected to mention their work relationship. This was the start of their new phase. Step one of what he was beginning to think of as his marriage plan was successfully under way. Tess was willing to give it a try. Which meant this evening was officially a date, not a business dinner.

Neither looking surprised to have found him dining with an attractive woman, the Crawfords murmured their polite "nice to meet yous," then gave in to their daughter's increasingly insistent urgings and made their exit. The toddler waved bye-bye over his dad's shoulder, making Scott chuckle and wave back.

"Cute kids," Tess said, drawing his attention back to her.

"Bryan's an old friend of Eli's. His daughter's in school with the twins, at Miss Bitty's. I think Libby had the girls on a waiting list for the place while she was still pregnant with them."

"I've heard of it. It's supposed to be one of the best. I know my sister looked into it when her oldest was a toddler, but it was too expensive for them then. She didn't want to admit that, so she just told everyone it wasn't her favorite option."

Was that another little dig at her sister? As close as he was with his own clan, it bothered him to think about Tess being estranged from the only immediate family she had left. From what he'd heard her say on the phone, it sounded as though Nina's nagging was most of the problem. So if his presence at the parties helped alleviate that problem, then maybe he didn't mind so much after all. Wasn't mutual benefit the whole point of this dating experiment?

"So," he said, "we're on for Thursday night, right?"

She gave him a too-bright smile. "Yes. We're on."

"Great." Personal business out of the way, he turned his attention back to business. "Now, about those meetings tomorrow..."

Twenty minutes later, he walked her to her car. Their breath hung in the air as they continued the work-related conversation they'd started inside, finishing up with a list of tasks he wanted completed the next day.

"I'll have Heather and Lynne start on those things in the morning," Tess agreed with a brisk nod, drawing her coat more closely around her against the chilly night air. "They should be able to finish most of it before the baby shower at four. I'll make sure your office is set up for the ten o'clock meeting, and the conference room upstairs for the one thirty. You should have plenty of time between meetings for that lunch with Garvey and Hannity."

It occurred to him that she was so confident, so at ease with him when they spoke of work, in marked contrast to the hesitation she showed when they veered into their new personal arrangement. Of course, she'd had several years to grow comfortable with him in the business setting; he supposed it would take a little practice in this new arena. And because there was no time like the present to begin…

He caught her arm as she reached for her car door. When she looked up at him, he lowered his head to brush his mouth against hers. "Your lips are cold," he said, smiling against them. "Maybe I should warm them up for you before you leave."

"That would be considerate of you," she murmured, and tilted her head into a more accessible position.

With a muffled chuckle, he kissed her. After only a heartbeat's hesitation, she was a willing and eager participant in the embrace.

His powerful reaction to their kiss in the office Saturday evening had caught him by surprise. He'd tried shrugging it off as first-time novelty, though technically it hadn't been a first kiss between them, if he counted that embarrassing, medication-fueled buss after his surgery. He decided not to count that one.

He'd tried blaming mistletoe, even though Tess had assured him there hadn't actually been any in the office. He'd even wondered if maybe he'd exaggerated the kiss in his memories, that maybe it hadn't been quite as spectacular as he remembered. He knew now that he had not. Kissing Tess felt so damned good that he had to ask himself now what had taken them so long.

Only his awareness of their very public surroundings made him draw back reluctantly when he would have liked very much to deepen the kiss. He opened her car door for her and then moved back to watch her slide in. Even as they said their good-nights, he was tempted to ask her to come home with him for coffee—but maybe it was a bit too soon for that.

Step one, he reminded himself while he watched her drive away. He climbed into his own car with a mixture of frustration and satisfaction with the way the evening had gone. They'd get to step two when the time was right.

"I don't know." Tess craned her neck to study her back view in the full-length mirror. "Does it seem a little tight to you?"

Jenny and Stevie answered in unison. "No."

A bold red sheath, the dress was closely fitted to her body, ending in a flirty double kick pleat just behind her knees. It wasn't overtly revealing, just brighter and snugger than her typical outfits.

"Your butt looks amazing in that," Stevie said bluntly. "I wish I could wear it, but that bateau neckline would never work with my boobs."

Tess's gaze was drawn to the reflection of her bust. The dress was definitely flattering there. As the least endowed of the trio, she couldn't help but push her shoulders back and pose a bit, making her friends laugh.

It was Wednesday evening and they had gathered in Jenny's fashion and accessories boutique, Complements. The store closed at seven on weeknights, staying open until nine Fridays and Saturdays, so Tess and Stevie often met there after-hours on Wednesdays to play in Jenny's new deliveries. They'd even been known to pitch in hanging up garments and setting up displays, mostly because they had fun doing so.

Tonight both Tess and Stevie were looking for outfits to wear to the Holiday Open Home cocktail party the next night. Stevie was attending as one of the donors; she'd been selected this year to design and oversee the kitchen update. It was for a good cause, not to mention she'd make the most of the professional exposure.

They stood in the dressing room area where several cushy benches were grouped around a large, full-length, three-way mirror. Six stalls with floral curtains for privacy surrounded them, but since they were the only ones in the store, they weren't overly concerned with modesty.

"The color is amazing on you, Tess," Jenny assured her. "I told you it would be."

Tess had worried that the red wouldn't go well with her auburn hair, but she should have known to trust Jenny's eye. "It does look festive without being too Christmassy. Not too splashy for the event?"

"You know what those things are like." Jenny waved a dismissive hand. "There will be people there in designer silks and others in jeans. If Sandy's there she'll have on a few strips of cloth and a boatload of diamonds. Trust me, this dress is exactly right for a charity holiday cocktail party."

Tess bit her lip against a grin at the description of their mutual acquaintance's fashion tastes. A notorious man-eater, Sandy had once made a fairly blatant play for Gavin. Not that he'd had eyes for anyone but Jenny.

"I'll give you the usual bestie discount," Jenny added persuasively.

"Okay, I'll take it."

Jenny smiled. "Great. And since you're in a buying mood, there's another dress I want you to try on. I think it's perfect for you, maybe for your cousin's party."

"I'm sure I already have something that will work for that."

But Jenny was already headed out to the showroom, saying over her shoulder, "Just try it, okay?"

"And that," Stevie said with a giggle, "is why Jenny now has two successful stores in the state and is considering a third."

"She is good," Tess admitted with a shake of her head. Twisting to admire the red dress once more in the mirror—her butt really did look good—she asked absently, "Aren't you going to try things on?"

"Oh, yeah, sure." Stevie turned toward one of the stalls. "Jenny hung some things in here that she thought I'd like. I just wanted to see that red dress on you first. I knew it would be amazing."

"It is pretty, isn't it?"

"You'll knock Scott off his feet," Stevie remarked through the open doorway to the stall, her voice muffled as if she were pulling her shirt over her head.

Tess's hand froze on the side zipper of the dress. She moistened her lips. Yes, she'd wanted something nice to wear to the event, and she'd been pleased that the dress had suited her so well, but she didn't want to look as though she was making any special effort to knock Scott off his feet. She turned when Jenny returned with a green garment draped over her arm. "Does this look like I'm trying too hard?"

Jenny sighed gustily. They were close enough friends that she understood the question immediately. "No," she said firmly. "Looking nice and appropriate for an event—even looking as beautiful as you do in that dress—is not trying too hard. It's simply putting your best foot forward."

Stevie stepped out of the stall wearing a filmy black dress shot through with silver threads. The skirt fit snugly at her hips, then flared out around her knees. She did a little spin and the hem swirled around her.

Tess nodded. "Pretty."

Shorter and curvier than her friends, Stevie's blond curls and large blue eyes made her look younger than her thirty-one years. She tended to be a more bohemian dresser, so Tess wasn't particularly surprised when her friend looked in the mirror, then made a little face at the reflection. "I don't know. Maybe."

"No." Jenny thrust the green dress at Tess. "Try this on while I help Stevie find something that suits her better."

"Yes, ma'am."

Stepping into the stall, Tess changed into the dress Jenny had brought her. A rich, dark green, it was another body skimmer, ending well above her knees to make the most of her legs without being too short for comfort. The neckline was a deep scoop outlined with a thin line of gold fish-scale sequins, just enough to add a little holiday sparkle.

It was a wholly impractical purchase, of course. Like the red cocktail dress, it would be something she'd wear only a few times. It was kind of hard to justify buying two party dresses at one time, but she loved them both.

"Gold earrings," Jenny said appraisingly from the open doorway. "Thin black tights and those high-heeled booties I sold you in the fall."

"You're killing me."

Her friend laughed without compunction. "Every girl needs to splurge occasionally. Especially when she's seeing a new guy."

Tess groaned. "Come on, Jen. Scott is hardly a new guy."

"He is when it comes to your social life." Jenny winked. "And I'm going to help you make sure he sees you as more than his trusty office sidekick."

Warmth flooded Tess's face, but she couldn't help glancing once again at the mirror. She did look different dressed this way.

"Okay, I like this one." Stevie danced into view in a short rose silk dress with a filmy mesh overlay. Gray beads and sequins were worked into an overall art deco–inspired pattern on the mesh, which ended in a beaded, scalloped hem. "I feel like a flapper. Makes me want to do the Charleston."

"T-strap shoes. Silver bracelets." Jenny nodded as if it was all decided. "Do your hair in that little twist off the face I like so much."

"Do you know how to Charleston?" Tess asked curiously.

Stevie laughed. "Not a clue. But it would be fun to learn, wouldn't it?" She glanced in the mirror again. "Sold."

Tess laughed. "Hooray for bestie discounts!" she

cheered as she went in to change out of the green dress that would be accompanying her home.

When she carried her purchases into the glittering, holiday-decorated showroom, Stevie was already paying for her choice and looking forward to wearing it at the charity event.

"I hope I'll get some new business," she added. "I can't wait to show you the kitchen. The updates are gorgeous, if I do say so myself."

"Will Joe be back from Austin in time to attend the party with you?"

Stevie's smile dimmed noticeably. "No, they're staying a little longer, making some good contacts in the Austin music scene. Joe thinks they have a nice gig lined up for next weekend."

"Good for them." Tess resisted an impulse to glance at Jenny, though she suspected they were both thinking the same thing—that this was the beginning of the end of Stevie's relationship with Joe.

Tess had heard all about Stevie's romantic history during late-night girls-only wine and confidences sessions. She knew her friend had a weakness for musicians, several of whom had broken her tender heart over the years. Would her heart be broken again, or was Stevie more prepared this time, more guarded?

At least she didn't have to worry about having her own heart shattered if this experiment with Scott didn't work out, she told herself. By approaching their relationship logically and cautiously, based on friendship and mutual goals rather than capricious emotions, they were protecting themselves against the sort of pain Stevie seemed to continually court with her impetuous infatuations.

"Well," Jenny said brusquely, breaking into Tess's somber thoughts, "it's Joe's loss that he won't get to see you in this dress, at least not this time."

"That's okay." Stevie's usual glint of mischief lit her eyes as she grinned at Tess. "That'll free me up to spy on Tess and His Highness all evening. After all, Jen, I promised you all the juicy details."

Tess rolled her eyes as Jenny laughed. "There will be nothing to report. We're just going to make an appearance at this thing, do a little networking and schmoozing for the business, then get out of there."

"To go where and do what?" Jenny teased lightly. "Do you and Scott have plans for after the party?"

"We haven't talked about it."

They hadn't actually had an opportunity to talk about anything but business since they'd parted in the parking lot Monday night. The past two days had been one pressing situation after another. Scott hadn't even had a chance to attend the office baby shower yesterday.

Only once had she suspected Scott's thoughts had wandered into personal territory. She'd caught him looking at her lips as she'd stood beside his desk waiting for instructions while he'd listened to a long-winded caller on his phone. Something had told her he was remembering their kisses—which, of course, had sent her thoughts, too, in that direction. Her lips had tingled as she'd instinctively moistened them. His eyes had narrowed and darkened, his expression making her pulse rate jump. She hadn't quite known whether to be relieved or a little disappointed when Andy had rushed into the room with another decision to be made, pushing all private issues aside.

"Has he said anything more about, you know, wanting to have your babies and stuff?" Stevie inquired, a little too artlessly.

Tess gave her friend a chiding look. "It's been a very busy week at work. And honestly, Stevie…"

Stevie shrugged. "You know I'm still concerned that you'll settle for Scott because of all the pressure your sister has been putting on you, and maybe the biological clock thing. I remember that silly, panicky feeling just before I turned thirty. I met Joe not long after that," she added quietly.

Was Stevie acknowledging that Joe had been a "Mr. Right Now" who'd shown up at a time when she was vulnerable? It was what Tess had always believed, but she hadn't thought Stevie was aware of it.

"A lot of people might be surprised to hear you suggest Tess would be 'settling' for Scott Prince," Jenny commented. "You are aware that he's one of this city's most eligible bachelors?"

Waving a hand dismissively, Stevie said shortly, "I'm not denying that Scott's a great catch. I'm just saying Tess deserves more than being a means to an end for a guy who's already accomplished many of his life goals and now wants to check marriage and kids off his list of aspirations."

Both Tess and Jenny stared at Stevie in response to that rather astringent assessment. Tess swallowed past a hard knot in her throat, while Jenny frowned in disapproval. "That was kind of harsh. I can't imagine Scott sees Tess as just a means to an end. I think it's more likely he's realized how lucky he is to have her in his life."

After a moment, Stevie held up both hands in apologetic surrender. "You're right. That was a tacky comment. Sorry, Tess, I certainly didn't mean to imply that Scott wouldn't be damned lucky to have you. I just hope he knows it, that's all."

Tess cleared her throat. "We're just exploring possibilities, Stevie. I haven't even decided what I'm going to do yet."

"Don't listen to me, okay?" Stevie's eyes were suddenly a glittering bright blue, glossed over by unshed tears. "Just have fun and make up your own mind what you want, with or without Scott. I just want you to be happy. I want all my friends to be happy."

Visibly concerned, Jenny moved around the counter to catch Stevie's fluttering hands. "What's going on, Stevie? Is this about Joe?"

Pasting on a semblance of her usual sunny smile, Stevie freed one hand to dash at her eyes and shook her head. "No. I'm fine, really. Just… I don't know, I'm kind of out of it today. I didn't sleep very well last night and I had to get up early this morning to feed Dusty before I left for work. Sorry."

Jenny patted her shoulder. "Of course. Do you need chocolate? I think I have some in my office. PMS is a bitch, am I right?"

Stevie's smile flickered momentarily, but she nodded and laughed cheerily. "You're so right."

Stevie was smiling again, but Tess still had some doubts about her friend's state of mind. Still, she went along with the change of subject. "You're still feeding your neighbor's cat? When is he supposed to be back from his business trip?"

"Tomorrow, thank goodness. Dusty's a sweetheart, and I don't mind sitting with her to keep her company when I have extra time, but I know she misses Cole."

To avoid any further potential pitfalls, they kept the conversation breezy for the short remainder of their visit. They parted on their usual affable terms, agreeing to get together again soon, with Tess and Stevie saying they'd see each other at the Holiday Open Home. Just to make it clear there were no hard feelings, Tess added a little extra warmth to her smile when they waved goodbye in the parking lot.

Still, Stevie's words echoed in her thoughts as she drove home. *Tess deserves more than being a means to an end for a guy who's already accomplished many of his life goals and now wants to check marriage and kids off his list of aspirations.*

She had a few life goals of her own, which just happened to be aligned quite closely with Scott's. Yet she didn't actually see him as just a means to an end, did she? Which brought up the question—what, exactly, did she want from Scott?

She almost chose not to wear the new red dress after all. For some reason, only minutes before Scott was due to arrive at her door, she glanced in the mirror and was taken aback by the reflection of the polished woman in the bright red dress with a glitter of diamonds at her ears. It wasn't that she hadn't dressed up for an event before, or worn bold colors. But something about that woman in the mirror looked different tonight, and she couldn't quite define what it was. Telling herself she was being silly, and that Stevie would certainly report to Jenny if she didn't wear the red dress, she turned away from the mirror and carried her tiny purse into the living room to wait for Scott.

She tried to remember if he'd ever actually been inside the condo she'd purchased two years ago. Had he come in the time he'd stopped by in his four-wheel-drive truck to pick her up for work after a late-January ice storm? No, she recalled, she'd met him downstairs.

She cast a quick glance around her place, trying to see it through his eyes. Stevie had helped her decorate in a warm, cozy style built around classic pieces with unexpectedly whimsical accents. The colors were greens, grays and off-white, her favorite combination. It was so well suited to her.

She sat down on the cushy sofa and sighed, trying to release some of her nervous tension about tonight. When her doorbell rang, she found herself wishing she could exchange the snug red dress for comfy pj's and spend the evening at home with popcorn and hot cocoa. Alone? Maybe.

Or maybe not, she thought, opening the door to find Scott standing there looking like sex in a suit.

"You look very nice," he said. "Are you ready to go?"

Maybe it wasn't quite the reaction she'd hoped for from all the effort she'd put into her appearance tonight. Still, she told herself it would have been foolish to expect Scott to be knocked off his feet, as Stevie had predicted, by a snug red dress. Whatever she wore, she was still just Tess. She supposed he knew her too well by now to see her any other way.

Chapter Five

Maybe it was the dress. It looked amazing on her. It was all he could do to keep his gaze focused on her face, especially when she happened to turn her back to him. She did so again, to reach for a glass of champagne from a passing server, and he couldn't resist noticing how the snug dress cupped her shapely bottom. He was only human after all.

"Scott. Good to see you. How's it going?"

Drawing his attention back to the networking he was here to do, he shook a couple of hands and exchanged meaningless small talk before his gaze was drawn inexorably back to Tess mingling on the other side of the crowded room. Even among the other guests crammed in the almost overly decorated large living area of the Holiday Open Home, she stood out—at least to his eyes.

There was something different about her tonight. He

couldn't quite decide what it was. She'd chatted easily enough with him during the drive. She worked the room like the pro she was, making nice with people who were either potential clients or referrals for PCCI. He was quite sure she worked his name into every conversation, subtly extolling his business acumen. She'd always been his most loyal cheerleader—and his most bluntly honest critic. His most valuable asset. But there was something different about her tonight.

Maybe it *was* the dress.

Or maybe it was the knowledge that tonight he'd be taking her home when the party ended.

As if in confirmation, she glanced his way, saw him looking at her and smiled. He lifted his champagne flute in acknowledgment. He took a sip, but what he really wanted was to taste her lips again.

A surge of hunger swept through him, and for a moment, he was unnerved by the strength of it. He reassured himself with the reminder that sexual appeal was a plus when it came to choosing a compatible mate. He wouldn't examine too closely how long he'd been aware of his attraction to Tess, but now that they were dating there was no real reason to continue to suppress it. He could handle, even welcome, a mutually gratifying physical relationship. It was romance he simply couldn't seem to comprehend, and at which he'd proved so incompetent.

He didn't want to mess this up. There was too much at stake to take unnecessary risks. But fortunately he and Tess seemed to be on the same page in both their business and personal agendas. Her sexy red dress hadn't changed anything. But she did look damned good in it.

For the first time since they'd arrived an hour earlier,

he'd found a moment to himself, sipping champagne in a relatively quiet corner of the two-story living room. Between the Christmas music playing from cleverly hidden speakers and the chatter of milling guests, not to mention that he'd been too busy to eat more than a few bites all day, his head was beginning to ache dully. He hoped he'd hidden his discomfort behind his best social smile as he'd worked the event. They'd already been given the official tour through the impeccably styled and glitteringly festive six-thousand-square-foot house, and now it was just a matter of making sure his company was represented to maximum effect before they could make a graceful escape. No one had seemed surprised to see him enter with Tess at his side; everyone who knew them probably assumed they were simply attending in a business capacity. It would take a few more appearances to get the message across that their relationship had changed.

A movement next to him made him glance around to find a petite blonde in a sparkly dress frowning at him. She smoothed her expression quickly, but not before he'd seen the disapproval on her pretty face. "Is something wrong, Stevie?"

"I was just looking for Tess."

"She's over there, by the Christmas tree, chatting with the mayor and his wife. Apparently Tess and the mayor's wife are on some sort of civic committee together."

"I'm sure she's worked you and your company into the conversation a few times," Tess's friend murmured, echoing Scott's thoughts from only moments earlier. "You have to admit she's your most dedicated ally."

"No argument here. I owe a great deal to her. She's

a big fan of yours, too. I've heard her directing several people to look at your kitchen this evening."

Stevie nodded. "She's the most loyal and supportive person I've ever known. Always the one in the background quietly doing all the work and getting too little of the credit."

Okay, there was definitely a message here. He just wasn't entirely sure what it was. Was Stevie implying that he hadn't given Tess enough credit at work in the way of salary, title, promotions? Or was there a more personal implication to her comments? How much had Tess told her?

"Tess has certainly been instrumental in the success of my business," he said to reassure Stevie that he was fully mindful of that fact. "I've told her many times, both publicly and privately, that I don't know what I'd do without her."

"You're lucky to have her. She has plenty of options, you know."

He was well aware that Tess had been approached by other employers, some who'd met her through his business and coveted her organizational skills for their own enterprises. One of his own friends had recently offered her a position as human resources director for his trucking company, promising he'd add 20 percent to whatever Scott was paying her. Lane hadn't even bothered to be subtle about trying to hire her away; he'd made his move in Scott's own office. Scott had been gratified when Tess had made it clear she wasn't looking for a new job, and he'd tried to be good-natured about it with Lane. But come to think about it, they hadn't really spoken since, though Scott wasn't carrying a grudge. Still, if the truth were told, he'd been annoyed. Maybe even territorial in a way that hadn't been entirely business related. Had it been about that time that the seed of this marriage plan had been planted unknowingly in the back of his mind?

"Anyway," Stevie said when he sipped his champagne to avoid having to figure out a way to respond to her, "I'm just saying I wouldn't want Tess to be taken for granted. I would hate for her to be hurt. By anyone."

He lowered his glass and met her eyes. "So would I."

"Good."

"Hey, you two. Sorry I got detained for so long, I got caught up in a conversation about the chances of my nephew's basketball team making the state playoffs," Tess explained as she rushed up to join them. "Stevie, the mayor's wife wants to remodel her kitchen within the next few months. I told her she should be sure to talk with you before she leaves. Be ready to make a pitch," she added with a smile.

"I'll be ready. Thanks, Tess."

Only moments later they were interrupted by someone who wanted to question Stevie about a function of a trendy new feature in the impressive chef's kitchen.

Scott turned to Tess after Stevie had moved away. "What's with your friend?" he asked quietly. "She seems unusually subdued this evening."

On the few occasions when he'd met Stevie before, she'd always been laughing, animated, a bundle of barely suppressed energy in a compact package. Tonight she'd seemed more serious than he'd ever seen her, and he didn't know if it was only due to her doubts about Tess and him.

He saw concern flit across Tess's face as she glanced in the direction in which Stevie had just disappeared.

"I think she's going through some issues with her boy-friend," she murmured. "But I don't really know, so I'm only speculating."

That seemed to be all she was willing to say about Stevie's problems, so he changed the subject. "I think we've put in our time, don't you? How about if we duck out now?"

"Sounds good to me."

"Do you want to say good-night to your friend?"

She shook her head. "Stevie's busy. I'll send her a text later. Let's go before someone else corners us."

Smiling at her eagerness to escape, he moved across the room with her, exchanging nods and quick hand-shakes on the way out. Tess shivered as she slid into the passenger seat of his car. She grabbed her coat from the backseat and wrapped it snugly around her over the seat belt. "I think the temperature has dropped a few degrees since we went inside."

He started the car. "Some people know better than to wear sleeveless dresses in December without a coat."

She laughed. "I brought a coat."

"And left it in the car."

"I didn't want to bother with having to check it and then wait to reclaim it. It was worth a few minutes of freezing to make a faster getaway."

"That was a bore, wasn't it? I was expecting live music or some sort of entertainment other than just walking through the rooms, then standing around with cheap wine and dry canapés."

"I have a feeling there will be a new chairperson for the Holiday Open Home committee next year," she agreed wryly. "It's been so much better planned in the past."

"Oh, well, as long as they met their fund-raising goals, I guess that's all that matters."

"True. And I'm sure Stevie will get some new business from it. Her kitchen was gorgeous, wasn't it?"

"It was very nice." It still bothered him a bit to remember the way Stevie had frowned at him, as if she had some valid reason to worry that he would hurt her friend, but he shook off the concern. Maybe it was only that Stevie was having relationship troubles of her own, as Tess had implied, and was subsequently pessimistic about any new relationship. Maybe if they'd been in a place where they could have had a private conversation, he would have assured Stevie more forcefully that he had no intention of hurting Tess. Considering his belief that broken hearts were the result of unrealistic expectations, his plan was much healthier and saner than Stevie's idealistic and deliberately naive approach to the search for a life partner. Would Tess's friend see his point if he explained, or would she still disapprove of his prosaic tactics?

Not that it mattered. The only concern to him was that Tess approved.

Feeling a bit more cheerful now that their first official outing had been generally successful, he said, "I'm starving. I've hardly had time to eat anything today and those little nibbles at the party didn't fill me up. Want to stop for something to eat?"

"I ate before the party. But if you'd like to come in to my place, I'll make you an omelet or something."

His fingers tightened a bit on the wheel, but he made sure to keep any hint of surprise from his voice. "Sounds good, thanks."

Oh, yeah, he thought. This was all working out just fine.

* * *

"And this," Scott said, his head close to hers as they peered down at the phone in his hand, "is Miranda holding Henry after Thanksgiving dinner. She and Madison love being the older cousins and taking care of the baby."

"Do you just remember who this is, or can you really tell those girls apart?" Tess asked with a laugh and a shake of her head. It always amazed her that Scott's family seemed to so easily identify each twin, though they looked exactly alike to her.

"I can usually tell. Their personalities are different enough that their expressions sort of give them away, even when they're dressed alike, which isn't very often. Eli and Libby think it's important that the girls develop their own identities, so that they aren't just known as 'the twins.' Still, every so often I mix them up, and they call me on my mistake pretty quickly."

They sat side by side on the deep-cushioned sage-green couch in her living room, flipping through family photos stored in Scott's phone. He'd already eaten and effusively complimented the generous omelet she'd made for him, and he'd quickly accepted her offer of herbal tea afterward. He seemed to be in no hurry to leave, and Tess was enjoying this relaxed, private time with him.

"Your nieces are really cute. And Henry's a little doll. Thanks for showing me the pictures. It looks as though you had a great Thanksgiving."

"We did." Setting his phone to one side, Scott touched her hand. "I'm sorry you didn't have a good Thanksgiving with your family."

Her first instinct was to deflect the sympathy with a

shrug and an assurance that her gathering with her sister's family had been fine and she'd had a lovely time. It was a bit embarrassing to compare her strained situation with his close clan. But if Scott was going to become a part of her life, he might as well know everything he was getting into. "I guess you know that Nina and I aren't close. I can never seem to live up to her standards, and I think it annoys her that I'm not jealous of her. Does that make sense?"

"It does, actually. You being jealous of her would be a validation that she's important. Impressive. If you don't want to be her, she probably wonders what you find lacking. Needing to be envied is a common weakness for people whose sense of self-worth comes only from the amount of admiration they receive from others."

He sounded like an amateur psychologist, but he was right. "That does sound like Nina," she agreed slowly. "It sometimes seems as though everything she does is slanted toward impressing others. She pores over fashion magazines and trend blogs trying desperately to stay current. She's raising her kids the same way. Nina would pretty much pawn her soul to buy them the 'right' label. She and Ken aren't wealthy, but they try so hard to keep up with the Joneses that it exhausts me just watching them."

"I've had friends fall into that trap before they realize it's a game they just can't win. There's always someone with more money, more toys, more admirers. I like nice things as much as anyone, but I buy what I like, not because someone else would be impressed by it."

She knew that about him, of course. She couldn't have worked side by side with him for six years without learning something about his core values. It was another point in their favor as a budding couple that they shared so many of those principles. Smiling, she waved a hand around her living room. "Same here, obviously."

"I've always admired your sense of style."

The compliment pleased her. She smiled. "Thanks. But I have to give credit to my friends—Stevie with her flair for design and Jenny for keeping my wardrobe reasonably up-to-date."

Draping an arm casually across the couch behind her, he ran a fingertip along the bateau neckline of her red dress. "If this dress is an example of Jenny's contribution, then I applaud her advice. You look spectacular tonight. I could hardly take my eyes off you at the party."

The brush of his hand against her throat made her pulse flutter there. She wasn't sure he'd even noticed her appearance this evening other than the perfunctory compliment when he'd greeted her. "Thank you. And yes, I bought the dress at Jenny's boutique for the party."

"Then, I can see why her business is doing well."

"She deserves every bit of her success. And her happiness." Tess thought of her best friend. "You know, Jenny got caught up in that game we were just discussing when she dated a man before she met Gavin. Thad Simonson runs in an exclusive crowd, and with his political aspirations, everything he says, does, wears or eats is shrewdly calculated. Jenny said she felt as if she was losing herself in that life. She spent so much time trying to please Thad and his followers—not to mention her overbearing grandmother—that she wasn't even sure what she wanted anymore. Since she married Gavin, she's happier than I've ever seen her. She says she feels as if she's just getting to know the real her, pursuing her own dreams. She and Gavin are planning a camping trip in the Smoky Mountains next summer. It's something she always secretly wanted to do, but Thad wasn't interested in sleeping in a tent and her grandmother would have called it a waste of valuable time."

"Sounds like fun to me. My brothers and I have been on several camping hikes."

"I know," she reminded him with a smile. "I was the one keeping the offices running while you were gone, remember?"

He tapped the shallow cleft in her chin in a teasing gesture. "You've taken a few vacations, yourself. We struggled to stay in business while you were gone, but somehow we managed."

She laughed, though she was increasingly aware of his proximity on the couch, the way his thigh brushed hers when he shifted his weight, the air of intimacy surrounding them in the quiet room.

"How about you?" he asked. "Do you like camping?"

"I don't know. I've never been."

He looked surprised. "You've never camped?"

"No. You have to understand, my dad was almost fifty when I was born. He had his first heart attack when I was only nine. My mom was forty-five when they were shocked by her pregnancy with me. She was diagnosed with lupus when I was still in junior high and her health was never good after that. Neither of them was interested in outdoor pursuits. Usually we just went out to eat or to watch Nina perform in pageants or at college. She majored in music, though she only attended for two years before she left school to marry Ken. She has a beautiful voice, but she sings only in her church choir now."

"What were your extracurricular activities in high school and college? Do you sing, too?"

"Oh, no, not really. I can carry a tune, but I don't have Nina's talent. By the time I was in high school my parents were both in such poor health that I had to help out at home a lot. I was on the school newspaper and yearbook staffs, because those were activities I could do during the schoolday. Nina was a young bride with small children, so she couldn't help much at our house. I contributed as much as I could preparing meals and doing housework."

Realizing she might sound as if she was whining, she shook her head and spoke more brightly. "Don't get me wrong, I've had a good life. My parents made sure I had everything I needed. They paid for my tuition and made sure I had a little nest egg to set me up in this condo when they were gone. I have good friends. I have a job I love, thank you very much. My relationship with my sister isn't really close, but it's not as if we're actually estranged. Considering the age difference and the lack of anything in common, we get by okay."

He covered her hand with his and gave her fingers a warm squeeze. "I'm glad you feel free to speak candidly with me. I don't think you'd have said those things to just anyone—not even to me had we had this discussion just a couple weeks ago. Right?"

"No, probably not," she conceded. "I'd have just said everything was fine. But if you come to my cousin's party with me, I'm sure you'll see how it is with my sister and me, so I wanted you to be prepared."

"*When* I come with you to your cousin's party," he murmured, emphasizing the first word, "I'm sure we'll get along fine with your family."

"Oh, undoubtedly. We're all very civil when we get together." Mostly because she bit her tongue until it almost bled to keep from snapping when they criticized her, she added silently, choosing to keep that comment to herself.

He laced his fingers with hers. "Maybe you and I could go camping sometime. I think you'd like it."

Her heart gave a quick thump at the thought of spending a night in a tent—or anywhere else—with him, but she managed to smile. "Both of us out of the office at the same time? Sounds like a recipe for disaster."

"I suppose we'll have to figure out how to handle that situation in the future," he said with a slight shrug and a smile that almost made her sigh aloud. "We've both been working damned hard for a lot of years. Now our company is well established, we have good people on our payroll that we can trust to take care of things occasionally, and we can be reached in a multitude of ways if we're needed. I think we both deserve to take some time away from work occasionally, don't you?"

Several things about that little speech stood out to her, but his use of the plural possessive was particularly startling. *Our company. Our payroll.*

"I've been giving it a lot of thought lately," he continued before she could answer what must have been a rhetorical question. "I'm closer to forty than thirty now, and all my energy thus far has gone into the company. Buying it, growing it, securing its future. As you know, I pretty much ignored my personal life. I made the one attempt at getting engaged, but that would have been a mistake even if it hadn't fallen apart due to my own negligence. Now I'm ready for more. Commitment. Marriage. Kids. Soccer games and teacher meetings and dance recitals. Eventually cutting back on work to travel and see the world with my wife."

"That sounds very nice." She almost sighed in response to the lovely images he'd invoked.

"But first," he said briskly, "we have to get through the holidays. What's next on our social agenda?"

There was that word again. *Our.*

She moistened her lips and drew her attention back to the topic. "I'm sure you remember that tomorrow afternoon is the reception at the Best Burger home office to celebrate the holidays and the opening of their twentieth restaurant." The relatively new, locally based fast-food chain was rapidly expanding throughout Arkansas and two neighboring states and had contracted with Scott to handle its new construction. It was one of the more lucrative deals Scott had signed during the past few years. He spent a lot of time making sure the owner of the chain was happy with the construction, including one currently under way in Little Rock. The three-to-five drop-in reception was for store managers, vendors and other professional associates, and Scott was expected to make an appearance. "I don't know if you want me to attend that with you...?"

"Absolutely. This was the deal, remember? We're doing all the holiday stuff together."

The deal. Was that the way he viewed their dating agreement? She supposed it summed it up well enough. She cleared her throat silently and nodded to indicate she was on board.

"So we'll stop by the Best Burger thing tomorrow afternoon. Do you have plans for tomorrow evening?"

This felt so familiar, she thought with wry amusement. How many hours had they spent coordinating their office calendars, planning business commitments for weeks or months at a time? She supposed it was only natural that they'd handle their personal plans in much the same way. "No, I don't have anything specific planned for tomorrow night."

"I have tickets for the symphony's holiday performance. I know it's short notice, but would you like to go with me? You know—a real date?" he added with a crooked smile that was too charming to resist. "Just the two of us."

"I would like that. I love the symphony."

Looking pleased, he nodded. "We'll pop back in to the office after the reception, then leave from there to have dinner and go to the concert, if it's okay with you."

She made a quick mental note to choose a day-into-evening outfit for the next day, and to take a sparkly jacket to slip on for the concert. "That'll work."

"What about the rest of the weekend? Do you have personal plans?"

"Saturday is my niece's birthday, and Nina has made reservations at that popular new Japanese restaurant."

Should she ask him to accompany her? She supposed the reservation could be changed to add one more, but was it too soon for Scott to join her at a family celebration? Would it make the evening better or even more awkward to have him there with her?

The possibility of joining her didn't even seem to occur to him. "I've got family stuff Saturday night, too. I told Jake I'd go to his house to watch the SEC West playoff game with him tomorrow night. Have fun at the party."

She nodded. It seemed that she and Scott were already beginning to define their future together: they would be free to pursue their own interests as individuals even as they attended some events as a couple. Practical and independent. The two adjectives had always been applied to her, so it made sense that they defined her budding relationship, as well. "Have fun with your brother."

It occurred to her that he was still holding her hand. It felt nice. His fingers moved on hers again, giving another little squeeze as he said, "Next weekend is fairly busy, too. We have our office Christmas party Saturday night. But before that, on Friday night, I have a dinner thing. Would you be free to go with me to that?"

"A dinner thing?"

He waved his free hand. "It's an engagement party. The couple sent out invitations a couple of months ago, I think, and to be honest, I'd forgotten about it until I got a reminder by email today. You know how hectic everything has been the past few weeks. This dinner totally slipped my mind."

This was the first she'd heard of an engagement party. She didn't handle his personal social calendar, but usually he mentioned upcoming events at least in passing. It did speak to his state of mind lately that he'd forgotten a commitment. "Did you tell them you'd be bringing a date?"

"Oh, sure. I figured I'd ask someone. I can't think of anyone I'd rather go with than you."

She swallowed. Accompanying him to the Holiday Open Home had been a relatively innocuous first social outing together. If anyone had been surprised to see them enter side by side, Tess hadn't noticed. She figured the Best Burger open house would be similarly easy. It was possible they'd see people they knew at the symphony performance, but then again, perhaps they wouldn't, nor would they likely be expected to explain why they attended together. But an engagement party… Well, that was very different. This would most definitely be interpreted as a date. "Are these close friends?"

He shrugged. "Bethany, the bride-to-be, is the youngest daughter of my mom's college roommate. I've known her all her life, but I wouldn't call us close friends. The groom just finished dental school in Louisiana and Bethany's mom talked Dad into interviewing him as a potential associate."

"So is he going to join your dad's practice?"

"Yeah, I think so. Dad's been wanting to add someone who specializes in pediatric dentistry, which apparently this guy does."

So the daughter of an old friend and his dad's new business associate. Which meant the entire Prince clan would probably be in attendance at this party. "You haven't, um, mentioned to your family that you and I are…"

"I haven't talked about us with anyone," he assured her. "But they'll probably get the picture when we show up at the party."

She nodded.

"Haven't changed your mind, have you?" He spoke lightly, but she sensed he was serious.

"No." In fact, now that he'd laid out such an enticing future for them, she was even more committed to their tentative plan. "I have to admit I'm a little nervous, but I'll go with you."

"Why are you nervous?" he asked with a little smile, holding her hand between both of his now.

"Well, it's your family and friends."

"Many of whom you've met several times. They already know you and like you."

"As your office manager."

"As a person," he corrected firmly. "My family doesn't tend to label people by their professions. The dinner's at Trapnall Hall and it shouldn't last overly long."

"I always enjoy events there this time of year. I'm sure the Christmas decorations are beautiful."

He lifted one hand to her face, running a fingertip lightly over her lower lip. "I'm glad you'll be going with me. It'll make the event much more tolerable."

Warmth seeped through her in response to his nearness, his touch. In some ways it still felt odd to be snuggled with Scott on her sofa, yet beneath the novelty was a growing certainty that it was exactly where they were meant to be. He'd simply realized it before she'd acknowledged it herself.

She rested a hand on his chest, allowing her fingers to curl a bit against his shirt to savor the warm strength beneath. He'd removed his jacket and tie and opened his collar, so he looked casually at ease, gazing at her in a way that made her heart beat a little faster. His eyes had darkened to a gleaming navy and his lips were curved into a faint sexy smile that made her ache to taste him.

"I'll try my best to make the party tolerable for you," she said, smiling.

His gaze was focused intently on her mouth. A low rumble of laughter escaped him. "I appreciate that," he murmured.

Silence fell between them then. Looking into his eyes, she realized that the time for conversation had ended. It was time for him to go...or not. Which didn't mean they had to rush to a decision about those options. She slid her hand up his chest to the back of his neck, her lips parting in an invitation he accepted instantly, eagerly.

Gathering her against him, he kissed her with a thoroughness and urgency he'd reined in previously. His mouth was hot, hungry on hers, his tongue sweeping deep to explore and challenge. She gave a little moan of surprise and pleasure, her arms closing around his neck to bring them even closer. His hand moved on her leg, toying with the hem of the dress and then sliding under to caress her thigh. She shivered in response to an image of his hands moving higher. Her breasts swelled against his chest, and a restless ache settled there. Just the thought of his hands closing over them made her tremble.

Slowly breaking the kiss, he lifted his head only a couple inches, his gaze sweeping her flushed face. Still nestled snugly in his arms, she was aware that he was breathing rapidly, that his eyes were dilated, his heart beating hard against hers. He was as aroused as she was, in control but reluctantly so.

She touched her fingertips to his jaw almost wonderingly. "Does this feel weird to you? Shouldn't it feel strange?"

His lips curved upward. "Maybe it should. But it doesn't. It feels...good. Right."

"To me, too," she confessed. "Maybe the strange part is that it *doesn't* feel weird."

He chuckled and set her a couple inches away from him. "I'm not quite sure how to unravel that statement, but I think I'd better go."

She blinked. "You're leaving?"

His voice was just a little rough when he nodded and said, "It's either that or I'm going to start trying to get you out of that pretty red dress. I'm not sure we're quite ready for that step yet."

Though a surprisingly insistent part of her wanted to argue, rational discretion prevailed. She scooted back another couple inches and reached up with unsteady hands to smooth her hair. "You should go," she agreed, pleased that her voice was reasonably normal. "We do have to work in the morning."

She walked him to the door to lock up behind him. With a hand on the doorknob, she smiled up at him, giving in to an impertinent impulse. "Scott? For the record—you wouldn't have to try very hard. With the dress, I mean."

His eyes widened, then narrowed. "You're determined to make me suffer tonight, aren't you?"

She patted his cheek. "Just saying."

His smile was decidedly lopsided. "So this is how it's going to go, huh? You're going to make me jump through a few hoops to prove myself worthy?"

Even though his amusement was obvious, she grew serious. "I know you're teasing—as I was—but let me make this clear. I don't play games. I don't expect you to prove anything to me. Outside the office, we're not boss and employee, but equals. Full partners. Yes?"

He matched her serious tone when he replied, "Absolutely. I've said from the start this has nothing to do with business. I expect you to speak your mind, state your wishes, read me the riot act when I deserve it, without fear of any professional repercussions." And then he looked thoughtful. "Actually, that's pretty much the

way you act in the office, too. You've never been intimidated by me, have you?"

She thought fleetingly of that first interview so long
ago, but merely smiled. "Not that I'd let you see."

He chuckled, then leaned over to brush his lips
lightly across hers. "And now you know why I'm convinced we make such a great team, inside the office
and out. Thanks for the omelet, Tess. It was delicious."

"You're welcome. Good night, Scott."

He hesitated for just a few moments longer and then
gave a decisive nod and let himself out. Tess released a
long breath and listened through the door as he walked
away. Only when she could no longer hear him did she
head for her bedroom to change out of the red dress
and into her nightclothes. For the sake of her peace of
mind, she made a deliberate effort not to imagine what
it would have been like if Scott had been the one to remove the dress.

Chapter Six

As Tess had expected, no one seemed to find it newsworthy that she accompanied Scott to the Best Burger reception. It was their biggest regular client, and everyone knew she'd interacted frequently with representatives from the chain. Andy and Lana, their architect and cost estimator, had already left for the reception, so PCCI would be well represented.

The reception was drop-in and very informal. Tess had met most of the higher-ups in the fast food chain's echelon at one time or another. Aware of her function as valued assistant to Scott, they welcomed her warmly to their base of operations. The owner of the chain even introduced her to a district manager as "the glue that held PCCI together." Grinning, Scott said he couldn't dispute that assessment. He stayed by her side during the hour they mingled, but she doubted anyone thought they were actually there as a couple rather than a work team. Still, as Scott had said, it was good for people to get accustomed to seeing them together in a variety of settings. They stood by the food table—laden, of course, with snacks available at any local Best Burger restaurant—chatting with a variety of local business-people, and when they thought they'd accomplished their purpose in coming, they made a gracious escape.

"That went well," Scott proclaimed in his car on the way back to the office, sounding almost smug about it. "This whole dating thing is turning out just fine, wouldn't you say?"

Tess laughed. "Scott, I refuse to acknowledge that as a date."

He slanted a grin her way. "Was the Holiday Open Home a date?"

"More so."

"How about the baby shopping trip followed by the barbecue dinner?"

"Less so."

He chuckled. "So by your definition, we're just barely in the honeymoon part of this relationship."

Her heart gave a little jerk, though she didn't know whether it was in response to the word *honeymoon* or *relationship*. Maybe it was something about the words used in combination. But because he was kidding, she chuckled and said, "Yes, I suppose."

"But tonight definitely counts as a date. Just the two of us at the symphony, no professional obligations, nothing to do but enjoy each other's company and the music."

"That sounds nice," she agreed, relaxing again. She really was looking forward to the concert. As much as she loved music, she was sure she would enjoy it even more with Scott by her side.

By the time they'd finished returning calls, answering emails, signing paperwork and placing orders, Tess and Scott barely got away from work in time. They acknowledged wryly that they should have known better than to stop by the office. "A couple of hopeless workaholics," Scott said with a laugh as he locked up behind them. "That's why we get along so well. You understand me because you're just like me."

Straightening the short sequined jacket she'd donned over her day-to-evening black jersey dress, Tess smiled in return. "Was that supposed to be a compliment?" she teased.

"Just an observation." He placed a hand on her back as they walked side by side toward their cars. "I can count on you to understand that sometimes I get distracted or held up by obligations to the company. You won't expect me to apologize when unexpected problems crop up or when I have to cancel social plans rather than risk losing a valuable contract."

"Well, of course not." She suspected he was thinking of his ex-fiancée. Sharon had made her displeasure clear to everyone when she didn't think Scott was paying her enough attention. She'd even snapped at Tess a few times when Tess had answered the office phone and had to explain that Scott was in an emergency meeting and couldn't be disturbed. Even though she knew he was comparing her positively to his high-maintenance ex, she would just as soon not be compared at all. She deliberately changed the subject. "So you're following me home to drop off my car and then we'll have dinner before the concert, right? We'll have to choose someplace with fast service in order to make the start of the concert."

They did make it to the concert hall in time, but just barely. The lights were already dimming when they slid into their seats. Tess wasn't displeased by that. This way they didn't have to wait very long for the music to start, nor had they risked running into mutual acquaintances on the way in. The concert was wonderful, a charming mixture of classical pieces and Christmas favorites. She relaxed into her seat, letting the music wash over her, not worrying about work or family or the future, just enjoying the evening. After one particularly rousing number, she glanced at Scott to find him gazing back at her. Though the lights were very low, she could see well enough to tell that he was smiling at her, apparently enjoying her pleasure.

He reached over to take her hand, squeezing her fingers. "Glad we came?"

"Very much."

They'd both needed a couple hours away from work and expectations, she decided. True, they were on a date, and there was still the novelty of that—but it was Scott. With their demanding work schedule, they'd spent more time together over the past six years than most married couples. They communicated so well silently that she could even tell which musical numbers he enjoyed most without looking at him—which was probably also true in reverse. They were comfortable together…and yet underlying that familiarity was a new awareness that gave her a delicious buzz when he touched her. Knowing there would be more kisses later caused little ripples of anticipation to run through her.

Thinking of where those kisses would eventually lead made her breath catch in her throat.

But no. She wasn't thinking ahead now, she reminded herself. She wanted to enjoy every moment of this evening, just sitting beside him and listening to the music.

They each saw a few familiar faces on their way out, but the crowded rush to the exits prevented more than nods and waves. If there were any mutual acquaintances in the audience, she didn't see them, but then she wasn't really looking. She and Scott didn't linger in the hall, but made their way to his car as quickly as possible. They'd accomplished their mission. They'd enjoyed a concert while growing more accustomed to being out in public as a couple. Maybe by the time next weekend rolled around, she would be a little less anxious about attending the party with his family and friends. Had that been part of his reason for bringing her to this concert tonight?

They talked about the concert during the drive home, comparing notes on their favorite numbers, expressing their admiration for both the musicians and the vocal performers. Arriving at her place, he parked next to her little blue sedan. Each unit came with two designated covered parking spaces, leaving her with an extra for her guests. He walked her inside, and her heart beat more quickly with each step they took toward her door. Should she ask him in? Of course she should. Were they ready for that next step they'd alluded to when he'd left her here last time? Part of her was most definitely ready.

He started to automatically follow her inside, then seemed to realize he hadn't technically been invited yet. He hesitated. It briefly crossed her mind to send him on his way with weariness as her excuse, but she decided she didn't really want to say good-night just yet. "Would you like some tea?"

"Sounds good." His flash of a smile made her hands tremble. He closed the door behind them with a firm snap.

She set her bag on a table and draped her coat over the back of a chair. "Would you prefer tea or decaf coffee?"

"Actually, I'm not very thirsty."

She turned toward him. "Neither am I."

Scott stepped up to her and cupped her face gently in his hands. His palms were still cool from being outside, but her cheeks felt very warm against them. His eyes locked with hers, and she could almost imagine he could see her thoughts, her doubts as he gazed somberly down at her. "You can kick me out at any time," he reminded her gently.

"I know. The problem is...I don't want to kick you out," she replied, resting her hands on his chest.

His eyes heated, but still he kept his tone even. "Is that really such a problem?"

"I'm still trying to decide."

He moved his thumb against her lower lip, tracing the shape of it. His gaze following the movement, he murmured, "I've been trying to take it slow. Give you time to adjust."

Take it slow? It had been only a week since he'd sprung this proposition on her. She felt a slight frown crease her brows. "How are *you* adjusting so easily?"

His smile was warm, understanding. "You know me. Once I make up my mind about something, I rarely second-guess myself. Now that we've acknowledged how great we are together, it just seems as if it was inevitable all along."

Inevitable. Was that enough? She doubted Stevie would think so.

"And now that we've spent this time together," he added, his mouth so close to hers that his breath was a warm caress on her lips, "I can't believe it took me so long to see what was right in front of me."

Okay, that sounded a little more intimate. A little less deliberate. Not exactly a declaration of devotion, but that wasn't what she was looking for from Scott. She'd heard flowery speeches and passionate promises before, and those relationships had ended in disappointment if not actual heartbreak. Maybe this time she should put her faith in actions, not words. And speaking of action...

She wrapped her arms around Scott's neck when he gathered her closer, capturing her lips with his. Despite the five inch or so difference in their heights, their bodies fit very nicely together. Each time they kissed, the sensations grew more familiar—and yet more urgent. He'd said he'd been taking things slowly, so perhaps he'd held back in those previous embraces. He wasn't holding back now. He drew her closer, letting her feel his body's response, making her intensely aware of his growing arousal. His mouth was avid, his tongue insistent. Faced with a choice between pushing him away and doing what she really wanted, she gave in to temptation. She crowded closer to him, returning the kiss with an answering demand.

Take it slow? Hardly. This had been building in her for six years.

He was quick to recognize the silent invitation and

he accepted it with an enthusiasm that soon had them both breathing heavily, shoving impatiently at clothing to access the warm skin beneath. Scott's jacket and tie fell onto the couch. She left her shoes behind when she led him to her bedroom. He had his shirt untucked and partially unbuttoned by the time they reached the bed. She reached for the zipper at the back of her dress, but Scott's hands were already there as he gathered her into his arms for another hungry kiss. By the time the black dress fell to the floor, she was too deeply lost in the embrace, too eager for more, to be at all self-conscious.

She'd seen him without a shirt only once before. It had been the day they'd worked at his house after his surgery. Still loopy from the meds, he'd accidentally tugged off a corner of his bandage. She'd smoothed it back into place and then helped him don a fresh T-shirt. Other than the necessary touching, she'd kept her hands to herself that day, resisting the then inappropriate urge to run her palms over the firm planes and hard muscles of his chest, to follow a thin trail of hair down his ridged stomach to his shallow belly button and below.

She'd never forgotten how appealing he'd looked that day, all rumpled and drowsy and half-nude. Unbidden memories had haunted her more than once during lonely nights since, though she'd quickly and firmly suppressed them each time. She didn't have to restrain herself now. She gave her curious hands free rein to explore and savor every inch of him, even as he pushed her beyond coherence with his own bold forays of discovery.

They communicated with soft moans and approving gasps, with kisses and strokes and urgent movements. His mouth on her breasts made her arch with a choked cry of pleasure. Her hands closing around him tore a low groan from him. They rolled and writhed, shoving pillows to the floor, covers to the side. He dealt with protection swiftly and deftly before returning his attention to pleasuring her, which he did with even more practiced skill. Their hands were interlocked when he finally, finally thrust into her, filling an emptiness that seemed to have been waiting for him all her life.

For only a raw heartbeat of an instant, she was aware of a sense of panic, an overwhelming fear that this was too perfect, too powerful. The knowledge that everything would change after this night swept through her, and for just that second she fought to cling to the safe, cautious status quo. The comfortable camaraderie that had carried no risk of disappointment or heartbreak, no fear of losing what they'd found...of losing herself. But then he began to move, and any hesitation was replaced by an almost desperate need for release. Her mind emptied of any thought except that very moment, that very place, the two of them entangled in the cozy cocoon of her bed, their bodies joined, hearts pounding in unison. Her climax hit with a force that shattered any illusion that anything would ever be the same for them again.

He didn't stay the night. Referencing an early breakfast meeting with a couple of job foremen, he slipped from the bed and dressed to leave while she wrapped herself in a robe to lock up behind him. He paused before opening the door, and she got the distinct impression that he was trying to come up with the right thing to say. It wasn't like him to be at a loss for words.

To help him out, she said simply, "Good night, Scott. Drive carefully."

He kissed her lingeringly. "Sleep well, Tess. I'll call you tomorrow."

She nodded and reached around him to open the door.

His jacket over his shoulder, tie hanging from his pocket, his finger-combed dark hair tumbling onto his forehead, Scott turned just on the other side of the door to smile at her. "I knew we made a great team," he said in visible satisfaction. "I really am a genius."

That made her laugh, as he'd surely intended. "Yes, you are," she said.

Because she didn't want him to leave feeling too sanctimonious, she reached out to grab his shirt, tugged his mouth down to hers and gave him a kiss that turned his laughter into a groan.

"Okay, maybe I could stay a little while longer," he said rather hoarsely when the kiss ended.

She tossed back her tumbled hair and took a step backward. "Good night, Scott."

She closed the door almost in his face. Through the wood, she heard him sputter a rough laugh, then listened as his footsteps faded away. Only then did she allow herself to release a long, slow exhale.

After fastening the door locks, she turned toward her bedroom, then realized she was biting her kiss-swollen lower lip. She released it with a reassurance to herself that things really were going well between them. It was probably only weariness and lingering disorientation causing the heavy feeling deep in her chest. The sensation felt much like apprehension, but she couldn't fully explain it and didn't want to examine it too closely tonight.

* * *

The positive side of the showy dinner party Nina threw in celebration of Olivia's fifteenth birthday was that she was too busy being the hostess and mistress of ceremonies to have much time to focus on Tess. She'd reserved a private dining room in the restaurant for some thirty guests. Most of the guests were related to Nina's husband, Ken—his parents and two siblings and a few of their progeny—in addition to a few church, social and business acquaintances. More to Olivia's taste, there'd been a teen party the night before at the indoor pool of a country club. Though she visibly relished being the center of attention again, Olivia made it clear she'd enjoyed last night's bash much more than this dinner party. She huddled with her boyfriend and the few other friends she'd been allowed to invite while her brothers played handheld video games and Ken quietly did his part by standing at his wife's side, following her directions and bankrolling the event.

Tess would rather be just about anywhere else, herself. She loved her niece, spoiled little princess that she was, but this was not her idea of a fun evening. All in all, she'd rather have been watching the football game. Either alone...or not.

She wondered if Scott was having a good time. If he'd thought of her at all this evening. She'd never been one of "those" girlfriends, she mused. Though she both practiced and expected monogamy during her relationships, she'd never expected to know where her significant other was or what he was doing at all times, nor did she report her movements to him. But it would be nice to know that she'd crossed Scott's mind today as often as he'd hovered in hers. That he'd mentally replayed their lovemaking and relived the excitement, that he felt the same anticipation she did about the next time they'd be alone together.

She wanted to be confident that when he thought of her now, it wasn't only with a list of tasks he needed her to oversee at the office.

It was a relief when the dinner was over. She exchanged farewells with the other guests, most of whom she'd met previously, then lingered to say good-night to her family.

Holding her boyfriend's hand, Olivia sauntered up to her. "Thank you for the bag, Aunt Tess. It's really cool. I love it."

Pleased by the girlish delight in her niece's voice, Tess smiled. "I'm glad. Jenny helped me find it for you. She thought you'd like it."

They hugged quickly, and then Olivia and her lanky boyfriend hurried off to rejoin their friends. Satisfied that she could make her escape now, Tess looked around for Nina, finding her on the other side of the room saying goodbye to some departing guests. She made her way to her sister's side. "I'm leaving now, Nina. It was a great dinner. Thanks for inviting me."

"Of course you'd be invited," Nina replied with an impatient roll of her eyes. "We invited all Olivia's aunts and uncles."

Resisting an impulse to snap that she'd just been trying to be polite, Tess drew a deep breath and held on to her smile with an effort. "It was good to see everyone again."

"Don't forget next week is—"

"Dana's party," Tess finished in unison. "I haven't forgotten, Nina."

"You've responded to the evite?"

Nina was very much in "mama mode" this evening, treating Tess exactly the way she would one of her children. Again, Tess had to cling to patience. "I have responded."

"Did you tell her you'd bring a guest? Because if you haven't invited anyone—"

"I'm bringing a guest. It's already arranged, Nina."

Her sister's eyes widened in curiosity. "Who are you bringing?"

"Hon, we need to help Olivia carry out her gifts," Ken interrupted the conversation to say. "The room's booked for another party so they're ready for us to clear out."

Nina lifted her chin. "We have it reserved for another ten minutes. I will not be hustled out."

"It'll take us that long to gather everything up and get the kids out to the van. Come on, Nina, grab a couple bags, will you?"

Tess moved a step forward. "Can I help?"

Her brother-in-law gave her a quick wink. "We've got it, thanks. Get out of here while you can."

She took grateful advantage of his suggestion.

A particularly boneheaded play in the football game would have made Scott curse in exasperation had a baby not been asleep on his chest. As it was, he grumbled beneath his breath, making little Henry squirm and nestle his nose into Scott's shoulder. Scott hoped fleetingly that it wasn't a snotty little nose, but it wouldn't be the first time he'd been used as a tissue by one of his brothers' offspring. He patted the kid's diapered bottom and Henry settled back into a limp slumber. Sprawled on Jake's couch with his stocking feet crossed on the coffee table, Scott glanced at the canned soda on the table and wondered if he could reach it without waking his nephew.

As if he'd recently mastered the art of mind reading, but more likely correctly interpreting Scott's expression, Jake snagged the can and handed it over. "Game sucks, huh?"

With a nod of thanks, Scott took a sip of the beverage, which had gone rather flat in the past hour since he'd opened it. "Yeah. I thought the score would be closer than this."

"You okay there? Want me to take the rug rat?"

"He's okay. We wake him up, he's just going to want to eat again, and we promised Christina we'd give her a little more time to herself. Might as well stretch it out as much as we can after the week she's had."

The virus Henry had picked up at Thanksgiving had held on for several days. He was recovered now, but his parents were tired and frazzled. Scott's mom had helped out when she could, but as a full-time accountant, she'd been busy with end-of-the-year work for her clients. Today had been a day for Christina to get some rest, with Jake and Scott taking care of the baby.

His eyes on the big-screen TV on the opposite wall, Jake munched a handful of popcorn, then asked idly, "You going to Bethany's engagement party next Friday?"

"Looks like. You know Mom would pout if any of us skipped out without a damned good reason, and unfortunately I couldn't come up with one."

Jake chuckled wryly. "Yeah, us, either. We've got a

babysitter lined up, so I guess we'll make an appearance."

"Lousy time for an engagement party, if you ask me. This time of year, seems like I'm running from one party or fund-raiser or holiday reception to the next one. Bethany and what's-his-name aren't even getting married until spring, so I can't imagine why they thought they needed an engagement party now."

"Mom said Jeremy—that's the groom's name, by the way—has an aunt in poor health. They aren't sure she'll still be around for the wedding, but they wanted to have her at the engagement party."

"Oh, well, now I feel like a jerk." With a grimace, Scott set the soda aside and patted the sleeping baby again. "I'll be there. With a smile."

"Are you bringing someone?"

"Yeah. Tess is coming with me."

He wasn't sure how he'd expected his younger brother to react to that, but it hadn't been with a laugh. "Tess? Man, she really is on call 24/7 for you, isn't she? Do you pay her overtime for keeping you company at parties you don't want to attend alone?"

Scott shook his head. "She isn't coming as my employee. Tess has agreed to be my date for the party."

"Your date?"

"Yes."

"Like…a *date* date?"

Scott scowled, hardly pleased by the disbelief in his brother's expression. "So we're back to high school now? Really?"

Jake shrugged. "I'm just surprised, that's all. I didn't know you and Tess ever hung out outside the office."

"It's a recent development."

"You and Tess, huh? Wow."

Wow pretty much summed up the last few hours he'd spent with Tess, Scott mused, though of course he wouldn't say that to his brother. Henry wiggled and made a mewing sound. Scott bounced him gently while saying, "Yeah."

"Since when?"

"We've been out a few times." He smiled as he remembered the teasing conversation he and Tess had about how many real dates there had actually been.

"So is it, you know, serious?"

An erotic memory of deep-throated cries of satisfaction whispered in the back of his mind. Scott cleared his throat. "Getting there."

"Well, that's great," Jake said, still sounding surprised.

Henry squirmed again, then lifted his head from Scott's now-damp shoulder to blink up at him. He looked a bit surprised to find himself in his uncle's arms, but with his usual happy nature, he grinned broadly, displaying two shiny new teeth. Scott couldn't resist smiling goofily in response.

"What's great?" Christina entered the room looking considerably more refreshed than she had when Scott arrived. Short and somewhat square in stature, she had red hair, numerous freckles, warm green eyes and a smile that could melt glaciers. Henry had inherited her coloring. His wispy hair was already a bright ginger rather than Jake's dark brown.

"Scott's dating Tess," Jake blurted.

Christina blinked a few times, then nodded. "Good choice."

"You're not surprised?" her husband challenged.

"Not very much." She crossed the room to take her son, who'd reached out in response to her voice. She smiled at Scott as she relieved him of his charge. "I think you and Tess fit very well together."

Oh, yeah. He and Tess fit very well together indeed, he thought, shifting restlessly on the couch.

"I guess it makes sense," Jake said after a moment. "Tess is great, and everyone likes her. Not sure what she sees in you, bro, but you'd be lucky to keep her."

"Thanks a lot." Scott laughed as he carefully straightened his left arm. The pins-and-needles tingling of returning circulation told him he'd sat in one position too long holding the baby, but he wasn't complaining. He'd enjoyed bonding with his nephew.

"So, Scott, when did you realize you had feelings for Tess?" Christina asked while trying to extricate her eyeglasses from her son's grasp.

He wasn't quite sure how to answer. He remembered clearly that moment of recognition when he'd found Tess under the office tree and had suddenly realized how perfect she was for him. It had just made sense to him. Was that what Christina meant by "having feelings"— or was she imagining some sort of epic Hollywood romantic epiphany that hardly applied to two generally levelheaded adults with common goals and wishes?

Okay, so maybe last night had gotten pretty hot. Maybe he'd tossed and turned as he'd tried to sleep alone afterward, regretting that he'd made himself leave her bed. Maybe he was counting the minutes until he had her in his arms again. Physical chemistry was a good thing between a couple, especially when they'd agreed they wanted children, he considered as his gaze lingered on his giggling nephew.

Maybe the attraction had simmered beneath the surface for quite a bit longer than he'd realized, judging by how swiftly it had come to a boil when he'd finally been free to express it. Her heated responses reassured him that the attraction went both ways, though knowing Tess, she'd probably suppressed any such awareness in the past for fear that it would be unprofessional.

"Scott?" Christina looked at him quizzically over Henry's head, and he suspected the trained psychologist was trying to analyze his facial expressions. "You and Tess?"

"We've just started seeing each other," he said, choosing his words carefully. "It's occurred to us both how well we get along and how much we have in common, so we figured it was worth exploring on a more personal basis."

The couple looked at each other and then back at him. Jake broke the momentary silence. "Wow. What a romantic story. Almost brought a tear to my eye."

Frowning at his kid brother, Scott grumbled, "Bite me, Jake. We all know I'm no good at the romantic stuff. I don't have to put on an act for Tess. She already knows me better than anyone outside of the family. Anything that develops between us will be based on honesty and mutual goals."

Jake raised both hands in surrender. "Whatever works for you both. I just want you to be happy, bro. You know that."

"Yeah, I do. Thanks."

Henry was beginning to fuss. Christina bounced him in her arms to momentarily soothe him as she carried him toward the couch. "I need to feed him and give him his bath, then put him to bed. Say good-night, guys."

Both Scott and Jake rose to bestow hugs and kisses on the youngest Prince. He gave slobbery smacks in return, then waved bye-bye over his mother's shoulder as she carried him from the room. She paused in the doorway to look back at Scott. "I like Tess a lot," she said. "I always have."

"I'm glad to hear that."

She looked uncharacteristically fierce when she added, "Don't hurt her."

"I won't."

Nodding decisively, Christina swept out of the room with Henry.

While he appreciated the sentiment, Christina should know that hurting Tess was the furthest thing from his mind. Wasn't that the whole point of approaching her the way he had with his proposition?

"So when *did* you—"

"Halftime's over, Jake," he cut in flatly. "Let's watch the game, okay?"

"In other words, you don't want to talk about you and Tess any more this evening."

"Exactly."

Jake directed his attention to the television screen, obligingly bringing the conversation to an end. But even though they weren't talking about it, Scott figured his brother was still mulling over this new development. He knew thoughts of Tess would hover in his own mind until he saw her again.

Although rather hectic and borderline chaotic, that second week in December was nevertheless enjoyable, as far as Tess was concerned. The business problems that cropped up were no more than expected and fairly easily resolved. Sofia started training with Heather and was obviously going to fit in well with the staff. People seemed to be in a generally good mood during the week, because of the approaching holidays or perhaps because the weather had taken a nice turn.

As for her personal life—that was going nicely, too. Though both busy with previously arranged after-work obligations, she and Scott managed to find time together during the week. Scott had business plans Monday evening and she had a civic club meeting. He called her just as she was getting ready for bed and they talked about their respective meetings, sharing a couple of amusing anecdotes. Something else that was new for them, she thought with a smile as she climbed beneath her covers afterward. A chatty personal phone call made for no other reason than to hear each other's voices, to stay in contact despite their individual pursuits. It was nice that his was the last voice she heard before ending the day.

They dined at a restaurant following a long day at work Tuesday, slipping out after the rest of the staff left. Tess had rather hoped the evening would end back at her place, but the muted beep of Scott's phone just as they finished dessert dashed that fantasy. Scott looked at her in apology after disconnecting the call. "I'm sorry."

"Something has come up," she said, easily reading his expression.

He nodded. "Apparently a bunch of punks climbed the fence around the rental units we're building in Sheridan and had a little vandalism party before the cops rounded them up. Andy and I are going to look around and see if they've done any permanent damage. I guess Andy could go without me, but…"

"But you need to go check it out yourself," she said

matter-of-factly, knowing him too well to imagine otherwise.

He grimaced and nodded. "We were so close to finished with that project. I'm hoping there's nothing that'll hold us up too long. I need to put the crew on the fabric store job after the holidays, and I'm sure we'll have weather delays in January and February. We always do."

"You don't have to explain. Just go. Let me know if there's anything I need to do."

"You're the best, Tess," he told her warmly.

He might as well have given her a cheery knuckle-chuck to the chin. Even though he gave her a fairly heated good-night kiss when he dropped her off at her condo, his attention was obviously focused already on what he would find at the job site. Tess let herself in her door with a wry smile. She honestly didn't resent him at all for rushing off to work. How many times had she walked out on plans with her friends because something had come up at work and Scott had requested her assistance? Her ex-boyfriend James had accused her of being at Scott's "beck and call" 24/7...and worse, liking it that way.

Still, she thought as she prepared for bed in her quiet home, it would have been nice if the evening had gone the way she'd hoped.

Fortunately the damages to the Sheridan job hadn't been too extensive, so Scott was able to make arrangements for fairly swift repairs. They got a great deal accomplished in the office on Wednesday, to everyone's satisfaction. She didn't see a lot of Scott that day, only when he dashed in with barked instructions and scribbled his signature on whatever she slapped in front of him.

Though she had to silently chide herself a couple of

times when she found herself watching his sexy mouth instead of listening closely to his words, Scott seemed to have no trouble at all seeing her as the same efficient assistant she'd always been to him. She was fairly confident the staff saw nothing different in their professional behavior, which was a relief to her even though she was aware it wouldn't be much longer before the news got out. She wasn't looking forward to that part, mostly because she suspected everyone would watch them surreptitiously when they were together, at least until they got used to the idea that the boss and the office manager were more than business associates. Considering that it had taken her more than a week to wrap her head around the idea, she expected the transition to be a bit awkward.

It would have been nice to think Scott was having just a little trouble keeping his personal feelings for her, whatever they might be, so well hidden. She'd hate to think she was the only one having to work at that.

Scott was scheduled for an overnight trip Thursday to a job site in Joplin, Missouri, planning to be back just in time to make it to the engagement party dinner on Friday night, and there was a long list of things to do to prepare for his meetings there. The sun had long set by the time Tess and Scott wrapped up their work. Predicting it would be a wearing day, she'd left a beef-and-vegetable stew in the slow cooker that morning, and Scott eagerly accepted her invitation to share it with her.

At his suggestion, they didn't discuss work during the meal. Instead, they talked about their families and friends outside the office. He shared stories about babysitting little Henry last Saturday, making her laugh at his description of changing a soaked-through diaper and onesie. "Jake just stood there and laughed at me," he added with mock indignation. "Didn't even offer to help."

She laughed again. "Did he take video?"

"No."

"Then, consider yourself lucky. The whole episode could have ended up on YouTube, you know."

He chuckled. "There is that."

"You enjoy being an uncle."

It hadn't been a question, but he smiled and nodded. "Very much."

He'd be a wonderful father, she thought with a little ripple of wistfulness. He was already comfortable with kids and experienced enough through his brothers that he was prepared for the reality of parenthood.

"I told Jake and Christina that you'd be coming with me to Bethany's party," he said, somewhat abruptly changing the subject.

They'd been clearing away the dishes when he spoke, and she paused in the act of loading the dishwasher. "Did you?"

"Yeah." He closed the refrigerator door after stashing away leftovers. "Christina said she likes you very much."

It was nice to hear. "I like her, too. All your family seems nice. Have you told them that we're…um…"

"Seeing each other?" he supplied with a smile. "By Sunday morning the whole family knew. They're cool with it."

She wondered what, exactly, his family had said, but she assumed he would tell her when or if he was ready. For now, he seemed to consider the question of his family's reaction settled. "What did your sister say when you told her I'm coming to your cousin's party with you?" he asked.

"I haven't actually told her," she admitted. "She knows I'm bringing someone but there hasn't been a chance to tell her it's you."

That wasn't entirely true, of course. She could have made time to talk to Nina. She couldn't even explain why she'd hadn't.

Scott studied her face a bit too closely. "Will you mention it before we show up?"

"If I speak with her. Hand me that ladle, will you?"

He let the topic go, but she knew he didn't fully understand her relationship with her sister. How could he, when she didn't herself? He would simply have to see for himself when they spent time with her family. As close as his clan was, he would surely be aware of the difference in hers.

He wiped his hands on a kitchen towel. "So what had you planned for the remainder of the evening, if I hadn't come to eat your food?"

"Promise not to laugh?"

He grinned. "No."

She wrinkled her nose at him. "Okay, fine. *Rudolph the Red-Nosed Reindeer* and *Frosty the Snowman* are on tonight. I've watched them every year since I was a little girl. Usually I make hot chocolate and curl up on the sofa for an hour of Christmas nostalgia before I take care of anything else that needs to be done, like laundry or paperwork or laying out clothes for tomorrow."

He didn't laugh. Instead, she thought he looked almost charmed by her admission—which, of course, endeared him even more to her. He reached out to smooth her hair in a casually affectionate gesture. "Do you have any marshmallows for that hot chocolate?"

"Of course."

"Then, may I hang around and watch the elf become a dentist with you?"

"I'd like that."

He brushed a kiss over her lips. "So would I."

They made it halfway through the first show before teasing chocolate-flavored kisses turned to aching, impatient need. Tess tugged at his shirt, needing to touch him, all of him, and his hands were busy beneath her soft sweater, stroking and circling and tugging lightly until her breathing was fast and ragged.

"What about your Christmas specials?" he asked when she jumped to her feet and held out a hand to him, making sure he couldn't mistake the invitation.

"I know how they end." She smiled. "I can always watch the DVDs if I want."

Taking her hand, he turned with her toward the bedroom. "I'll buy them for you," he promised with a low laugh.

"I'll buy them for myself. There are other things I want from you, Scott Prince."

Grinning, he swept her against him. "Happy to oblige, Tess Miller."

They proved without doubt that the first time hadn't been a fluke. Their lovemaking this time was just as spectacular, just as breathtaking. As much as Tess hated clichés, she had to admit if only to herself that she'd honestly never felt anything like that before.

Because he'd be making an early start the next morning, Scott didn't stay long. He left her with smiles and kisses at the door.

"Be careful during your drive," she urged him.

"I will. You know how to reach me for whatever."

"Yes. See you Friday."

"Friday," he repeated, stepping out her door. He glanced over his shoulder with a rather odd expression. "I'll miss you."

Why did he sound almost surprised? "I'll see you Friday," she repeated and gently closed the door.

Was it really such a surprise to him to think he might miss her? True, they hadn't really talked about their feelings for each other—they'd talked about common dreams and goals and values, about families and children and other interests, but they hadn't said anything about love. They'd shared fiery kisses and mind-blowing lovemaking, but even in the throes of passion they'd whispered only encouragement and pleasure. She didn't expect flowery declarations from him; she knew him too well. But "I'll miss you" sounded innocuous enough. Why had it seemed so hard for him to admit?

And why hadn't she told him she would miss him in return? Because she realized now, as she climbed into the sheets still warm from his body, that she would miss him very much, even though she would see him again in only two days. And that was a bit daunting, indicating that she was investing a great deal in this budding relationship.

Apparently he wasn't the only one getting a little nervous with the speed and intensity with which this momentous development was taking place between them.

Chapter Seven

With Scott out of town and it being Heather's last day, Friday was particularly busy at work. By the time Tess arrived home, she was already tired, though she still had a party to get through that evening. A fairly momentous party, actually. She would be spending the evening with all of Scott's family for the first time since they'd become lovers. She doubted he'd shared such details with his relatives, but would they be able to sense the differences between her and Scott?

Scott arranged to pick her up at seven thirty, giving her just enough time to freshen up and change into the green dress she'd bought at Complements. He'd texted that he would be on time, but she knew he was rushing to make it after driving all afternoon from Joplin. She turned in front of her mirror. She'd followed Jenny's advice of thin black tights and heeled booties, and was glad she had. The dress was a bit shorter than usual for her, though perfectly appropriate for a party this time of year.

"Let me guess," Scott said when she opened the door to him a few minutes later. "Another purchase from your friend Jenny?"

Her coat draped over one arm, a small gold clutch in her hand, she smiled. "Yes. I bought it the same day as the red one. My holiday splurge for the year."

"And worth every penny," he assured her. "You look great. I suppose it would ruin your lipstick if I were to kiss you right now?"

She tilted her face up to him with a smile. "I can reapply it."

Grinning, he swooped in. "Always resourceful," he murmured just before his lips covered hers.

It was so good to kiss him again. Just to be with him again. Though they'd spoken by phone several times for business and once just for themselves, it still seemed as though the past two days had passed much too slowly. She'd had dinner with Jenny and Stevie last night and both had commented that she'd been unnaturally distracted.

"You're thinking about Scott, aren't you?" Jenny had accused her.

Feeling her cheeks warm, Tess had shrugged sheepishly. "A little."

"This courtship is moving fast, wouldn't you say?" Jenny had asked with raised eyebrows. Both she and Stevie had studied Tess's face closely when they'd gotten together, and Tess wouldn't be at all surprised to know that her friends could tell she and Scott had taken the next natural step in their relationship.

"It's not as though he's someone I just met," Tess had replied logically.

"True. It's just a big change, and it's happened almost overnight."

Tess could have responded that once Scott got a plan in mind, he rarely saw a reason to delay implementing it. She was his new plan, she'd thought a bit wistfully. And he seemed quite satisfied with how it was coming along.

Stevie, who'd been so perky and bubbly that Tess had wondered if there was some overcompensation involved in the cheeriness, grew a bit quieter when Scott's name came up. "I talked with him a little at the Holiday Open Home," she'd confessed. "I have to admit I was trying to read his feelings about you, just for my own curiosity."

Lifting her eyebrows, Tess had asked, "And...?"

"And I still don't know," Stevie had said. "He's a hard guy to read. He told me he values you highly. When I told him I'd hate to see you hurt, he assured me he would hate that, too."

Tess didn't know how she felt about Stevie issuing warnings on her behalf. She was certainly capable of taking care of herself, of course. Still, it was so characteristic of Stevie to feel protective of her friend. Hiding her annoyance, she'd let it go.

It was the same tonight, though as she entered the engagement party, it was nervousness she hid, this time behind a forced smile. Scott's hand at the small of her back was reassuring, reminding her she wasn't in this alone. They'd passed the test of whether they could continue to work efficiently despite their personal relationship. Tonight it was important they not be seen as boss and office manager, but as equals. To that end, she held her head high and her shoulders back as she and Scott entered Trapnall Hall, the historic antebellum home that had been rented for tonight's event.

Built in 1843, the Greek Revival–style brick house had been meticulously restored, and served as the Arkansas governor's official receiving hall. Tess had been here a few times in the past for various events—business gatherings, a couple of weddings, a charity fashion luncheon, among others—but it had been a while and she was struck again by the beauty of the place. Decorated for the holidays and the reception, it was undeniably the perfect setting for a momentous celebration. The guests mingled around impeccably set round tables with white cloths and glittering tableware, and Tess was secretly relieved to note that her green dress with its touch of glitter had been just the right choice for the evening.

She suspected that Scott's family had been waiting for them to arrive. The whole clan descended on them almost immediately, greeting them both with warm smiles and cheek kisses.

Short and plump, Holly Prince was towered over by her husband and three sons, adored and healthily feared by all of them. Tess had always liked the cheerful, gregarious woman, but suspected no one had better hurt anyone in Holly's family lest they feel her wrath. Her husband, Barry, like their sons, was tall and naturally slender. His thinning silver hair topped a face that Tess had always thought looked like Scott in one of those age-progression drawings. Eli and Jake bore a resemblance to their dad, but Scott was his younger duplicate.

"We're so happy to have you here with us this evening, Tess," Holly assured her. "You look lovely. What a pretty dress."

Scott's sister-in-law Libby studied the green dress with envious dark eyes. "I've been looking for something similar for a Christmas party next week. Do you mind if I ask where you got it?"

Tess was always happy to plug her friend's boutique. She chatted for a few minutes with the Prince women until Holly towed her into the room to present her to other guests, including the happy young couple. No one seemed surprised Scott was there with a date, reminding her that he'd never had trouble finding female companionship, an uncomfortable thought she immediately pushed away.

Tess and Scott dined at a table for eight with his parents, two brothers and their wives. Because she already knew everyone, Tess was able to join in the lively conversation easily enough, though it once again amused her that the Prince clan tended to talk over one another when they got deeply involved in a topic. They were so obviously close-knit, sharing quick grins and private jokes and good-natured insults, yet making Tess feel welcome among them.

She could see both Libby and Christina felt close to their in-laws, as comfortable in the circle as if they'd been born into the family. Tess suspected the ease was partially a result of Holly and Barry Prince's warm, laid-back parenting style. Scott had informed her his parents had been fairly strict when their sons were in their formative years, but they made it a practice not to get overly involved in their adult lives. They were always there for their sons and grandchildren, but they kept their advice and opinions to themselves unless asked—a policy that served them well with their daughters-in-law, Scott had added with a smile.

Dinner was followed by half a dozen heartfelt toasts from family and friends of the bride- and groom-to-be and then a twenty-minute performance by a smooth-voiced, Arkansas-born pop singer who'd performed well on a nationally televised talent show. The party pretty much ended with the resulting applause.

Scott gave her a sign that he was ready to slip out as soon as possible. She thought he was probably tired after being in meetings for two days, then on the road for four hours that afternoon. He got delayed for a few minutes of conversation with his father, and Tess hovered patiently nearby, watching in amusement as various starstruck party guests posed for snapshots with the singer.

Her attention lingered for a moment on the engaged couple, who were saying goodbyes to departing guests at the door. They were holding hands, she noted, their fingers interlocked at their sides. Every few minutes their gazes held and they smiled just for each other. They looked young and happy and visibly in love, she thought with a funny little pang she couldn't quite define.

"Tess, it was lovely to see you this evening," Holly said warmly as she, too, prepared to leave.

"You, too, Mrs. Prince."

The older woman patted her arm. "Please, call me Holly. There's no need to be so formal now that you and my son are seeing each other."

Was that Scott's mother's way of giving her blessing? Tess smiled but had no chance to respond before Scott returned to take her arm. "Okay, now we can leave. We've done our duty, right, Mom?"

Holly rolled her eyes comically. "Yes, Scott. You may go now. Thank you for coming. I know Bethany and her family were happy to have you here."

"As if I'd have had the nerve to skip it," he muttered, kissing his mother's soft cheek with a fond impertinence that displayed absolutely no wariness of her. "G'night, Mom."

She stroked his cheek. "Good night, sweetie. Drive carefully."

Tess bit her lip as another twinge rippled through her. Maybe she was just weary from a long, busy week, but she was feeling a bit more sentimental than usual tonight.

"You've been quiet since we left the party," Scott observed as he walked her to her door a short while later. "Is everything okay?"

"Of course." She tucked a strand of hair behind her ear and smiled faintly up at him as she unlocked her door. "Just tired, I guess. Probably not as much as you, though. You've had a very long day, haven't you?"

He didn't look entirely reassured. "No one said anything to you? Upset you in any way?"

"Of course not, Scott. Everyone was very nice. Frankly, I was expecting some personal questions or comments, but between dinner, speeches and the musical performance, there wasn't a lot of time for personal conversations."

"Yeah, that worked out pretty well, huh? Folks could get used to seeing us together without getting nosy about the details." He looked rather pleased with himself, as if he'd arranged that in advance.

She stepped inside her living room and looked over her shoulder. "Are you coming in?" she asked when he seemed to hesitate.

He took a couple steps forward, his smile faint. "Sorry. I'm a little slow this evening."

"You're tired." She studied his face, seeing dim shadows beneath his eyes, slightly deeper than usual lines around the corners of his mouth. To what lengths had he gone in order to get back in time for the party? "Go home, Scott. Get some sleep. I know you have that project manager meeting in the morning. Are you sure you don't need me to be there?"

"No, I'll text you if we have any questions for you. I'm sure you have things to do."

She nodded. "I do have shopping to finish and errands to run before Dana's party. Um, you're sure you still want to—"

"I'm going to the party with you," he said flatly, brooking no argument. "I keep my word."

She offered to drive the next evening, but he insisted that would be out of her way. "The party starts at seven, right? So I'll be here around six thirty."

"No rush," she assured him with a wrinkle of her nose. "It's not as if I care if we're the first ones there."

He chuckled and shook his head. "I'm not having your sister blame me for making you late. I'll be here on time."

He continued to stand in the center of the room, one hand squeezing the back of his neck. She got the distinct impression that he was torn between staying and leaving. But just as she hated sending him away, she knew it was best tonight.

"Go get some rest," she repeated quietly. "I'll see you tomorrow."

He reached out to pull her into his arms. "I am tired," he admitted. "I'm afraid once I get horizontal I'll be out for a while, and I do have that early meeting. So maybe it's best if I head home."

Nestling her cheek into his shoulder, she gave him a hug, savoring the feel of him before she had to let him go. "We'll see each other tomorrow."

He kissed her lingeringly, then took a step back. "Maybe we should start thinking about having only one place to go to when we're not at the office."

Was he really talking about moving in together? They'd been moving fast to this point, but that was kicking the relationship into hyperdrive!

He laughed wryly in response to whatever he saw on her face. "You don't have to respond to that tonight. Just leaving you with something to think about."

"As if you haven't given me enough to think about lately," she muttered with a shake of her head. "Go get some sleep, Scott."

"Yes, ma'am."

She moved to lock the door behind him. "Scott?"

He turned just on the other side of the doorway to look at her. "Yes?"

"I'm glad you're back. I missed you."

This time he was the one who seemed caught unprepared. After a moment, he said simply, "Good night, Tess."

He turned and walked away before she closed the door.

He'd been in an odd mood this evening, she thought

as she secured the locks. Maybe it was simply that he was exhausted.

It would have been nice if he'd said he missed her, too.

Tess's phone rang late the next morning just as she was loading a few bags of groceries into the backseat of her car. Slamming the door, she lifted the phone to her ear as she slid into the driver's seat. "Hi, Jenny," she said, having checked the caller ID screen before answering.

"I'm just calling to let you know that Scott's sister-in-law came into the shop this morning looking for a party dress. She ended up buying two outfits and some accessories, even a couple of Christmas presents. She said to tell you thanks for sending her to me, so thank you from both of us."

"You're both welcome."

"We were very discreet and didn't gossip about you and Scott."

Tess chuckled. "I appreciate that."

"She did, however, make it clear that the family approves of you and Scott dating."

"They seemed okay with it at the party."

"More than okay, I think. They think you and Scott are a good match."

A good match. A great team. Inevitable. The labels echoed through her mind.

Their relationship sounded so ordinary when described that way. Unexciting. Even calculated. Was that how their friends and families saw them? The way Scott saw them?

"I'm glad to hear they approve," she said, keeping her tone steady.

"You're okay? You sound a little funny."

"I'm in my car in a parking space. Just finished running some errands and buying groceries."

"Oh, sorry, I didn't mean to catch you at a bad time. We're going to have to get together soon, right? I want to hear details of how things are going with you and Scott, of course. And we need to talk about Stevie. I'm getting a little worried about her."

So Tess wasn't the only one who'd noticed that Stevie hadn't quite been herself lately. "I'll call you to set something up," she promised.

"Great. Gavin has three days off, so I'm planning to work here until three or so this afternoon and then he and I are heading up to the cabin until Monday evening. We're looking forward to a few days away. But as soon as I get back, you and I are making plans, okay?"

"Absolutely."

She put her phone in the console after disconnecting the call and backed out of the parking space. Her errands were done, so her intention was to head straight home and rest awhile before the party. Tonight was going to be a more emotionally stressful event than the previous ones. She expected her family to be much more nosy and critical than Scott's had been. Would her sister be able to tell by looking at them exactly how much had changed in the past couple of weeks?

Her concerns about the evening were driven from her mind a few minutes later when a car ran a stop sign in an intersection near her condo and crashed into the back-passenger side of her car. Her seat belt tightened, holding her in her seat, and she gripped the wheel with white-knuckled fists as she brought the car to a stop. The jarring, sickening sound of the impact rang in her ears, her heart pounded and her knees shook beneath the steering wheel. After a quick visual self-exam that told her she was still in one piece, she opened the door with trembling hands to assess the damage to her car and the other driver. To her relief, she could see that he was already out of his car and seemed unharmed.

She was grateful no one was hurt, but really she hadn't needed this today, she thought with a groan. As she leaned back against her dented car, one thought rang through her mind: Was this an omen for how things would go tonight?

"So meeting her family tonight, huh? The big audition."

Standing on a ladder outside his parents' home, Scott looked down at his older brother, who stood below him, steadying the ladder. "I've met Tess's sister before. They don't have much family left except for a cousin I'll meet tonight."

"You've met the sister as Tess's boss, not her boyfriend," Eli pointed out. "That's different."

"True." It was still a bit odd to hear himself referred to as Tess's boyfriend, but he supposed that was a close-enough description outside the office. For now. "Okay, the bulb's replaced. Mom can quit fussing now."

He and Eli had both just happened to drop by that afternoon. Taking advantage of their presence, their mother had talked them into replacing a burned-out bulb on the strand of Christmas lights strung over the portico entrance. That dark bulb had been driving her crazy for the past week since they'd paid a neighborhood teen to hang the strand. Scott's dad had wanted to take care of it, but only three months past knee-replacement surgery, he'd been forbidden by his wife and sons to climb the ladder.

Scott descended the rungs, then jumped the last couple of feet to the ground. He brushed off his hands on his jeans and reached for the ladder. "Grab the other end and help me carry this around to the shed," he ordered his brother. "Then I have to get out of here and get changed into my party clothes."

Eli chuckled and gripped his end of the ladder. "If you're anything like me, you're already tired of Christmas parties. I've lost track of the number of invitations Libby has accepted on our behalf. And that doesn't even count the open house we're hosting at the clinic next weekend."

"Know the feeling. Tess and I have already been to several."

"So the family's still trying to figure when and how you and Tess got together. It's as though one day you were business associates and the next day you're a couple. Unless it's been going on awhile and you've been keeping it quiet for some reason?"

"No. It's a recent development." He'd found himself using those words a lot lately. Maybe he should think of a new phrasing.

"Mom's a little worried."

Frowning, Scott stopped walking, causing his brother to stumble at his end of the ladder. "Why is she worried? I thought Mom liked Tess."

"Dude, give me a heads-up when you're going to stop like that, will you? Almost gave me whiplash. And Mom likes Tess very much. Which is why she's concerned."

"Because…?"

"She said you aren't acting like a man at the early

stages of a romance. She said she remembers how I was when I fell for Libby. Goofy. Distracted. Kind of hyper."

"Young," Scott added with a shrug. "You were just a kid when you met Libby."

"I was in med school. Not that young."

"A decade younger than I am now. I'm a little past the goofy, hyper stage."

"You and Tess are hardly a couple of senior citizens," Eli scoffed. "You're both younger than I am—and trust me, Libby still knows how to make me go all goofy."

Scott opened the door to their dad's backyard garden shed. "You can spare me the details, thanks."

Now that he thought about it, he was a little distracted today. He'd had to focus a bit more than usual on conversations because his mind kept wandering to a condo on the other side of town. He could hardly remember what he'd eaten at his breakfast meeting, but he still vividly recalled every touch, every taste, every sensation of making love to Tess. But that was only to be expected, right? He was a red-blooded guy with a healthy appreciation for great sex—and sex with her had most definitely been great. He wasn't the type to kiss and tell—or bag and brag, as a few of his buddies termed it—so he wouldn't discuss his intimate relationship with Tess even with his brother, but it had reinforced his certainty that he and Tess were well-matched in every way.

They stored the ladder, then brushed off their hands as they stepped back. "Anyway," Eli continued, seemingly determined to make his point, "Mom is worried that you aren't fully emotionally invested in this courtship, or whatever you're calling it. She thinks you're following your usual pattern of getting involved more because you think you should than because you've lost your heart."

Taking after their dad in personality more than appearance, Eli had always been the most sentimental of the Prince brothers. He'd had his heart broken, or at least painfully bruised, a couple of times before he'd found his Libby. So was he expressing their mother's concerns—or his own?

"You can tell Mom to stop fretting. My heart is exactly where it's supposed to be," Scott replied lightly. Losing one's heart—what a weird saying, he mused. His beat steadily in his chest. It had most definitely raced when he'd made love with Tess, but he'd never felt in danger of "losing" it. He knew what the metaphor meant, of course, but it had just never seemed to apply to him.

"She's afraid you're going to hurt Tess."

Scott heaved an impatient sigh. "Everyone keeps saying that. Isn't anyone concerned that maybe the opposite could happen?"

"No, not really."

"Thanks a lot. But you can all quit worrying. As I have said to anyone who's expressed concern, I'm not going to hurt Tess. I would never hurt Tess. She and I have talked extensively and we both know exactly what we want, what we're doing."

"So you are thinking long-term?"

"Yes," Scott replied simply.

"Okay, then." Eli nodded and locked the storage shed. "I'm happy for you, bro. Tess is a fine woman who'll fit right in with our family. You're damned lucky she's interested in you. Don't screw it up."

It might have been nice for his brother to have a little more faith in him, but still Scott was satisfied that his family approved of his choice. As Eli had said, Tess fit in well with the independent, capable women in the Prince family. Everything was falling into place very nicely. As he knew it would. When he had one of his brilliant ideas, he was very rarely wrong.

Which didn't explain the odd feeling that had hovered in his belly since he'd left her place after making love with her Wednesday night. He still remembered that moment when the words "I'll miss you" had left his mouth, before he'd even realized he was going to say them. When it had hit him that he would, indeed, miss her, even though he would be gone only one night.

He'd made trips before, several considerably longer than one night, and yet it seemed different now. Like an inconvenient necessity from which he couldn't wait to return. What the heck was that?

He'd done it again last night. Blurted out a thought he hadn't taken time to consider. He'd come close to suggesting that Tess move in with him. Granted, it was the logical progression of this courtship, but were they really ready for that just yet? He hadn't been flattered by the way she'd all but jerked back from him in response to his hint. She kept assuring him she was on board with his long-term plan—and she certainly seemed more than amenable to exploring all the possibilities—but there had definitely been doubts in her eyes when he'd even hinted that they give up their separate homes.

He and Eli walked into the kitchen to say goodbye to their parents—then both recoiled in exaggerated horror at finding their mother bent back over their dad's arm being soundly kissed.

"Jeez, I didn't need to see that," Eli grumbled, waving a hand in front of his eyes as if he'd gone blind.

"Get a room, people," Scott muttered, copying his brother's gesture.

Laughing, their parents straightened, though their dad kept his arm around his wife's soft waist. "Holly just said she'll make fettuccine Alfredo for dinner. I've had a hankering for that for weeks, and I've finally worn her down."

Shaking her head in exasperation, his wife muttered about all the rich foods they'd be eating during the holidays, but she was already pulling supplies out of the pantry.

"And garlic toast on the side?" their dad asked hopefully. "With plenty of butter? Maybe a chocolate cake for dessert. I'll make the cake."

"Don't push your luck." Their mom looked at her sons with a roll of her eyes. "You see what I have to put up with? Tomorrow I'll have to nag him onto the treadmill to make up for this meal and he'll pout like a toddler. Mark my words."

"She takes good care of me because she's crazy about me," their dad boasted, winking at his smiling bride. "I'm a lucky man."

His sons heartily agreed.

Dressed for the party in a sport coat and slacks, Scott drove into Tess's parking lot, eager to see her again. He frowned as he turned toward her unit and saw a dark compact parked in her slot. Frowning, he checked to make sure he hadn't made a wrong turn, but the painted numbers assured him he was in the right place. Noting a rental car sticker on the back bumper of the compact, he parked beside it. Was Tess's car in the shop?

She opened the door to him with a smile that showed no evidence of awkwardness. He kissed her in greeting.

"You look nice," he said with a glance at the boxy black jacket she wore with a silver tank, subtly striped black and charcoal pants and chunky jewelry. Another outfit from her friend's store? Wherever it had come from, it looked great on her. But then, everything did.

"Thanks. So do you," she returned with a cheeky pat on his jaw.

He chuckled, then asked, "So what's with the rental car downstairs? Where's your car?"

She groaned and rolled her eyes as she collected her bag and coat. "I was in an accident this morning. My car had to be towed to a body shop. I'm waiting to hear about the damage."

Scott froze, trying to process her words. "Wait. What? You were in a wreck?"

"Yes. Obviously I was unhurt, and so was the guy who ran a stop sign and hit me, but it was a nuisance to have to deal with it. I had groceries in the car that had to be salvaged and a few other things I had to take out before it was towed off. Now I'm sure I'll have to fight the guy's insurance company to get everything I should—you know how they try to pay as little as they can get away with. I hate that part."

He was still trying to wrap his mind around this. "How did you get the rental? Was it delivered to you at the scene?"

"No, I called Stevie. She came to pick me up and drove me to the rental lot."

His jaw going tight, Scott made a show of pulling his phone from his pocket and checking the log.

Tess raised her eyebrows. "What are you doing?"

"Just checking my missed calls. I thought maybe I hadn't heard you trying to reach me."

Something in his tone must have warned her he was annoyed. She eyed him guardedly when she said, "I didn't try to call you."

He stashed the phone again. "You had a car accident and you needed help. Why didn't you let me know?"

"I guess I didn't even think about it. I knew you had that meeting this morning and Stevie was—"

"You didn't even think about it," he cut in to repeat slowly.

"As I said, I knew Stevie was available and she wouldn't mind helping me out. She was just the first one I thought of."

He told himself he had no reason to be angry with her. No right, to be honest. But still it irked him that she'd turned to someone else for help. He drew a deep breath and touched her arm, searching her face. "You're sure you're okay? Any pain or discomfort?"

"I'm fine. Really, I wasn't hurt at all, just shaken up."

"So you still feel up to the party?"

"Of course."

"If you get a headache or anything..."

"Scott." She patted his hand on her arm. "I'm fine."

He nodded, trying to lighten his expression, though he wasn't sure he succeeded. "We should go, then."

She moved toward the door and he followed, still trying to decide why it bothered him so much that she hadn't even thought to call him after her accident.

Chapter Eight

Tess had always been able to read Scott's moods fairly accurately. Some of their coworkers claimed to have a hard time telling what he was thinking when he got quiet or preoccupied, but it had always been easier for her. She couldn't read his mind, of course, but she could usually tell when he was working out a problem in his head, when he was making mental lists or plans, even when he just wasn't feeling well. Tonight she could see he was annoyed—and his irritation was directed right at her.

It had never occurred to her that he'd be upset with her for not calling him after the accident. Stevie was almost always the one she called when she needed a hand, and Stevie knew, of course, that Tess would gladly return the favors. That was what one did in a personal predicament such as a fender bender—call a friend, a family member, a significant other.

Not the boss.

Apparently she was still in the process of adjusting to the major change in her relationship with Scott. Was that why he was so cross with her? He'd taken her unintentional slight as an indication that she wasn't invested in their relationship. But seriously, shouldn't the past week have convinced him otherwise?

She turned to ask him, but they'd arrived at their destination. Dana's party was being held in her west Little Rock home, a sprawling Mediterranean modern–style house built beside a golf course in a gated community. Dana had married into money, becoming the second wife of a considerably older investment banker who indulged her shamelessly. Though she considered her cousin rather materialistic and showy, Tess still liked her well enough. In small doses.

"Nice house," Scott commented as he parked among the other cars in the big circular drive. Knowing Scott as she did, Tess was sure he thought the place was overdone, particularly when it came to the holiday lights and decorations that covered nearly every square inch of the house and grounds.

"Dana does like her flash."

"I see that. I'm sure your sister approves."

"My sister is so jealous her brown eyes turn green here," Tess corrected him wryly.

He looked a bit puzzled. "So Nina won't be here this evening?"

"Oh, Nina will be here to spend time with her dear cousin Dana. Snuggly selfies will be taken and posted to Facebook before the evening is over. Probably in front of a sixteen-foot Christmas tree done up in real gold and crystal."

Scott laughed. "Okay."

"Trust me. My sister will bask in our cousin's social glory all evening, even as she secretly hopes every bite Dana nibbles goes straight to her thighs."

He laughed again. "Sounds like a fun party."

"Well, I can assure you the food will be amazing. Dana always puts out a great spread."

"That sounds promising anyway." He unfastened his seat belt and reached for his door handle. "Tell me again how she's related. Your mom's side or your dad's?"

"Her mother and my mother were first cousins. But they were very close, almost like sisters, so we saw Dana quite a bit growing up. She's five years older than I am."

"Got it." He opened the door and climbed out.

At least he'd seemed to have put her car wreck out of his mind for now, she thought. She needed to do the same. She'd worry about insurance and repairs and a man's prickly ego after the party.

She had to admit it felt good to walk into the soaring foyer with Scott at her side. The two-story entryway was anchored by a curving staircase laden with garland and lights leading up to a balcony-railed second floor. Beyond the staircase was the ballroom-size great room, from which guests could see into the formal dining room and elegant music room. The whole place looked as if Christmas had exploded inside, coating every surface with glitter and garland.

She couldn't help noticing the women whose eyes widened in appreciation at seeing Scott, then in surprise at recognizing her with him. It occurred to her that she'd attended the last social gathering here solo, and she'd been perfectly comfortable doing so—but she didn't mind having a polished, handsome escort, either. Was that shallow? Probably. She'd do some sort of penance tomorrow to make up for it.

Nina spotted them almost immediately, most likely because she'd been watching the door. Tess saw the startled expression on her sister's face when she recognized Scott. And then Nina shook her head. Tess knew her well enough to recognize the expression. Why was Nina exasperated with her now? Seriously, what could she possibly find to criticize about Scott?

Towing Ken in her wake, Nina made a beeline straight for them. "I'm glad you could finally make it, Tess."

It was all of five minutes past seven, Tess thought with a stifled sigh.

"And Scott. It's so nice to see you again." Nina offered her right hand with its gaudy profusion of diamonds. "Such a nice surprise."

He shook her hand lightly. "It's good to see you, too, Nina. It's been a while, hasn't it?" He'd met her a few times during the past six years when she'd dropped by the office.

"Yes, it has. Tess doesn't invite me to join her for lunch very often these days."

"Actually, I've invited you to lunch several times in the past few months," Tess refuted evenly. "You're the one who always has something else to do."

Nina heaved a sigh. "Oh, hon, I know. When you're the mother of three popular and active students, it seems as if there's always a demand on your time." She turned to Scott.

She turned then to Ken. "Scott, I don't believe you've met my husband, Ken Wheatley. Ken, this is Tess's boss,

Scott Prince. Wasn't it nice of him to do her a favor and accompany her this evening?"

Nina was really in a mood this evening. Tess didn't know what had gone wrong that day for her sister, but she was getting the sharp edge of it.

She glanced at Scott. He was still smiling, smoothly civil. Probably only she could tell that he was irked when he said lightly, "Actually, this party was just an excuse for me to spend an evening with Tess away from work."

Ken gave Tess a perfunctory kiss on the cheek. "You look nice tonight, Tess."

That drew Nina's gaze to Tess's clothes. "Pants? Oh, well, I suppose you're comfortable. Come in and say hello to Dana and Lloyd. Jolie and Cam are here, and Mary and Bill. Oh, and Glenn's here. He came stag. He asked about you."

She was not the only woman at the party in pants, Tess fumed with a quick glance around that showed her a wide variety of outfits. Hers fit in just fine.

"Glenn?" Scott murmured into Tess's ear when her sister turned away. "The guy you dated? Mr. Boring?"

She gave him a look. "I thought we'd agreed you weren't to mention anything you overheard during that phone call," she said, keeping her voice as low as his.

His smile was unrepentant. "I don't think I agreed to that at all."

She looked past him to smile and return a wave from an acquaintance just inside the doorway of the grand room. "I think I feel a headache coming on," she said to Scott through a forced smile. "It would be such a shame if we have to leave early."

He laughed softly and put a hand at her back as they

followed her sister and brother-in-law into the gathering. "Introduce me to our hosts, Tess. I need to compliment them on their very tasteful decorations."

This time a sputter of laughter did escape her. Perhaps the party wouldn't be so bad after all, not with Scott at her side.

The gleam of amusement in Tess's eyes was reward enough for the effort he'd made to come to this thing with her, Scott decided. No wonder she'd been so stressed at the thought of attending. Her sister treated her like a recalcitrant child, while their cousin was too busy showing off to make a real connection with anyone at the party. Tess seemed to know quite a few of the other guests, but not in a close way. Most of them mentioned how they rarely got to see her. When Nina made a point to introduce him as Tess's boss, they nodded knowingly.

He got the distinct impression that he was known among Tess's friends and family as a somewhat demanding employer. Totally unfair. He never required Tess to be at work all the time. She just happened to be as committed to the company as he was, as conscientious about her responsibilities there. Had Tess used him as an excuse to escape to the refuge of the work she loved rather than tolerate the condescension of her sister and cousin? Okay, he could live with that. He couldn't even blame her for latching on to any excuse she could find.

He did wish Nina would back off the "Tess's boss" introduction, though. His family had accepted that he and Tess were a couple now. Hers seemed to think she'd brought her employer as an escort for lack of another option. He was doing his best to change that impression. He stayed right by her side all evening. He deflected conversation away from work as much as possible. He mentioned other functions they'd attended together. He did everything but plant a kiss on her mouth to demonstrate that his presence at her side was anything but business related.

At least Tess didn't refer to him as her boss, but tended to say simply, "This is my friend, Scott Prince."

Friend. Better than *boss*, he supposed, but still he found himself vaguely dissatisfied by the introduction. But really, what else could she say, he asked himself as he shook the hands of yet another couple whose names he would surely forget. *Boyfriend* seemed juvenile. He supposed *friend* would have to do. For now.

Tess hadn't been wrong about the food, he thought as he popped a lobster puff into his mouth, followed by a spinach-and-goat-cheese mini quiche. Both were delicious, as was everything he'd sampled on the bountiful buffet. He already had his eye on the desserts table, his sweet tooth kicking into high gear at the sight of all the delicacies available there.

"You were right about the food," he said to Tess as they took a seat at one of the little tables artfully scattered about the great room. "Good stuff."

She smiled and picked up a wild-mushroom toast square from her own plate. "Dana would love hearing you say that. She takes great pride in her parties."

He could tell she was fond of her cousin despite their dissimilarity. "I'll be sure to compliment her when we take our leave."

"There you are, Tess. I saw you earlier but couldn't make my way to you."

Scott felt her stiffen a bit, though she turned in her seat with a smile in response to the male voice. "Hi, Glenn. How have you been?"

The portly, broad-faced man who appeared to be in his midthirties, perhaps a couple years younger than Scott, took Tess's outstretched hand and pumped it a bit too enthusiastically. "You look great tonight," he said, seemingly unable to look away from her. "It's been too long since we've seen each other."

"Oh, you know how it is," Tess replied, skillfully extracting her hand. "Work responsibilities get pretty crazy this time of year."

She turned to Scott, who rose to offer a hand to the other man. "Glenn Stowe, this is my friend, Scott Prince."

Glenn shook Scott's hand with an expression that made it clear he wished he was the one with Tess, instead. "Prince," he repeated, glancing from Scott to Tess and back again. "You own the company Tess works for?"

"Yes, I do."

He could almost see the change in Glenn's posture. It couldn't be more obvious that Glenn took encouragement from learning Scott's identity. "It's nice to meet you. Tess has spoken of you often."

In a business context, Scott silently finished.

Glenn had already turned back to Tess. "I'm so glad you weren't injured in that car accident this morning. You're sure you're all right? I can't help worrying that you should have had a doctor check you, just in case."

"I'm fine, Glenn, really. No sore neck or anything, just impatient to get my car back."

"So you knew about Tess's wreck?" Scott asked, working hard to keep his tone politely neutral.

Tess explained quickly, "Didn't I mention it? Glenn is my insurance agent."

"Yes, I see why you had to call him."

She cleared her throat, then glanced around. "Excuse me, guys, my cousin is motioning for me," she murmured, taking a few steps away. "I'll catch up with you later, okay, Glenn? Scott, I'll be right back."

"I'll guard your food," he assured her with a somewhat strained smile.

She gave a quick laugh. "That's leaving the fox in the henhouse. My crab Rangoon better still be on my plate when I get back."

Though it was hard to take his gaze from her as she moved so gracefully away, he turned back to the table. He was almost surprised to see Glenn still standing there.

"There are more of the crab things on the buffet table if you want your own," the other man offered helpfully.

"Thanks, Glenn, but she was teasing."

Glenn nodded. "It's hard to tell sometimes with Tess. She has a very subtle sense of humor."

Scott didn't think the reference to a fox in a henhouse had been all that subtle, but maybe Glenn just had a different sense of humor. "Yeah, I guess she does."

"Working so closely with her for so long, I suppose you've gotten to know her pretty well."

"Yes, I think I know Tess quite well." Was he being too subtle for Glenn, or had the other man picked up on the hint? He didn't consider himself the possessive type usually, but occasionally deeply ingrained male instinct just took over.

"She and I have been out a couple times," Glenn confided. "I'd hoped to attend this party with her tonight, but I guess I waited too long to ask. I sent her a text last week but she said she had already made plans. With you, I suppose."

Obviously, Scott almost said, but he merely nodded.

"Maybe I'll see if she's free for New Year's Eve. I should ask earlier this time. But it's nice that Tess wanted her family and friends to meet her boss this evening. We all know how much her career means to her."

Scott didn't know if this guy was doing some clumsy fishing or if he really was as socially clueless as he acted. But Scott was getting fed up with this "boss" crap. "Tess won't be available on New Year's Eve," he said bluntly. "She'll be with me."

"Oh?" Glenn blinked, finally catching on. "Ah. So you and Tess are..."

"I'm going to marry her," Scott replied clearly, succinctly.

He heard a gasp behind him. Maybe a couple of gasps. With a slight wince, he looked around to find Tess a few feet away, staring at him in disbelief. She stood between her sister and her cousin, with her brother-in-law only a few steps behind them. All of them were looking openmouthed at him.

"Oh, my gosh, Tess, why didn't you tell us?" Dana squealed, clapping her brightly manicured and bejeweled hands together. "You're engaged!"

Her head spinning, Tess stammered, "I, um—"

"Yes, Tess, why *didn't* you tell us?" Nina demanded, still looking as though someone had knocked the breath clean out of her. "How long has this been going on?"

"I want to see the ring," Dana insisted, snatching at Tess's bare left hand. "Oh...no ring?"

"Not yet," Scott supplied, giving Tess a look that was a mixture of sympathy, apology and...defiance? Daring her to dispute him, perhaps? "Maybe Santa will bring her one for Christmas."

"Oh, how exciting!" Dana giggled. "Bet it'll be a good one."

"Congratulations, Tessie." Ken kissed her cheek. "I hope you're both very happy," he added, reaching out to shake Scott's hand. "Welcome to the family, Scott. You've got yourself a treasure here."

Scott looked at Tess again when he responded, "Yes, I'm aware of that."

They were suddenly surrounded by well-wishers, hugged and congratulated and barraged with questions neither was prepared to answer. She noted that Glenn had disappeared into the crowd after unwittingly initiating this excitement. Standing at Scott's side, she gritted her teeth behind a bright smile and settled for a couple of stock answers. "It's a recent development" and, "No, we haven't set a date yet." She appeased her sister somewhat by promising to visit the next afternoon with all the details.

"We weren't planning to announce it just yet," she added with a chiding look toward Scott. "He just got carried away."

"My bad," Scott agreed. "I guess I'm just too excited to keep it to myself."

"Oh, that's so sweet," someone crooned while Tess fantasized about strangling him.

They took their leave as soon as they could politely do so. Dana's husband cracked a suggestive joke about the newly engaged couple wanting to be alone together, earning himself a cold stare from Nina that made him swallow visibly. Tess clutched Scott's arm in a white-knuckled grip and almost dragged him out the door.

A taut silence surrounded them in Scott's car as he drove through the gates of the neighborhood. Only when they were on the highway headed toward her condo did he sigh and say, "Okay, let me have it."

She twisted beneath her seat belt to face his profile. "I can't even come up with the words."

"Look, I'm really sorry, Tess. I know that was awkward for you—"

"Gee, you think?"

He winced. "It got away from me. That Glenn guy was grilling me about our relationship, talking about asking you out, brushing me off as nothing more than your boss, and I simply told him the truth. I didn't realize you and your family were within earshot, though I guess I should have checked before I spoke."

"Or maybe not have spoken at all?"

"Maybe."

She could tell he wasn't entirely sorry. Just what male ego button had Glenn pushed? Surely it hadn't been intentional; Glenn wasn't exactly the territorial type. For that matter, she'd never thought of Scott that way, either.

"Technically, I didn't say we're engaged," he added somewhat stiffly. "I told Glenn I'm going to marry you. I just didn't mention I haven't officially asked yet. You could have made it clear you haven't given me an answer yet if you didn't want everyone to start congratulating us."

"Oh, that wouldn't have been awkward at all."

"Sorry, Tess. But we knew when we started attending these things together that people would want to know what's going on with us. Like I said, Glenn asked about our relationship and I told him the truth. I want to marry you. I thought we'd already established that."

She couldn't quite define the emotions crashing through her. She wasn't surprised, exactly. Scott *had* made it clear that this was the direction in which his thoughts had been headed. All that talk of what a good team they made, what a brilliant idea he'd had about them, how nicely she fit in with his family, how well she understood his demanding obligations and responsibilities. Yet in all of that talk, not once had he mentioned love. He'd even had a hard time telling her he'd miss her while he was out of town.

She rode without speaking for the remainder of the drive, and he didn't push her to express her thoughts. He turned into the parking lot of her condominium compound. "Are you going to invite me in?"

With a little sigh, she reached for her door handle. "Of course. Come in."

They really did need to talk. The problem was that when they were alone together in her condo, talking was too often the last thing on their minds.

Inside her living room, she dumped her coat and bag on a chair, then turned to face him as he waited patiently for her to speak first. After a moment, she gave a wry laugh and pushed back her hair. "One thing about you, Scott—dealing with you is never boring. Neither at the office nor, it turns out, at parties."

"I hope that's a compliment."

"Not entirely. Every once in a while it might be nice to be prepared for what you're going to do next."

Taking a step toward her, he caught her hands in his, gazing somberly into her eyes. "I really am sorry I embarrassed you in front of your family, Tess."

She bit her lip, then couldn't resist saying, "Did you see Nina's face?"

A sudden grin tugged at his lips, though he seemed to be trying to contain it. "Yes. I'd say we surprised her."

"It's one of the few times in my entire life I've seen my sister struck speechless."

"How did that feel?"

"It didn't suck," she pronounced after another moment.

Scott chuckled. "She does like to get in her digs against you, doesn't she? I don't know how you keep from losing your temper with her."

She shrugged. "I have a few times. I learned long ago that it doesn't really accomplish anything. She gets all chilly and defensive and makes a grudging apology she doesn't really mean, and then everything goes back to the way it's always been. I've conceded that if I'm going to have any sort of relationship with my sister in the future, I just have to bite my tongue and accept the way she is."

He looked annoyed on her behalf. "But you don't have to let her push you around."

"I rarely do. I just let her speak her mind and then I pretty much do what I want."

Running a hand up and down her arm, he laughed softly. "Much as you do with me?"

She shrugged.

"I have always admired your quiet determination," he told her, and though his tone was still light, she could tell he was serious.

As always, his compliment touched her, weakened her resolve against him, dampened her annoyance. Releasing a low sigh, she shook her head slowly. "I guess you know word of this will be all over town by tomorrow. We had mutual acquaintances there, and Dana's love of gossip is second only to her passion for shopping."

"Then, we should probably tell my family. I heard you tell Nina you'd be at her house early afternoon tomorrow—why don't I join you for that and then you can come with me to my folks' house. We'll get it all out of the way in one day."

Out of the way. She frowned at him. "You're assuming quite a lot, aren't you?"

He grimaced. "I'm not trying to railroad you. I'm being clumsy again, I'm afraid. This really isn't my forte, is it?"

He drew a deep breath and asked, "What do you say, Tess? Will you marry me?"

She bit her lip.

"I'm lousy at the romance stuff, you know that," he said. "I'll probably forget birthdays and anniversaries and special occasions—hell, I've always depended on you to remind me of that stuff anyway. I'll cancel our plans when work issues come up. I'll get caught up in mulling over a dilemma and I won't hear your questions or comments. I'll be short-tempered and impatient sometimes when I let stress get the better of me."

"I'm used to all of that," she reminded him.

He smiled ruefully. "Yeah, I guess you are. I guess what I'm trying to say is you know me better than anyone. I can't be any different at home than I am at the office because that's just who I am. Other women didn't like that. They wanted more from me than I was able to give."

Lifting his chin, he added proudly, "And by the way, I think I have a hell of a lot to give. I can promise absolute loyalty and faithfulness. I'll be a good provider, a devoted father, a steadfast supporter of your dreams and ambitions. You can depend on me to be there for you whenever you need me. You and I have always gotten along amazingly well without either of us trying to be something we're not. We've proved that we have a strong, more than satisfying physical connection. I think we can carry our solid partnership into a marriage that will last a lifetime. I know what I want. But it's in your hands now. I can give you more time, even though I know I rushed things this evening. As much time as you need."

No, it wasn't a particularly romantic speech, but she couldn't deny that he'd laid out a very convincing argument. He was offering everything she'd looked for when she'd signed up with those online dating services hoping to make a connection. Well, almost everything. Maybe there was a bit more of the romantic in her than she'd realized. Most of the single women she knew would probably tell her she was crazy not to snap this guy up before he had even a chance to change his mind. And here she was dithering because there was some indefinable something missing from his earnest proposal.

Studying his face, she asked quietly, "What would you do if I were to tell you that I don't want to marry you? That I've decided we're not a good match after all?"

A muscle jumped in his jaw, but he spoke in an even tone. "I'd be disappointed. Very disappointed. But I would accept your decision and I'd continue to focus on my work. Maybe I was meant to be a workaholic bache- lor. Whatever happens between us, I would still treasure our friendship and your contribution to my company."

"You honestly believe we could still work together if this experiment, as you called it, didn't succeed?"

"I'd like to think so. It could be a little awkward at first, but I think we could manage it. Which doesn't mean I wouldn't have moments of regret that it didn't work out," he added candidly.

Moments of regret. Hardly a description of a broken heart, but then they'd made a concerted effort from the beginning of this plan to avoid that drastic outcome, right? He'd steadfastly asserted that avoiding unreal- istic expectations would protect them both from bitter disappointment. It sounded so logical and honest that she couldn't think of a sound argument.

"Is that what you're trying to tell me, Tess? That you don't think we're a good match?"

"I think we're a very good match," she replied, draw- ing a deep, bracing breath and lifting a hand to his cheek. "We'd never have made it through the past six years working together if we weren't. I'm willing to gamble with you that we're equally well suited outside the office."

The tension in his face eased. His smile broadened, as his face moved against her palm. "That's a yes?"

She swallowed. "Yes."

"We should seal the deal." He stuck out his right hand. "Put 'er there, partner."

A laugh sputtered from her. "I know you said you're no poet, but honestly, Scott...a handshake?"

Grinning, he swept her into his arms and spun her

around once. "I can do better than that," he said, and smothered her laughter with his kiss.

They took their time making their way to her bedroom. Whether because of their new status or because they were becoming more comfortable with their lovemaking, they weren't as frantic and impatient this time, but more deliberate, savoring every touch, every kiss, every slow caress. Clothes were smoothed out of the way rather than stripped off, falling softly to the floor beside the bed. Their bodies were illuminated by the dimmed light on her nightstand, an intimate circle of light in the otherwise shadowed room.

Scott frowned when he saw the bruise on her left shoulder that ran a few inches down onto her chest. He traced it very gently with one fingertip. "Does this hurt?"

"No, not really." Caught up in the pleasure of being snuggled against his warm, bare body, she couldn't care less about a couple of minor bruises.

"It's from your seat belt, isn't it? From the accident this morning."

"I guess. It locked up hard to keep me in my seat. I'm fine. I've just always bruised easily."

A lump formed in her throat when he pressed his lips very tenderly to the bruise. He lifted his head and smoothed her hair from her face, looking into her eyes with an almost fierce expression. "I don't want anything like that to happen to you ever again. But if it does, call me. Wherever I am, whatever I'm doing, I want you to call."

She'd had no idea it would bother him so badly that she hadn't called him that morning. She'd planned all along to tell him about the accident, of course. But she hadn't realized he would take the delay so personally. "I'll call," she promised.

He gathered her closer, lowering his mouth to hers. "Good."

Scott lay on his side, propped on one elbow as he looked down at the woman sleeping on the pillows beside him. He'd smoothed the covers over her and she'd snuggled into them, drawing them to her chin in her sleep. It was the first time she'd slept with him there. Was she growing more accustomed to his presence in her bed, or was she simply tired after a long week, a long day? He thought of the bruise on her shoulder and scowled, hoping she hadn't underplayed the physical effects of the accident. Should he be monitoring her sleep? No, he was overreacting. She hadn't hit her head. Even the bruise was mild, just a smudge of purple against her fair skin.

He was satisfied that she would remember to call him now should anything similar happen in the future. Now that they were engaged, he wanted to be the first one she thought to notify in an emergency, even a minor one.

Engaged. To be married. Tess Miller had agreed to be his wife.

He mulled the words over in his mind, getting used to the feel of them. They felt...pretty good, he concluded. Really good, he added, his body still warm and heavy with satisfaction.

He was still a little dazed by the way the evening had progressed. He hadn't intended to propose tonight, certainly not to announce their engagement before he'd even confirmed it with Tess. Hell, she'd have had every right to toss him out on his ear for his arrogance. Why hadn't she? Considering that Tess wasn't one to allow herself to be railroaded—not at work or in her personal life—he could only conclude that she'd accepted his proposal because she wanted to marry him. He'd made some good arguments in his own favor. Presented his case with the same enthusiasm and persuasion he used when making a pitch to a potential client. And he'd convinced her to say yes.

He always reacted to victorious presentations with pride, gratitude, personal validation. He supposed he felt those things now, but in a deeper, quieter way. Losing a bid, even a big one, was hardly devastating. Disappointing, perhaps, but there were always more jobs, more opportunities to make money. Having Tess turn down his proposal would have been harder to swallow. Since he'd concluded she was the perfect mate for him, he couldn't imagine anyone else in her place. He'd set his sights on convincing her and he'd been persistent. And now it was going to happen. He'd won again.

So why was there a nagging feeling deep inside him that something could still go wrong? That maybe he was forgetting something or overlooking some detail?

Perhaps it was simply all too new. Hadn't sunk in yet. Maybe it was the abrupt way the engagement had come about, as opposed to his usual practiced sales style. He'd been left with the feeling that something was still unfinished.

She stirred in her sleep and tugged the covers to her ears. He smiled. Tess was a cocooner. She'd probably nestle into his arms if he settled in beside her. Because that sounded so appealing, he did so, finding that she did, indeed, fit perfectly into the hollow of his shoulder. He hadn't intended to spend the night, but what the heck. He had no plans in the morning. It seemed like the right time.

He brushed a kiss across her warm forehead and closed his eyes. By tomorrow, he was sure this funny feeling inside him would be resolved.

Maybe he was just tired.

Tess wondered how long it would take for the novelty of waking up with Scott to wear off. She thought it might be a while. As for the novelty of having him join her in the shower and linger there with her until the water ran cold...well, she couldn't imagine that ever growing mundane.

They cooked breakfast together. She made French toast while he sliced fruit and brewed coffee. They didn't talk much as they prepared the meal, but worked in companionable silence in her small kitchen.

"So what time are we supposed to go to your sister's?" he asked.

"She sent me a text this morning. She ordered me to be there at two. I told her you'd be joining us."

"What did she say to that?"

"'Don't be late. I have plans for the evening.'"

"I can tell she's very happy for us."

She gave him a look over her coffee cup. "Delirious."

"Okay, two o'clock. That gives us time to stop by my place so I can change into clean clothes." He was wearing the slacks and shirt from last night.

"Plenty of time."

"Maybe we could run by the office, too. I have a couple of things I need to take care of there."

"Fine. But if we're late, you'll have to explain to Nina."

"Trust me. We won't be late."

She laughed in response to his fervent tone. Apparently Scott had decided it was best not to be on the receiving end of one of Nina's icy looks.

An hour later he ushered her into his house, a three-bedroom traditional-style home in a peaceful development filled with upscale professionals with families. Because it had begun to rain, and occasionally heavy downpours were predicted all day, he'd parked in the garage and brought her in through the kitchen. She had always admired the granite counters, the cherry cabinets, the state-of-the-art appliances. The room was almost exactly what she'd have designed herself, given the choice. Scott hadn't employed Stevie for the kitchen remodel because he hadn't yet met her at the time, but Tess doubted her friend would have any criticism of the beautiful and functional space.

Scott had bought the house at about the same time he'd been involved with Sharon, though Tess had gotten the impression even back then that Sharon hadn't been particularly enthused about living in this neighborhood with its families and minivans. Saying they could always flip the house for a profit and invest in something more to Sharon's tastes, Scott had boasted about having gotten a very good deal on the place. He'd had it remodeled to his own satisfaction after Sharon had taken off. Sharon had never lived there. Tess doubted Sharon had ever even spent a night in the house.

She was ruefully aware she found that fact gratifying.

The high ceilings and open floor plan gave the first floor an airy, inviting feel. Having toured the home previously, Tess knew a private office and the master suite were located downstairs while two smaller bedroom suites and a media room made up the second floor. He favored a traditional style inside, too, with matte walls, clean lines, leather and wood and stone. Not too masculine, but well suited to a nesting bachelor.

"You have a new sofa," she said as they entered the great room, nodding toward the large oxblood leather sectional positioned to face a big stone fireplace. Behind the sofa, glass doors led out to a travertine patio with teak furniture, a large fountain and a tidy expanse of privacy-fenced lawn beyond. He'd done little holiday decorating, but an artificial tree with multicolored lights and coordinated red and silver ornaments stood in one corner with wrapped gifts stacked neatly beneath. "Nice."

"Thanks. I'd had the old couch for ten years. It was ready to be retired." He motioned back toward the kitchen. "Can I get you anything?"

"No, I'm good. Go ahead and change. I'll make myself comfortable on your new sofa."

He moved toward the doorway. "Feel free to explore, if you want. After all, this will be your home, too, soon. Unless you want to sell both our places and find a different one," he added, pausing with a thoughtful expression.

She waved him on. "We'll talk about that later. Go change."

She pressed a hand against a little flutter in her stomach after he left. Glancing around the room, she pictured herself living here. Waking in the mornings, having breakfast with Scott, perhaps riding to the office together. Sleeping in that big master suite. She'd bet he had a nice big shower in there.

She cleared her throat and sank onto the new sofa. Very comfortable. Maybe she wouldn't have chosen leather, but she could get used to it quickly enough. She looked around. A beautiful house with a couple of extra bedrooms waiting to be filled, a handsome husband... Yeah, she could fit in here nicely, she assured herself.

He rejoined her a few minutes later wearing a royal blue shirt with khakis, clean shaven, his hair neatly combed. Her very own Prince Charming, she thought with a little smile, thinking of Stevie's nickname for him. "So what do you think?" he asked. "Do you approve of the couch?"

She patted the soft leather. "I approve."

He leaned over for a quick kiss. "We could always break it in," he murmured, waggling his eyebrows.

"Mmm." She ran a fingertip from his throat down the center of his chest to his belt buckle. And then she flattened her hand on his chest and pushed him away. "Later."

Scott groaned. "So cruel."

She stood and spoke with determination, "Okay, let's do this. We'll stop by the office and then find out exactly how our engagement is complicating my poor sister's life."

Scott gave one last wistful look at the new sofa, then turned with her toward the door. She paused on the way out to glance over her shoulder at the house that would be her home soon. She was sure she'd be very happy here. After all, she asked herself again, what more could she want?

Chapter Nine

The softly glowing numbers on the nightstand clock read 2:25 when Tess rolled over in the bed to check the time. She groaned and pushed at her pillows, trying to fluff them into a more comfortable position. It was a futile gesture and she knew it. Her sleeplessness wasn't caused by physical discomfort. It was too bad she couldn't unravel the tangled thoughts in her head as easily as she could smooth out the lumps in her pillow.

The sound of the rain hitting her windows should have been soothing, but it was only annoying instead. It had been raining on and off for hours. Turning over to put the clock behind her, out of sight, she found herself gazing instead at the empty pillow on the other side of the bed. She rested a hand on it, wondering fancifully if she could still feel Scott's warmth there. But no, it was cold. Claiming apologetically that he had a list of things to do to prepare for the to prepare for the busy upcoming workweek, he hadn't stayed tonight after they'd returned from dinner with his family. He'd left her with kisses and reluctance and a comment that he was looking forward to the time when they made their home together.

They still hadn't talked about a date for their wedding. Scott had implied that he'd like for it to be soon, which was no particular surprise to her. Once he had a plan in place, he was always impatient to get it under way. They'd talked about a wedding, both with her family and his, but had made no specific plans as of yet, agreeing that they should wait until Christmas was behind them to focus on the logistics.

Something about the word *logistics* made her wince. It was such a…businesslike word, taking the practicality of their engagement to an uncomfortable extreme. Scott could make her head spin with how smoothly and easily he transitioned from teasing, affectionate, even passionate to briskly realistic and deliberately prosaic. He claimed not to be the romantic type, and seemed to even take pride in the fact, but it was almost as if he were afraid of taking that final step into deep intimacy. Was it fear of being hurt? Of doing something wrong?

Now that she'd agreed to marry him, shouldn't he be more confident about it? Should she really have seen the faintest hint of panic in his eyes yesterday whenever anyone in their families had alluded to how romantic it was that their working relationship had turned into an engagement?

She thought about her sister. Maybe Ken had given Nina one of his rare lectures about how she should act that afternoon, because she'd been on her best behavior.

She'd served tea and pretty little cakes to Tess and Scott in her parlor and congratulated them on their engagement. True to form, Nina hadn't been able to resist a few complaints that she'd been left out of the loop and that she'd heard about their engagement in such an abrupt, public manner. Tess couldn't totally blame her sister for feeling slighted, which made her more patient in dealing with the censure. Nina had regally accepted Tess's apologies, then proved no more resistant than most to Scott's charming smiles and winsome contrition.

Nina had insisted she would do everything she could to help with the wedding—though of course her schedule was so very full, her presence so in demand, that she wasn't sure how much she could physically contribute. "We'll try to arrange lunches during the weeks ahead," she'd said to Tess. "You can bring photos and samples and I'll be happy to give you my input."

Tess could easily imagine how those meetings would go. She would potentially spend hours choosing colors and dresses and music and other details, and Nina would shoot down every option with an indulgent comment about how Tess's ideas were "cute," but perhaps she should consider Nina's much more fashionably inspired suggestions instead. Tess had smiled noncommittally and politely promised her older sister she'd let her know when she needed advice.

The only truly personal moment between her and her sister had come just as the visit was ending. Scott had dashed out in the downpour with an umbrella, having chivalrously volunteered to bring his car close to the front door for Tess. Waiting just inside the door with her sister, Tess had been surprised when Nina gave her a firm, apparently impulsive hug.

"I am pleased for you, Tess," she'd said. "I hope Scott will make you very happy. You deserve to have someone take care of you for a change."

Startled, Tess had almost replied that she was more comfortable taking care of herself, but sensing a rather touching sincerity in her sister's words, she'd said only, "Thank you, Nina."

Dinner with Scott's family could not have been more different. The whole Prince clan had been there, including the twins and baby Henry, all gathered around the big farm table in Holly's dining room, all talking at once, laughing, teasing, treating Tess as if she was already part of the family. They, of course, had already been aware of the change in Tess and Scott's relationship, so it was easier for them to process the announcement of their engagement.

"When's the big day?" Jake had demanded.

"We haven't set a date," Scott had replied, squeezing Tess's thigh beneath the table, "but I'd like for it to be soon."

"It takes a while to plan a wedding," Libby had warned. "You have to reserve a space for the ceremony and the reception. Caterers and florists and cake decorators and musicians are often booked well in advance, so as soon as you choose a date, you should start putting down deposits. I have a friend who's an excellent florist, Tess. I'd be happy to go with you to talk with her, if you like. Bet I can get you a discount."

"My cousin is a caterer," Christina had chimed in. "She did our wedding and it was great, wasn't it, guys? And I'll get you the number for our videographer and photographer. Jake and I were very happy with their services."

"I would love to help you with whatever you need from me," Holly had added eagerly. "I can make calls or address envelopes or anything else you want me to do. And I have a connection with a cake decorator who does some of the most beautiful work I've ever seen. I'd be pleased to introduce you to her, though of course I won't be offended if you decide to use someone else."

They had all been so excited, so eager to help, yet Tess hadn't felt at all as if they were trying to take over. They were just making themselves available to her in any way she needed them. She'd found that incredibly sweet.

All in all, it had been a very nice day. So why was she lying awake in the middle of the night, thinking back over the gatherings and trying to analyze why the more thrilled everyone seemed to act about them, the more Scott had seemed to withdraw into himself? Oh, nothing of the sort had shown in his behavior. He'd laughed and conversed as heartily as anyone else at his mother's table. He'd participated in the discussion of possible wedding venues and teased Tess about hiring an '80s-revival heavy-metal band for the reception. He'd kissed her good-night with the same heat and hunger that had made their previous embraces so exhilarating and he'd looked genuinely regretful when he'd made himself leave her.

Was she only imagining that he was holding a small part of himself back? Was she mistaken in sensing a tiny kernel of doubt deep inside him—or was that a projection of her own lingering misgivings? It had all happened so fast. She'd been swept along by his enthusiasm for his brilliant idea, his enticing verbal pictures of an ideal future together, her own yearnings and long-suppressed attraction. And now that everything seemed to be settled, now that everyone knew about their plans, now that it would be incredibly awkward to call it all off, now that she couldn't imagine not marrying Scott— a tiny part of her feared that she'd made a mistake.

With a groan, she punched her pillow again. She really was an idiot.

Maybe she was just tired.

Pulling the covers to her ears, she sank into the bed and squeezed her eyes shut, trying to push those silly doubts and foolish fears away. And wondering why she, who almost never cried, felt suddenly on the verge of tears.

Scott spent most of the following week out of town visiting job sites and attending planning meetings for the new year. Their hectic work schedule prevented them from spending much time together, but they spoke by phone every evening and managed to share a couple of pleasant nights together. By the beginning of Christmas week, both were tired and looking forward to the end of this hectic holiday season. Tess was ready to focus on their future together outside the office, something they'd barely had time to even think about since they'd become so unceremoniously engaged.

The shortened workweek ahead made Monday ridiculously busy in preparation. Wednesday was Christmas Eve, and Scott had announced the offices would close at noon that day and wouldn't officially reopen until the following Monday, which would also be a short holiday week. If any crises occurred, essential personnel could be called in, of course, but they all hoped the holiday would be problem-free.

The stressful day finally over, she was driving to Stevie's for a pre-Christmas celebration. But her mind was preoccupied by what had happened that afternoon.

Scott had called an early staff meeting to confirm the week's schedule. Then he'd wished everyone a merry Christmas as he handed out generous gift cards to an upscale local restaurant. End-of-the-year bonuses were included in their paychecks, but this was a little treat he'd been in the habit of providing on his own behalf for the past few years, telling his employees they deserved a nice night out to relax after working so hard and so loyally for him.

"Before we adjourn," he'd added, holding out a hand to Tess, "there's one more announcement I need to make. I'm sure the rumors have already begun and I want you all to hear the news from Tess and me."

Moistening her lips, Tess had pasted on a confident smile and taken her place at his side. Some of the staff looked puzzled, and she figured they wondered if a promotion or resignation was being announced. A couple others smiled knowingly, which meant the gossip had already made its way to the office.

After a slight nod of approval from her, Scott turned back to their team. "Tess and I are engaged," he said simply. "We haven't determined a date yet, but we're going to be married."

Amid the startled cries and happy claps, Scott held up a hand to add, "You all know how valuable Tess is to this company. Just so you know, we aren't making any immediate changes in her responsibilities here in the office. So carry on, and here's to another great year for all of us who make up PCCI."

She'd appreciated his attempt to make sure she was

treated no differently by the staff now that she was marrying the boss, but she knew some changes were inevitable. If there was any resentment, she didn't see it at the moment. Still, she and Scott would have to be very careful in the future to keep their personal life clearly separate from work, just as they had to this point.

The phones had begun to ring and everyone went back to work. Scott left soon after the staff meeting and was out of the office most of the day, though a series of terse phone calls and texts from him kept Tess and the rest of the staff busy trying to keep up.

He hadn't returned by the time Tess had to leave, so she sent him a text reminding him that she had plans with Jenny and Stevie, and that she'd see him at work in the morning.

I'll call you tonight, he texted back. Have fun with your friends. Tell them hello for me.

She arrived at Stevie's place for their own little Christmas celebration. A cozy bungalow, Stevie's house was the one in which she'd grown up with her mother and brother, located in a neighborhood that had briefly declined and was now undergoing a revival. Her white frame home sat on a corner lot, so her nearest neighbor was a '60s-style brick ranch on her west side, the one in which the widowed cat owner lived. Tess glanced automatically that way as she parked at the curb in front of Stevie's house. A dark car sat in the carport and lights burned in the windows, so she assumed Stevie's neighbor had returned from his business trip, though she caught no glimpse of him. She'd bet Stevie was glad to be done with her cat-sitting duties for now.

The neighbor hadn't decorated for the holiday, but other houses on the block were festooned with festive lights and oversize Christmas inflatables in their yards. Stevie had arranged a string of white lights around her little porch, and a Christmas tree with white lights was visible through the lace curtains at her front window. A big wreath with a red velvet bow decorated the front door, which was painted blue to match the shutters at the windows.

Stevie and Jenny both greeted Tess with such expectant expressions that she shook her head wryly. If they were trying to be subtle, they failed miserably at it. She'd told them individually about the engagement, sending messages to them both before they heard through the grapevine, and she'd promised to give them details tonight.

"At least let me set this stuff down before you start pelting me with questions," she said, handing over two wrapped gifts before peeling off her coat.

Jenny set the gifts beneath the tree while Stevie stashed away Tess's coat and bag. "Did Scott really blurt out that the two of you were engaged at Dana's party?" Jenny asked avidly. "Before you'd even told your sister?"

"Even worse," Tess replied with a groan, glad she could finally speak frankly about that night. "He told everyone we were engaged before he even got around to asking me."

"Oh, we definitely need to hear this whole story," Jenny said after a moment of stunned silence.

"Tell us while we eat," Stevie ordered. "I didn't cook all this food to serve it cold." She loved to cook, and she'd insisted on preparing the meal without any contributions from her friends.

An hour later, stuffed with delicious food and emotionally drained from talking, Tess sat with her friends in the living room, preparing to open gifts. Stevie was leaving the next morning to spend Christmas with her brother in Tennessee, while Tess and Jenny both had plans with their families here in Little Rock, so this had been the only night they could get together for their own little celebration.

"I'm so glad we decided not to have a big party this year. I prefer that it's just us," Jenny said as she leaned back against a throw pillow. "Though I would like for us to all get together soon to get to know Scott better. Gavin met him briefly when he responded to that break-in at your office earlier in the year, but they should get to know each other socially since I'm sure they'll be seeing quite a bit of each other through us. And Stevie will bring Joe, of course."

Stevie cleared her throat. "That's not an 'of course.'"

Tess and Jenny exchanged looks.

"Are you and Joe breaking up?" Jenny asked quietly.

"Looks like it." Stevie raised both hands to stave off any comments. "Would you mind if we talk about this later? After Christmas? I need some time."

"Absolutely."

"Whenever you're ready," Tess assured their friend.

Blinking rapidly, Stevie nodded. "Thanks. Besides, tonight is all about you, Tess. Jen and I hope you and Scott will be very happy together."

"Thanks, Stevie." But now it seemed completely wrong to discuss her engagement when her friend was obviously in pain. "You know, I have an idea. Let's not talk about men or relationship issues for the remainder of the evening. Let's focus on ourselves. Our friendship. Our jobs. Stevie, I want to hear all about this busy season for you. I know it's been great for your reputation and your bottom line. And, Jenny, tell us about your idea to open a store in Fayetteville. How exciting would it be to own a chain of three boutiques, maybe more? And I need to tell you about the new accounting clerk I hired this month."

Her eyes brightening, Stevie smiled. "I'd love to talk about my business, but first," she said, tugging impatiently at the red mesh bow on the gift Jenny had brought for her, "I have just got to see what's in here. I can't wait any longer to open presents!"

Laughing, Tess and Jenny ripped into their own gifts. They were still laughing two hours later when the night came to a close.

Stevie gave her a warm hug as Tess prepared to leave. Jenny had stepped into the restroom, so Tess and Stevie had the moment to themselves.

"Merry Christmas, Tess," Stevie said, pressing a kiss to her cheek. "Thank you so much for the bracelet. I love it."

"And thank you." Stevie had given her a hand-thrown pottery serving bowl. "It's gorgeous."

Her friend smiled with a little wrinkle of her nose. "I knew you'd like the colors. I hope they work in the new kitchen you'll be sharing with Scott."

She could already picture the bowl on the big island in Scott's kitchen. "It will work just fine. I'm sure he'll like it, too."

"I hope so." Stevie hesitated a moment, then blurted, "I know we said no more talk of relationships tonight, but I have to ask. Just for my own peace of mind..."

"What is it, Stevie?"

"Do you love Scott?"

"I—" It was such a simple question. It shouldn't have taken her by such surprise. And yet it occurred to Tess only then that Stevie was the first one since this had all begun to even think to ask.

"Tess?"

"Yes," she whispered as sweet memories of laughter and kisses, long conversations and leisurely lovemaking, flashed through her mind. "I love him."

Should that answer really make Stevie look only more worried? Shouldn't she have found it reassuring?

"Just one more question," Stevie said. "Does he love you?"

Tess swallowed. "He said there's no one else he'd rather marry."

Stevie held her gaze for a moment, letting her silence express a great deal, and then she reached for the door. "Thanks for being honest with me. I hope to God you're being honest with yourself. Good night, Tess."

Placing the bowl from Stevie and a beautiful spring cardigan from Jenny on the passenger seat beside her, Tess fastened her seat belt and started her car, her movements deliberate. Her gloved hands gripped the wheel tightly enough to cause pain in her knuckles as she drove away from Stevie's little house.

I hope to God you're being honest with yourself.

"So do I, Stevie." Her strained voice echoed hollowly within the darkened interior of her car. "So do I."

It wasn't uncommon for Scott to stumble into his house past 10:00 p.m., weary and ravenous yet satisfied after a long day of business operations. Particularly at this time of the year, he hardly had a minute to himself. Fortunately most of the professional and social obligations were out of the way now, with this week being reserved for family celebrations. He opened the fridge and drew out a container of yogurt, a little hungry but too tired to make a meal. He hadn't forgotten that he'd promised to call Tess that night, but he needed to catch his breath a minute first. He hoped she would still be awake by the time he finished his snack.

He was sure she'd had a good time with Jenny and Stevie. The three women had formed a tight friendship. A man would do well to keep in mind that he'd better not attempt to come between them, not that he would even want to try. He remembered before Tess met Jenny and Stevie. Though he hadn't given it much thought at the time, blindly ambitious as he'd been back then, he realized now that she must have been lonely, working long days while attending classes and taking care of her parents until she'd lost them so close together. He'd tried to be a supportive employer to her during those days, a good friend, even though he'd worked to keep the friendship professional. Perhaps getting involved with that guy James not long after her mother died had been a result of her loneliness. She'd done well to dump the jerk; Scott had met him only a couple times, but he hadn't liked him.

It was only during the past couple of years that Tess had really come into her own as a strong, competent, satisfied adult. Earning her degree, buying her condo, meeting her friends, taking on more supervisory responsibilities in the office, establishing her independence from her overly critical sister—all those things had contributed to a new confidence in her, a difference he'd observed and admired. She'd been looking for companionship on her own terms, unwilling to settle despite her expressed desire for home and family, and he was damned lucky she'd considered his proposal worthy of her. That she considered him worthy of her, despite his limitations when it came to romance.

How many women would have forgiven him for that boneheaded blunder at her cousin's party? Or would be so patient with his crazy schedule and his some-times unpredictable moods? He hadn't showered her with compliments or gifts, as Sharon had pointedly and repeatedly informed him most women desired from a man. In fact, he hadn't given Tess anything at all, in-cluding an engagement ring, he thought with a frown. Hell, he hadn't even given her one of the restaurant gift cards he'd distributed to the staff.

Tossing the empty yogurt container in the trash and the spoon in the sink, he carried a glass of water into his bedroom to make the call he'd promised. He could at least do that, he thought guiltily.

"How was your evening with your friends?" he asked after they'd exchanged greetings.

"We had a wonderful time. Great food, good conver-sation, and we exchanged gifts. How was your day?"

"Long," he said with a sigh, and gave her a quick summary of what he'd accomplished since he'd last seen her. "Tomorrow's going to be just as long," he warned.

"Yes, I figured. I have a lot to do tomorrow myself. I'm hoping to finally have time to finish wrapping gifts and do my Christmas baking. I always take stained glass cookies and pear tartlets to my sister's house for Christmas dinner, and I haven't even started them."

"I've had your pear tartlets," he reminded her. "You made me a batch last year, remember? They were out of this world."

"I thought I'd make extras of everything to take to your family's house Christmas. Do you think they'd like them?"

"Are you kidding? They'll love them. Jake and Eli will probably arm wrestle for those tartlets."

She laughed musically in his ear. "That won't be necessary. I'll make plenty. Your mother was so insistent that as a first-time guest I shouldn't have to bring anything this year, but I feel as though I should take something."

"That'll be fine. It feels kind of strange to work around two family schedules for Christmas, huh?"

"It does. My social calendar was much busier this year than usual." Fortunately her family celebrated together on Christmas Eve, while his gathered for a big Christmas Day lunch, so the traditions hadn't overlapped.

"Mine's been packed, too," he said. "But I'm not complaining. I've enjoyed the past weeks with you."

"So have I," she said.

Had he heard something a little odd in her voice just then? He wished he could see her face. He wished he could touch her. Kiss her. The intensity of the hunger that shot through him so unexpectedly shook him. It had only been a few hours since he'd seen her, but here he was missing her as if it had been days.

"Tess? We can have as big a wedding as you'd like, but I'd like to put it all together fairly quickly. I don't know about you, but I'm hoping for a short engagement."

She hesitated only a beat, as if surprised by the abrupt change of subject, then replied, "I don't need a big wedding. Family and a few close friends are all I really want to be there."

"That sounds about perfect to me. The sooner the better."

"We'll talk about it."

"It's late. I'm sure you're tired. I'll see you tomorrow—though maybe only for a few minutes at a time."

"Okay. Good night, Scott."

The pause then felt oddly heavy, as if she was waiting for him to say something more, while he felt as though there was something he should say. He settled for "Sleep well."

And then he disconnected, feeling vaguely unsatisfied with the call's conclusion.

Don't screw this up.

Why did he feel the need to keep saying that to himself?

Chapter Ten

Christmas Eve was a great success so far, at least where Scott was concerned. For the first time, Tess had brought a bag and had spent last night at his house, a momentous occasion for both of them though they hadn't expressed it in so many words. They'd made dinner together in his kitchen, then watched a Christmas movie afterward while her pear tarts for the next day baked in the oven. They'd held hands during the movie like giddy teens in a theater. Afterward, she'd stashed the tarts in the fridge, playfully slapping Scott's hand when he tried to pinch a few. She had distracted him easily enough from the Christmas sweets by enticing him into the bedroom. It had been quite a while before they'd fallen asleep.

They'd talked of wedding plans that afternoon, and they'd agreed that a spring ceremony in his parents' sprawling backyard would suit them nicely. It was where Jake and Christina had exchanged vows, and Scott said theirs had been a very nice little wedding. Eli and Libby had married in the big Catholic church in which she'd grown up and had treated themselves to a lavish celebration with a couple hundred guests. Also nice, Scott had admitted, but not to his taste. He'd been relieved, but not particularly surprised, when Tess had heartily concurred.

Now, as it grew closer to time to leave for her sister's house, Tess donned the red dress she'd worn to the Holiday Open Home, and he was still struck by how good it looked on her. "You got your money's worth out of that dress," he assured her, looking at her in the mirror as he fastened his tie. "It's really pretty."

"Thank you. Sorry about the tie. Nina insists on fancy dress for her Christmas Eve meal."

He chuckled. "I don't mind. But tomorrow we get to be comfortable. My family's not nearly so formal."

"No surprise. I'm crazy about your family, by the way."

He grinned in pleasure. "Thanks. They feel the same about you."

It was all going so well, he thought in satisfaction. He must have misinterpreted whatever funny tone he thought he'd heard in her voice the other night. She seemed perfectly content with him now, visibly enjoying their time together. If there were moments when he caught her studying him with an expression he couldn't quite interpret, fleeting impressions that she was waiting for something he couldn't explain—well, this was all still very new for both of them, he assured himself.

It was only natural that it would require a bit of adjustment on both their parts.

When they were dressed in their finery, he asked her to wait a moment in the living room before they left. They'd already loaded his car with the gifts and baked goods they were taking to her sister's house, so all they had to do was collect their coats and her bag. She looked at him with a question in her expression.

"Have you changed your mind about going?" she teased, obviously knowing he hadn't.

Still, he gave an exaggerated shudder. "And risk Nina's wrath? I wouldn't dare."

She laughed. "Well, as least you're getting to know my sister. Since she's going to be your family, too, now."

"I can deal with your sister."

"Right."

His smile fading, he bent to pluck a small gift box out of the stack beneath the tree. "There's something I want you to open before we leave," he said, his heart beating just a bit more rapidly than usual.

Her eyes widened as she studied the gold-and-white wrapped box in his outspread hand. It would have been hard for her to mistake the size; he hadn't bothered with clever camouflage. She accepted it from him when he held it out to her, but didn't immediately open it.

"I have a gift for you, too," she said, her voice a little breathless. "I put it under the tree if you want to—"

Aware that she looked a little nervous—as he was himself, for some reason—he spoke gently. "I'll open mine later."

Moistening her lips, she nodded and tugged at the ribbon on the box. Moments later, she opened the hinged lid of the small velvet box she'd unwrapped to reveal the ring displayed in white satin inside. He'd selected a traditional round diamond engagement ring mounted in a platinum setting with three smaller diamonds on each side.

"I hope you like it," he said, growing a little anxious when she didn't immediately say anything. "It looked to me as though it would suit you—elegant but not too splashy, fashionable but not trendy." Again, he was quoting the jeweler, but the words had seemed to fit Tess. "If you'd rather have picked out your own rings—"

"This is beautiful, Scott. I can't imagine I'd have picked one any more perfect for me."

She looked up at him then and he was shaken by the sheen of tears in her eyes. He hoped they were happy tears. She'd said she liked the ring, so...

"Um, should I have gotten down on one knee?" he asked with a grimace. "Sorry, I—"

"No." With a misty smile, she placed a reassuring hand on his arm. "Please don't. We've said we aren't playing games, remember?"

Had he gotten on one knee when he'd proposed to Sharon? He couldn't remember. But come to think about it, he wasn't sure he had officially proposed at all to his former fiancée. He sort of suspected that an engagement had been mostly her idea. He'd just gone along for the ride because he'd thought himself ready to settle down and...well, because he'd been dazzled by her skills in the bedroom. A fascination that had worn off rather quickly when lust had turned to almost constant fighting.

But why was he thinking of Sharon now? Tess was nothing like his ex. He couldn't imagine his feelings for her ever turning as bitter and angry as he and Sharon had eventually become.

"No games," he promised. "We've already done the proposal and acceptance, even if I was fairly clumsy about it. But I will do this part right," he added, taking the diamond ring from the box. He slid the ring on her finger, then lifted her hand to his lips to kiss it in place. "There."

"It fits perfectly," she said in wonder.

"I guessed at your size, but the jeweler said it would only take a couple days to size it if it needs adjustment."

"I don't think it will. It's beautiful, Scott. I love— I love the ring."

He heard the little stammer and he attributed it to emotion. He thought that had gone very well. He believed Tess when she said she loved the ring. Seeing it on her hand gave him a wave of deep masculine satisfaction. From now on, he thought, all other men would know she wasn't free for New Year's Eve or any other night.

It occurred to him again that it wasn't like him to be the possessive type. At least he knew better than to say it out loud to Tess.

Don't screw this up.

"Let's see that ring! Oh, my gosh, it's so beautiful!" Clutching Libby's hand, Christina Prince turned to motion expressively. "Libby, Holly, come see. Scott gave Tess her ring and it's gorgeous."

While the men watched indulgently, Tess held out her hand for Scott's mother and sisters-in-law to examine the ring. All of them pronounced it exquisite, and just perfect for Tess.

"You picked it out all by yourself, Scott?" his mother asked in surprise.

"With a little help from the jeweler you've always used," he admitted.

"Patrick? Oh, yes, he has wonderful taste."

Tess couldn't help comparing this family's reaction to Nina's last night. Nina had studied the diamond with the shrewd eye of a well-trained jeweler, all but pulling out a loupe to assess the color and clarity before pronouncing it "very nice."

"Tess wouldn't have liked a big, gaudy diamond," she had assured Scott. "You were wise to choose such a pretty little stone for her."

Amazingly, Scott hadn't displayed any desire to strangle her tactless sister. He'd merely agreed that the ring seemed to suit Tess well.

Christmas Eve dinner with her family had been very nice, on the whole. With a newcomer in the midst, and with gifts on the line, the kids had been mostly on their best behavior. Scott had chatted easily enough with Ken, who was another college football fan caught up in postseason bowl hype, and it wasn't long before they'd drawn the boys into the conversation. Nina and her teenage daughter had spent the evening offering increasingly extravagant ideas for the wedding, from Nina's outlines for possible themes to Olivia's television-inspired suggestions of a Cinderella carriage with white horses, and doves for the guests to release after the ceremony. Tess had simply smiled and nodded a lot, mentally vowing to stick to the plans she and Scott had made.

Scott's family, on the other hand, seemed genuinely enthused about the ideas Tess and Scott presented, all agreeing that a wedding should reflect the individual couple's tastes and wishes.

"Both my sons had perfect weddings for them," Holly declared happily. "I know you and Scott will have just as nice a celebration."

"The wedding is just a party, really," Barry agreed, wrapping an arm around his wife's shoulders. "It's much more important to plan a marriage than a wedding. Holly and I were married by a justice of the peace in front of her grandmother's fireplace three days before I shipped out to Vietnam. We'll be married forty-four years next month. And I love her as much today as I did then," he added without embarrassment.

As if in echo of the sentiment, Eli and Jake hugged their wives. The love in the room was almost palpable. Tess swallowed a lump in her throat that seemed to be sharp edged. She glanced through her lashes at Scott and found him studying the back of his hand as if there were something fascinating to be seen there. He was obviously avoiding her eyes.

She was grateful when Madison—or was it Miranda?—interrupted the awkward moment. "We want to open presents," the little girl insisted. "Please, Grammy. May we please open presents now?"

"Lunch first and then presents," their grandmother said, smoothing the child's fine hair.

At the resulting protest, their parents reminded the twins that they'd already opened presents from Santa that morning and they had to be patient before opening the family gifts. They weren't happy about it, but the girls acquiesced and the family moved into the dining room to begin the meal.

Tess couldn't help watching the individual family members as they ate. She noted the little things—affectionate touches, shared smiles, teasing pats and pinches. She even heard a murmured "I love you" between Jake and Christina when they thought no one was listening.

As the day passed, she found herself working harder to keep smiling. She wasn't sure why, because she was having a lovely time with this endearing family.

"Tell us about when Scott gave you the ring," Libby said when the women were alone in the kitchen later. "Was it romantic? Did he get down on one knee?"

Tess forced a laugh. "I asked him not to do that. We've agreed that there's no need for pretense between us. We're just ourselves with each other. That has always worked well for us."

"Good idea," psychologist Christina approved. "You know each other so well after working together for so many years. It would be counterproductive to start acting differently with each other now. As long as you love each other for who you are, there's no need to try to change for unrealistic reasons."

"It's such a romantic story, though," the more sentimental Libby said with a sigh. "The boss who falls in love with his valued assistant and finds that she loves him in return. All these years you must have had secret feelings for each other. Now you can openly admit you're in love. That must be so liberating."

Tess twisted the ring on her finger, which suddenly seemed heavier than it had before. "Scott and I agree that we're very well suited," she said.

The brief silence that followed her words let her know it hadn't been an ideal response.

She was relieved when Jake barreled into the room.

"Tess, you have got to give us the recipe for these pear things. Man, they're good! Eli's been into them all afternoon, so I've hidden a couple for myself for later. Scott suggested we arm wrestle for the rest of them, but I know Eli would cream me at that, so I'm not taking the chance."

She was so relieved by the interruption that she spun to him with a too-bright smile. "I'd be happy to send you the recipe. They're really not that hard to make."

"These are good, too," Eli said, munching on a stained glass cookie as he followed his brother into the room.

His wife planted her hands on her hips. "Just how many sweets have you had today, Dr. Prince?"

Her husband grinned. "Calories don't count on Christmas, remember?"

"Sounds good to me," Christina said, heading for the dining room. "I'm having one of those pear things. You better not have hidden all of them, Jake."

Tess was smiling again until she looked around and accidentally locked eyes with Scott's mother. There was no mistaking the concern on Holly's face. It hadn't been there before that awkward conversation about Scott's feelings.

A hand fell on Tess's shoulders. "I told you your baked contributions would be a hit," Scott said with a laugh. "My brothers would marry you themselves if they weren't already taken."

She tried to laugh, failed, turned it into a cough. "I think I need a glass of water," she said, avoiding Holly's eyes as she moved toward the sink.

"You've gotten very quiet," Scott said in his car on their way back to her place. "You must be tired."

"A little," she conceded. She realized she was holding her hands in her lap, twisting the ring again, and she made herself stop before he noticed.

"Want some music?" He tuned the radio to an adult contemporary station, knowing from past conversations that she had a weakness for pop music, though his own tastes leaned toward classic rock. "I think we've had enough Christmas carols for a while, don't you?"

"Yes. This is fine, thanks." She was glad for the music, actually. She could pretend to listen and avoid having to make conversation for the duration of the drive.

Looking out the window at the passing holiday decorations, she let her head fall back against the headrest. A song ended and a new one began. She bit her lip when she recognized the opening piano notes to A Great Big World's "Say Something." The lyrics expressed the singer's longing to hear that his love was returned before he gave up on the relationship. He'd have swallowed his pride and followed his lover anywhere, he insisted in audible pain. All he'd needed were the words.

Say something, I'm giving up on you.

Funny. She'd heard this song dozens of times during the height of its popularity. She'd always liked it.

Only now did she fully understand it.

The last mournful note faded away just as Scott parked in the space beside the rental car. She'd have her own car back next week, she thought in relief. It was taking longer than she'd have liked, but that was probably to be expected this time of year.

Her car, at least, could be repaired. Brought back to its original condition, she'd been told, with no one the wiser at a glance to the damage that had been done to it. As for herself—well, maybe the damage wouldn't be visible at a glance, but she wasn't sure it would ever be fully repaired.

She and Scott both had their arms full of bags and gifts when they entered her condo. "Just dump it all on the couch," she said. "I'll put everything away later."

He turned to face her, his now empty hands planted on his hips. "All right, Tess. Spill it. What's wrong? Did someone in my family say something to upset you or make you uncomfortable?"

"Of course not." Not intentionally anyway. "Your family is wonderful. They were all so gracious to me."

"Then, what is it?"

She pushed a hand through her hair, her restlessly wandering gaze pausing on the Christmas tree. She hadn't turned on the tree lights so it was dark, the symbolism not lost on her. Should she wait? Was it horrible of her to do this on Christmas? But no. It would be worse to lie and tell him everything was fine. She and Scott had insisted on honesty from the start.

With her back to him, she slid the beautiful ring from her finger and looked down at it for a moment, struggling for composure. Only when she was sure she had her emotions under control did she turn to him, the ring closed in her fist.

"I asked you once what you would do if I told you I didn't want to go along with your plan. If I decided I'd rather not marry you."

His eyes wary, his expression guarded, he nodded. "I remember."

"Do you remember what you said?"

He nodded again. "I said I would be disappointed but I would do everything I could to put it behind me. I said I wouldn't let it affect our work relationship or our friendship. We could agree that it had been worth a shot and then go on with our lives just as we've been doing for the past six years."

She swallowed in pain before asking softly, "Do you still think you could do that? Even now?"

"Tess—"

He took a step toward her but she held up her free hand, palm out, and stopped him. "Please answer my question."

Lifting one hand to squeeze the back of his neck, he gave it a moment's thought before replying slowly, "I'm not saying it would be easy. As close as we've been the past month, as much as we've shared—hell, it'd be hard. But yeah, eventually, I could do it. Whatever happened between us, I would do anything I could to make you comfortable at the office, to assure you that your job would not be affected by any personal decision you make about us."

"And you'd be able to go back to seeing me as your office manager? Your employee?"

Again, a lengthy pause followed her question.

Say something, Scott.

"Yes," he said finally, the word a knife straight through her heart. "I could get to that point again. It might take a while, but we're adults, right? It would serve neither of us well to mope about our plans not working out."

"That's very...practical of you," she whispered. "You've always been so proud of your ability to compartmentalize your life. I guess that's part of what has made you so successful in your business."

She thought back to the end of his previous engagement. How long had it taken him to get over Sharon? A week? A day? She'd thought at the time he'd seemed almost relieved the relationship had ended, freeing him to concentrate again on the business he truly loved. Maybe it would take him a little longer this time.

But maybe not.

"Tess, you're really confusing me." He dropped his arm to his side. "I don't know where this is coming from."

She took pride in the fact that her eyes were dry when she looked at him. "I'm so very sorry, Scott. I wish I'd understood sooner what I wanted. What I needed. It wasn't your fault that I let myself get swept up into a fantasy. You did everything you could to warn me. You were nothing but honest with me from the beginning."

His eyes were wide now. Dark with dawning comprehension. "What are you saying?"

She held out her hand. Turned it palm up so that the ring was visible to him. "The life you've described would be a very good one. I'm sure you'd work as hard at being a husband and father as you have at running a business. Only a romantic idiot with totally unrealistic expectations would turn you down."

"You aren't an idiot, Tess."

"Apparently, I am."

The ensuing silence was almost suffocating. She drew a ragged breath into her aching lungs, her hand shaking a little as she continued to hold out the ring to him.

Say something. Please.

"What do you want from me?" He sounded honestly bewildered.

"Everything," she answered simply. "I needed to know that losing me would break your heart. But that's not something you were either able or willing to offer. And this pretty diamond isn't enough to make up for that."

"Tess, you don't understand. I can't... I'm not the kind who... I've tried before and I failed. And if I've hurt you now, I've failed again. I'm so sorry."

She took his hand and made him accept the ring. "It's not your fault," she repeated, tormented by his obvious distress. "You did nothing wrong. You offered everything you had to give. I'm the one who got greedy. Like I said, I'm an idiot. I fell head over heels in love with you, Scott. I've probably been in love with you for six years. Isn't that pathetic?"

"No." His voice was a little choked as his fingers closed hard around the ring. It would probably leave a mark on his palm. "Not pathetic."

"But foolish."

He couldn't seem to argue with that.

"I think you'd better go now," she said with a strained, sad smile. "I'd hate to complete my humiliation by bursting into tears. Neither of us would care for that."

"I don't want to leave you like this."

"Please." She almost flinched at the entreaty in her own voice. The one thing she was determined not to do was to beg. "Just go."

He walked slowly to the door. "Will I see you at the office next week?"

"I'll come by to get my things and to make arrangements for a replacement. Maybe Damaris could take over my duties until you can hire someone permanent. Actually, you'll probably have to hire a couple of people to replace me," she added with wry candor. "You'll need an office manager and a human resources manager."

"You're quitting?" So many emotions swirled in his face that it was hard to identify them all, but she saw the first glint of anger then. Good. Maybe it would make this easier if he got mad. At least that was a real, honest emotion. "You're seriously giving notice?"

"Yes. Unlike you, I can't go back to the way it was before. I can't just stop loving you. And I won't punish myself for it by working with you every day and watching you get over your disappointment and then move on. I deserve better than that."

"Yes. You do. You deserve everything you want." With that quiet statement, he turned and let himself out. He didn't look back as he closed the door behind him.

She didn't know how long she stood there just staring at the door, unable to move, unable to cry, unable to think beyond the dull realization that she had just ended her relationship with Scott and quit her job. She knew which loss was more devastating—but she'd loved her job, too. She would miss it almost as much as she would him. Or had she loved the job so much because of him?

The numbness began to wear off and the pain came in waves that crashed through her, slammed the breath from her lungs. A sound escaped her that was part sob, part moan. Nothing had ever hurt her as badly as this.

She needed not to be alone. But Stevie was out of town and she couldn't crash Jenny's first Christmas with her new husband. On an impulse she snatched up the keys to her rental car, tucked her bag under her arm and headed for the door.

Somehow she made it to her sister's house without being in another car crash. Shivering in the cold that seemed to be coming more from inside her than outside, she huddled into her coat and rang the doorbell.

Having checked through the security window, Nina opened the door. "Tess, what on earth are you doing here? It's nearly ten o'clock. On Christmas night! We're already getting ready for— Oh, my God. What's wrong? What's happened?"

The tears had started, and there was no way she could stop them now. "Can I—can I come in? Please."

"Of course." Nina took her arm and drew her inside. "Let me make you some tea. You're freezing. You can tell me all about it once you're warm."

Tess allowed her big sister to lead her toward the kitchen, even though she wasn't sure she'd ever be warm again.

Chapter Eleven

Scott hated failure. Hated it. He'd spent his entire life doing everything he could to avoid dealing with it, which meant he'd never really learned how to handle it. Failure had been such a rare thing in his life. Oh, sure, there'd been the broken engagement to Sharon, but that had been easy enough to wave off. Maybe because he'd never really considered that failure his fault. Sharon had demanded too much from him, made it impossible for them to continue. She might have been the one to officially call it off, but he would have done so eventually if she hadn't. So he'd always told himself that had all been more of a misstep than a failure. Still, it had left a few scars, along with more determination than ever to avoid future potential failures at all costs.

He'd been so confident that he'd minimized all the risks with Tess. That he'd looked at every angle, foreseen every potential problem, dodged any complications. With the experienced skill of a successful entrepreneur, he'd presented his case, brought her on board with his plan, followed a step-by-step progression from first date to engagement, a path that should have continued on to the cozy little wedding and a couple of kids to fill those empty upstairs bedrooms. He'd pretty much won over her sister, and his family had all but adopted Tess. The staff at work seemed okay with their arrangement, so that potential complication had been avoided. He'd done everything right. She'd said so herself.

But still he'd hurt her, the one thing he had vowed from the start not to do. He'd lost her as a fiancée, as a friend, even as an office manager. He hadn't just failed, he had failed spectacularly.

On Saturday, two days after Christmas—a month after he'd come up with that so-called brilliant idea—he sat in his empty office staring at a phone that wasn't ringing, looking at a doorway no one would be walking through today. The job sites were idle, his business associates all busy with their holidays, so there was nothing to distract him from his glum thoughts.

He hadn't broken the news to his family yet. He'd managed to avoid calls and respond to texts in brief, nonspecific replies, so they probably thought he and Tess were utilizing the time off to celebrate their engagement. Which was exactly what they should be doing, had it not all fallen apart.

He shoved himself to his feet, unable to sit still any longer. He didn't know what he was looking for when he wandered into the lobby. Everything was as tidy as they'd left it at early closing time on Wednesday.

The garland and other decorations still hung in place. He'd always thought there was something forlorn about Christmas decorations hanging around after the holiday passed. Today was no different. The tree sat in the corner, lights off because he hadn't wanted them on. Tess had been sitting right there under that tree when his brainstorm had hit.

The door to her office was open. Her desk was clean, organized. He tried to picture Damaris sitting there, or some other future employee. His brain just couldn't process it. Tess was the only one who'd ever sat at that desk. How could he ever find anyone to replace her? Here—or in the rest of his life?

Why would he want to replace her?

He could go on, he told himself. He could put it behind him. Shake off this misstep and focus on what he was good at. His business. He didn't need a wife he'd probably just neglect, or kids he didn't have time for anyway.

For Tess and the kids they'd have made together, he'd have made time.

He thought of the upcoming Kilgo job, the new Best Burger restaurants on the long-term plan, the apartment complexes and strip malls and other construction jobs waiting to be bid on and won and implemented. Maybe he'd get back his enthusiasm for the projects before long, once he figured out how to tackle them without Tess at his side.

Maybe he just had to get through that stages-of-loss thing. He'd already dealt with shock and denial. He was still struggling with bouts of anger.

What the hell more had she wanted from him? He'd

offered her his home, his business, his family, his future. What more could he have given her?

I needed to know that losing me would break your heart.

There wouldn't have been any need for heartache if she'd just gone along with the plan. She'd said she wanted the future he'd outlined, the same things he desired. Why had it mattered so much to her to hear the words, the things so many people said and didn't really mean? How many of his friends had tumbled into love, rhapsodized about their undying devotion to their new someones, thrown themselves headfirst into fairy-tale weddings, only to end up angry and disillusioned, bitter and resentful? Words held no guarantees. Actions were what counted. And he'd been prepared to follow through on all his promises.

I fell head over heels in love with you, Scott. I've probably been in love with you for six years. Isn't that pathetic?

What was more pathetic? The one who confessed love—or the one who was too cowardly to surrender to it?

I deserve better than that.

Yes. You do. You deserve everything you want.

He'd meant what he'd said. He wanted her to be happy. She did deserve it. He was sure there were plenty of men who'd be more than willing to offer Tess everything he had held back. Men who would think they'd just won the lottery of a lifetime if they were lucky enough to earn Tess Miller's love. Scott doubted that the boring Glenn was the only other man smart enough to figure out what a treasure she was. And choosy as she was, she would find someone worthy of her someday.

Maybe someday soon. And then he'd have lost her forever. That stupid plan of his would have cost him everything. More than he'd even known he'd placed at risk.

He leaned his throbbing head against the doorjamb
of her office and pressed a hand to his aching chest.
He'd never had his heart broken before, so he didn't
know what that felt like. He suspected it felt a hell of
a lot like this.

"You didn't turn on the security system. Don't you
know just anyone could break in?"

He froze, his wounded heart clenching in his chest.
And then he turned, very slowly, wondering if he'd
only imagined her voice because he'd wanted so badly
to hear it.

But no. She was here, standing in front of him looking a little pale, a little worn, but her chin held high
and her shoulders square. Tess might have been hurt
by his stupidity, but she would spring back to her feet.
She was a survivor. He suspected she was a hell of a
lot stronger than he.

"Why are you here?"

"I thought I'd start cleaning out my desk," she said
quietly, dashing his hopes that she'd come to find him.
"It's not something I want to do in front of the staff."

"You're really quitting."

She nodded. "I think it's best."

"I don't want you to go."

"I know. It won't be easy for you to replace me," she
said with a frank shrug. "But you'll manage."

"And if I don't want to manage?"

"I'm sorry," she said, but he could tell she wasn't
going to change her mind.

He pushed his fingertips into the pockets of his jeans. "I respect your decision."

"Thank you."

He moved to one side to allow her to enter her office. She set a tote bag on the desk. He hadn't even seen it in her hand. She opened her desk drawer. "Are you going to stand there and watch me?"

"Tess." Exploding into action, he reached around her and slammed the drawer shut. "Damn it, this is wrong. You can't do this."

He heard the edge of desperation in his tone, but there was nothing he could do about it.

She looked for a moment as though she was about to snap at him, but something in his expression must have caught her attention. She went still. "Why can't I do this?"

"The company needs you."

She shook her head. "Not good enough."

"*I* need you."

Her expression didn't change. "You'll find another office manager. No one is irreplaceable."

"You are," he said roughly. "Maybe I could replace you here in the office, though I'd never find anyone as competent and dedicated. But I could never replace you in my life. I don't even want to try."

"Why, Scott?"

"Because I love you, damn it. I don't want to lose you."

The words echoed in his ears as she studied him in silence. He grimaced. He'd screwed up again. That was probably the least romantic declaration she'd heard since...well, since he'd made such a mess of proposing to her.

"I really am hopeless at this," he muttered. "I can't

blame you for wanting to get as far away from me as you can, but I'm asking you to stay. If it means getting down on one knee—hell, on both knees—I'll do it. Don't give up on us, Tess. Don't give up on me."

She'd said she loved him. Had she changed her mind? Had she come to her senses?

She took a step toward him, searching his face intently. "You've really suffered the past two days, haven't you?"

"Yes," he admitted in a growl. "Hell, yes."

Incredibly, she smiled. "Good."

"Well, I'm glad that makes you so happy," he grumbled.

She threw her arms around his neck so abruptly he staggered backward. He righted himself quickly, gathering her close. "Tess?"

She drew back just far enough to gaze fiercely into his face. "I don't want to be married because we make a great team. I don't want to be the one you choose because I'm practical and sensible and fit in well with your family. I don't want you to marry me because I'm low maintenance or easygoing or understanding. I want the romance, darn it, just like any other woman. You don't have to get down on your knees, but you'd better be willing to admit you don't want to lose me. You'd damned well better fight for me if you want me."

He studied her flushed face and wild eyes, utterly fascinated by this new side of her. How could he ever grow bored with Tess or take her for granted when she never ceased to surprise him?

"I'd fight dragons for you," he said in growing wonder. "I'd give up everything I own to keep you, including this company. I'll give you every material thing I own because none of that matters. You already have the rest of me."

"Including your heart?"

"You're the only one who's ever had it. I was just too damned scared to admit it."

Rising on tiptoes, she lifted her mouth to his. He kissed her thoroughly, intensely, pouring all the emotion she demanded from him into the embrace. All he wanted to give her.

"You'll have to be patient with me," he said when they could finally speak again. "I'm going to make a lot of stupid mistakes."

She nodded. "I'll probably make a few myself. We'll deal with them together."

He set her a few inches away and dug into his pocket. Holding out his hand, he offered her the ring on his palm. The ring he hadn't been able to put away since she'd returned it to him. She hesitated only a heartbeat before smiling and reaching for it. Scott caught her hand and slipped the ring on her finger himself. Once again, he kissed it into place.

"This time it stays," he said in steadfast resolve.

Cupping his face in her hands, she brushed her lips against his. "This time it stays."

Feeling whole again for the first time since she'd sent him away, he grinned and swept her into his arms.

They really did make the perfect team. In business. In love.

It turned out he'd had the perfect plan all along.

* * * * *

SOMEONE LIKE YOU

SHIRLEY HAILSTOCK

To my dear and supportive friend and fellow
author Candice Poarch.

Chapter 1

Blind date! Theresa Granville, Teddy to her friends, drummed her long red fingernails on the white table-cloth. She was waiting for Adam Sullivan, a man she'd never met, and she could just as easily spend the rest of her life happily oblivious of his existence. But that was not to be. She'd been set up. Teddy hated blind dates and she didn't need anyone to find her a man, especially not her *mother*. The truth was, she was capable of meeting men on her own and dated often. But she'd been goaded into agreeing to have dinner with Adam Sullivan. Since she didn't like to go back on her word, she was stuck.

The restaurant was crowded for a Thursday night in Princeton. It was fall and the majority of the university students returned a month ago. Most of the restaurant's patrons were around the bar cheering on some sports team's efforts to statistically capture a spot in the history books. Teddy had long since stopped hearing the triumphs and groans of their participation in the televised game. She'd relegated the sound to white noise. Her attention was on the restaurant's entrance. From her solitary perch on the second-floor dining area, where private parties were usually held, maybe she'd be able to spot her date when *and if* he arrived. Maybe he hated blind dates, too. And Teddy would feel no disappointment at being stood up. If she didn't have to gently explain to her mother yet again why she didn't want to be set up, she wouldn't be here, either.

Frowning, she watched a short guy with round-rimmed glasses enter. Her fingers went to the phone in her pocket. Diana, her friend and business partner, was only a call away. The two had worked out a signal if Teddy wanted or *needed* to be rescued.

Again, she glanced at the man below, taking in his height or lack of it. One of Teddy's requirements in a man was height. At five feet nine inches, she didn't want to stand with a man whose head only reached her breasts. Thankfully, Mr. Glasses lifted his hand, acknowledging his party, and joined a group at the end of the bar. She breathed a sigh of relief that he wasn't her blind date.

Three other singles and two couples came in before the seven o'clock appointed hour. Then *he* walked in right as the clock struck the hour. Teddy did a double take when she saw him. Shaking her head, she immediately rejected him as someone who'd never need a blind date. He couldn't be the one. Her mother didn't have taste that good. Except for her father, who was still a handsome man in his fifties, the men her mother usually chose looked like the round-rimmed-glasses guy.

For a moment Teddy wished her date *was* the man at the door. Leaning over the banister, she watched the stranger move toward the receptionist. The two had a short conversation and she checked her seating chart. Then she shook her head. As she gathered a couple of menus and led him toward a table, the room was momentarily quiet, allowing Teddy to overhear her own name.

"I'll bring Ms. Granville over as soon as she arrives, sir," the woman said.

Teddy gasped. Her stomach lurched and her heart jumped into her throat. This couldn't be Adam Sullivan. He was gorgeous. Where did her mother find *him?* He was tall, at least six foot two. His shoulders were broad enough to rest any available head and for a moment she thought of hers resting there. Why would this guy need to be set up on a date? It took her a moment to gather herself. This was still a blind date and, as far as she knew, the two of them had nothing in common. Meeting him could be a disaster despite his looks. In fact, she expected it was. A man this good-looking could stand on his own. Yes, she decided, there had to be something wrong with him.

Rising, Teddy tucked her handbag under her arm and left her solitary seat in the upper balcony. She took the back stairs that led to the main floor. Entering through the bar, she was assaulted by the noise. The crowd was wall-to-wall and a whoop of pleasure went up as she wove her way toward the crowd. She smiled here and there, gently warding off interested men. At the entrance to the restaurant section, she peered through the vertical columns separating the dining area from the den of sports enthusiasts.

Adam Sullivan had no smile. He looked comfortably about, taking in the other diners as if he'd need to recall their exact positions at some later date. He wore an open-neck shirt and dark jacket. Masculinity exuded from him. Even sitting alone, he appeared in command. He was clean-shaven with dark tanned skin, hair cut close and neat, no mustache. Other than the I'm-in-command aura he wore, there was something else about him. Something that said "Sex!"

That's what it was. Sex appeal. Tons of it. More than any one person should be allotted. From across the room, he had her breathing hard and all she'd done was look at him. She wondered again what was wrong with him that he'd even consider meeting a stranger for dinner. He didn't look as if he needed help in finding companionship. From the stares of the other women in the room, they'd gladly leave their own parties to join his.

The receptionist was away. Teddy passed the receptionist's station and walked with measured steps toward his table. He looked up as she approached. His face remained serious, no smile, no outward sign of approval. She was slightly disappointed and a little bit insulted.

"Theresa Granville?" he asked as he stood.

She nodded, looking him straight in the eye. He

passed the height test. Teddy wore five-inch spiked heels and if she took them off, she'd only reach his chin.

"Adam Sullivan," he identified himself.

Teddy extended her hand. He took it in his larger one. It was warm and strong. She'd never been one to use clichés to describe people, but there was no other way to think of him.

Adam Sullivan was *sexy as hell*.

Conversations clashed with plates and silverware, bringing the sound in the room to a wealth of indistinct noise. Occasionally there was a burst of laughter from the bar area that drew everyone's attention for a few seconds.

Adam pulled out a chair next to his and Teddy took a seat. She waited for him to say something, but the moment stretched into awkwardness. She thumbed the edge of the menu but did not pick it up.

"Why did you agree to this?" she finally asked.

"To what?" His eyebrows rose as if he hadn't understood her question.

"Going on a blind date."

"Are you blind?"

She rolled her eyes. So that was his problem. His humor sucked. What else was wrong with him?

Then she saw a slight smile lift the corners of his mouth. Not a full smile, but it made her wonder what one would look like.

"Sorry, I had to say that. I hoped it would break the ice."

"So blind dates aren't your thing, either?" Teddy said.

"I'd rather be boiled in oil."

"Well," Teddy said, "I guess that sums it up." She felt slightly put out, even though she felt the same. She'd never been turned down for a date and frankly she didn't really like this guy. And even though she didn't want a blind date, she wanted to be the one to make the decision to end the night. "I suppose we should just shake hands and return to our lives."

She waited again for him to do something, but he seemed to be waiting for her. She stood up and extended her hand. He stood and took it.

"It was nice meeting you," he said.

His voice was perfunctory. There was nothing nice about the meeting, but Teddy was relieved she wasn't going to have to sit through an awkward getting-to-know-you discussion.

"Sorry it didn't work out." She wasn't really sorry, but the words seemed appropriate. And she wouldn't have to call Diana for rescue. As she picked up her purse, her stomach growled.

"It wouldn't have worked anyway," he said. "You're not my usual type."

"What type is that?" For some reason Teddy's back went up. She'd never been dismissed before she even got a chance to prove herself.

"You're too tall, too intelligent."

Teddy blinked. Was he real? "You can tell my intelligence level from a couple of sentences?"

"My mother gave me a little information," he explained.

Teddy's mother had told her nothing. "I see. You're

looking for arm candy. Petite, long wavy hair maybe, big brown eyes. The kind you could get lost in." She paused, giving him a moment.

"Someone who isn't very smart, but good in bed," he admitted.

Not to be waylaid by the good-in-bed comment, Teddy asked, "So I'm being dumped because of my height?"

"Not exactly dumped," he said.

Teddy took a breath and calmed down. She smiled sarcastically. "You're right. I am not the one. I'm not arm candy and I don't want a man who is. No matter how good-looking you are, I prefer a man I can talk to both before *and* after sex." She hooked her purse farther up on her shoulder. "And I am not just good in bed, I'm *great* in bed."

Pivoting on her high heels, she moved away from the table. She'd only taken a step when he called her name. "Theresa?"

She turned back.

"I probably shouldn't have said that. It's been a long day and I've forgotten my manners."

"Is that an apology?"

He nodded.

She had the feeling that he rarely apologized. He was a man in command. She could tell he was confident and obviously chose his own road. This date orchestrated by his mother and her mother was outside his developed character.

"Teddy," she said. "Everyone calls me Teddy."

"Teddy," he repeated. "Since you're obviously hungry, and we're already here—" he spread his hands encompassing the room "—we might as well eat. That way I can answer truthfully when asked how my night went."

"It hasn't begun on a high note. You sure you don't want to stop here? If we go on, things could get worse."

He laughed. The sound was deep and infectious, but Teddy refused to join in. She kept her features straight and unsmiling.

Teddy shrugged and returned to her seat. Undoubtedly, she'd be questioned, too. They ordered, and as she cut into a prime rib so tender she could have used a butter knife, Adam opened the conversation.

"While I was arguing with my..." He stopped. "I hear you're in the wedding business."

Teddy didn't like his tone. She nodded. "I design wedding gowns and I'm a partner in a wedding consulting firm."

"So you believe in orange blossoms and till death do us part?"

She refused to rise to the obvious bait. "Orange blossoms would be very expensive on this coast. But there are some brides who insist on them."

He raised a single eyebrow and sipped his drink.

"I take it you are a nonbeliever?" Teddy asked.

"I'm a realist. I've seen too many of my friends walk down that aisle only to end up hating the person they vowed to love."

Teddy was in trouble. She should have taken the opportunity to walk out the door when she had it. Now she was as stuck here for as long as the meal lasted.

"You've been married," she stated. He had all the earmarks of a man who'd been hurt in a relationship, but his tone regarding orange blossoms told her he'd been down that aisle himself. His nod was barely perceptible.

"And you hate her now?"

He shook his head. "Quite the opposite. We're very good friends."

She frowned. This was an exception to the rule of divorce. "What happened?" she asked, realizing it was probably the wrong question, but it was already out.

He spread his hands and hunched his shoulders. "We were too young. We got married for all the wrong reasons. Mainly, we didn't know each other, didn't understand that our dreams weren't the same."

"What was her dream?"

He smiled. Teddy liked it. It was the good-memory smile, the one that appears when a person looks back and only he understands the happy place he's entered. She was glad he had good memories of his marriage. She'd seen her share of people who only remembered the wedge that separated their relationship and not what created it.

"Her dream was to be an actress." He took a moment to eat some of his steak before continuing. "After our divorce, she moved to L.A. and got a part on a soap opera."

A light dawned in Teddy's brain. *Chelsea Sullivan?* She rolled the name around in her mind. "You were married to Chelsea Sullivan?"

He nodded. "She kept the name."

Chelsea Sullivan was the lead actress on the top daytime television program. From what Teddy read in the entertainment magazines, she was about to move her career to feature films.

He sat back in his chair. "And you? What did you dream of being?"

"I have my dream. I wanted my own design business."

He smiled fully. "Then you're ahead of most of the world. You have everything."

Not everything, she thought. Her partner, Diana, married last year, and while the two of them had been friends for years, Teddy wondered at the happy changes she saw in her friend. There was a newness, a happiness that hadn't been there before. While they both loved the work, for Diana there was something more to look forward to at the end of the day. Teddy had begun to wonder what she was missing.

But as she sat across from Adam, Teddy wondered how anyone could talk him into meeting someone whose business was weddings when he didn't believe in them. And so far she was sure he wasn't the one for her.

"What about marriage?" he asked.

The word hit her like a spray of ice water. "Me? Married? Never made the trip."

"I see," he said. "You give the story to everyone else but stand clear of it yourself?"

"You say that as if it was by design."

"Is it?" Adam asked. He stared straight at her.

"No, I suppose I'm the cliché," Teddy said.

"Always a bridesmaid, never a bride?"

She shook her head. "I haven't met the right man, yet."

"But your parents are determined to find him for you if you don't do it yourself?"

Teddy nodded. "My mother for sure. But isn't marriage a taboo conversation for people on a first date?" Teddy asked.

"I suppose it is, but we decided this is dinner, not a date." He laughed again. This time Teddy laughed, too.

"What do you do?" she asked. In speaking with her mother, she'd never asked anything about him. She'd been too busy arguing that she didn't want to go on a blind date to think about his profession.

"Investments. I own a brokerage house."

She was impressed, but kept it off her face and out of her voice. "So, I deal in dreams and you in cold, hard cash."

"Not cold or hard. Just ones and zeros." There was no censure in his voice. It was also devoid of pride or arrogance.

"Computer transactions." Teddy nodded, understanding that everything today was done on a small machine you could put in your pocket.

"Actual money is on the way out." He turned to her, pulling his chair an inch closer. "How much money do you have in your purse right now?"

Teddy glanced in surprise at the clutch bag that lay on the table. Tossing her head, she said, "Enough for a taxi and a phone call."

Adam smiled. It was the first time since they met that his face showed any emotion. "I remember hearing my mother telling me about taxi fare and carrying cash when she and my father were dating. Of course, their generation can remember life before cell phones."

"I got that story from my father. He wanted to make sure I could get home or at least call if some guy got out of hand. He said I could lose the phone or forget to charge the battery."

"Did it ever happen?" he asked.

"The phone, no. The date, nothing I couldn't handle."

Adam gave her a long stare. She wondered what he was thinking. She hadn't issued a challenge, yet she felt as if he was thinking of one.

"What about you? Any sisters to give that message to?"

"No sisters, two brothers."

"Where are you in the mix?"

"Right in the middle."

Teddy nodded. Spoiled, she judged. It rang true for middle children. Teddy was one of four siblings. She was the second child, the one who never got her way. Adam, as a middle sibling, would have always gotten his. And probably still did.

"What about you? Any brothers or sisters?" he asked.

"Two sisters, one brother."

"Do they live close by?"

Teddy shook her head. "We're pretty spread out, but we all make it home for most holidays."

"Where's home?"

"Maryland. Bentonburgh, Maryland. It's near Hagerstown, not that you've heard of either of those places."

"Actually, I have," he said.

Teddy looked at him for further explanation.

"A while ago I met a woman studying hotel management. She worked in Breezewood, the Town of Motels, for three years."

Teddy wasn't surprised he knew a woman there. She supposed he knew women in lots of places. That fact also surprisingly left her slightly cold. Deciding to move away from discussions about herself and her family, Teddy asked about him, "How did you get into investing?" He smiled at that. She recognized that type of smile. She'd seen it a hundred times on the faces of mothers or grandmothers of the brides. They were usually remembering their own weddings and knew how in love the bride was. The smile took them back in time. Adam had that look.

"My parents let me try it."

"How?"

"I had a teacher in high school who told us about the stock market. It intrigued me. It was one of the few classes I had where I sat up and listened to what he had to say." He spread his arms and hunched his shoulders. "I was fascinated by the possibility of turning a little money into a lot of it. I told my parents I wanted to try investing. They said it was too risky. That I would lose anything I had."

"And you proved them wrong," she stated.

"Very wrong, but it was a turning point."

"How?" Teddy took a sip of wine.

She gave him her full attention, just as he must have done to that high school teacher all those years ago.

"I wasn't the best kid. But in high school, who was?" He paused and gave her a long stare. "I was sixteen and rebellious. I guess I was at that age where a turn one way or the other could make me a man or send me to jail. My parents talked over the idea and agreed to let me have a thousand dollars to play with."

"Play with?" Teddy's brows rose. Her parents weren't poor, but she couldn't imagine them giving her that much money when she was in high school.

"Money was the first thing that really interested me. They would try anything that would hold my attention and keep me out of trouble," he explained. "The money was enough that I would be careful with it. So I read all the reports, learned the language, took small steps. Within a year, I'd turned the thousand into five thousand."

"You're kidding." Teddy stared at him. She knew that kind of return was unheard of.

He shook his head.

"That's a phenomenal return on investment," she said.

"It was. I made good choices and I learned that I was good with money. After that I took every class I could on investing and wealth management. After college I took a job on Wall Street, got my feet wet and struck out on my own."

He smiled, proud of himself. Teddy liked that he put his mind to something and stuck with it. "So if you're ever looking to invest…" He left the sentence hanging.

"You're not going to give me a sales pitch?"

"Why? Are you a hard sell?"

"Extremely hard," Teddy said.

"I'm good at what I do," Adam challenged.

"I see," Teddy said flatly. "So you like handling other people's money?"

"As much as you like the weddings you plan, I like building wealth."

Teddy thought about the wealth they had built, she and Diana. Both had come from humble backgrounds. Diana had been a scholarship student at Princeton, and Teddy, too, had had scholarships and had worked partially through Stanford. Both understood the need for capital and they learned management of money as a necessity to their business.

Teddy wasn't wealthy, but she was comfortable. Her designs were selling for thousands of dollars and she had a growing portfolio. It wasn't managed by Adam's company.

"What is the name of your investment firm?" Teddy asked.

"Sullivan Brothers Investment, Inc." He slipped a business card across the table to her. The ease with which he did it showed a practiced salesmanship.

Teddy had never heard of his company. That was probably a good thing. If they weren't maintaining or increasing wealth for their clients, she surely would have heard something from the many brides that came in for planning. And there was the trade show that had financial planners in attendance every year. She didn't know if his company had ever been represented.

"Your brothers are part of the business?"

He shook his head. "Initially, my brother Quinn went in with me, but quickly decided it wasn't for him. I bought him out for all of three dollars." He stopped and laughed at that.

"I suppose that laugh means you didn't actually cheat him out of a good deal?"

"He hadn't invested any capital into the setup. He did the legwork of finding the offices and his muscle in helping me buy and set up furniture. That was years ago now."

"Are you at the same location?"

He shook his head.

Weddings by Diana had moved twice. Once for a medical project, and the second time because she and Diana needed more space and they could afford a more prestigious area.

"With both of us in Princeton, I'm surprised our paths haven't crossed before," Adam said. "Of course, my hours are unpredictable when I'm dealing with overseas markets."

He gave a reason for them not seeing each other. Teddy also had an explanation. "My weekends are often taken up with weddings. And unless you attend as many as I do, we'd never meet."

"Not unless our mothers had something to do with it," he said.

The streets of Princeton were nearly deserted when Teddy and Adam left the restaurant. The September night was clear and unseasonably warm. Teddy couldn't believe they'd stayed so late. Talking to Adam had been mostly pleasant after they broke the ice and agreed that they would eat together only because they were hungry. And when she realized they wouldn't be seeing each other again, it was easier to relax.

He had a nice voice, deep and rich. It reminded her of late nights listening to "music for lovers only" on the radio. The DJs always had devastating voices that tended to reach through the woofers and grab hold of you. Teddy hadn't thought of that in a while. Mainly her radio listening was done in the car while returning from a meeting or a wedding.

Yet, Adam had that DJ kind of voice. It was reaching for her. And she was willingly leaning toward it. His breath had stirred her hair when he leaned close to her. And her own breathing became shallow and labored. Teddy's gaze dropped to his lips and she wondered what it would feel like if he kissed her. Then she snapped back, stopping herself. What was happening to her?

It was good to be outside, where the coziness of their surroundings didn't play into a fantasy world. She thought about whether she would like to see him again. Of course, she would rather he liked weddings and respected what she did, but marriage and the business of marriage wasn't for everyone. Adam had declared he was one of the ones who'd rather do without it. And that probably meant he'd rather do without her as a reminder.

"My car is parked in the lot," she said, looking behind them.

Together they turned toward the nearly deserted area. Other than their cars, she was sure the remainder belonged to the restaurant staff who were cleaning up and ready to end the night's work. Why hadn't she noticed the bar noise dying down? Or the other dinner patrons leaving? She and Adam had been engrossed in conversation, but it was the first time ever for Teddy to be so oblivious of her surroundings that she didn't realize they were alone.

Adam didn't touch her as he walked beside her to her car. Neither did he speak. She wondered what he was thinking. They could have gone on talking as long as they kept away from certain subjects, like weddings and marriage. Two that shouldn't be discussed on a first date anyway. Except this was not a date.

"Thanks for sharing my meal," he said when they stood next to her car.

Teddy thought he was being careful with his words. "I enjoyed it." It wasn't totally a lie, but it also wasn't fully the truth. She pressed the button on her key fob and heard the door unlock. As she reached for the handle, Adam called her name. She stopped. Could she have imagined the softness of his voice? She turned back.

Adam stepped closer to her. For no reason, her heartbeat accelerated. He leaned forward. Teddy leaned back an inch or so. Then his cheek brushed hers. Other than their initial handshake, this was the first time he touched her. His skin was smoothly shaven and warm. He held her for a short moment, not even long enough for her hands to reach his arms as they lifted to grasp him. Teddy didn't move. She thought he was about to hug her. Her breath caught and held, but he only reached around her to open the car door. She got in and, without a word, Adam closed the door. He stepped back and she looked up at him.

She started the car and, with a wave, pulled out of the parking space. As she reached the street, she glanced in the rearview mirror. Adam stood where she'd left him.

Color me confused, she thought.

"How was the date?" Diana asked, setting a cup of coffee on Teddy's desk.

Teddy wasn't working. Usually she would be. They had five weddings coming up in the next three months, but today her mind was on the man she'd had dinner with.

She reached for the coffee and took a sip. "He's got a dry humor. He hates weddings, doesn't believe in happily ever after, he's arrogant as hell and we won't be seeing each other again."

"That bad?"

"Right off, we agreed to shake hands and say good-bye. But it wasn't all bad. We had dinner." Teddy noticed Diana's eyebrows raise. "*Only* because we were both hungry," Teddy finished.

"What does he do?"

"He's the wizard of Wall Street. That's Wall Street in Princeton."

"Investments?"

Teddy nodded. "And he's good at it. His words, not mine. So, if we're ever ready to ditch our investments firm, I'm sure Sullivan Brothers Investments, Inc. would give us a personal presentation."

"You didn't like him even a little bit?" Diana asked.

"You know how I hate blind dates."

"I met Scott on a blind date."

Scott was Diana's husband of six months. "How you met Scott is not the same. You and he had talked to each other online for months before you decided to meet. You knew a lot about each other. Even more after you discovered you'd known each other in college. Being set up with a total stranger in a bar is not the same thing."

"Well, at least you satisfied your mother's requirement," Diana told her. "The two of you met and had dinner."

Teddy took another sip of her coffee. And they talked. Teddy thought about the night and how they had been unaware of other people around them.

"He was good-looking, though," she mumbled, almost to herself.

"Oh." Again, Diana's eyebrows rose.

Teddy blinked, bringing herself back to the office and out of the restaurant where they'd talked. "He was very direct—"

"Just like you," Diana interrupted.

"I am not direct," Teddy protested.

"Sure you're not." Sarcasm was present in her tone. "But don't get off the subject. You were saying he was good-looking…"

Teddy gave her a hard stare.

"Was he tall enough? I noticed the shoes you

changed into before you left yesterday had very high heels."

Diana knew Teddy's height requirement. "He was tall enough."

"So he was tall and good-looking. And he owns an investments company."

"And he's not The One," Teddy said, intent on ending the conversation. "Not even close."

"All right, I get it." Diana raised her hands in defeat. "Conversation over. But I have hope for you. You'll stop playing the field and find the right man one day." Diana gathered her cup and smiled. "Just like I did."

Diana headed for her office, and when Diana could no longer see her, Teddy repeated, "Not even close."

Chapter 2

Soft music played in the massive cathedral in New York. Saint Patrick's had sat on Fifth Avenue since 1858. Teddy wondered how many weddings had taken place there as she looked over the assembly of friends and relatives invited to the fourth marriage of Jessica Halston. Teddy didn't want to think about the number of favors she'd called in to make this ceremony happen. A three-time divorced non-Catholic being married at Saint Pat's. Even Cardinal Richelieu was probably turning over in his seventeenth-century grave. It was truly a miracle.

Teddy glanced around. People seated in pews spoke in low tones, but the sound rising to the high arches made even a whisper loud. Along the sides Teddy saw someone she thought she knew. She blinked. She had to be mistaken. What would Adam Sullivan be doing here? The man moved behind one of the huge columns that supported the massive structure. She waited, watching for him to reappear. Before that happened, she heard a voice through her earbud.

"The bride needs you." Renee, one of her consultants and Teddy's right hand, spoke in her ear. She pressed the earpiece closer and lowered her head to hear over the noise made by the many tourists admiring the massive building. "Where is she?"

"Dressing room."

Teddy was already moving, forgetting the man she was following. "Is she all right?" Many brides got cold feet even this close to saying "I do." It didn't matter if the bride had already been to the altar three times, she could still be plagued by reservations.

"She needs a little encouragement."

That could mean anything from a full-blown refusal to leave the dressing room, to a broken nail. Teddy moved down the stairs to the dressing room, going as fast as she could. She knocked quietly and entered. Jessica stood in the middle of the room—alone. For a fourth wedding, she looked as fresh and bright as she had at her first. Teddy had been present for all three of them.

"You look great," Teddy said. It was always good to let the bride know that her appearance was perfect. "When Donald sees you, he'll be bowled over." Teddy moved closer to her. "Would you like me to get the veil?"

"Is everything ready?" Jessica asked.

Teddy recognized the unspoken question. Most

brides had the same fear. They were afraid of being left standing at the altar. Even making the trip down the aisle for the fourth time, the fear was still there. Teddy understood how to answer her, so Jessica could conceal her fear and save face.

"Everything is ready. The bridesmaids are all here, dressed and looking like a picture. The best man and groom are in the vestibule. He's got cold hands by the way."

Jessica laughed. "Cold hands, warm feet."

Teddy felt her relax. Some of the tension left her body. Teddy lifted her veil and brought it to her. "The church is packed. Everyone is in place. All we need is you." She gave Jessica a reassuring smile. "Ready?"

"Ready."

Saint Patrick's Cathedral did not stop the tourists from walking around while services were in progress. When the strangers realized there was a wedding, they lowered their voices but did not leave the building as good manners dictated. Teddy, sitting on the last pew next to Renee, had long since relegated them to an inconsequential nuisance.

She surveyed the party in the front of the church, smiling at the perfect photo they made. Teddy's mind, however, was on the minister. Not a priest, but the result of calling in another favor. No matter how many times she heard the wedding vows, they still commanded her attention. From the corner of her eye, she saw several people moving along the outside aisle that led to the exit. A man stepped into the pew she and the three junior consultants sat on, but she wasn't looking at him. Her attention was on the bride and groom, and she thought he was being courteous to other visitors coming in the building. But when he stopped directly next to her, she turned to glance at him.

"Adam?" she whispered. "What are you doing here?"

Stunned, Teddy was so focused on Adam's unexpected appearance that she missed the last words of the ceremony and the kiss. The sudden sound of organ music snapped her out of her trance. She had to move. Adam didn't have a chance to answer her question before she was needed to take care of more details. The three consultants were all on their feet and moving outside. The bride and groom were on their way up the long aisle preceded by a photographer and a videographer. Teddy lost sight of Adam as she followed them, all the while speaking into the headset she wore.

Bright sunlight blinded her. Using one hand to shade her eyes, Teddy directed the security staff she'd hired. They were already in place controlling the crowd of well-wishers and onlookers. Teddy and her assistants helped to place the wedding party for the photographs. Adam Sullivan came into view and the two shared a moment of staring at each other before she turned back to her charges.

It wasn't like they found each other across a crowded room, she told herself. And what was he doing here, anyway? She'd seen the guest list. He wasn't on it. She had a job to do and she didn't need him here as a distraction. Jessica wanted everything to go smoothly and

Teddy prided herself on giving the bride her due. One of the security guards tapped Adam on the shoulder and he moved to the back of the crowd.

For forty minutes the photographers took pictures. Teddy held flowers, smoothed hair away from a face, pushed a bridesmaid's errant bra strap into place and even stood completely concealed behind a bridesmaid as she held the woman's dress in place for a better fit. As she did this, Teddy searched the faces on the sidelines for Adam's.

When they moved inside, Teddy stayed with the bridal party while the others headed for the reception at the Waldorf Astoria. The photographer had things under control and one of his assistants had put the items not needed on a pew. He was likely to be another forty-five minutes before finishing his capture of this moment in time. Teddy took the moment to look around for Adam.

He stood along the rear wall. She headed for him. "Your presence here can't be a coincidence," Teddy said when she was close enough to him that no one else would hear her.

"Apparently, I'm here for you."

"Me?" She frowned, her hand going to her breasts. "Why? I'm in the middle of a wedding and I didn't…I mean, we didn't agree to meet again."

"It's out of our hands."

"I don't understand," Teddy said.

"You have to pick up something this afternoon before you go back to New Jersey."

"A painting," she said. "My moth—" Teddy suddenly stopped. She fully understood. Her mother had called Adam and told him she was going to the gallery today to pick up a painting and bring it back to Princeton. When she went home in a few weeks, she'd take it with her.

"Another setup, I see," Adam said.

"You don't have to do this," Teddy protested. "I'm sure you're busy. It's a small canvas and I can carry it on the train."

"I'm here now. I don't mind driving you since we will be heading in the same direction."

"You drove?"

He nodded.

"Teddy?"

She looked back at the photographer and waved at him to indicate she'd be a moment.

"I have to go now. The reception is at the Waldorf. When I leave there I'm going—"

"I know," he interrupted. "I have all the details."

"Of course you do." Teddy knew her mother was nothing if not thorough.

"I'll see you at the reception."

Teddy nodded and rushed to the front of the church. As she went to work on the necessary details that needed attention, she couldn't help but look over her shoulder to see if Adam was still standing there.

He wasn't.

Two hours later Adam caught up with Teddy just inside the main ballroom. "Would you like to dance?" he asked.

"I'm not a guest here," she told him. "And neither are you."

"Your duties are over. You were invited to the reception, so you're free now." He took her hand and pulled her close. "Would you like to dance?"

He didn't give her time to answer. And he didn't put her hand on his waist. Her hand rested below his belt on the strong haunches of his lower back. She didn't move it—not away at least. He felt her hesitation and she pushed it down an inch. Heat rushed through his clothes, up his back and into his neck. Adam felt the scorching flame beneath her skin.

His eyes were staring at her. He had to move, snap out of the paralytic state he was in. Moving his feet, he circled her onto the floor and she fell in step with him. He knew she wouldn't fight him. That would cause a scene, and at a wedding this important or even one that wasn't, Teddy wouldn't ruin the day for the newly married couple. He'd garnered that from talking to her during their blind date.

She danced well. She was light in his arms as he led her from one step to another. She followed him as if they'd practiced for hours. Adam enjoyed it. He didn't dance much, but in his youth he'd been known to command the floor.

When the music stopped, they headed toward the staff table. Adam grabbed two bottles of water and they both drank thirstily.

"You two looked great out there." Renee smiled as she joined them. She was shorter than Teddy with light brown eyes and hair the same color that was pulled back, exposing her entire oval-shaped face.

"Adam, this is Renee Hart. She's a fantastic assistant."

Renee blushed as the two shook hands and exchanged the customary greeting. The assistant began clearing away the few things on the table that he assumed would go back to the office. Turning to Teddy, she said, "Your bag is over there." She pointed toward the wall behind the table. Adam saw a small canvas bag lying there. "We're all packed and about to head back."

"All right," Teddy said. "I'll see you on Monday."

Renee said goodbye, leaving the two of them alone.

Teddy turned back to him. "I'm finished now. I guess we should go get the painting, unless you want to dance again."

Adam drove the SUV expertly through the crowded Manhattan streets. Yellow cabs, buses and New York drivers proved no match for his skill.

"How was the wedding?" he asked.

"Do you really want to know?" Teddy remembered his comment on weddings in general. "I thought you didn't go in for the happily ever after."

"I don't. I was only making conversation."

It was a long ride back to Princeton. It would be even longer if they didn't talk. "The wedding was beautiful. The bride was beautiful. Several of her bridesmaids cried. You saw the church."

"How long does it take to plan a wedding?"

"I thought you were married before. How long did yours take?"

"We didn't have all the bells and whistles. We went to the justice of the peace and got married," Adam said.

Teddy was surprised. "Your wife didn't want a big wedding?"

"She did, but we couldn't afford it. So we decided to use the money we had for the honeymoon."

"Maybe next time," Teddy said, forgetting his beliefs.

"There will be no next time," he said. His voice was final.

"Then you better stop your mother from setting up blind dates for you."

"Oh, it's on the top of my list of things to do."

Teddy laughed. "If you find a solution to that, please send me an email and share it so I can stop my mother."

Teddy reached down and opened the small package she'd brought with her. Inside was a pair of shoes, which she traded for the ones she was wearing.

Adam glanced at her.

"Different muscles," she explained.

"What does that mean?"

"After a wedding or a long day on my feet, changing my shoes means I use different muscles in my legs and they don't get as tired."

"From the way you were all over the place, you must be tired of running."

Teddy sighed. "This one wasn't that bad. The cathedral was huge, but everything ran rather smoothly. Jessica will be pleased."

"Jessica is the bride, I take it?"

Teddy nodded. "For the fourth time."

"Four husbands?" he said.

"She keeps us in business."

He must have mulled that over. Adam lapsed into silence while he maneuvered through the traffic. Teddy realized she'd given him more ammunition to support his impression about weddings and marriage. Thankfully, traffic was clogging and Adam kept his attention on the road.

Finally they reached the gallery. Adam pulled into a space someone vacated and the two of them went inside. The place was bright with light. Huge windows covered the entire first story. Interior lights were placed strategically toward paintings to give them the best appearance.

A man came from the back of the small building. He was about six feet tall with gray hair, a potbelly and a welcoming smile. "Ms. Granville?"

Teddy nodded.

"I'm Gene Restonson, the gallery owner."

"I'm Theresa Granville, Gemma Granville's daughter, here to pick up a painting you're holding for her." Teddy introduced Adam. Gene shook hands with them both.

"We were just finishing packing it up. Give me a moment," he said with a smile that took in both her and Adam. "Excuse me."

Teddy nodded and he left them to go to the back.

The huge windows looked out on the afternoon traffic. Teddy moved away from them, going to a painting on a back wall. It was a landscape of the sea and sky. Adam came up behind her. "You know what they're doing, right?"

She turned to him. "'They'?"

"Our mothers."

"What?"

"They're going to keep throwing us together in hopes that we finally decide to date."

"I'm sure I can handle that," Teddy told him.

"I can, too. We're both very busy, but I think there's another option that will satisfy us all."

Teddy was intrigued. "What is that? You're not going to propose?" She held her breath. It wasn't possible, but she was unsure of what he might do. He'd appeared out of the blue today and after their conversation on weddings at dinner, he could be setting her up for anything.

He shook his head. "No, that's not it."

"You have my attention. What do you think we should do?"

"I think we should give them what they want."

"I thought you weren't going to propose." Teddy had no idea where this was going. "They want us to fall in love and get married."

"So we pretend to fall in love," Adam said.

"What?"

"It's not so strange."

"Pretend lovers. Those plots don't work in books, let alone with two people who don't know each other."

"That's what makes it perfect. We can spend the

time getting to know each other. At least, that's what we'll tell them."

"And how do we get out of this, when my mother starts making appointments for the church, the cake and asking me for the wedding gown design?"

"It won't go that far. We'll keep it up until Christmas. Then we'll tell them it didn't work out and we'll be free of each other."

Teddy stared at him. "Free of each other," she repeated.

"I didn't mean that the way it sounded. We'll have satisfied our parents for the time being. Mine will usually not bother me for a year after a breakup."

"And with the new year," Teddy said. "They'll be too busy to bother us for several more months. By then, maybe we can convince them that their meddling produced disastrous results and we're in command of our own love lives."

"Giving each of us time to find our own partners, if that's our intention."

Teddy shook her head, indicating that was not her intention.

"We'll call it the Marriage Pact," Adam suggested.

Teddy glanced up at him skeptically. "You know, you're way too into this."

He smiled, showing his even, white teeth.

"Shouldn't it be the Pretend We're Falling in Love Pact? After all there will be no wedding planning."

"Too many words." He frowned as if he was seriously considering it. "Are you in?"

"I'm not sure…" She hesitated. "I hate to deceive my mother." She paused a moment. "Although…"

"Although what?"

"Although she'd deceived me a number of times." Teddy remembered when her mother threatened to send out wedding invitations with "Groom: TBA" on them if Teddy didn't find her own date.

"Well?" he prompted.

"I think we should think this through more. For example, we don't know much about each other."

"We'll go on a few dates and come up with our story."

"How are we going to handle the holidays? You said this would be over by Christmas. A lot of planning goes into the family holidays."

"We'll have everything in order," he told her.

"All right," she said on a sigh. "Conditions." Teddy wasn't convinced this would work, but she'd give it a try if it had the possibility of giving her a few free months from her mother's relentless pestering.

"What conditions?"

"We go on these dates and we talk about the implications of this approach. We think this through."

"Agreed," he said.

Teddy believed he wasn't really thinking it through. "I mean, with the same consideration you give to your investments, you give to this plan."

He took a moment to consider it. Then he nodded and said, "Will do."

"Here it is," Mr. Restonson said.

Teddy turned. The gallery owner was a few feet behind her. She'd nearly forgotten about him in light of Adam's plan. She wondered if he'd heard them.

Moving across the floor, Teddy met him in the middle of the room. "It's huge," she said when she saw him carrying a package longer than her arms. The painting had been wrapped and she couldn't tell what the picture was, but she could see its size. No way could she take that on the train back to Princeton.

And her mother knew it.

Chapter 3

Adam wrestled the painting into the back of the SUV as Teddy watched. Several times she jerked her hand to help catch the falling canvas. "I apologize," she told him when they'd managed to get it in without a mishap. "Mom said it was a small painting."

"Relative term," he replied. "Compared with the murals at Times Square…" He left the sentence open, but Teddy knew what he meant. The advertisements in that area of Manhattan were described by the number of stories they covered. The smallest one she could think of was about ten-stories high.

There was that dry humor again. Teddy didn't mind it. In fact, she found it likable. They climbed into the plush cabin and Adam started the engine. He pulled into the afternoon traffic. Teddy thought about the suggestion Adam had brought up in the brightness of the gallery.

"Thinking about my proposal?" Adam broke into her thoughts.

"It isn't a proposal, not by my definition. But it is on my mind," Teddy said. She lapsed into silence. She knew he was waiting for her to continue by the way he glanced at her.

"Afraid pulling it off might be an issue?"

"Aren't you? After all, these are *our* parents. And what about girlfriends? I can't imagine you don't already have one." He had met her for a blind date. That should indicate that he was unattached, but Teddy didn't want to assume. She noticed him stiffen. Hands that had been relaxed now gripped the steering wheel harder.

"I did," he said quietly. "We broke up six months ago."

Teddy intentionally kept her voice low. "Is it over or do you think you'll reconcile?"

"No reconciliation." The note in his voice was final, even if it was a little higher pitched than she remembered. Teddy knew that wasn't the end of it, but she didn't know him well enough to continue questioning.

"What about you? Beautiful, confident, business owner. There must be a man in the wings."

"Several," Teddy said.

"Anyone in particular?"

"They're all particular."

He took his eyes from the road to stare at her with raised eyebrows. "How many is 'all'?"

"Not a relevant question, or one I'll answer," she told him.

"So the Marriage Pact won't work for you?"

"I didn't say that," Teddy said, a teasing smile curving her lips.

"What are you saying?"

"I'm not sure. There are complications that could happen from this action and I don't know what they are yet."

"Does that mean you'll think about it?"

After a long moment, she said, "I'll think about it."

They were both quiet for the rest of the drive. When they entered the Borough of Princeton, Teddy directed him to her house.

"Where do you want it?" Adam asked, carrying the painting.

"In here, slide it between the columns." She led him to the area between her living and dining rooms. They were separated by a pair of columns. Teddy pointed to a spot that didn't obstruct her entry or exit. Adam leaned the painting against the wall and followed her back to the kitchen.

"Would you like something to drink?" she asked.

"Thank you, but I need to go. Japanese markets are open and I have some transactions to take care of."

"Of course," Teddy said. She was slightly disappointed that he wasn't staying. She headed back toward the front of the house. At the door, she turned to thank him for his help, but a sudden and unexpected emotion gripped her. She looked up at him. The idea of a pretense with him wasn't sitting as badly as it should.

Her eyes roamed his face, settling on his mouth. Teddy thought of leaning toward him but stopped herself.

"Is something wrong?" he asked.

She shook her head.

"You will think about the pact?" he asked.

Teddy nodded. "I promised." Then surprised herself by adding, "We could talk more about it sometime." She hesitated and that was unlike her. "After the markets close, maybe."

"We need to know more about each other," he agreed.

She nodded.

"While you're thinking, here's something to help you along."

Before Teddy knew what he was going to do, he leaned toward her and she couldn't help but lean into him. Her head tipped up and her heels came off the floor at the same time. His mouth hovered over hers. He took her face in his hands, first one hand, then the other, cradling her. She took in his scent. Images swam before her eyes. She closed them as emotions burned within her. Intense heat flashed through her until she was sure she was glowing yellow. His mouth settled on hers. Easy. He didn't rush or plunge. His fingers threaded through her hair, combing it with ease as if he savored the texture and feel of the dark strands. Palms slid across her shoulders and with slow, caressing movements skimmed over her arms and sides before wrapping around her waist. He pulled her against him, possessively, his mouth mirroring the actions of his body. She felt the fire of his hands searing her suit fabric.

Teddy had been kissed before, but never like this, never with this tenderness, this softness that was as unnerving as if he were devouring her. Her arms reached upward, sliding over arms that were rock hard. On tiptoe she circled his neck and pressed herself into him. Just as her mouth began to mate with his, he lifted his head.

She said nothing. Her eyes closed and opened in answer. His finger on her lips made her incapable of speech. The emotions rifling through her were new, untried, outside her realm of experience. But they were there—prickling electrical points that dotted her body, vibrated over her skin like a formfitting acupuncture machine that dealt only in pleasure. The sensation was new.

Adam moved his hand and the moment snapped, a tenuous thread broken.

"Now we know what it's like to kiss each other."

Reaching around her, he opened the door. She was already close enough to him that the smell of his heady cologne clouded her senses. Brushing against his hard body as she made room for him had her responding to the pure sexual drive of him.

The door clicked shut and she let out a long breath. She was incapable of speech. When had a man ever caused her to react like this?

And one her mother *handpicked!*

Teddy understood that if she agreed to Adam's suggestion, the two should keep it secret, but she told Diana everything. In this she needed a second opinion.

"So, what do you think?" Teddy asked as she finished explaining Adam showing up at the wedding, the painting and his suggestion. She omitted the devastating kiss at her front door.

Diana stared at her with openmouthed amazement. "He suggested you pretend to be in love?"

Hearing it put like that and in a tone that said it was incredible, Teddy was sorry she'd brought up the subject.

"Do you think it will work?" Diana asked.

"I'm not sure. I'd rather just tell my mother to back off, but we both know that won't work."

Diana leaned forward, her arms folded on her desk. "Let me ask a different question. Are you considering this because you're attracted to Adam?" Teddy hesitated. It was apparently too long for Diana. "I guess that's my answer."

"I told you he was good-looking." Actually he was gorgeous. He had the most amazing eyes, light brown with a fringe of lashes that any female would be jealous of. His hands were soft when he had them on her face, but she could feel the strength in them. His body was solid and that bedroom voice could possibly undo her.

"At the time you didn't say you wanted to spend time with him. What is this, your third date?" Diana asked.

"We haven't been on a date yet."

"What was dinner last week and the wedding on Friday?"

"Those were chance meetings."

Diana frowned at her, but her face showed the opposite. "Sure they were," she said sarcastically. "But as far as your question goes, you'll have to decide. If you're doing it to ward off your mom, that's one thing. But if you just want to spend time with the guy and he with you, I'm sure neither one of you needs a guise."

Teddy thought about that. She was confused about her reasons for considering the Marriage Pact. She'd never wanted to be married in the past. Even though she loved the planning of someone else's wedding, she'd never thought of doing it for herself. So Adam should be a perfect candidate in her life. He didn't like weddings, didn't want to have anything to do with happily ever after. So why didn't Teddy just take him up on the Marriage Pact and fall in with his plans? It would make everyone happy. Did she really want to continue seeing Adam? Granted, if she'd met him on her own, she'd have no problem going out with him. But in her usual manner, as Diana put it, Teddy would quickly move on to someone else.

There was a certain chemistry between them. Teddy felt it. Her mouth tingled just thinking about the kiss the two of them had shared. Was that the reason? Was she afraid of spending time with him? They could become close. Was that so bad? Diana and Scott hadn't begun on the best foot and they were happily married now. Was Teddy protecting herself, putting up barriers to prevent her life from changing?

Neither she nor Adam really needed to fall in with their parents' wishes. She was her own woman, with her own needs and plans. So why was she so undecided about Adam?

* * *

Adam stared at himself in his bedroom mirror. Who was this guy, he mentally asked himself? He'd never acted this way before. He liked Teddy. He really liked her. And that was his problem. He *really* liked her. In fact, he felt as if his feelings were morphing into something else, something more. It didn't make any sense. If there had been a lineup of beautiful women before him, Adam would never have selected her as someone he wanted to get to know, but he did want to know her.

Grabbing a sweater from the drawer, he shrugged into it, dropping the one he'd spilled beer on in the hamper. Then he went into the kitchen and popped the top off another can of beer. Joining his brother in front of the big-screen television in his family room, he dropped down next to him and tossed him a can.

There was a baseball game on ESPN and Quinn was watching it. The moment he arrived, he went straight for the TV and turned on the game. When Adam joined him, he took his eyes away from the screen for a moment. Quinn was the athletic brother. He not only watched every sporting event possible, but in high school and college, he played baseball and tennis, and competed in track. He was still active in tennis and jogged several miles a day. Adam didn't envy him his biceps. Adam had his own workout routine that could rival his brother's.

Adam knew Quinn had been observing him closely for the past few days. He didn't think he'd changed since he and Teddy talked about their Marriage Pact, but he knew his observant brother must have noticed a change in him. Anything that removed Quinn's attention from a game in progress had to be important.

"What are you thinking?" Adam asked.

"That something is wrong with you."

"I'm fine," Adam said.

"Since Mom fixed you up with that blind date, you haven't been the same."

"Which blind date? There have been several. Often I can get out of them." Adam knew the routine with his mother. She would call, pretend to ask him something about investing or going through some amount of small talk, before mentioning that she'd run in to so-and-so from his past or that she'd met a very nice woman who was unattached and who would like to meet him.

Other than giving her an out-and-out no, which he'd done on one occasion, he put them off by telling her he already had a date. Sometimes that was true. Sometimes he then found a date to make the lie come true.

"You know which date," Quinn said. "The one you had a few weeks ago."

Adam took a sip of beer. "How have I been different?"

"You're quieter."

"Aren't you the one who's always telling me to be quiet so you can hear the television?" Adam said, glancing at the TV screen, and sipped his beer to cover the uncomfortable feeling that washed over him.

"I never thought you'd actually do it."

"I'm getting older...and wiser."

"Nope," Quinn said.

"Nope?"

"You're getting older, but I think we can thank Ms. Theresa Granville for the change."

Adam stiffened. "She has nothing to do with this."

"Not what I heard."

"What do you mean?" Adam frowned. "What have you heard? And from whom?"

"I mean, the word is that the two of you are a couple."

"Yeah?"

"It's true." A commercial came on and Quinn hit the mute button on the remote control. He turned to Adam. "Someone's gotten under your skin?"

Adam understood what Teddy meant by not truly thinking through the deception angle. He'd intended to fend off his mother. He hadn't thought that he'd have to keep the pretense up with everyone else, including his brothers. But the fewer people who knew the truth, the better. And while Quinn could keep a secret, Adam decided it wasn't the time to reveal what he and Teddy had talked about.

"It had to happen sometime," he answered Quinn. Adam hated lying to his brother, but if their deception was to work, only the two of them could know about it. And Adam was confused by Teddy. She seemed to tap into something deep inside him and he was unsure of what it was. Keeping it under wraps was the right thing to do, he told himself.

"This from the man who said falling in love wasn't for him. That he intended to play the field the rest of his life. Then you meet Veronica." Quinn paused, giving Adam a long look. "Then that didn't work out

and you find Teddy. Two out of two. Or is Teddy a re-
bound love?"

"Teddy is nothing like Veronica."

"Is she more like Chloe?"

Adam tensed. His brother knew better than to bring
up Chloe. But Adam didn't want to let on that her name
disturbed him. Chelsea, who he parted with on a mutually friendly basis, was never the subject of their man-
woman discussions. But she had an impact on his life
as did the other women. Chloe was a different story.

"She's nothing like Chloe," he said. He hadn't compared them, but Teddy was her own person. Maybe that
was why he couldn't identify her. Adam thought of
their kiss. For days afterward, he couldn't get the feel
of her in his arms out of his mind. He liked the way her
body folded into his as if she belonged there. As if she
wanted to be there. As if it was the right place for her.
And he wanted nothing more than to go on holding her.

In the time since he decided to never marry again,
he hadn't met anyone who captured his mind days
after meeting the way Teddy had. Pushing himself up
straight on the sofa, Adam became very serious. He
scrutinized Quinn for a moment before asking, "Have
you ever been in love? I mean, really in love? Have
you ever wanted a woman more than you've wanted
anything else?"

Quinn pointed the remote control at the television
and clicked it off. "This is going to take some time."

For a long moment Quinn stared at Adam. The two
brothers were close and rarely held anything from each

other. Adam wanted to tell him about the pact, but not yet.

"You think you're in love?" Quinn asked, breaking Adam's train of thought.

"No."

"Then what *do* you think?"

"I'm not sure. I think I might be going through some kind of phase."

"Phase?" Quinn grunted. "You're way too old for phases."

"Has it happened to you, Quinn?" Adam asked seriously.

His brother hesitated. Then said, "Once."

"With who? What happened? Why didn't I know about this?"

"You have your own life and mainly you work after dark."

"I work with world markets. They're open late," Adam said. "What about the woman you were in love with?"

"Obviously it wasn't the can't-live-without-you love, since I am still here. And this conversation is not about me," Quinn countered. "Does Mom have anything to do with this?"

"Not much. She's always meddling in my love life."

"Well, you haven't been seeing anyone on a steady basis," Quinn said. "And that's a cue for her to take control."

"So she finds me dates. Blind dates."

Quinn smiled. "So that's what this is about. She got you a date and you're having feelings for her."

"Not totally. I mean, Teddy is a nice person. I'd have dated her on my own if Mom hadn't interfered. But I'm not in love with her."

"What about Veronica and Chloe? Weren't you in love with them?"

"I thought I was. Veronica was all flash."

"And Chloe?"

"I'll never know."

The parking lot was nearly empty when Teddy returned from her last appointment. She usually loved it when there was a lot of activity going on, but she was in no mood to deal with overzealous mothers or brides who wanted a wedding the size of a Hollywood star on a budget that wouldn't support a B-level film. For the past three days, Teddy felt as if she'd been on a merry-go-round. She had rushed from one meeting to another, juggling details, approving orders and trying her best to put Adam out of her mind. The work was nothing compared to thoughts of Adam. The effort resulted in a headache as both sides of her brain warred with each other.

The offices of Wedding by Diana had recently moved from a scenic but cramped building in downtown Princeton to more spacious surroundings on the fringe of the township. They had a large parking lot and easy access to the major thoroughfares. The offices were brighter and much better organized, although Teddy knew that happened because they had moved and put everything in a new and neat place. Maintaining it would be a chore, but Diana was good at that.

Opening the glass double doors, Teddy balanced the bundles in her arms and headed for her office. A peal of laughter had her stopping just inside. The receptionist looked up and smiled. Teddy was used to hearing happy female voices when she returned from afternoon appointments. She wasn't used to hearing male laughter unless Diana's husband, Scott, had dropped by. This was a decidedly female domain. More laughter rang out. Her heartbeat quickened as she recognized the low masculine sound. Adam! What was he doing here? Again here he was, unannounced and throwing her emotions out of kilter.

Dropping her portfolio and packages in her office, she took a deep breath, squared her shoulders and entered Diana's office.

"Hello," Teddy said.

All conversation stopped. Adam stood up. His smile brightened when he saw her and for a moment Teddy almost forgot she was angry with him. This was her workplace and she didn't need him dropping by and confusing her. She had too many details to remember and he was somehow invading her thoughts and making it difficult for her to concentrate.

"You didn't tell me Adam was a stand-up comic," Diana said, a smile brightening her face.

Teddy looked from Diana to Adam. His humor with her hadn't been comedic.

"He's been regaling me with stories about some of his clients' questions while he waited for you."

"Sorry I'm late." Teddy acted as if she had expected him all along, which she hadn't.

Adam said goodbye to Diana and followed Teddy to her office. "Did we have an appointment that I don't know about?" she asked the moment she closed the door. "Because I don't have you on my calendar and I'm very good at keeping track of the people I'm supposed to meet."

"I couldn't wait any longer," he said.

"For what?" Teddy frowned. Confusion had to show on her face.

He took a moment to look around. Wedding portraits hung on the walls. Fabric books sat in a corner. Samples of netted veils hung from a rack near a conference table.

"To get your answer. I thought this setting might generate a positive response."

"And that's what you want?"

"I think it could benefit us both."

For some reason, Teddy thought he was referring to their kiss.

"And…my mother called," he finished. "Are you done for the day?"

The question was an abrupt change in subject and just as abruptly her heart lurched. There were a few hundred details that needed her attention, but they could wait until morning. She nodded.

"Why don't we go somewhere and talk?"

Teddy looked at the pile of bundles she'd brought in with her. Usually she would spend time organizing them. She'd check the notes she'd made during her meetings and put them in the proper files or set up her to-do list for the next day. Yet, when Adam asked about her time, her heartbeat increased. She wanted to go with him.

A moment later they said good-night to Diana, whose face hid a smirk, and left the office. Ten minutes later, they sat at a small table in a local bar where the waitress addressed Adam by name.

"Come here often?" Teddy teased when the woman left to get their drinks.

He smiled and appeared uncomfortable.

"You don't have to answer that," she said, teasing still in her voice. "This is a small town."

"I'm sure there are places where you're recognized," he told her.

"Many of them," she admitted. "My job requires it."

"Mine, too," he said. "Really," he repeated at her skeptical look. "Depending on the market, my hours can be unpredictable. Often this is the only place to get food after midnight."

"No snack bar at the company you own?"

"By midnight it's empty and I prefer more than a diet of potato chips and chocolate."

Teddy didn't reply. He reminded her of chocolate, the kind that was dark and bittersweet, but with a good measure of milk. For a moment, she wanted to taste him, see if that body had the same feel and texture of melt-in-your-mouth chocolate. Teddy had once planned a chocolate wedding. Everything from the cake to the trays that held the multiple sugary concoctions had been made of chocolate: dark chocolate, milk chocolate, white chocolate. Some with nuts. Others with designs made of dried strawberries, raspberries or blueberries. She imagined Adam fully sculptured in a rich, milky flavor that would make her teeth ache.

"White wine," the waitress said, setting a glass in front of Teddy and snapping her mental musings. She set a beer glass in front of Adam, poured the honey-colored liquid into the cooled glass and left them with a friendly smile.

Teddy sipped the dry wine.

"What's it to be?" Adam brought up the subject she'd been dreading.

"You're sure this will work?" Teddy wavered in her decision. She'd spoken to Diana, but thinking of her mother had set her pulse on edge.

"How can it fail?" Adam asked. "Going on a few harmless dates will play right into their plans."

"And the girlfriends?" Teddy asked, intentionally using the plural. "Suppose we commit to this and the one woman you want above all others walks into your life? How are you going to explain me to her? Or the change in women to your mother?"

She'd seen the expression on his face change. There was a woman in his past. The proverbial one that got away.

"That's not likely to happen," he said.

"What about me? My one and only could show up unexpectedly."

He tried to cover his surprise, but Teddy saw the eyebrow rise over his left eye before he forced it back in place.

"Is there a chance of that?" He leaned forward, cradling his beer in both hands, and spoke in a low voice.

"It could. I don't live in a convent."

He waited a moment as if he was weighing his options. He had no options. "I wouldn't hold you to the terms. I'm sure your mom would be even more pleased to know her daughter had found the *right* man."

Teddy understood the implication. *He* wasn't the right man. This wasn't going the way she expected it would. She felt as if she'd somehow hurt Adam, although she didn't know how.

"In that case," Teddy began, "knowing that a true romance with someone else can and would complicate things, we agree to end this pretense early should that happen." She stared at him. "Agreed?"

"Agreed." Adam raised his glass and clinked it with hers to seal the deal.

"So, how do we begin?" she asked.

"We've already begun."

The kiss they'd shared came to Teddy's mind. She didn't know if he was into public displays of affection, but her brides and grooms had no problem letting the world know they'd found that special someone.

"We need to get to know each other, so if our parents quiz us we'll have similar stories."

"Similar? Not the same?"

He shook his head. "When my dad tells a story, my mom is always correcting his details."

"Does that happen in reverse, too?"

"You bet it does and it's amusing to watch."

For the next two hours, over a variety of tasty appetizers, Teddy and Adam enjoyed their first date. They exchanged stories about siblings, colleges attended, pros and cons of their jobs, past jobs, foods they liked and disliked, favorite colors, pet peeves. Teddy found him extremely easy to talk to and his humor wasn't as dry as she'd originally thought it was.

As the waitress replaced Teddy's third glass of wine with a cup of coffee, Teddy brought up the subject every serious relationship couple should know about—past relationships.

"Why did you and your last girlfriend break up?"

Adam coughed and shifted in his seat. Teddy had asked her question after he finished a sip of coffee. She expected his reaction and was not disappointed. She had to stop herself from laughing at his surprise.

"Why is that relevant?"

"For several reasons," she said, leaning toward him. "It'll give me insight to your character if you're totally honest. And it'll tell me some of the pitfalls I should avoid. It can also tell me some qualities your parents will compare in me. But we'll get to parents later. Let's stick with the girlfriend for now."

Adam leaned back in his chair and crossed his arms. He wore an ecru Irish knit sweater that contrasted with the darkness of his skin. "Her name was Veronica and we weren't compatible."

"I'm sure there's more to it than those few words. And your reluctance to discuss her tells me the end of the story is still unfolding."

"It's over," he said. "We didn't really like each other. She didn't make an effort to get to know me." He paused. "She never delved into my likes or dreams the way you have in the past few hours. And you're doing it on a pretense basis. With her it was supposed to be real."

"So how did you become a couple?"

"With my hours it's hard to meet and maintain relationships. Hence, my mother." He stopped a moment to flash her a grin.

"Your mother introduced you to Veronica?"

"I met Veronica at a party given by a business colleague. She was fun, lots of laughs, beautiful. I ran into her several times randomly. One day we agreed to meet. From then on, we were a couple."

"And then you found her with another man."

Adam gasped. "How did you know?"

"I had a few clues. Your hours. The fact that you never said anything about being in love. It was either another man or you didn't meet the approval of the king. The king being her father. And since you also omitted a king, it had to be a man." Teddy gazed at him, but he said nothing. "And now you've sworn off my entire sex?"

"Something like that," he admitted.

"Veronica couldn't have been the first. But you must have felt something for her that she didn't feel for you. Something deep and fearful."

Adam cleared his throat. "Can we change the subject? I believe it's your turn now. Who's the one who got away in your past?"

"I haven't met him yet."

"And how old are you?" he asked with a humorous, skeptical eye.

"Thirty, why?"

"I know there's been someone special in your life, other than the *they're-all-special* types. Which one stood out?"

Teddy hesitated for a long moment. She knew she had to answer. Adam had answered her questions. And she was the one who opened this dialogue. It was only fair that she tell him the truth.

"We called him Chad, but his name was Charles Davis. We were high school sweethearts." She stopped, gazing at Adam, remaining quiet for a few moments. "We'd known each other since the cradle. In grammar school, when boys and girls discover we aren't the sorrowful creatures we each thought the other was, Chad and I were a couple."

Teddy smiled, remembering the good times they had.

"What happened?" Adam asked quietly.

"We stayed together all through high school. He was my date to the junior and senior proms."

"Then college came," Adam added.

Teddy nodded. Her smile was gone and the heartache she'd felt all those years ago rushed back. Not as sharp. Not as raw. But still present. Teddy guessed that until someone replaced those feelings in her, she would have this spot that wasn't filled.

"He went to Northeastern. I went to Stanford."

"Let me guess. He found someone else in college."

She shook her head. "Not in college. He did a summer internship for an international bank. He was extremely excited that he was going to spend the summer in Switzerland. That's where he met her."

"How long did it take to get over him?"

Teddy lowered her chin and looked up at him. "Is that the question you really want to ask?"

"Perception kicking in again," he admitted. "Have you ever gotten over him?"

"I think so."

"But…" he prompted.

"Diana wouldn't agree with me." Before he could ask what that meant, Teddy explained. "Diana thinks I don't date seriously because I never got over Chad."

Adam leaned in close and his voice was conspiratorially low when he spoke. "Since we're baring our hearts here, in your heart of hearts, is that the truth?"

Teddy didn't have to think about it, but she took a moment to let the question gain weight. "At first I did. After a couple of years, I discovered it was up to me to decide if I was going to let my life be determined by that one incident or if I was going to pick up the pieces and build on my abilities."

"Since college you haven't been in a serious relationship?"

"Like I said, I just haven't found the right guy." She smiled and sipped her coffee again. "And that's why my mother is on the husband-hunting warpath." Teddy laughed hoping to lighten the mood. "Was Veronica the catalyst for your mom?"

Adam shook his head. "My mom has been on the marriage path since I was old enough to date. We have a family joke, that we can see the wheels in her head turning every time one of us goes on a second date."

"I guess she's not one of those mothers keeping her sons tied to her apron strings."

Adam shook his head. "She's the kind running with scissors. Secretly, I believe she's always wanted a daughter."

Teddy wondered what his mother had thought of his ex-wife, Chelsea, and Veronica. Had she embraced them, thinking they would be her daughter-in-law? Had she dreamed that one of them would be the daughter she wanted?

Teddy wondered where she would fit in the mix. Could she fulfill those requirements? Would any woman do, or did his mother have specific requirements that she wanted in her son's wife?

"What's she going to think of me?"

Adam reached over and took Teddy's hand. "She'll be more than thrilled."

Chapter 4

Cocking her head to the side, Teddy listened. She heard the slamming of car doors. Her parents had arrived. Her mother was already rushing to the door when Teddy opened it. Grabbing Teddy and folding her into a bear hug that could break a normal person's back, her mother was genuinely happy to see her. Released, Teddy hugged her dad—not quite as exuberantly as her mother's hug. Still she was happy to see her parents.

Out of the blue, her mom called on Monday to say they were coming up midweek. Teddy had to work doubly hard to get everything in order for the weekend wedding she had on her calendar and take a day off to spend with her parents.

"This is a surprise. Did you just decide to drop by

for a visit?" Teddy asked. "Not that I'm not glad to see you." When her mom called, she didn't give any other information except they were coming up for two days and that she had to rush and finish packing.

"I'm giving a lecture," her dad said. "Apparently the main speaker for Princeton's journalism symposium is ill. They asked me to fill in."

"I'm impressed," Teddy said with a smile and a hug.

As the owner/editor of a small town newspaper, Kevin Granville found wide distribution due to his various editorials. This wasn't the first time he'd been asked by universities to speak, but it was the first time he'd be going to Princeton University. And it gave Teddy the opportunity to see her parents other than over holidays like Thanksgiving and Christmas.

"Come on in. I've made lunch," Teddy told them. "I'll help you with your luggage."

"No luggage," her mom said. "The university put us up in a hotel. We've already dropped our bags."

They entered the house and Teddy went straight to the kitchen.

"I'm not going to eat much," her mom said. "We have plans for dinner. We're going to Smithville."

This was the first time Teddy had heard anything about this. Of course, the university could be taking them out to dinner, but Smithville had to be a hundred miles south of the university town.

Over a lunch of cold salads and broiled salmon, Teddy's dad outlined his lecture. Teddy asked a lot of questions. She could tell her mother was antsy to discuss Adam, and while Teddy's interest in her father's program wasn't that strong, holding her mom's crusade at bay was both humorous and tiring.

"Teddy, not to change the conversation, but where is the painting you brought for me?" Her mother finally managed to wedge into the discussion.

"It's in the dining room." She turned to her dad. "You'll have to carry it out. It's a little larger than Mom led me to believe."

"You had Adam there to help you," Gemma Granville said. "I didn't think you'd have a problem."

There it was, Teddy thought. She'd gotten Adam's name into the conversation. This was the opportunity she'd been waiting for. And there'd be no stopping her probe for details.

"Thanks to you and his mother." Teddy glanced at her mom, giving her that stop-interfering look. But Gemma just smiled.

To her husband, she said, "Kevin, would you get it and put it in the car?"

The look her father gave her mother was one Teddy had seen many times. He knew she was on a crusade and whatever his efforts, she wouldn't be derailed.

"It's between the columns," Teddy directed.

Alone with her mom, Teddy took her favorite mug from the cabinet and one for her mom. She filled them with coffee and returned to the table.

"I was surprised Adam wasn't with you," her mother said as she sipped the hot liquid.

"It's his parents' anniversary and he's having a dinner for them."

"Oh, he didn't invite you?"

"Mom," she warned. "We're not joined at the hip."

"Not yet," her mother whispered. Teddy didn't think she was supposed to hear that. At least she gave her mom the benefit of the doubt.

"I do like him," Teddy said, sipping from the mug and beginning her subterfuge.

Her mom smiled. "Do you think he might be The One?"

The hopeful lift to her voice made Teddy feel guilty. She hated deception, but she'd agreed to this fake proposal so she had to go through with it.

"I'm not sure," she said. "But we're going to keep seeing each other. Wherever it goes, it goes."

"That's a start."

She patted her daughter's hand the same way she had when Teddy was a gawky teenager in need of her motherly advice.

"Mom, don't get your hopes up. This may not work out. We've met a couple of times."

"But you agreed to another date," her mother stated.

Teddy nodded. "We liked each other enough to try it."

"Good." Her mother clasped her hands together.

"Stop," Teddy said. "You'll get excited about this and it could be over in a matter of weeks." Teddy knew it would be over in a short time period. She and Adam had already set their expiration date.

"Oh, don't be so negative," her mother said. "He could be the best thing that happened to you. Give it some time." After another sip of her coffee, she said,

"Speaking of dinner, you're invited so I hope you have something dressy to wear. I mean, something special."

They hadn't been discussing dinner, but it was a safer subject than Adam, so Teddy let the change happen. Of course she had a nice dress. Her mother knew Teddy had a closet full of clothes for every occasion. Yet she felt Teddy needed to make an impression on someone who would be attending the dinner, someone who could probably help her father. She wondered what her mother was wearing. "The university must be going all out for Dad."

"Oh, they are."

Teddy found out why she needed the *special* dress several hours later when her father pulled into the parking lot of a restaurant too many miles from home for Teddy not to be suspicious.

"This is a really long way from Princeton," Teddy commented as they exited the car.

"I hear the food is good," her mom said. "Have you been here before?"

"I've done a couple of weddings here. And the food *is* really good."

"It's beautiful." Her mom took a moment to look at the small village. Every shop was completely outlined in tiny white lights. Teddy knew the area was lighted this way year-round.

"If you ever do your own wedding, you can probably use this as a place for a reception."

Her mother's message wasn't lost on Teddy. She ignored it and looked at the building. The place was huge and it had a large parking lot. When you lived in Princeton, you understood the need for adequate parking since it was at a premium in the college town.

Inside the place was warm and inviting. She didn't hear her father give his name, but they bypassed all the people in the waiting area and followed the receptionist to an adjacent room.

All Teddy's training and experience at remaining calm and keeping her emotions in check deserted her when she entered the private party room. She gasped. Adam sat at a U-shaped table with people who were obviously his parents. She assumed the others were his brothers and their dates. He'd told her neither of his siblings were married.

Adam stood up slowly and stared at her. "Wow," he said, taking a long moment to look her up and down. Teddy felt a blush cover her, but couldn't deny that she liked the way he made her feel. Now she understood why her mother insisted on checking to see what she was wearing. The black knee-length sequined dress lay haphazardly on her closet floor where it had fallen when her mother rejected it for the scarlet strapless chiffon she now wore.

Disengaging himself from the group, Adam came to stand in front of their three-person party. He kissed her lightly on the lips. "I don't know what's going on," he whispered. Then in a louder voice, he said, "Let me take your coat," as if he'd been expecting her. She handed him the drape she had over her arm and he placed it on an unoccupied chair at an empty table. Apparently, the assembled party of guests were the only occupants of the room.

Teddy introduced her parents. Behind him Adam's mother and father had risen and now stood in front of her. Adam introduced Merle Sullivan and Dr. Ann Sullivan, and Teddy already suspected her mother knew Adam's mom. Adam's father was the CEO of a mid-size insurance company. He was a portly man, over six feet tall with thinning hair that was a mixture of gray and black. Dr. Sullivan was short and petite. Her hair was cut almost to her scalp, making her face strong and prominent. Yet her smile was beautiful and Adam had gotten his eyes from her. Teddy didn't have time to process all the information because the other family members quickly joined the small congregation. Galen and Quinn were Adam's brothers. Both had dates and Teddy wondered if they were also on the receiving end of their mother's quest for married sons.

Adam slipped his arm around her waist and she felt heat flow to her toes. As everyone headed for the table to retake their seats, Adam took her hand. The two lingered behind the others, staying close to the entrance.

"It wasn't my idea. I nearly swallowed my teeth when the three of you walked in," he said. He stopped and glanced over his shoulder. "But I can see my mother's hand in this…coincidence."

"Well, I suppose it's time we went into our act," she said, her voice low. "Get ready."

"For what?"

"The *Gemma Granville Marry My Daughter Show.*"

Adam almost laughed at that. Teddy had no way of knowing that his mother could hold her own when it came to her sons and the marriages that were still to come. Quinn and Galen weren't immune to their mother's machinations, but tonight they weren't on the front line.

Glancing at Quinn, Adam noticed the shadow of a smile on his brother's face. He could almost hear him asking, *Is she the one?* Adam had no answer for that. There was something indefinable about Teddy, but so far the two were only trying to solve the problem between themselves and their overzealous mothers.

"Are you two going to hover over there all night or join the rest of us?" Quinn called from his place across the room.

Adam and Teddy turned to face Quinn and the waiting table. Adam put his hand on her back and urged her toward the U-shaped table that had been laid out festively for an anniversary. Both the chairs and tables had been covered in white. Place settings were laid out for a six-course meal. Adam wasn't sure he'd survive it.

The two took seats. "Sorry for holding things up," Teddy apologized to Adam's parents.

"Don't worry about it." His mother brushed her apology aside. She placed a hand on her husband's and continued. "We remember how it was to be newly in love."

Adam's ears should have slid off his face at the amount of heat that flashed within him so fast the entire room had to see it. Glancing at Teddy, he was surprised to see her smiling.

"You think this is funny?" he whispered.

"Hilarious." Then she gave her attention to his parents. "Adam didn't tell me how long you've been married."

"Tonight we celebrate thirty-eight years," his father responded for the first time since their introduction. He smiled, one Adam had seen many times and knew was genuine.

"Happy years." Quinn raised his glass and toasted them.

"Can you imagine being married that long, Teddy?" her mother asked.

"Mother, I can't imagine being married for one year, let alone several decades. But…" She paused and took Adam's hand. Hers was warm and calm, while his, despite the heat generating in his body, was ice-cold. He wondered where she was going with this. "…maybe one day we'll all meet again for an anniversary and I'll answer that question."

Adam thought his mother was going to beam out of her chair. The smile on her face rivaled the size of her dinner plate. Quinn looked stunned. His brother Galen's mouth dropped open and Teddy's mother's face mirrored that of her coconspirator.

"Wait a minute," Galen said. "Are you telling me, you two are serious?" He pointed from one to the other with the index fingers of both hands.

Adam cleared his throat. "Well, we haven't known each other that long, but…" he stopped for effect and the need to swallow the lump of lies he was about to tell "…things are progressing."

"Progressing?" Galen repeated.

Teddy nodded. "I hope you have no objections." She gazed directly at Galen, then turned to his parents.

Adam's mom spread her hands. "We're thrilled." Then a moment later, she continued, "Of course, we want you two to be sure."

Adam watched the bobbing heads. He knew the two mothers in this room had already decided that they were more than sure.

Teddy held her sides, hesitating on the steps to her porch, as she laughed for the hundredth time during their ninety-minute drive back to Princeton. She and Adam had reviewed the evening's events since leaving the restaurant and climbing into his car. Adam drove and Teddy was glad she didn't have to negotiate the dark roads as tears sometimes trickled down her cheeks over some comment or action one or both of their mothers had made.

She opened the door to her house and both entered the dimly lit foyer.

"If you don't stop," she informed Adam, "I'm going to have to go to the hospital so they can stitch up my sides." She took short breaths, trying to control the pain in her sides, but she started to laugh again. Hiccupping, she stopped.

"I apologize for my parents," she told him after a moment.

"It was just as much my mother's fault as yours."

"They ambushed us."

"But we were ready. I'm sure both of them went home as happy souls."

He smiled at Teddy and it was almost her undoing. Every time she saw him, her heart fluttered and her stomach felt as if butterflies were playing inside her.

"Do you want something to eat?"

"I'm starving," he said. "I couldn't eat anything during dinner."

"I know." Teddy headed for the kitchen. "Between your brothers and our parents, I was afraid I'd choke if I tried to swallow anything."

Teddy started to laugh again. Tears cornered in her eyes and she used her fingertips to wipe them away.

"Quinn." She paused, taking a sobering breath. "When Quinn asked your mom where she was hiding my wedding gown and the room went deathly quiet, I thought she might answer that it was in the coat closet."

Adam laughed. "Then Galen joined with…" He stopped as they both remembered his brother coming up with the same thought about where the gown was located. "And then adding that the minister was probably coming in for dessert and would perform the nuptials."

"The look on your mom's face was priceless, even though I was totally afraid my mother might say it was all true," Teddy said.

The gales of laughter continued. Teddy held her head. All the laughing was making it throb. She forced herself to control it and went into the kitchen.

Adam followed her. "Can I help with anything?" he asked as she opened the refrigerator.

Teddy stopped and stared at him. "Can you cook?" she asked.

"I've been known to boil water," he said. "And I

make a mean macaroni and cheese. If pushed, I can boil spaghetti and open a jar of sauce."

Teddy smiled. "I'm not used to having anyone in my kitchen, so why don't you set the table?" She pointed to the cabinets holding plates, glasses and silverware. "Does your mother also find dates for your brothers?" Teddy asked.

"Often," he said. "They threatened to accept jobs far from home if she didn't stop."

"And that worked?" It seemed an easy solution. Teddy knew it wouldn't work for her. Her mother still found blind dates for her and she lived two hours away, plus she worked a lot of weekends.

"For about a week."

"Who were the women at the anniversary? Were they mother-finds, too?"

Adam shook his head. "During the planning process, they both stated they were bringing their own dates. Even though we were only going to be a family, we knew our mother would do something unexpected."

"Me," Teddy said.

Adam nodded. "I should have had a clue when I noticed the extra place settings, but I never thought I'd see you come through the door."

"My mother let me believe we were going to a dinner with the university organizers. The fact that it was in Smithville was a little unusual, but I wasn't expecting to join in on your parents' dinner."

Minutes later they were sitting down to a meal of omelets, sausage, toast and decaf coffee. It only took a few minutes to cook and even less to eat. Filling their cups with more coffee, Teddy added cream to hers. Adam drank his black.

"This is a better meal than the steak I had earlier tonight," Adam said.

"Last night," Teddy corrected. "It'll be daylight in three hours."

Adam took their dishes to the sink and rinsed them. Teddy got up and joined him. Together they finished the dishes and took their cups to the living room.

"Tired?" Adam asked when Teddy sank into the sofa. He joined her there.

"A little," she said, stifling a yawn. "You're going to have to go straight to the office, if you shouldn't already be there."

"I checked in before we left Smithville. I imagine the world of finance won't collapse before morning."

He put his arm around her and she leaned into him. Teddy started to giggle.

"What's so funny?" Adam asked.

"My mom, when she asked me if I could imagine being married thirty-eight years."

Adam laughed, too. "I'm sure your answer wasn't ideal for her, but you weathered it."

"I wonder what she would have thought if I'd really said what came to my mind first?"

"Which was…" Adam prompted.

"Thirty-eight years with the same man. I shudder to think." She mock shuddered and laughed, but Adam didn't join her despite his arm being around her shoulders.

"Have you ever really given it thought?" His voice

turned serious. He was holding Teddy in his arms and she couldn't see his face, but she could feel the tension that had somehow crept into his body.

Teddy moved back to look at Adam. "I never thought of being married," she answered.

"Really?" Adam's brows arched.

"Really."

"You plan weddings. Marriage ought to be the first thing on your mind."

"Or the last," she said.

"You see hundreds of couples pledging their last breath to love. You design the perfect gown and give the fantasy wedding to strangers. And not once have you ever imagined it would one day be your turn?"

Teddy hesitated a long time. "I did once," she said. "The first gown I ever designed was the one I wanted to be married in."

"The groom?"

She smiled briefly. "There was no groom. Only my fantasy of the perfect man. But I made the gown, added the finest lace. It was perfect, inside and out, and it fit every part of me."

"I bet you were a beautiful bride. I'd like to see it."

Teddy was shaking her head before Adam finished his sentence.

"Why not?" His arms tightened around her.

"I sold it."

"Why?"

"After I finished it, I took it into the office for Diana to see. She insisted I put it on. While I was dressing, a client came in. Diana was helping her when I came back. The woman saw the gown and loved it. She loved it so much tears rolled down her face. She wanted to buy it. Diana told her it wasn't for sale, but she kept asking what we'd sell it for. She was willing to pay anything. The business was new. We needed the money."

"So you sold it?"

"I sold it."

"Regrets?"

"For a while, but not anymore."

"Now you're a cynic?"

Teddy laughed. "Me? What about you?"

"Okay, we're both cynics," he agreed.

"It's a good thing we found each other."

"You know you are the most intriguing woman I've ever met?" he said.

"Really?" Teddy smiled. "Why is that?"

"I never know what you're thinking or what you're going to say."

Teddy nodded, an impish smile on her face.

"And you like that?" Adam asked.

"Absolutely."

Adam looked at her for a long time before he said, "Yeah." But he didn't stop staring at her. His eyes made Teddy warm. She saw the heat there, watched it build into desire. Her mouth went dry, and it was hard to swallow. She endured his gaze as that now-familiar blanket of warmth settled over her. She knew the heat between them would build. This time there was more. She wanted more. Anticipation, need, want. She had many names for it, but she wanted him. The slow cravings inside her spoke of arousal. Her body ached for his. She wanted his mouth on hers, his body working its primal magic with hers. She wanted to feel the weight of him, know that sweet moment of initial penetration. And she wanted to take it all the way.

Then he leaned forward. His eyes dropped to her mouth and settled there for a charged moment. Teddy licked her lips, unable to stop herself from wetting the dryness. Adam kissed her lightly, his lips brushing hers, but she felt the world tilt. She tasted the coffee from their breakfast on his mouth. It acted as an elixir, a fantastic drug with powers to transform her into the wanton tigress that was waking inside her.

The intimacy was tantalizing. Hands slipped under her hair and lifted her head to his.

Teddy's body went soft and liquid. She felt pliable, her movements like syrup, able to flow into the contours of Adam's frame as he brought her closer. Her arms, which still had substance, circled his neck, and she closed the small space separating them, connecting their mouths.

His lips changed from the soft, teasing kiss to a hard, hungry one. Adam bent her over his arm, his mouth locked on hers possessively, demanding acquiescence. Heat burned between them. Teddy gave as she got, embracing him, loving the feel of his body as her hands roamed the muscles of his back, muscles that contracted and relaxed under her sensitive fingers.

Heat built between them like the onslaught of a forest fire. Their heads bobbed one way, then the other. Teddy slid under Adam and he slid over her in a choreographed movement. His heavier frame pressed her deep into the sofa cushions. The length of him spread over her, his erection pushing against her stomach. Need sang in her veins. Adam's tongue invaded her mouth, searing her to him so tightly her breath ran out.

Teddy had never had this all-consuming experience before. She wanted to feel him all over, run her hands over his skin, feel it next to hers, have his body connect with hers and join in the ancient dance known to lovers since the beginning of time. Her dress, a thin chiffon, was a barrier to her needs.

She needed Adam, wanted him. Wanted the hot thrust of his body inside hers. Teddy always played the field. She never got close to a man. She could always control her reactions. She liked sex. She enjoyed men, but she'd never had this strong sensation of need, of anticipated release that was designed for one man. But that was what was happening with Adam. With him there was no other. Had never been another. They were forging a new frontier, terraforming a world into existence.

She wanted all of him, wanted to devour him. She wanted to get into his pants and his mind, imprint herself on him so thoroughly that her name would be visible to any other woman he ever saw.

"Have you got a condom?" Teddy asked with the small amount of breath she had.

"Yes," he said just as breathlessly.

Teddy slid off the sofa and grabbed Adam's hand. The two rushed up the steps and into her bedroom.

Adam pinned her to the door and clamped his mouth to hers the moment they were inside. For eons it seemed they stayed suspended in their own world. Then his mouth moved from hers to nibble kisses along her neck and bare shoulders. Heat mounted in the room. Teddy raised her head, giving him access to skin so sensitive she could feel the blood rising to the surface. Then Adam pulled her away from the door and reached behind her. The zipper's teeth on her dress opened with a low ripping sound as Adam pulled it down. His fingers against her back were like a match to kerosene.

Her back arched and the dress slipped to the floor. Part of the bodice contained her bra, leaving her dressed in only her panties, hosiery and high-heeled shoes. Adam opened his mouth to speak, but said nothing. He stared at her until Teddy's skin burned.

Finally, Adam slipped his arm beneath her knees and lifted her. Teddy was tall and no one had ever carried her, but Adam made her feel petite and light. He took her to the bed and laid her gently on the comforter as if she was the most precious baby. He sat next to her, one hand caressing her shoulder. It dipped down and his thumb brushed across her nipple. It sprang to life with an inner passion that was like a wave crashing against her insides.

Teddy reached up and undid the top button on his shirt. Her hands moved to the second button and released it. Adam, apparently thinking it would take too long, grabbed the back of the fabric and pulled it over his head. In the darkened light he was beautiful. His chest, bare of hair, was muscularly defined. If he carried an ounce of unneeded fat, it was well disguised.

She ran her hands over smooth skin, rising up from the bed to again join him in a kiss. This time Teddy took charge, pushing past his teeth and sweeping her tongue in his mouth. She pressed herself against him, reveling in the hardness of his chest against the softness of her breasts.

Sounds, guttural, raw and hungry, mingled about in the electrified room. Adam's hands traversed her back, angling her from side to side as their mouths danced. Suddenly, he stopped and stood, removing the remainder of his clothes, and protecting himself and her with a condom. Teddy removed her shoes, hose and panties.

Together they joined each other on the bed. She realized they both had been holding back, but now the thread that was binding their emotions snapped and they wrestled together, yearning for each other. Adam's erection pressed hard against the juncture of Teddy's legs. Sensations spiraled through her like circular lightning. She felt lit inside and out, straining for him to enter her, to make good on the promise his body invoked. With one knee he spread her legs and entered her. Teddy clamped her teeth on her lower lip but couldn't stop the sound of pleasure that escaped. Adam moved inside her, his body connected to hers, enkindling an urgency that had the two of them writhing for dominance. They rolled back and forth across the bed, their arms and legs tangling as each gave the other the joy they sought.

This was a completely new plane for Teddy. She'd never felt like this. Never had a man demanded all from her. Never was there a man she was willing to give all to before Adam. She wanted to give all. Wanted to give whatever he demanded, whatever she felt like giving.

She wanted to take it all, wanted to have him in her forever, have this feeling go on until she could no longer stand it, then have it go a little longer.

Teddy could barely breathe, but she didn't care. Her palms felt the tiny electrical impulses that ruptured off his skin as she skated her hands over the lower curve of his back. Her touch seemed to push him on. His body moved harder, faster into her. Each time his powerful body thrusted into her, the sensation of pleasure escalated. Her breath hitched as time stopped. The earth no longer moved for anyone but the two of them. Then the wave began. A huge internal signal that told her a moving ridge of passion stronger than the last was about to engulf her. She braced for it, writhing beneath him. Her body strained for the rapture, wanting it, needing it, reaching for it in every way. But it waited, a breath away, a torment so sweet that she rallied for its touch.

From a distance she heard the moan, not knowing if it came from her or Adam. Their bodies twined together, each fighting for the brass ring, identical need grasping for the golden key. Finally, Teddy heard her own voice as her climax began and ended in a scream of release.

Chapter 5

Adam rolled on his back, breathing hard. He pulled Teddy into his side and held her there, his legs entwined with hers. He didn't want to let her go. What had just happened to him? They hadn't taken the time to pull the covers down, but the bed still looked as if a war had taken place. The cover was bunched under him, although most of it had spilled to the floor. Blood throbbed in his head, yet he felt euphoric. He'd never made love like he and Teddy had just done. It was as if he was another person with her. He wanted to please her more than he ever wanted to please anyone. His own satisfaction wasn't as important to him as hers was. That had never happened before.

And he hadn't wanted to stop. He'd have gone on and on if he could, if they could. Adam ran his hand over her naked shoulder and arm. She was warm and smooth and she felt so right in his arms. The room had that electric smell of love. Adam took a deep breath, filling his lungs with their comingled scent, wishing he could capture it and save it, be able to take it out and relive this moment.

"What are you thinking?" Teddy asked. Her voice was deeper than usual, sexy in the dark, filled with satisfaction and something he couldn't define.

Adam turned to her and pushed her hair off her forehead. He kissed her lightly there, then worked his way to her lips, each kiss a thank-you for what she'd given him. Even if she was unaware of what she'd done, he thanked her.

"I was thinking that I've never felt anything like I did tonight." It was an unguarded comment. He'd never have said it in the past, but for some reason he wanted to tell her the unvarnished truth. They had been truthful with each other from the first. From the moment they met on the blind date, both had said exactly what was on their minds. Adam liked that about her.

"I felt the same way," Teddy whispered. She snugged against him. His body was cooling and he could feel the air. Teddy must be getting cold, too. Adam reached for the part of the comforter that lay on the floor and pulled it over the two of them. Like curling in a rug, they had to get closer to each other. Teddy's arm went around his waist and her body touched his from breast to his knee. Without volition he began to respond. His erection grew hard again. He wanted her again. And he wanted her now.

Pushing her back into the mattress, Adam kissed her hard. His legs covered hers and his hands trailed up and down her body, touching her skin, learning her curves, learning the zones that gave her pleasure. Because he wanted to give her pleasure. He wanted her to feel good. He wanted that more than he wanted his own gratification.

He mounted her, his body joining smoothly with hers as if they had been lovers all their lives. Adam couldn't stop the movements that seemed to come from somewhere deep inside him. Every brush of their legs together caused friction that ignited him more. He wanted to take it slower this time, but it felt like the first time. He couldn't stop the momentum that had him filling Teddy to the hilt time and again.

He heard her female sounds, listened for the pleasurable noises she made. Those sounds drove him, forced him to push harder, faster, but not over the limit. Adam waited. He needed her to join him, be with him in the frenzy of movements that would satisfy them both.

He felt it as Teddy moved. Together they convulsed, joining and separating, taking on the rhythm of their own, giving, taking, moving, writhing, learning each other. Taking the greatest pleasure on earth.

Then it happened. Adam couldn't hold back any longer. He felt Teddy climbing with him, the two of them entering that singular place that was theirs alone, the place where they burst through time and where everything was suspended. A place where their rapture had substance and the world was theirs.

Adam held her there for as long as he could. Eons

passed as his body was racked with wrenching excitement. A shocking torrent of emotion thundered through him until he thought he'd explode. Then he dropped back to earth, landing on a soft cloud. For the second time tonight, his breath came in ragged gulps. He was weak like a toddler spent from a full day of playing in the sun and sand.

And he never felt better in his life.

An insistent buzz woke Teddy. She ignored it, hoping it would stop. It came again and again. Groaning, she opened one eye. Hair obscured her view. Pushing it out of her face, she groped for her cell phone. On her first attempt, she missed, pushing the device farther away.

"Damn," she cursed. Whoever it was should call back, she thought. Glancing at the clock, it was only six o'clock. Who would be calling her this early?

Then she remembered Adam. Quickly turning over, her hand slapped the phone to the floor. The phone continued its persistence, and she expected to find Adam lying next to her. The bed was empty.

The buzz stopped.

Teddy ran a hand through her hair, sighing heavily. Disappointment flowed through her. The pillow and sheets were rumpled; he'd straightened them because their bedroom gymnastics had worked them off the bed. The night had been indescribable. But this was morning. A new day. Fantasy over. Time to return to reality.

The phone buzzed again. Teddy groaned, more at Adam being gone than the phone.

Maybe it was him, she thought and picked up the device.

"You are there," her mother said. "I thought you might have your phone off."

"Mother?" Teddy questioned, as if she didn't recognize her mother's voice.

"Of course, dear. Did I wake you?"

Teddy's mother was very active. She played tennis three mornings a week at seven o'clock. The other two mornings she swam laps in the pool at the local health club. She could swim in the university pool where she worked as an economics professor. They could also afford to have a pool in their yard, but Gemma Granville was a socializer and she met more people if she left the house than if she stayed in it.

"You were asleep. I'm sorry I woke you. I wanted to know how it went with Adam last night."

Teddy's entire blood supply bubbled to the surface, turning her red with embarrassment. She couldn't answer that question, at least not with the truth.

"What do you mean?" She stalled.

"You two were very close-headed when you left the restaurant."

"Close-headed?" Teddy didn't know what that meant.

"Close together, speaking softly, secretively, holding hands, acting like you wanted to be alone."

She was fishing for information. "We're fine, Mother. He drove me home, saw me safely into the house and..."

"And?"

Teddy heard the anticipation in her mother's voice.

"And we agreed to see each other again."

"Wonderful! I knew you two would hit it off." Gemma Granville was probably jumping up and down. "So I was right," she said.

"Right about what?"

"About Adam. He's The One."

"Mother," Teddy warned. "Don't go jumping to conclusions."

"I'm not."

"Sure you're not. You'll probably be looking at wedding gowns as soon as the stores open."

"I wouldn't look at gowns. I assume you'll design your own. After all, you *are* a designer."

Teddy rolled her eyes. "We only agreed to go on a date. Let's see how things work out?"

"But you do like him?"

Her mother was determined to get a commitment out of her. The truth was, Adam was gone. They hadn't set a date for anything else, although after last night, she was sure they would.

"Yes, Mother. I like him."

"Good."

"I have to go now, Mother. My other phone is ringing." There was no phone ringing.

"Teddy, you are coming to your dad's lecture today, right?"

"I wouldn't miss it."

"You can bring Adam."

"I'm not sure. Adam has overseas contacts and he may not be available."

"Give him a call and see. We'd love to see him again before we go back home."

"I'll see. Gotta go now." Teddy hung up, not giving her mother time to stop her.

Pushing the cover aside and untangling her legs from the bedding, she swung her legs to the floor and stood up.

She was naked.

Adam had covered her with his body and kept her warm during the night. But without the cocoon of heat the two generated, she felt the chilliness of the room.

It didn't take her long to shower and dress. Pulling on gray wool slacks and a bulky sweater, Teddy headed for the kitchen and her first cup of coffee for the day. On the counter sat a note propped against a mug with a single red rose in it. Teddy smiled. She lifted the note and read.

Sorry to leave without waking you, but you looked so adorable with your hair spread across the pillow.

It was signed, "Adam." There was a P.S. that read, "You smile in your sleep." Teddy's hand went to her hair and she pushed it through with a smile. She picked up the cup and smelled the rose. Where could Adam find a rose at this early hour or at whatever hour of the night he left?

Minutes later Teddy poured herself a cup of coffee and carried it to the table. Her phone buzzed as she sat down.

"I guess this means you're awake," Adam said.

"My mother woke me, but I got your note and your rose. Thank you."

She heard the smile in his voice. "I'd have left you a bouquet if I could have found one."

That would be romantic, Teddy thought.

"But I'm calling for a different reason."

Teddy listened, waiting for him to continue.

"My mother called this morning, too," Adam said.

"What did she want?"

"She invited us to Thanksgiving dinner."

"We knew we were going to have to be somewhere for the holiday. Although I thought that would be when our parents met. Ah, too late. We've already done that." Teddy lightened the moment she felt was getting heavy. "I guess we can split the day—do the meal with one family and dessert with the other."

"It's at least a two-hour drive to Bentonburgh and my mother had another suggestion."

Teddy set the coffee cup down and bit her bottom lip. "What is it?"

"Joint families. She'd like to invite you and your family, sisters, brothers, spouses, significant others—everyone—to Thanksgiving dinner."

"Does she know how many people she's talking about?"

"I told her you had a brother and two sisters and they may have dates. She's okay with that."

Teddy sighed.

"Are you all right?" Adam asked.

Teddy ignored his question. "I suppose she's already contacted my mother?"

"She didn't say that, but I had the feeling the deal was already done. We're the only two wild cards in the mix."

Teddy laughed. "I guess we'll be having dinner with your parents." Even though they were on the phone, Teddy thought she heard relief in his voice.

"I'll let her know."

"One more thing," she said.

"What's that?"

"My father's lecture today. My mother asked me if you would come with me. I told her you had duties at work."

"What time's the lecture?"

"Three o'clock."

"I'll pick you up at two."

"Are you sure? I mean, you—"

"Will you be ready?" he cut her off.

"Sure." This deception hadn't set well with her in the beginning. Now they were acting as if it was *real*. Combined families for Thanksgiving, joint invitations. Complications were setting in. These were minor. She couldn't imagine what was in store for them as the holidays approached.

"Teddy?" Adam said.

"I'm still here."

"I agree with you."

"About what?" she asked.

"You aren't just good in bed. You're great."

* * *

Plans were made and often they changed. Teddy knew this from her business. Working with brides, she knew that the beginning plan was not the final plan.

So when Adam called and asked if she could meet him at his condo instead of him picking her up, Teddy agreed. She wanted to see where he lived and going to his condo would give her the chance. He'd been to her house more than once, had eaten breakfast in her kitchen and spent the night in her bed. This would be her first visit to his house.

Adam lived in one of the new condo units built on the outskirts of the township. The buildings resembled town houses, but they were sold as condos. His was near the back of the complex, close to the trees that lined the property and gave the area a parklike setting.

The weather yesterday had been mild, but had turned much colder overnight. Today it was windy and bone-chilling. She thought it was ushering in November and reminding them that winter was on its way. Teddy pulled into a parking space near the front door. Shutting down the car's engine, she got out. Her booted heels clicked on the concrete. She still wore the gray slacks and sweater, but had added the pant boots, earrings and took care with her makeup.

Adam opened the door as soon as she rang the bell. He smiled when he saw her, and took her hand to draw her inside.

"Oops," she said, facing him. "I forgot to get you a gift."

"Gift?"

"My mother says the first time you go to visit someone, you should bring them a gift. I don't have one." She spread her hands, showing their emptiness.

"I'll take this instead."

He leaned forward and kissed her. It was short and only intended to be a friendly kiss. But when he pulled away, the two looked at each other and in the next moment, she was in his arms for a full never-let-me-go lip-lock. It went on for several seconds, before he raised his head.

"That will take the chill off the weather outside," Teddy said to cover the fact that if they didn't have to go to her father's lecture, she'd push him to the floor and make love to him right here. She needed to control herself around him. This was a deception for their parents, but she was having trouble separating fact from fiction.

Adam laughed. "I'm almost ready. Make yourself comfortable. I'll be right back."

"Isn't that a woman's line?"

"It's interchangeable. You can use it next time I come to pick you up."

He disappeared up the stairs and Teddy turned around. The prickles on her arms were receding. Removing her coat, she laid it on a chair inside the living room. There was a fireplace and a fire burned in the hearth. Teddy spread her hands, taking in the warmth while she looked about. The room had that decorated-by-a-decorator look. Everything coordinated: the walls were a soft blue-gray, blond hardwood floors that glowed warm in almost any light. The furniture was black leather, soft as butter with gray and white pillows. Fresh flowers were set strategically about the room, giving unexpected pops of color and a fragrance that had her thinking of romance. Spying a vase of roses, she went to it, bending down and smelling their fragrance. Now she knew where he got the rose he'd left her. He'd driven all the way home and come back to leave her a rose. Emotion welled up in her throat and she had to blink away the tears that filled her eyes. The simple act of kindness was unexpected.

There were pictures on the walls, not anything personal. These were oil paintings. Teddy didn't know art, but she knew these weren't the kind of paintings you find in local department stores. Looking in the corner of one, she checked for a signature. It was hard to read and meant nothing to her. Despite the room's perfection, it was cold. There was nothing here that said Adam. None of the personality she was coming to know was reflected in the blacks and grays of the room.

He was a warm man, sensitive and loving. Of course, his humor could use some work, but that was one of the things that made him different from all other men.

"Ready?" Adam asked, running down the stairs.

Teddy faced him. Wearing pants that hugged his thighs and a blue shirt open at the collar, he looked both casual and good enough to eat. Teddy curled her fingers in her hands to keep them from reaching out and touching him. She knew that body, knew the hardness of his chest, the strength of the muscles in his arms and the tenderness they could enfold. She knew his mouth, the way it fit perfectly over hers. The way his tongue felt sweeping into her mouth and removing everything from her mind except him.

"You brought me a rose," she said, placing her hand on one of the buds in the vase.

"Sleeping so soundly, you reminded me of a delicate flower."

"So you drove home, picked a flower and drove back."

"It was on the way to work."

She knew he was making light of his actions, but she appreciated it. Teddy went to him and kissed him on the cheek. "I liked the rose."

"You're easy to satisfy."

"Am I?" she questioned, knowing the innuendo in her voice.

Adam darkened, but recovered almost immediately. "I'm not sure. I'll have to try it again just to make sure."

She kissed him again, this time on the mouth. "Now?"

He let out a long breath. "I would sure like to, but we'll miss your father's lecture and your mother will never let us live it down."

"True." She pouted.

"We'd better go before I change my mind. And if we don't leave now, we're bound to get caught in traffic."

"Right," Teddy said.

"Would you hand me the phone in that drawer?" He indicated an end table. Teddy hadn't seen the drawer when she looked around the room. She heard Adam exhale a long breath when she was no longer looking at him. The thought that she affected him made her feel good.

Pulling the drawer open, she saw a phone lying in the bottom. The only other thing in the drawer was a charger the phone was connected to. She didn't see how it fed out the back or bottom of the drawer and connected to an outlet. Reaching inside she disconnected the phone. The password screen came up as she handed it to him.

Adam slipped it into the pocket of the leather jacket he'd added to his wardrobe.

Lifting Teddy's coat from the chair, he held it as she slipped her arms inside. For a brief moment he squeezed her shoulders. She wanted to step back into his embrace, feel the warmth of him, but she knew where that would lead. Where she wanted it to lead. But they didn't have time for that now.

"We've been invited to a Christmas party," Adam said.

"Really?"

"One of my VPs holds a holiday party every year. Since we'll still be together then, would you like to go?"

"I haven't been to a party just for pleasure in a long time," she said. "I'd love to."

"Good. I'll let him know we're coming."

"Now, we'd better get to this party."

With his hand on the small of her back, the two went through the front door. Teddy opened her car door and slipped inside. The decision of who would drive had been solved without discussion.

As an honored guest, Teddy had a pass to park on campus. They entered the lecture hall several minutes later and took seats near the middle of the auditorium.

"What's your father speaking about?" Adam asked. "I know it has something to do with journalism, but I didn't get the specific topic."

"I'm fuzzy on that," Teddy said. "He told me, but I wasn't paying close attention. My mother was trying to get into the discussion and I was blocking her. It has something to do with the future in the digital arena of journalism."

Teddy turned her attention to the program, looking for the topic. She didn't get to read it due to the interruption.

"There you two are," her mother said, coming to where they sat. Her voice sounded like a proud parent on the night of her daughter's first date. "I thought you'd like to sit closer to the front."

Teddy shook her head. "If we sit up there, Father will embarrass me. This is fine." They were sitting in the subdued light halfway up the hall. Teddy wasn't sure they could be seen from the front.

The room got quiet. "They're about to start," her mother whispered. "I'll see you when the lecture is over." She got up and rushed back to her seat near the front, hunching down as if she didn't want to be seen.

When the president of the symposium introduced her father, he said the speech was on the coexistence of the internet and the small newspaper. Adam took her hand as her father walked to the podium and began his speech. Neither she nor Adam had anything to do with newspapers. The subject sounded boring, but her father had a knack for entertainment and he had the audience laughing as he delivered anecdotes on his experiences as a newsman from the big papers to the one he managed now. His lecture was followed by an active question and answer period.

The crowd thinned until only Adam, Teddy and her mother remained in the audience. Several organizers of the event cornered her father and congratulated him.

"Are you going back to work after this?" Teddy asked Adam.

"I thought we might have an early dinner with your parents."

"You're ready to endure my mother again so soon?" Teddy's eyebrows went up while her voice went down.

"I can take it." He smiled, glancing at the woman sitting in the first row.

"They're not staying," Teddy told him. "They decided to return home right away. My father can't be away from his paper too long. He gets withdrawal symptoms."

"So, it's just you and me?"

"If you can endure me so soon after the last time," she teased.

Adam's eyes turned dark and hot. She meant to be flippant, get a laugh out of him, but the impact of her words after the night they'd spent together came to her in a rush of heat. By the look on Adam's face, he was obviously remembering that night, too.

"Teddy?"

She didn't even hear her mother until she'd called

her name twice. Turning, she looked at her, hoping it was too dim in the room for her mom to see her clearly.

"We're going to head for home as soon as your father finishes up." She glanced at the three men still talking at the front of the room.

"We want to get there before dark," her father was saying.

It was only a couple of hours to Bentonburgh. They should make it with time to spare. But it was rush hour and that would slow them down a bit.

Teddy and Adam stood up and went to the end of the aisle. Adam followed. Teddy hugged her mother. And then her mom hugged Adam. It appeared as if she was welcoming him to the family.

"Adam, it was good seeing you again. And I spoke with Ann this morning. We agreed to spend Thanksgiving as a family."

"Mom," Teddy warned again.

"What?" She looked at Teddy. "It'll be good to spend the day with friends and family."

"Thanksgiving is a month away."

"But these things must be planned, the same as weddings."

"Mrs. Granville, I'm looking forward to it," Adam cajoled, slipping his arm around Teddy's waist. She let go of her rising anger.

Her mom stepped back. "You two do make a lovely couple. And I can see how much you love each other."

Teddy grabbed Adam's hand and squeezed. Neither of them agreed or disagreed with Gemma Granville's comment.

Finally her father joined the group. The four of them left the auditorium and walked to his SUV.

"I wish we could stay longer, but I have to get back to the paper," Merle Sullivan said. He reached around her to Adam and shook his hand. The two men nodded mutually. Both knew it wasn't necessary. Then her dad kissed her on the forehead and climbed into the driver's seat. Her mom got in the passenger seat and fastened her seat belt. With a honk of the horn, they pulled out of the parking lot and headed south toward Maryland. Teddy stood with Adam's arm around her until the SUV was out of sight.

"What do you think they're planning for Thanksgiving?" Teddy asked.

"I have no idea. But I realize this was just a warm-up. The main event is being planned as we speak."

"I can only hope we'll be ready for it," Teddy said.

"We'll surprise them."

Chapter 6

Both Teddy and Diana were early risers. This was something that made them compatible. They had time to spend a few minutes being friends and then get a jump on the day. The calm before the storm, before the other associates came in and before the phones started to ring.

"You're here early," Diana said. "You're always early, but today you're really early."

"After spending two days with my parents and the weekend, I have a thousand things to do. Why are you here at—" she looked at her watch "—six o'clock?"

"Scott had an early flight. I dropped him at the airfield."

Scott usually drove himself to the airport, but he and Diana were still technically newlyweds. She made no excuses about wanting to be with him as much as possible. And Scott had told her he loved finding her at the airport waiting for him when he returned from his flights.

Diana took a seat and handed Teddy the cup of coffee she often brought in with her. "When I spoke with Renee on Friday, she seemed to have everything under control."

"She did. I told you she's ready to go out on her own. I'm going to hate losing her as an assistant."

"I'm sure you two will work something out." Diana leaned forward, putting her arm on the edge of the desk. "Tell me about your weekend. Did you have a good time?"

Teddy leaned back. "Picture this—two mothers, both wanting their children to find someone and get married. Send them all out to dinner and miraculously discover they are all at the same restaurant and in the same room."

Diana was holding her mouth closed. "You met Adam's parents."

"And his two brothers and their dates."

Diana was laughing. "What an ambush."

"That's exactly the word Adam used."

Teddy explained that her mother led her to believe they were going to dinner as guests of the university, but it was really to join the Sullivans for their anniversary, and for them to push Adam and her toward each other.

"Stop laughing," Teddy said, trying to keep from joining her. "It's not funny."

"It's hilarious, and to think they aren't even trying to hide their strategy." She took a drink of her coffee. "How's Adam taking it?"

The mention of his name had Teddy's body reacting as if she could touch him from this distance. She hoped Diana didn't notice the change.

"He's better than I expected he'd be. This was his idea, but I thought he hadn't thought it through. Yet, he falls into the act as if it was natural."

Teddy looked up and saw Diana staring at her. "Are you falling for him?" The scrutiny in her eyes was serious.

"Of course not." She wanted to stop there but knew she needed to reinforce her statement. "He is easy to look at."

"And he's got a great body."

Teddy nearly choked.

"And he loves to touch you," Diana went on.

"What?"

"Don't tell me you haven't noticed."

"He's only doing that for show," Teddy explained.

"Yeah," Diana said. "It isn't only that he touches you, but the way he touches you."

"The way?" Teddy frowned.

Teddy knew exactly what Diana meant. She loved being touched by Adam. Whenever he put his hands on her, she felt his tenderness. She wanted to turn into his arms and settle there forever.

"Teddy, you're blushing."

Teddy snapped out of the reverie she was falling into. "I am not."

Diana didn't respond. At least, not in words. She gazed at Teddy for a long time.

"All right, I'm attracted to him. And yes, I've noticed that he touches me a lot."

"And you like it." It was a statement.

"I shouldn't. I shouldn't feel anything more than a warm hand, but for some reason my entire body almost glows."

"I am so glad to hear this."

"Why?" Teddy asked.

"Because you deserve to be happy."

"You're only saying that because you found Scott and you think everyone should feel like you do."

"You're right," Diana said. "What I feel for Scott is amazing. And I never thought he'd be the man for me, but since that time long ago, you've sort of given up on ever finding someone. But with Adam—"

"Stop." Teddy put her hand up. "There is no Adam and me. We're not a couple. We're only together for this short period. He and I set the rules and we'll live by them."

"Teddy, things always change. You know that."

"Not this," Diana said.

"Does he feel the same way about you?"

"I don't know," Teddy said, sorry this conversation had taken this turn.

"Does he know how you feel?"

Teddy shook her head. She hoped he didn't know.

The jewelry store on the corner of Nassau and Williams Street had sat there for decades. Adam passed it almost daily, but he'd never stopped to look into the windows. Yet today he stood there, staring at a setting in the window. *Would Teddy like that?* he wondered. He pictured the ring decorating her elegant hand.

"Never buy the ring unless she's there to pick it out," someone said behind him. Adam turned to find Veronica Woods standing behind him. She was the last person he ever expected to find on a street in Princeton.

"Veronica, this is a surprise."

"A good one, I hope," she said. She leaned forward to kiss him. Adam pushed his cheek to hers and stepped back. Veronica was dressed impeccably in black and white, looking like someone he'd see on the cover of a glossy magazine. Her long coat was ringed with white fur around the neck and sleeves. On her head sat a matching hat. This framed her face, softened her features and made her desirable to any man—except him.

"What are you doing here? I thought you moved out to Chicago."

"I did. I'm only back for a visit, but I'll be here for a couple of weeks. When I left, I took a job working for a decorator. After a few years, I joined the partnership. A while after that, I was about to strike out on my own when we decided to open another office. I'm running that office."

"Here in Princeton?" Veronica represented betrayal to him and he didn't want to be reminded of it constantly. He knew she'd never really been in love with him, but the humiliation she heaped on him was not easily forgotten.

"Philadelphia," she corrected with a shake of her

head. "I came up today to see some old friends. I didn't know one of them would be you. I take it you're still running that investment company."

He nodded, disappointed that she didn't remember the name of his company. He could tell Veronica hadn't changed much. She looked better than she had five years ago. Her clothes were designer originals, but her values were the same. She acted as if they'd parted as friends, as if nothing had occurred between them.

"Things must be going well if you're looking in the window of a jewelry store." She indicated the display windows behind him. "Who is she?"

Adam glanced at the window. The setting he'd been looking at sparkled. "You wouldn't know her," he replied. Adam hadn't seen anyone on a steady basis since he and Veronica's relationship had ended. He wasn't about to let her think he was harboring any residual feelings for her.

"It must be serious. I never thought you'd give up your bachelorhood."

"Change happens," he said, refusing to mention anything about their past.

She smiled. Adam knew that look, knew that the sweeping down of her eyelashes meant she was covering something she didn't want him to see.

"Why don't you buy me a cup of coffee and tell me about her?"

He looked over her shoulder at the university that dominated the college town. "I'd love to, but I have to get back to that investment company. I only stepped out to pick up my lunch, which is probably ready by now. But it was great seeing you again." He knew he was dismissing her. "Good luck with your design firm."

She opened her purse and pulled out a business card. "Call me sometime."

He took the card. "If I need a decorator."

"Or if you just want to mull over good times."

Adam doubted he would call for that reason, but he nodded. Veronica again leaned forward. This time she kissed his mouth. And of course it would happen then. As he raised his head he saw two women turn the corner and walk toward them. Immediately he recognized them both.

Teddy and Diana.

It took a moment since they were talking to each other before Teddy recognized him and smiled. The two approached.

"Hello, Adam," Teddy said. She glanced at the woman and nodded.

"Veronica, this is Theresa Granville, my fiancée, and her business partner, Diana Thomas."

As the women acknowledged each other, Teddy reached into her purse and extracted a tissue. She held it out to Adam.

Red wasn't his color.

At seven o'clock that night Teddy stood outside Adam's condo. She pushed the doorbell and heard it chiming through the ornate entryway.

"So that was Veronica?" Teddy stated by way of a greeting as Adam opened the door.

"That was Veronica." Adam sighed. He stood back

and allowed her to enter the foyer. Taking her coat, he hung it in the hall closet. "I assume you're hungry and since I didn't know what you might want to eat, I bought a variety of entrées."

He led her into the dining room, where several bowls of Chinese food sat on a table set for two. She'd glanced in the kitchen on the way and saw the paper containers whose contents he'd transferred to china bowls. She wondered what Adam was trying to do, what he might want to tell her.

"Sit down," he said and poured her a glass of white wine.

Teddy took a seat and because she was hungry, she filled her plate with a small sample of everything and ate heartily. Adam, on the other hand, pushed his food around but ate very little. He felt guilty, she thought.

"Adam, is something wrong?"

"Why do you ask that?"

She was sure something more was wrong than she thought. In her experience, any time a question was answered with a question meant something was wrong. Their meeting on the street this afternoon had prompted her to rethink their plan.

"What is it?" she asked.

Adam got up and took his wineglass. He offered his hand to Teddy and they moved from the dining table to the large family room. This one also looked as if a decorator had a hand in the furnishings and wall art. It had a large circular sofa facing a gigantic television and a fireplace with a fire that crackled and popped, adding ambiance to the evening meal. Teddy took a seat on the sofa.

She finally spoke. "Is this about Veronica?"

Teddy felt the tension rising in her. She didn't know how this was going to end, but she didn't think it would come out in her favor. Adam turned to her and Teddy knew the look. It was an ending. Everything had been packed and was ready for release. Teddy just needed to wait for the last train.

"Is she your one and only? I know the rules we set in place when we started this. But if you want to end the pretense so you can be with—"

Teddy didn't get any further. Adam moved faster than lightning. He was in front of her, pulling her up from her seat. His face was so close to hers it scared her. "This is not about Veronica. I saw your face this afternoon. You looked as if I'd kicked you."

Teddy pulled back, taking a step to straighten herself. "Things are getting complicated," she said. "More so than we thought they would. Now you have a former lover in town."

"Emphasis on 'former.' Our relationship ended long ago. It's old news."

"Is it?" she asked.

"Very old," he confirmed.

"It didn't look old. In fact, it looked as if there would be a new edition. And I thought in light of that, you might want to end this. Now." He was holding her so close and so tight, she could hardly breathe. "I thought you and Veronica wanted to get together. After all, you *were* wearing her lipstick."

Adam's head moved with the same speed as he'd crossed the room. His mouth clamped on hers and held for a long moment, long enough for Teddy to cling to him. These days that took less than a second.

"Now I'm wearing yours," he said.

Teddy couldn't stop the smile that turned her mouth up. The smile became a giggle and then a laugh. Adam put his arms around her and together they laughed. The tension that had settled between them on the main street in Princeton that afternoon lifted.

Adam took her hands and they sat side by side on the sofa. The fire gave the room a rosy glow. Teddy slipped her feet out of her shoes and tucked them under her.

Adam smiled. "Comfortable?"

She nodded. "Tell me about her?"

"I told you the story before."

"And there's nothing more?"

"Nothing."

"But she's back now. More than likely you'll run into her from time to time."

"She's a decorator. She's opening a business in Philly. Probably more of her clients will be in that area than here."

Teddy felt he was giving her excuses, rationalizations that could boil over and change at any given moment.

"Was she The One, Adam? Did you think the two of you would have the forever kind of love?"

He hesitated a long time. He took a drink of his wine but didn't move away from Teddy. She felt for a change in his body, a stiffening of muscles that indicated an increased heartbeat or a rush of blood to the head, even a raised eyebrow. None of the cues were present.

"My brother Quinn says there comes a time when you have to risk your heart. I thought I was doing that with Veronica. I thought she felt the same about me. That proved not to be the case."

"So you're no longer willing to risk your heart?" Teddy asked. "I guess that makes me perfect for you."

His head snapped up. "How so?"

"Your plan. The Marriage Pact. It's perfect. There's no chance of you risking anything. You can satisfy your inner logic of never letting a woman entangle you the way Veronica did without the burden of complications."

"That's not what this is about," he protested.

"Are you sure?" Teddy raised her eyebrows, giving him an inquiring look. Her heart was beating so fast, she didn't know if she could speak, but she understood everything now. She knew there was more to this deception than just eluding his mother's attempts to have him find a bride. He'd built a wall around his heart and Teddy was the temporary guard who would keep the wall intact for a while. Then he'd move on to the next guard or retreat into his overseas connections as a method of keeping himself free of risks.

"What do you think this is about?" he asked.

"That's a loaded question. Are you sure you want the answer?"

His face wasn't exactly blank, but Teddy could see he was trying to keep it free of expression. He nodded. "I'm a big boy. I can take it."

Teddy uncurled her feet and stood up. Taking her

wineglass, she walked about the room. "A decorator did this room, didn't she?"

Adam frowned. She knew he didn't understand the question.

"Veronica has never been here," he said.

"I didn't think it was her," Teddy told him. "It's a beautiful room. I could see it in one of the glossy magazines."

"But," he prompted.

She came back to him. Faced him. She sat on the huge coffee table that held only a glass vase of flowers, her knees only an inch from his.

"There's nothing of you in this room. There's nothing of you in the entire house. Not even in the bedroom." She paused, giving him a long look. "Maybe the flowers are your reflection, which are surprising since most men would never think of flowers, especially fresh ones. Few would buy them or replace them when they died."

"Or drive home to get a single red rose?"

Teddy smiled remembering the mug on her kitchen table the first time they made love. The thought nearly undid her. That warm blanket began to settle, but she pushed it aside. She needed to stay on track. Allowing thoughts of their lovemaking would send her soaring in a different, although wonderful, direction.

"That, too," she said. "Only the flowers say you have a heart, much less want to risk it." She took his hand. He didn't pull it away, but it had gone from warm to slightly cold. "I'm sorry your don't like what I'm saying, but you did ask. I hope you see that, like your brother said, without risk there is no love, and without love, you'll have a very lonely existence."

Adam pulled her up from the table and onto his lap. "So you believe I should let go of the past and open my heart?"

Her own heart was beating a drum in his ears. She nodded.

"Are you also saying I should approach Veronica and see if what I thought we had in the past could be rekindled? Bring the fire back to life?"

Teddy forcibly controlled her urge to move out of his arms. "If that is what you want," she whispered.

"That's not what I want."

She raised her eyelids and stared directly at him. She knew she shouldn't ask, but she had to know. "What do you want?"

"Right now? Right this very moment?"

"Yes," she said, drawing the word out as if it had several syllables.

"I want you."

"I want you" wasn't the same as "I love you." Adam knew that. He wanted to say it, wanted to let Teddy know that she meant more to him than any woman ever had, but he couldn't get the words out. So he retreated, retreated into what any man would do in his situation.

He kissed her.

Teddy didn't protest. She was pliant in his arms. He wanted her there, wanted to tell her everything she wanted to know, but he'd been burned before.

* * *

It was hard to think there was hunger in the world when Teddy looked at all the food on the tables in Dr. Sullivan's dining room. She said "tables," since there were at least three. They were covered with turkey, salads, sweet potatoes, green bean casseroles, corn bread dressing, pies, cakes and even more dishes, all smelling delicious and making her stomach growl.

Just as both mothers were trying to get their offsprings married, both mothers were outdoing the other with the amount of food they cooked and delivered. Her sisters Sienna and Sierra brought their signature dishes. Emory, her brother, was exempt since he'd proven years ago that cooking wasn't something he would excel at. Teddy arrived with a dish of macaroni and cheese.

"Who do you think will win?" Galen whispered in Adam's ear.

Adam glanced at the football game on the big-screen television, but he knew his brother wasn't speaking of the game.

"You don't even want to go there," Adam said. "It could get bloody."

"Just remember," Quinn joined in. "Everything is delicious. Nothing is better than the other."

"They are all equally great," Adam and Galen said in unison.

"Obviously you three have gone through this routine before," Teddy said.

Quinn nodded. "And we learned early not to play favorites."

"Remember that time everyone made the green

beans and wanted all the cousins to judge them?" Quinn asked, laughter in his question.

Galen frowned. "That year I was sure someone would die."

They were all laughing at a shared memory. Teddy knew from her own family that the rivalry was all in good fun. She hadn't made a green bean casserole. Her dish was macaroni and cheese, which sat on a warming plate in the dining room. Teddy was free to join the others and enjoy the game. Dr. Sullivan had already refused any additional help in the kitchen.

"So," Galen said, looking at Adam, "when are you two getting married?"

The room went quiet. Everyone stared at Galen.

"What?" Galen asked, spreading his arms in innocence, one of them holding a beer. "You've been going out for months. This is the second family dinner you've appeared at." He glanced at Teddy. "It must be time for marriage."

"We'll set ours when you set yours," Teddy told him.

"Me?"

"Yes, I have a sister and I see how you look at her." Teddy checked that her sister Sienna couldn't hear her. "I'll point that out to your mother. Then all we'll need is one more dinner and it can be a double wedding."

Again, the room stared at the youngest Sullivan son.

Finally Quinn laughed and, pointing at his brother, said, "She got you." Everyone burst into laughter.

Obviously embarrassed, Galen was the first to stand up when his mom announced the meal. The dining room didn't have the same dimensions as the restaurant where their anniversary dinner was held. Instead of a U-shaped arrangement, two parallel tables had been set up. Adam steered her to one the farthest from both their parents.

For the next twenty minutes, food was passed around, plates were filled, and the only sounds in the room were those of the dinner forks and "Mmm, mmm" of appreciation.

"Overwhelmed yet?" Adam asked.

"I'm actually enjoying myself," Teddy told him. And she was. "How about you?"

"I love my family. We don't get together often enough."

"I know. Despite our parents' meddling, we have so much to be thankful for."

Adam gave her one of those looks, the one that said so much but told her so little. It was confusing, making her wonder what he was thinking. What was behind the look? And what did it mean?

"My brothers really like you." He took a moment to glance around the table. Teddy followed his gaze. Everyone was eating and talking, smiling, making comments on how good the food was. Galen sat next to Teddy's sister Sienna, and the two seemed to be hitting it off.

"You have a nice family," Teddy said.

"Even my mother?"

"Especially your mother. She's only looking out for your best interest."

Adam's eyes opened wide. "Who are you and where have you hidden Theresa Granville?"

She laughed. "Every parent wants their children to be happy."

"And they want grandchildren."

"That, too," Teddy agreed.

"But most of them don't size up dates for them," Adam said, keeping his voice low enough that no one else could hear him.

Before Teddy could answer, Dr. Sullivan announced dessert. The groan of being too full to take another bite came up like the roar of a football goal.

"I'll have some later," Quinn said.

"Then I guess we can fill our glasses with wine. And you guys can clean up the plates," his mom said.

En masse, the women left the room and by mutual agreement, the guys cleared away the dishes. By the time they finished and joined the group in the great room, the first game was almost over.

"Wine?" Adam asked, coming to stand by Teddy. Teddy nodded, handing him her glass. Instead of him leaving, he squatted down beside her. "Anything happen while I was gone?"

She shook her head. "Everyone was really into the game. I see your mom is a big fan."

"She is now." He glanced at her. "My father recruited her, and when she was the only woman in a house of men, it was conform or be left out."

Teddy watched him smile. He really loved his family. She liked that about him. When they'd first met, she'd classified him as a loner, someone you assumed sprang full grown without the aid of parents. But in the past weeks, Teddy had come to know the man inside and she was falling further and further in love with him.

"What's that look for?" Adam asked.

"What look?"

"The one on your face. It's an I've-got-a-secret face. Like you know something no one else does."

"I might," she answered honestly, but couched it behind an impish grin to throw him off. Then she leaned over and kissed him quickly. "That's my secret."

"Not anymore," Adam said. "My mother saw that."

"Good," Teddy whispered. "Let's give her a show." Her mouth was only a shadow away from his. "Just a short comedy, not a Broadway musical." She kissed him again, a slow sweet touching of lips. Adam slid his tongue between the seam of her lips. Lightning strikes thundered through her blood. She moved back before a production number started and she was unable to stop.

"I'll get that wine now."

Chapter 7

The last bottle of wine on the table was empty. Adam took it to the kitchen and dropped it in the recycle bin. Getting a new bottle, he pulled the cork out. Ann Sullivan entered the kitchen as it popped. She took a seat on one of the high stools in front of the large center counter. The food from dinner sat in myriad plastic containers stacked at the end closest to the refrigerator.

"Did I hear you talking about setting a date earlier? Was that a wedding date?"

His mom didn't begin with small talk. She went right to the subject on her mind.

"Mom, don't go jumping over the horse." Adam poured wine in the two glasses. Teddy's glass had her lip print arched on the delicate crystal. He had the urge to drink from that glass, placing his mouth on the exact spot where hers had been.

"I'm not, but my hearing is excellent."

"It was a joke. Galen was teasing Teddy. Did you hear her reply?"

Ignoring his question, she said, "All teasing aside, the two of you have been seeing a lot of each other. And from what I saw in there, you both seem to only have eyes for each other. Is this arrangement exclusive?"

"We've never discussed that specifically, but I'm not seeing anyone else at the moment. I'm sure Teddy isn't, either."

His mom smiled, obviously pleased. Then her face became serious again. "You'll never guess who I saw yesterday while I was running some last-minute errands."

Adam moved to the seat next to his mother. He slipped into the chair and looked directly at her. "Let me guess. Veronica Woods."

She raised her brows in surprise. "You know she's back?"

"She's not back. She says she's here to do a job based in Philly. She was only here visiting."

"Where did you two meet?"

"I ran into her outside of Varrick's and before you ask, there is nothing left between us. We've been done for some time now."

"Varrick's? Varrick's Jewelry?"

"One and the same," Adam said. "But I'm sure you already know this. Veronica isn't one to keep information to herself if she can use it."

"You were looking at rings." It was a statement.

"I was out for lunch and looked in the windows. I wasn't shopping."

"So you didn't buy Teddy a ring?" Adam's mother's voice went slightly up at the end of the sentence in hope that he'd tell her he had bought a ring.

"Isn't it true that the woman should always be there to pick out her own ring?"

She nodded. "Are you in the market for a ring?"

"Do you think it's too soon? We've only known each other a few months."

She shook her head. "I don't think it's too soon." Ann Sullivan slid down from her chair and folded Adam in her outstretched arms.

After a second, Adam pushed her back "You're not just saying that because you want grandchildren, are you?"

"Of course not." She feigned hurt. "You know I want grandchildren, but I also want you to be happy. You *are* in love with Teddy, right?"

There it was, Adam thought. He'd walked right into that question. And it had to be answered. If he were a lawyer, he would never set himself up for a question he didn't want to answer. But Adam wasn't a lawyer. And he'd drawn the question.

"Yes," he said. The word came lowly as if he was talking to himself. He did love Teddy. He only realized it this minute. When had that happened?

"Are you going to ask her to marry you?"

Adam was having difficulty processing this newly discovered information, but his mom's question penetrated his brain. "Mom, slow down. Let me do this in my way. Teddy may not feel that we've known each other long enough. She may not feel the same way about me."

"From what I saw a few minutes ago, her love is something you should have no doubt of."

"In any case, I'll tell her when the time is right," Adam said.

"Of course. You know I would never interfere."

Adam picked up the two wineglasses and howled.

A loud shout punched the air in the family room as the supported NFL team scored a touchdown. Hands slapped in the air. Calls of success, as if they were the actual player, filled the airspace from floor to ceiling. It appeared the Sullivans and the Granvilles had bonded. Teddy's brother and sisters were in the mix of Adam's family, comfortable and easy as if they had been friends for years.

Teddy looked over her shoulder for any sign of Adam. He came out of the kitchen first. His mother followed. Teddy watched, hoping to find something in his expression that would tell her what his mom thought of their demonstration before he left to get her wine. Adam's face was unreadable, but his mom had a smile on hers and a gleam in her eyes.

Teddy got up and met him near the dining room door. "What happened in there?" she asked as soon as his mother passed out of earshot. He set the wineglasses on the table and the two took seats. She had her back to the room. Taking a sip of the wine, she felt she might need fortification.

"She wanted to know about Veronica."

"What about her?"

"She asked if I still had any feelings for her."

"And…" Teddy wanted to know the answer to that, too.

"You're not jealous, are you?" He smiled at her and took her hand.

Teddy understood he was teasing, and she *was* jealous. But she couldn't tell him that. "Of course I'm not jealous." She paused, both hands cradling her glass. "We already discussed this and resolved it. I don't think your mother was really interested in Veronica," Teddy said.

"You weren't even in there. How could you know?" Adam asked.

"She was probing you for information about us." The look on his face told her she'd hit the mark. "What did you tell her?"

"That I was in love with you and planning to ask you to marry me."

Teddy laughed. "Sure you did."

"You don't believe me?"

"If you'd told her that, she'd have come out of that kitchen singing your praises." She stopped him from responding by going on. "I know because it's what my mother would do."

Behind her, Teddy heard a commotion. Her mother was making a beeline for her. Teddy stiffened, understanding that something was about to happen. Teddy glanced at Adam. "You didn't," she said.

"Teddy, is it true? Why didn't you tell me?" her mother said. She was excited, her color heightened and a smile on her face like George Bailey's when he realized it really was a wonderful life. "I should have been the first to know."

"What?" Teddy asked. She felt Adam's hand tighten on hers. She looked at him, but his eyes were piercing his mother's as if she had also betrayed him.

Teddy's mother looked at Adam. "I believe Adam has something to ask you."

Teddy swung her gaze from Adam to her mother. She saw his face fall.

"Mom, I asked you—"

"I'm sorry, Adam. I didn't think Gemma would rush over and spill the beans."

"I don't understand," Teddy said, but apprehension gripped her.

"Go on, Adam," his mom prompted. "The cat's out of the bag now."

Teddy looked at the room. The television commentator continued his play-by-play. The field of bulked up men scrambled and ran for a goal line, but no one in the household watched them. All eyes were trained on her and Adam.

Adam curled his hand in hers. "This isn't how I pictured it," he told her. "I thought we'd have a romantic evening and then I'd ask you."

"Ask me?" There was a warning underlying Teddy's

question. He couldn't be about to do what she thought he would do. This was not part of the plan.

"Will you marry me?"

Collectively, the room held its breath. Teddy held hers, too. Her hands went ice-cold. Adam felt it, but he didn't take his gaze away from her. She had to answer. She couldn't wait too long or her mother would begin to worry or she'd answer for her.

Teddy looked at him. An unexpected film of mist blurred her eyes. "Yes," she said.

The breaths were exhaled.

Adam got up and pulled her into his arms. He kissed her. And then hugged her to him.

"You are so going to pay for this," Teddy whispered into his neck.

Adam held on to Teddy. He didn't want to push her back. However, this time it wasn't because he loved holding her. He didn't want to see the look in her eyes. She had tears in them and while the others would interpret them as those of a blushing bride, Adam knew they weren't happy tears. He'd just been forced into a corner, behind a web of lies that was tightening with every day and every step they took.

Pandemonium broke out. Teddy was pulled away from Adam and hugged by her mother, then her brother and sisters in turn. Adam's mother and his family followed. Everyone was congratulating them.

The wine was exchanged for champagne, and toasts to the happy couple were shared. Adam kept track of

Teddy. He wanted to get to her and explain, but something or someone stopped him.

"This is great, Adam," Quinn said. "Now Galen and I will be released from the pressure chamber." He laughed and slapped his brother on the back. "Seriously, though, I like Teddy. I'm sure the two of you will be happy."

"When are you going to get the ring?" Adam's mother asked.

"I have an idea." Teddy's mom cut in. "I have to return that painting to the gallery in New York. Why don't we go up there next week? I can return the painting and get the right one. You two can go pick out a ring and we can all have lunch at The Gaslight."

"No," Teddy said. Her voice was a little more emphatic than Adam knew she'd expected it to be.

The two mothers stared at her.

"I'm sorry," she apologized. "This has been a little overwhelming. Adam and I need a little time to discuss things." She reached for Adam's hand and he immediately took it and pulled her into his side.

"Of course," her mother said. She came forward and hugged Teddy again. "We can talk about this later."

Gemma Granville turned back to Adam's mom. With all the excitement of a bride herself, she said, "Ann, we're going to have a wedding in the family." The two women hugged and jumped up and down like children.

Adam closed his eyes and wondered how this had gotten so out of control.

* * *

Snow! The white puffy flakes should have surprised Teddy when they left Adam's parents' house and headed back to Princeton, but she was in no mood to care about the weather. Her life was falling apart. Both families were still celebrating, hugging them, waving goodbye, wishing them well as if they had already married and were off for their honeymoon.

Teddy's parents and three siblings were staying with her. She knew they had taken a turn about the house looking for evidence that she and Adam were living together or at least leaving clothing and various grooming items around.

While Adam had spent the night several times, he'd left nothing behind, no toothbrush in the bathroom, no forgotten clothing in the closet or drawers. If he had, Teddy would have found and returned them before her family descended. She'd given the place a good cleaning. Although neither her mother nor any of her siblings were white-glove people, Teddy always cleaned like a mad woman when they were planning to stay over. Now she wouldn't be going back there tonight. She and Adam had a lot to talk about, if she could even begin to talk.

"What were you thinking?" Teddy attacked him the moment they were in the car. "This was not part of the plan. We never talked about getting engaged, never discussed an engagement. This…this sham is supposed to be over by Christmas. Now what are we going to do?"

Adam glanced at her and sighed heavily, but he said nothing. In fact, the two of them remained quiet for the duration of the twenty-minute ride. When he made the turn that led to her house, Teddy spoke. "Don't take me home," she said. "I'm not going there tonight."

Adam turned the car around and headed for his house.

"My entire family is staying with me. There's no telling what I'll admit if I have to continually be hugged and congratulated," Teddy said. "And believe me they will want every detail that a newly engaged person should know."

"I apologize," Adam said as they walked into his house. He turned the light on in the living room and Teddy went in.

Nothing about their situation was black-and-white. There were too many shades of gray, too many shadows that hadn't been lighted.

Teddy sat down heavily. Adam came to her and sat facing her on the sofa table. He took her hands.

"I'm sorry," he apologized again. "I never told my mother we were engaged."

"Then where did she get the idea?"

"We were talking about Veronica like I told you. Remember where we were when you and Diana met us that day?"

Teddy thought a moment, wondering how that could matter. "It was on Nassau Street near the sandwich shop."

"We were standing in front of Varrick's Jewelry."

Teddy frowned. "So?"

"Veronica told my mother I was looking at wedding

rings. She jumped to conclusions. Then everything got out of hand."

"What are we going to do now?" Teddy asked. "An engagement wasn't part of the deal."

"It doesn't change anything. We know we're not really engaged."

"Adam, it changes everything," Teddy said in frustration. "Don't you see? Our parents are so happy. We made them happy with this…" she faltered "…with this false engagement. It's going to break their hearts when we split. If we'd just been going out together, even exclusively, the split doesn't have the same impact. But someone you're engaged to, someone you pledge your heart to enough to want to walk down the aisle with, that's a completely different level."

"Well, if we don't make a big deal of it, they can't. And they aren't with us every day, so they won't really be involved."

"Didn't you hear my mother as we left tonight? She wants me to email her a photo of the ring as soon as I get one."

"We can do that."

"Adam, we're not getting a ring."

Teddy was working herself into a frenzy. She wished this episode was over. She wished she'd never agreed to this plan. Christmas couldn't come fast enough for her.

Adam moved from the table to the sofa. He hugged her close. Teddy leaned against him, turning her face into his shoulder. His arms hugged her tighter. Teddy's head was pounding. She closed her eyes and tried to relax, tried to let the events of the day float away as if they had the substance of dreams. But she knew they didn't. They were as anchored to the earth as the Empire State Building.

"We can stick to the original plan," Adam whispered above her head.

"We didn't account for things well enough," she said. Her voice was low and sleepy. "From the very beginning we didn't have all the information we needed."

"What was that?" Adam asked.

"Our mothers already knew each other."

"They belong to the same sorority," Adam said.

"It's more than that." Teddy pulled back, out of his embrace. She slipped her feet out of her five-inch heels and tucked them up on the sofa. Hugging her knees she looked at him. God, he was gorgeous. "Things got too complicated. It seemed like a simple plan. That was the problem. It was *too* simple. We didn't think about the after."

"After?" Adam questioned.

"After we broke up. After we told our parents that we were no longer a couple. We didn't consider their feelings. Who knew the families would get together, that they would bond so quickly or at all. After ten minutes it was like they'd known and *liked* each other since childhood. But now, when we part..." She stopped, not wanting to think about that, but also not wanting Adam to know the kind of effect he had on her. "When we part, it's going to cause a rift."

"I can't dispute that." He paused, then stared at Teddy for so long she felt scrutinized, felt he was trying to commit everything about her to memory. Maybe he was thinking of the time when they wouldn't be constantly together. Teddy admitted she enjoyed being with him. Thinking of not seeing him again was like cutting off her arm. Hugging her knees tighter, Teddy made sure her arm was still intact.

"I have another plan," Adam said.

Teddy tensed. She looked at him with hard eyes. "Need I remind you that the first plan was your idea? Look where that's gotten us."

"It has you sitting in my living room with your shoes off and your feet up, looking every bit the confident woman you are. We'll get through this," he continued. "I promise."

Teddy hoped he could keep that promise. Skepticism must have been on her face, because Adam renewed his promise.

"Come here," he said.

She lowered her feet to the floor and went into his open arms. Teddy felt safe there. She felt as if he could make everything all right. That he could keep his promise.

"What will your parents think if you don't come home tonight?"

Teddy sat up straight. "Oh," she said, her hand going to her breasts. "I never asked if I could spend the night. I don't want to presume."

Adam stopped her. "You can spend the night."

"I'm sure my parents will be okay with this. They might even expect it. After all, we were engaged tonight."

"That's very progressive of them."

Teddy laughed against his chest.

"What?" he asked.

"It's not that they're progressive. You're the one who's old-fashioned."

"I am not." After a second, he added, "Why would you think that?"

"My parents lived together for three years before they got married. I'm sure in that time, they had sex and slept in the same bed."

"Ah, but did their parents know?"

She smiled. "I don't think they ever actually walked in on them, but pre–cell phones and pre-email and pre–caller ID, I'm sure one of them answered the phone when the other parent called. And barring all that, Thanksgiving dinner would be a clear giveaway when family comes to stay and finds toothbrushes, shoes and clothes hanging in the closet that don't belong to their child."

"We don't have any of that," he said.

She looked up at him. "No," she said, her voice conveying her feelings. "We don't."

Adam bent down and kissed her. Teddy should be used to him touching her tenderly. She should also be used to knowing that he could unleash an animal so ferocious it devastated her. That's what he was doing now. His mouth changed. His lips tantalized, promised, worked magic on her. Teddy could feel the prickly electricity that accompanied his touch.

His hands moved over her, skimming over her arms and finding the zipper at the back of her dress. He didn't immediately pull it down. His hands played over the fabric as his mouth sought and found the skin of her neck. Teddy gasped at the sensation that pulsed through her at his touch.

Her inner body responded, becoming aroused by the movement of his hands. They captured her curves, running down her body as if it was his and he needed to learn each indentation, every soft contour of the skin that covered her. Skin that was burning with anticipation. Fire burst inside her.

Teddy grew bold. Her hands touched Adam. He was covered. His shirt long-sleeved. His pants over long legs. Teddy began a crusade to remove them. Reaching for the first button, she slid it through its hole. One by one, she released them, freeing the shirt and exposing his chest. Her hands went inside it finger by finger. Skimming them over the skin, she felt the moisture the building heat was rendering. Bowing her head, Teddy pressed her lips to his nipple. It was hot, searing hot. Her tongue came out and she tasted him. He groaned, both holding her and pushing her back. Then, in an immeasurable amount of time, Adam's hands caught her head and pulled her mouth to his.

His tongue slipped inside, joining her, mating with her, sweeping deep into her mouth and holding her until breath demanded they part.

"I need you," he said, his voice so deep Teddy could only understand it because she had entered the same private world where the language was known by only the two of them.

"I know," she said. "I need you, too."

Pinning her to the sofa, Adam stretched out over

her. His body moved over her, working her dress up to her knees and then higher. His mouth devoured hers. Hands raked her sides, slid down her breasts. His mouth moved to her neck and her shoulders. The clothes were too much of a barrier. Teddy needed to, had to, get rid of them.

"Now," she said.

Adam reached under her dress and removed her stockings and panties. In a flash of speed, he stood, pulling her up. Her zipper was dispensed with, and her dress dropped to the floor. Teddy pushed the shirt over his shoulders and down his arms. It fell away. In the half light, she looked at his form. Her hands sculpted him, created him. First bones, then muscle, sinew, skin. Pouring on the color of dark brandy, she painted his arms, his shoulders, his belly. She angled into his tight waist and followed over the curves of his hips and butt until she reached his strong legs and feet. Then she circled his erection. Not an inch of his frame had been left to chance. She caressed him, covered all of him.

His body was hard and ready. She ran her hands over him, feeling the throb of blood that rushed to her hands. His hands tightened on her, squeezed her back as desire stormed through him. His mouth opened and his hands moved like speed demons over her flesh. The heat generated called for second-degree burns.

Together they fell from the sofa to the soft carpet. Adam pushed the coffee table aside and quickly they removed the last of their clothing. Like the opposite poles of a magnet, they snapped-moved together, returning to the positions they had before. Adam pulled a condom from his pants pocket and quickly covered himself. Then he reached for her. His massive body covered her as his erection penetrated her.

"Sweet," Teddy moaned, holding the word for an interminable amount of time. It was the sweetest feeling, the entry point. The center of her being and Adam had found it. He pushed into her until there was no more of him to give. Then he started the race. It was slow and easy, belying the pulsating rapture that it created. Blood raced through her at a pace equal to the sensations rioting within her.

Linking her fingers to his, Adam stretched them over her head. He dragged her upward, pulling her with him as they reached the limit of their horizontal height. He thrust into her, hard and fast. Like a drum, the rhythmic sound of percussion set them off. Teddy heard it in her head. Connecting with the beat, she worked with it, allowed it to lead her, fill her. She worked with the sound, keeping time with it. As the sound roared and the tempo increased, she exerted a greater effort. It was faster and faster, as if some insane drummer was setting the pace. Inside her the world was erupting. Bright rivers of passion pushed her on, egged her forward and upward, taking her to heights previously unreachable.

Hunger led her, forced her to go one more round, then another until she was unable to stop the shattering rhythm they'd set. Teddy thrashed and writhed under Adam, her body working at a demonic pace. Sounds ripped from her as she grunted with each fierce shock wave that seduced her body. The beast was within her, taking over. It was huge, hungry, with an undeniable need. It wanted more. It wanted it all. She wanted it all.

The explosion came. Her voice joined Adam's in an all-consuming cry of release. They collapsed on each other. The sound of ragged breath filled the room. Neither tried to be quiet. They needed air and each dragged it into their lungs as if they'd been on a planet without oxygen and had quickly returned to the earth.

Adam still lay on Teddy. Both were soaking wet. Both were still trying to get their breath to return to normal. Teddy felt the coolness of the room's air. The fiery equator of heat was subsiding. Adam shifted off her, a low groan escaping him.

"Each time," he began, needing to take a breath between each syllable, "each time we're together, I don't think it can get any better. And then it does."

Chapter 8

Adam now had clothes at Teddy's house. She couldn't leave his house wearing the dress she'd had on for Thanksgiving. She wore a pair of his shorts and a T-shirt with Invest Now written across the front. Teddy didn't know what time her family got in, but when she quietly opened the door just after sunrise, the house was still quiet.

She went to her room and quickly changed into jeans and a sweater. After her morning ritual of brushing her teeth and cleaning her face, she made sense of her hair and went to the kitchen to begin breakfast. No one showed up for another hour. Teddy was on her second cup of coffee by then and knew today would be at least a three—if not four—cup day.

"You're up early," her father said, coming into the kitchen."

"Breakfast?" she asked.

"That bacon sure smells good," he said.

"You can have one slice," Teddy told him. "Mom said so."

"I guess she's been giving orders already."

"You know Mom," Teddy teased.

Teddy made breakfast and one by one her family showed up.

"Did you enjoy the party yesterday?" her father asked. He was right in the middle of things, but pretended like the party was news to him.

"I had a wonderful time," Sienna said.

"Planning to see Galen again?" Teddy asked. She was teasing her sister, hoping they wouldn't get into any discussion about Adam and her. And the wicked engagement blunder that had set off a hailstorm of fear within her.

"Not sure," Sienna said. "But I'm sure Mother will let you know."

Conversation at the table reviewed the uneventful events of Thanksgiving. But then Gemma Granville came to the table and the dynamics changed.

"I'll fix you a plate," Teddy told her mom.

"It's all right, I can get it."

The room was full of happy voices. Teddy's mom took a place and made her own breakfast. They sat around the table for nearly an hour.

"I have to go or I'm going to miss my plane," Sienna said.

Traveling activity filled the house with each of her siblings getting their suitcases and travel bags.

"What time is your flight?" Teddy asked Sienna.

"I have a ride," she said.

"With who?" Teddy asked.

Sienna only smiled. "He'll be here soon and I need to go put my makeup on."

Sienna didn't need any makeup and rarely wore much. Teddy was in no doubt that Galen would be arriving to pick her up.

As it turned out, Teddy didn't have to take anyone to the airport or train station. Apparently, they'd all made arrangements for themselves. She waved good-bye and hugged her sisters and brother as they climbed into a car that Galen Sullivan was driving and headed to the airport.

Forty minutes later, her parents were climbing into their SUV for the trip home.

"Mom, did I hear you say the painting was wrong?"

Gemma Granville nodded. "You didn't look at it?"

"When he brought it out, it was already packaged and ready to go. Not that I would know it wasn't the right one anyway. You never told me what it was a picture of."

"I'm sorry, but don't worry about it. I've made arrangements to go to the city and do some Christmas shopping. I'll return it and get the right one."

Teddy thought she was going to get away without a discussion related to the engagement, but she should have realized that was a fool's logic.

"Have you and Adam thought about a wedding date?" her mother asked from her seat in the SUV.

"We only got engaged less than twelve hours ago."

"June is a good month," her mother said as if Teddy had given her a date.

"You realize it takes a year to plan a wedding. June is an extremely popular month. We could be talking about a year from June."

"You're in the business, Teddy. I'm sure you won't have to wait that long. Call in some favors." Her mother waved away her argument as if it meant nothing. "I'll tell you what. I'll come up in a couple of weeks and we'll begin planning it."

"Mom, I have four weddings this month. I won't have time for another one. Why don't we make it after Christmas?"

Teddy knew the entire business would be over before any planning was necessary.

Her mother looked as if she was thinking this over. "I suppose that would be better," she agreed. "I'll just book the church and the reception. Think I can do that with a couple of phone calls."

"Don't, please." There was pleading in Teddy's voice. "Adam and I need to discuss it first. Then I promise, we'll give you a date and you can go crazy with details."

That seemed to placate her. Her smile was huge. She reached through the window and gave Teddy a tight hug.

"Bye, dear."

"Bye." Teddy waved to her father and he backed down the driveway.

She should be angry with Adam for putting her in this predicament, but she couldn't. She remembered last night. And if an engagement could result in that, they should get engaged more often.

Teddy loved her family, but she was so glad to see them go. Her mother and sisters extracted a promise from her to send them photos of the engagement ring as soon as she got it.

By Monday, Teddy had spent two days washing sheets, towels, clearing away dishes and restoring her home to the place where she lived. The city was in full shopping mode. Roads were constantly clogged with drivers in pursuit of Christmas bargains. Getting anywhere on time was purely coincidental.

It was also a busy time for Weddings by Diana. Teddy had four weddings in December. And there was the annual winter fashion show that the office sponsored. In the beginning, she and Diana established two shows a year to bring in business. The two had morphed into huge events with SRO attendance and sales to match.

The van was packed and ready for her and Diana. Renee and several other associates left yesterday to get everything set up and ready. Only two people would remain in the office and Teddy should also be gone, but she was still in her office going over the final details, searching for a particular veil that Renee had called and asked her to bring.

"Have we got everything?" Diana asked, coming in. She was holding a dress bag needed for the fashion show.

"I thought everything was in the van." Teddy indicated the bag.

"This is a surprise," Diana said. Then noticing Teddy fumbling through things, she asked, "What are you looking for?"

"The clover veil." Teddy pulled a drawer opened and shuffled the contents aside. Then she closed it and looked in another drawer. It wasn't there, either. Leaving her office, she went to search Renee's. She found the veil in the third drawer, already in a box with a label on it. She returned to her office.

"The keys," she said to herself. "Where did I put the keys?"

"I'll drive," Diana said, lifting them from beneath a pile of fabric samples. "You appear to be in no condition."

Teddy wasn't. She didn't argue with her partner. "I'm sorry. I just have a lot of details on my mind." She knew Diana had seen her stressed before, but not this stressed. It wasn't the work. It was Adam and their engagement. How could she go and fall in love with him? How could she fake the engagement?

The two headed outside and climbed into the SUV bearing the logo for Weddings by Diana. Diana put the vehicle in gear and drove out of the driveway. The fashion show was taking place in New Brunswick, less than an hour away if traffic didn't slow them down. Neither woman said a word until Diana pulled onto

Route 27 and headed north. At this hour the interstates would take a long time to reach and be packed when they got to them.

"Teddy, you're obviously tense. What happened? You said Thanksgiving went well, but I'm thinking that wasn't how it actually turned out."

Teddy leaned her head back and closed her eyes for a moment. "Adam asked me to marry him."

"What!" Diana took a long glance at her.

"In front of everyone. My sisters and brother. His brothers. Both sets of parents. I couldn't say no. My mother and his mother stood in front of us practically panting for me to accept the proposal. I thought they were going to hug and jump up and down like happy children when I said yes." She glanced at Diana. "Then they did just that."

"You said yes?" Diana nearly screamed.

Teddy nodded. "There was nothing else I could do."

"Teddy, I thought this was a temporary arrangement."

"It is," Teddy said, but she wasn't sure anymore.

Diana lowered her voice. It was compassionate. She understood part of what Teddy was feeling. "What happens now?"

"I don't know. We haven't figured that out yet."

"When was the last time you talked to Adam?"

"Friday morning." It was when she left his bed, but she kept that tidbit of information to herself.

The phone rang and Teddy automatically punched the media button on the Bluetooth phone then spoke into the air. She listened for a few seconds. "You're kidding?" she said.

More time passed. Teddy listened again. Diana watched anxiously.

"What about Grace?" Teddy asked whoever was on the other end of the line.

"Never mind. I'll handle it when I get there."

Irritated, she hung the phone up.

"What's wrong," Diana asked.

"Brianna caught a cold. She won't be able to model. And Renee has no substitutes for her."

Diana looked at the dress bag. "She has a lot of outfits."

"And they're already at the hall. Renee said they tried to find a replacement, but no one is available." Teddy put a hand to her temples and squeezed. She'd had a headache since Thanksgiving. It didn't help that this show was adding to her stress, and now she had no one to model a huge collection of gowns.

"You and Brianna are the same size. And you were one of the first models—"

"No," Teddy said.

"We have to have someone model the gowns. She's got some of the best of your creations and the back-stage dressing and getting ready will be totally off if someone doesn't fill in."

"Can anything else go wrong today?" Teddy asked rhetorically.

Diana looked at her and smiled. "Adam could show up."

* * *

The snow didn't last long. The temperature climbed into the mid-fifties melting all vestiges of it away two days after Thanksgiving. By the day of the fashion show, the township was shades of winter gray and brown, but the holiday lights swinging from every streetlight and lamp pole gave the place a festive look.

"What are we doing here?" Quinn asked Adam. The two men had gotten out of Adam's car and headed for the door. Quinn saw the sign announcing the fashion show. "I get it. Teddy must be here."

"She is."

"Can't the two of you be without the other for a few hours."

"We can, but why should we?"

"You know this place will be full of women?"

"When did that ever bother you?" Adam asked.

"When they are already engaged."

The two men went inside. Not only was there to be a fashion show, but a trade show was also in progress. Everything anyone could want or need for a wedding was on display. Adam and Quinn passed china, cookware, photographers, invitations, florists, bakeries and jewelers. Even Realtors, furniture stores and design firms were represented.

Quinn stopped him in front of one display. Adam looked down. Trays of engagement rings gleamed brilliantly against a black velvet background.

"How about that one?" Quinn pointed to a platinum setting with a large stone perched on top of it. It appeared to be floating in the sea of black.

"I've been told to never buy an engagement ring without the bride's approval."

"Who said that?"

"I did."

Both turned to find Veronica standing there.

"The last time we met, you were standing in front of a jeweler," she told Adam. "Hello, Quinn."

"Veronica, this is a surprise. What are you doing here?" Quinn asked.

She laughed. "Obviously you've never been to one of these shows."

"Guilty," he said.

"Newlyweds want newness in their lives. They are into decorating. Anything from an apartment to a mansion is open to change. And I'm a decorator." In her hand was a stack of business cards and flyers. "Our booth is over there." She pointed to the end of the row. "The other financial managers are at the end of that row next to the wedding gowns and tuxedo groups. You guys got the best location. Everyone goes for the gowns."

"Financial managers?" Adam questioned.

"Isn't that why you're here?" She raised her perfectly arched eyebrows. "People are looking at their long-term financial goals earlier and earlier." She swung her gaze between the two men. "You mean you're not here to gain potential clients?"

"We're here for the fashion show," Adam said.

"I hope you have tickets."

"Tickets?" Quinn said.

Veronica laughed. "You guys are so out of your element."

Renee was equipped with pins, buttons, tape measure, needle and thread, and extras of everything. She had to take over for Teddy, who had to take over for their model Brianna.

"You look stunning," Renee told Teddy, who stepped back and admired the wedding gown she was wearing.

Teddy took a long breath. She wasn't afraid of the runway. She'd been on plenty of runways, although not in the past few years. The mirror in front of her reflected her image. Teddy tried to smile at the tall, thin woman who'd been her right hand for the past three years.

"Renee, you've seen hundreds of brides."

"I've never seen you in a gown, only that one picture that used to hang in your office at the other location."

That photo had been of Teddy in the gown she'd modeled for Diana and sold right off her back. Every now and then she wondered about the woman who bought it and if she was still happily married.

"How much time do we have?" Teddy asked, slipping a ring on her finger. It was a faux diamond engagement ring similar to the ones the other models wore.

"About ten minutes. Practically all the seats are taken. If we can get through the chaos back here, the show should go fine."

It was always chaotic behind the scenes of the fashion show, but every year it turned out fine. Teddy clung to that thought. Diana would act as emcee as she always did.

Teddy saw Diana coming. She was walking fast and her face showed the stress Teddy felt. Something else had obviously gone wrong.

"I'm going to check the stage one more time," Renee said. There was a full crew taking care of it, but Renee was a detail person and she would make sure everything was fine before she returned to be the dresser for Teddy and three other models.

"Ready?" Teddy asked Diana.

"I need the train pulled up," she said.

Diana turned around. Teddy found the loop in the middle of the train and pulled it up to the third button on the back. She looped it twice to secure it.

"There," Teddy said.

"Now I can turn around without tripping or kicking the dress."

Teddy knew she was teasing. The dress was one of Teddy's designs. It was a new one. Diana always wore a new design for the show.

"Time to start," Diana said.

Teddy turned for one last check in the mirror. She was the third gown out.

"There's one more thing I think you should know," Diana said.

"What's that?" This was the real reason her friend had come over.

"Remember on the drive here, when you asked if anything else could go wrong today?"

Teddy nodded. Her breath suddenly died, and then she was heaving for air.

"He's in the audience. Last row on the right."

Teddy stepped onto the runway. Bright lights blinded her, but she didn't squint and didn't look to the last row on the right. With a smile on her face, she concentrated on Diana's voice as she described the gown. Teddy pivoted and turned on cue at the end of the extrawide runway. Using her hand, she swirled the train up and around to the unexpected gasp of appreciation from the audience.

She displayed the dress for about a minute before she headed to the back and exited through the curtain that raised as she approached it. Teddy went left. The next model entered from the right.

Teddy exhaled with a hand on her breasts as her knees grew weak. Adam was indeed in the house. Renee rushed over to help her down the three steps and into the dressing area.

"What's he doing here?" she muttered to herself.

While she hadn't looked directly at him, Teddy noticed Adam and his brother. She wasn't sure if it was Quinn or Galen.

Renee immediately started releasing the buttons on the gown and getting the next dress she was to model.

"Do we have any financial investment companies in the trade show?" Teddy asked.

"We have some financial planners from big firms. So yes."

That must be why he was here, Teddy thought. But why didn't he tell her he was coming?

She stepped out of the gown and someone whisked it away to rehang it in the numbered bag that corresponded to its order number. Teddy stepped into the next gown and Renee zipped and buttoned her in. Another associate wrapped the veil around the crown of her head. Teddy could have been a robot. She raised her arms when told, lifted her feet and stepped into shoes, bowed her head for veils, and closed her eyes or opened them for makeup. Her mind wasn't on dressing.

It was on Adam.

Adam was president of his investment firm. Someone else could be in charge of sales and not mentioned this particular trade show. Or not mentioned it by name. She looked for excuses for him, for a reason he'd be here.

And Thanksgiving, that disastrous day, had provided such an unexpected turn of events that thinking about a trade show couldn't have been on the top of his mind.

Twelve other models had gone up the steps and back in the time it took for Teddy to change. She went to the edge of the curtain and waited. Then she moved into the center space. Her train was adjusted so it would drag behind her in a perfectly straight line. Her veil covered her face giving her a small sense of invisibility and allowing her to look in Adam's direction.

The curtain rose. She stood there a second. The audience applauded. Teddy stole a glance at Adam. His smile had her heart lurching. Clinging more tightly to the fresh flowers in her hands and mentally counted the steps she went through before returning to the dressing room.

"Teddy, don't crush the flowers," Renee admonished as she took the bouquet. "We want to use them more than once."

Teddy hadn't noticed the flowers. They were donated by one of the florists participating in the trade show. Looking at them, she was surprised to see the mangled stems. Renee took a towel and cleaned her hands of the green stains.

Teddy followed the routine four more times, careful to keep from destroying the bouquets. She checked Adam's position each time and never once did he move. She wondered if something had happened. Was he waiting for her to be free to tell her something, like maybe he'd confessed their deception to his parents? Or he'd taken one of his brothers in confidence and they spilled the beans? One unwelcome scenario after another ran through her mind.

Her cell phone was on silent and carefully tucked away in her purse. She wondered if there was a message from her mother. She wondered if Veronica, whom she'd seen immediately after entering the building, had somehow lured Adam here. Telling herself she was being paranoid, Teddy concentrated on not tripping over her feet.

"Last one," Renee said, breaking into her thoughts as she placed the last gown over her head. "After this there's the finale."

The words should have made her feel better. The

show was coming to an end, but Teddy knew when it was over, there might be bad news on the other end.

"Teddy?" Renee called to her.

Teddy was standing in front of a three-way mirror that had been brought in for the models. She looked at Renee. The other woman looked confused.

"What is it?" Teddy asked.

Renee had swept Teddy's hair to the side and anchored it with an S-shaped rhinestone clip that had veil netting attached to it. The veil didn't cover her face, but hung down the side of her head balancing the asymmetrical shape of the dress bodice.

Teddy adjusted the veil.

"You're very distracted today," Renee said. "Is everything all right? Diana told me to keep this one as a surprise for you. That you'd love it. But you barely looked at it."

Teddy looked down and screamed, her hands going to her mouth and cutting off the sound.

"I don't understand," Teddy said. "Where did she find this?"

"Is it all right?" Concern entered Renee's voice. "What's wrong?"

"Nothing, nothing." Teddy lowered her voice to a calming level. She placed her hand on Renee's arm to assure her. "I just wasn't expecting this."

"What is it?"

"The first wedding gown I ever designed and sold." Teddy turned all the way around, looking at the way the dress moved. She took a few dance steps. When she'd conceived the idea, she'd wanted to make sure the bride's grown swayed like those of a professional dancer. She stopped and looked at herself again. It was perfect.

"This is the one from the picture," Renee said. "I almost didn't recognize it. It's so much prettier in person."

"Where did Diana find this?"

"She didn't say. Only that it was a surprise." Renee straightened one side and admired Teddy in the glass. "It's beautiful. When I get married, I want one of your designs."

"It'll be my present to you." Teddy smiled and squeezed Renee's shoulder.

Renee beamed, then continued her duties. "Time to get you on stage."

Teddy went through the curtain. A chorus of oohs and ahhs came from the audience, and then a long moment of applause. Teddy glanced at Diana with a smile on her face. In the audience she saw the owner of the gown who gave her a thumbs-up signal.

Teddy began the final walk, holding her head a little higher. This time her smile wasn't plastered on her face. It was genuine. Her groom, in this case it was Diana's husband, Scott, who'd been commandeered to play one of the male models, offered his arm and escorted her down the aisle. After she finished showing the gown, he took her to her final place in front of the chapel setting that had been erected for the finale.

She felt good in the dress. This is the way she wanted to feel on her wedding day, dressed in a gown of her own design and heading for the man she loved. Her eyes went directly to Adam when that thought came. Again he smiled at her and Teddy's insides did a meltdown. Scott gripped her arm tighter and she steadied. The other models finished their routines and at the end they stood as a fifteen-bride wedding party, each woman with her groom. Teddy imagined the picture they presented.

As each of the models took her place in the finale line ending her presentation, thunderous applause erupted in the hall. The brides remained as they were, everyone smiling. Teddy knew they were relieved that the show was over, but also proud that it had gone over without too many glitches, all of which were backstage. The hired photographer and many of the guests took pictures.

Adam and his brother—she now recognized him as Quinn—came forward, each with a cell phone snapping photo after photo. Teddy wanted to leave, but she was trapped until the last camera flashed and the last question was answered. Adam didn't ask any questions. He stood with his arms crossed and watched and waited.

Why wasn't he at his station, talking to people about investing in their future? Why was he remaining in the background, like a suitor waiting for his bride? They both knew that despite his actions on Thanksgiving, the two were not engaged and not likely to be.

Traditionally, when the show ended, the models kept the finale gown on as they mingled with the crowds, allowing the crowd to see the designs and imagine how they would look in the dress. There was an information and order desk with forms, business cards and brochures about the wedding planning services. Brides could also make appointments for fittings or consultant services.

Normally Teddy and Diana would remain at the desk after the show while the consultants packed everything up. Today, both worked the room, leaving the job to two other consultants who'd volunteered for the duty.

As the models left the stage, Adam came forward and took Teddy's hand. His brother was behind him.

"You look beautiful," Adam whispered. He pulled her into his arms and kissed her on the cheek. Teddy was nervous. Why, she didn't know. When he pushed back, his hand went down her arm and lifted her hand. The faux diamond ring gleamed there. His eyes came to hers and she saw the question in them.

"We all wear rings," she explained. "After all, the bride is engaged." Teddy regretted the words as soon as they fell.

Quinn excused himself to look at the trade show. "He's really going to look at the models," Adam said when he was gone. "Are they all engaged?"

"A couple. The others are mainly models we hired for the day."

"Why are you modeling?"

"One of the models is ill. We're the same size. I stood in because she had some of the newest gowns and without them there would have been a large hole in the presentation." She paused for a moment. "And Diana talked me into it."

He nodded and dropped her hand.

Teddy felt a coldness settle in when he was no longer connected to her. "Shouldn't you be at your booth, talking to prospective clients?"

"We don't have a booth here. But if I'd known there would be this many people interested in investments, I'd have passed the idea on to Marketing."

Her brows rose. "If you're not here on business, why *are* you here?"

"We haven't talked since Thanksgiving," he said. "And that day didn't turn out the way we expected. I wanted to make sure you were all right."

"So you came here." Teddy spread her hands.

"So I came here," he said. "To this female dominated den where people are talking about crystal, lace and honeymoon destinations."

The crowd around them pressed closer, forcing them to step closer to each other. Teddy could smell Adam's cologne. The heady scent reminded her of when their bodies were separated by nothing but sexual desire.

Her heartbeat increased. She was jostled from behind, pushing her into Adam's arms. Even without the push she was already about to hug him.

"I know we're not really engaged," she whispered. "But you coming here, to a place you said you don't want to be, is the most romantic thing anyone has ever done for me."

Adam pushed her back and Teddy knew she was

about to be kissed, but he was stopped by a voice behind them.

"You two make a lovely couple. I can only imagine what your real wedding will be like."

Adam kept his arm around her waist as they turned to see Veronica.

"Congratulations." She glanced at Teddy's hand. "Beautiful ring."

Teddy raised her hand. Both she and Adam stared at the large stone. Neither of them corrected Veronica. She wanted to know what Adam was thinking, what he was feeling. Teddy was the one supposedly engaged to Adam, yet her heart felt as if there was a tear in it. When their camouflage ended, who would Adam seek out? Was he ready to take the risk again? Had Teddy made him see that he could love again?

"Have you set a date yet?" Veronica asked.

"Not yet," Adam said.

"Well, congratulations again." Veronica looked at Teddy as if she'd lost a prize. But Teddy knew *she* was the one who'd lost.

Chapter 9

Teddy flopped on the sofa, tired from the exertion of helping Adam carry a gargantuan pine tree from the garage to his condo.

"Why did you have to park so far from the door?" she asked, out of breath.

"You're not that much out of shape." He turned from leaning the tree against the wall next to the fireplace and looked at her. "You're not out of shape at all."

"Well, I'm used to running and lifting weights, not carrying awkwardly shaped objects that stab my hands and face with needles."

"Remember, this was your idea," Adam reminded her. "And you only carried it from the car."

"I might regret it before this is over."

"I don't think so," he said.

Teddy heard the need in his voice. Earlier she'd commented on the lack of Christmas decorations in his condo. When she was young and all her siblings lived with their parents, they always put their tree up right after Thanksgiving. Teddy asked where he kept them, and she was surprised to learn he had none. It was her idea that they go shopping. Together they bought a tree, a world of colorful bulbs and lights, a garland for the fireplace, and an assortment of ornaments.

Adam put on some Christmas music and Teddy went to the kitchen. She poured two cups of apple cider and warmed them in the microwave. When she got back to the living room, Adam was lighting the fireplace. The condo had all the modern touches and supported a glass-enclosed built-in structure that burned gas and could be lit with a match. It sat high on the wall and produced no smoke and no fumes.

Adam accepted the cup and took a sip. He set it on an end table and attacked the many boxes and bags littering the floor. Finding the tree stand, he worked quickly to set it up. Teddy opened the bags and organized the contents into sections: lights, ornaments, angel for the top, timers, extension cords, tree skirt, garlands and more. Even with organization, the room was strewn with discarded store bags and boxes.

"I think we overbought," Adam said.

Teddy shook her head. She watched as Adam worked. For a long moment she couldn't take her eyes off him. He had his back to her and she was free to stare at him. His arms were strong under the sweater he wore. It filled out his form and Teddy was in no doubt of the muscles it concealed. She wanted them around her.

"There," Adam said. He shook the tree to make sure it was sitting in the stand and held sturdy enough that it wouldn't fall over. He turned to Teddy. "Your turn."

"This is a group effort," she told him. "We decorate together." She handed him a box. "Lights first."

As they moved back and forth and around the tree for the next hour, the decorations quickly disappeared from their boxes, turning the tree into a brightly lit work of art. A garland of pine branches was arranged around the fireplace. The holiday cards he'd stacked on a table were tucked in the garland they hung around the room's entry. Adam moved his cup and interspersed the table with scented candles and several Santa Claus statues. Teddy lit the candles and the fragrance of Christmas cookies permeated the air.

"That's it." Adam stood back and checked their work. Dropping down on the sofa, he checked the boxes still unopened. "We did overbuy."

"We're not finished," Teddy said. Taking his hand, she pulled him up. He came forward, his arms going around her waist as his body came in contact with hers. Teddy looked up as his head swooped down and he kissed her. Teddy wanted to stay in his embrace. She raised her arms and circled his neck. For a long moment the kiss went on. Her knees weakened and she forced herself to push back.

"We need to keep our heads," she said.

"I have my head," he said, kissing her again. "It's your head that I'm working on."

"We have to finish these," she insisted.

"I thought we *were* finished."

Teddy moved back. "This room is done, but there are other rooms."

"We decorate the entire condo?"

"Didn't you ever do this when you were younger?"

"We decorated the family room, where the tree was. In the kitchen, Mom put out some red-and-green dish towels, but that was it."

Teddy picked up a small lighted tree from a box.

"Where is that going?"

"Follow me."

She went into his bedroom.

"I was wondering how I was going to get you in here."

Teddy shot him a warning glance. "Bring the small box with the Kwanzaa kinara," she told him. She set up the tree on a table and plugged it in. The white lights gave the room a soft glow. Adam came up behind her and put his arms around her waist. Kissing her neck, he set the candleholder next to the tree and gathered her close against him.

"Need anything more?" he asked.

"Not a single thing," she said. Sidestepping him, Teddy left the room and finished the decorations. She placed towels in the kitchen as Adam said his mom had done. In the dining room, she placed a red-and-gold runner on the table and set a basket of silver bells in the center. Ten minutes later, she looked around.

"Is everything done now?" Adam asked.

"All except plugging in the lights."

Back in the living room, Teddy turned off the room lights and took a seat. Adam threw the plug-strip switch and the tree lights blinked on.

Adam joined her, his arm along the back of the sofa and resting on her shoulder.

"You're right," he said.

"About what?"

"The decorations. I didn't know how much I missed them. Thanks for today, for shopping and helping me trim it."

Teddy looked up at him. In the subdued light of the tree, he was even more handsome. Her eyes rested on his mouth. Biting her lip, she tried to keep from moving toward him. She put her head on his shoulder, snuggled into his arm and faced the tree.

"It looks so much better than if you'd hired a decorator to do it," she said.

Adam's arm tightened on her shoulder as he helped her settle into his side. "I was thinking the same thing."

"Great minds…" They were a pair, Teddy thought with a smile. If only he felt the way she did. Teddy was quiet for a long time. She and Adam watched the fire and watched the tree. Previous conversations they'd had came to mind. But the Thanksgiving proposal was at the top.

"I have a question," Teddy said. She knew it was an inappropriate time to ask it, but she couldn't keep it in any longer. She was in his arms. She felt safe and warm and wanted to stay there, but she had to know.

"Shoot," Adam said.

"Remember when we had the conversation about meeting someone? Finding your one and only?"

She felt the arm about her stiffen. His entire body did the same, although she knew he was trying to control it. They were too close, too connected to each other.

"You've found someone?" His question was stated as distinct words, each one given equal weight, as if they needed to struggle to reach an audible sound.

"Not me," Teddy said. "I thought, since you ran into Veronica, you might have second thoughts about us." The impact of the word *us* hit her. It sounded as if they were a real couple and this was a defining moment in their relationship. She rushed on. "About what we're doing."

Adam put his hand under her chin and lifted it until she was looking in his eyes. "She's not my one and only."

Teddy didn't think she could hold the tears back, so she closed her eyes. She felt his lips brush hers and it turned into a kiss. Adam's hand combed through the hair above her ear as he kissed her deeply.

Varrick's Jewelry was founded the same year as Princeton University and had maintained its present location as the tiny college town grew to its present size. Teddy wondered how many graduates had crossed the main street in Princeton and bought an engagement ring in all the time the store had existed?

Adam opened the glass doors with gilded handles forming a V. The store housed some of the most beautiful jewelry in the world. Teddy pushed the door closed and stepped aside. She stood in front of one of the windows. Behind the glass was a diamond necklace. A huge stone was set at the center, completely surrounded by rubies. It was beautiful.

Teddy turned away from it. She didn't want Adam to see the awe on her face at beauty so exquisite it took her breath away.

"Adam, why are we here? There's only a few weeks left before we end this charade. I don't need an engagement ring."

"Your mother wants a photo and mine calls me nearly every day and asks if we've got the ring and have we set the date."

"I can wear that ring I had on at the fashion show. It's hard to tell the difference between that and a real diamond."

Adam frowned. "You don't think our mothers will be able to tell the difference?"

Teddy knew they would. "Not in a photograph and I'm sure I can avoid your mom for three more weeks. I'll be working several weddings in that time and I won't be available for visits."

"And when they show up on your doorstep, unannounced. What will you do then?"

"I'll think of something," Teddy told him. She knew it could happen. When her dad spoke at the symposium, that had been impromptu. Her father could have come alone as he often did when he went to speak at colleges. Her mother had come to Princeton to check on her and Adam.

"Why don't we just go in and look," Adam suggested. "We're already here."

That sounded a lot like the first dinner they had together. They ate because they were already at the restaurant. And look where that had led her.

Despite her protests Adam ushered Teddy inside. With all the holiday traffic, entering Varrick's was like finding a sanctuary. There were no crowds rushing past her, no frantic mothers vying for the hot toy of the season.

Teddy followed Adam. He went straight to the counter holding engagement rings as if he'd been there before. Then she remembered he had been married. But he was very young then and his business was new. She doubted he could have afforded a ring from Varrick's.

"Adam, I really don't need a ring." Even as she said it, Teddy looked in the case at the settings being displayed. She held her breath so she wouldn't gush over what she saw. "I'm sure we can tell our parents that we want to find the right one before committing. Or that you're planning to give it to me on Christmas. Since this will be over by then, we shouldn't go through buying one."

"If we don't choose a ring, they'll probably choose one for us, and tell us it's a wedding present. Like I said, let's just look. If you don't like anything, we can leave."

When they emerged an hour later, Teddy was wearing a square-cut flawless diamond engagement ring. It felt heavy and foreign on her hand. She knew she'd tried to talk Adam out of a ring altogether, but secretly she loved it. Even though their pretense wasn't going to last much longer and there was no reason for her to have a ring, especially one that was over five carats and cost enough to rival half of the inventory at Weddings by Diana. Still, Teddy loved it.

Adam took her hand and looked at the huge stone. "My mother would expect it and I'm sure yours will, too." He could practically read her mind.

Of course he was right. Teddy stared at it in the bright December sun. It was a gorgeous stone. And she liked the way it looked on her hand. It made her fingers appear long and elegant. She was going to be sorry to give it back.

"Why did you ask the jeweler if it could be returned?" Adam asked when they were on the street.

"You don't think I would keep it," she said, amazed that he thought she would. "Although it does look great on my hand." She stretched her fingers open. She'd done it at least fifty times since Adam lifted it and placed it on her finger. It wasn't like the one she'd worn for the fashion show. This was a real diamond. It had significance. It represented two people who wanted to live their lives together.

"Feeling like a bride?" Adam asked.

"I am," she said in surprise.

"Next time our parents show up, you can show them the ring."

"We won't have to wait for that," Teddy said.

Adam opened the door to his car and Teddy got inside.

"Why not?" he asked when he was seated and pulling out of a parking space that another car was waiting to take.

"My mother already called, asking if I'd chosen something and not to forget to send her a photo."

"So she knew you were getting a ring."

"She assumed."

Moments later Adam pulled the car into her driveway. "Looks like you won't need to send a photo," Adam said. "You have guests."

"I don't recognize the car," Teddy said.

"It belongs to *my* mother," Adam said. Stopping next to it, Teddy saw her mother in the passenger seat.

"Mom," she called. Teddy got out of the car and rushed around to greet her. "I thought you were—" Midway to where Gemma Granville stood, Teddy stopped. By the look on her mother's face Teddy knew something was wrong.

Thinking something might have happened to her dad, she rushed forward.

"What's wrong," she asked. "Dad? Is Dad all right?"

"This has nothing to do with your father."

"Sienna, Sierra—"

She put her hand up to stop Teddy from going through the full list of relatives. "Nothing to do with any of them. It's about you."

"And you." Adam's mother leveled her comment to him. The harshness of her words were enough to hold back a flood.

"How could you?" Gemma Granville said, with the slight hitch in her voice.

"How could I what?"

"Fake your engagement?"

The four of them stood in the crisp December air—speechless. Teddy fingered the ring on her finger, feeling like a child caught doing something wrong. Tension around them was like a chill factor, reducing the trust and love that had always been part of their collective lives. Teddy felt numb. How did they know?

"We'd better go inside and discuss this." Adam appeared to remain rational. He took Teddy's elbow and led her toward the door. Their parents followed.

Teddy found her key with some prompting. Adam took it and opened the front door. Warmth hit her as she led the small procession through the foyer and into the living room. The coldness of the outside was gone. She felt hot and tense. They sat facing each other, she and Adam on one side, their parents as accusers on the other.

"How did you find out?" Teddy asked her mother.

"As if that matters," she said. "Gene Restonson told us."

Teddy frowned. "Gene who?"

"The gallery owner in New York. Remember I told you I got the wrong painting? Well, Ann and I returned it today. And while I was telling Gene how romantically Adam proposed to you on Thanksgiving, he told us about you two agreeing to deceive us."

Teddy winced, remembering that conversation. She hadn't thought anyone could hear them. The gallery was empty. But when he brought the painting out, he was right behind her. It was unimportant now. Their parents knew the truth.

"I am so hurt and angry," her mother said. There was that hitch in her voice again. "Why did you two think you needed to lie to us?" She looked at Teddy, then at Adam and back again.

"Mom, we didn't really. You wanted us to like each other...and we do." Teddy glanced at Adam for confirmation. He took her hand in assurance, but it didn't seem to affect the two mothers. They sat across from them in individual chairs. Teddy had the feeling this was a court and she and Adam were on dual witness seats. The problem was they *were* guilty.

"We thought if you believed we were really getting close to each other, that you would stop..." She trailed off, not wanting to make matters worse by telling them to stop meddling.

"Go on," her mother said, raising her chin slightly. "What would we stop?"

"Sending us blind dates, commenting on our single status," Adam said.

"And you were so happy when I told you we were going to continue to see each other," Teddy explained.

"You think I, we—" she used her hand to encompass both Adam's mother and herself "—want you to be married so badly that you needed to fake a relationship?"

Teddy refused to answer. She held her mother's gaze but did not reply to the question.

"And what about that proposal on Thanksgiving?"

Adam's mother asked him. "Were you going to go as far as planning a fake wedding?"

"Of course we weren't," Adam replied. "We were going to break up just before Christmas. You'd be disappointed, but you'd stop with the marriage tests for a while."

"Mom," Teddy hesitated. "I'm sorry. I never meant to hurt you."

"Well, you have. The whole family, in fact. Your sisters were already talking about being bridesmaids. And even though your father never said it, he was glad you'd finally found someone to care for you."

"And I was thinking of finally being the mother of the groom," Ann Sullivan addressed them both. "I thought you'd be over Veronica and Chloe by now and ready to start a new life, but I see I was wrong."

Teddy looked at Adam. "Who's Chloe?" she asked.

Ann Sullivan froze. Teddy noticed her reaction, but the question went unanswered when Teddy's mother spoke.

"Can I take it you two are not in love with each other?" Gemma Granville asked. It took all the courage Teddy had to look at Adam. She didn't know what to say. She wanted him to answer first. She wanted to know why he'd told her about Chelsea and Veronica, even introduced her to the woman, but failed to mention anyone named Chloe.

"We're not," he finally said. His answer was for the two mothers, but his gaze never left Teddy's face.

Teddy felt a dagger plunge into her heart.

* * *

The two mothers looked as if they'd been shocked. Even if they were expecting confirmation, they weren't prepared for it. Dr. Sullivan stood up and Gemma Granville did the same.

"There's to be no wedding?" Gemma said.

Teddy shook her head. Her hands were in her lap. She'd pulled the one Adam was holding away when his eyes told her that his mother's comments were true. She felt the weight of the square-cut diamond on her third finger. She twisted it around so the stone wasn't visible.

"No wedding," Teddy said.

"Well," Dr. Sullivan said on a resigned sigh. "Then I'll be leaving." She turned to Gemma. "I'll see you later."

She went to the door and pulled it open. Adam stood up. "Mom," he called, but she continued walking, going out into the December afternoon. Moments later they heard her car start.

"Teddy, I'll call you later," he said over his shoulder as he, too, headed for the door.

Teddy got up and called him. She followed him into the foyer. At the door she took his arm to stop him. Immediately, she dropped her hand as if his touch burned. They watched his mother back down the driveway and drive away.

"Don't forget this." Teddy looked at the huge ring on her finger for several seconds. Then she pulled it off and handed it to him. "We only got it today. I'm sure they'll take it back."

"I need to go now, but this isn't over. I'll call you."

Adam quickly kissed her cheek and left. Teddy knew their show for the parents had become so natural that his kiss was still part of the charade. She couldn't see a need for further conversation. They hadn't wanted a relationship from the start. Now that everything was out in the open, there was no need to do anything except hope they could mend the open rift with their families.

She watched as the second car in her driveway exited and headed in the same direction as the previous one. Back in the living room, her mother was standing in the same spot.

"Can we talk?" Teddy asked.

"Is there anything more to say?"

"I'm sorry," Teddy began.

She could see emotions playing across her features, then disappear as a new one replaced the last.

"I know you're disappointed in me. But I had a good reason. At least, I thought I did. I love you and I only wanted to please you."

"You thought a fake romance would please me?"

"You were so happy when you thought we were dating. When Adam proposed, I thought your heart would jump out of your chest."

Her mother looked down at the floor, then back at Teddy. "I was. I thought you'd finally found the man of your dreams and instead of running everyone else's wedding, you could finally have your day."

Teddy moved to where her mother stood. Only a foot separated them. "That happened, Mom." She took a moment to swallow.

The expression on her mother's face turned from confusion to apprehension and finally to understanding.

"You *are* in love with him." She said it like a person struggling with a foreign language, and comprehension finally made all the words make sense.

Teddy nodded, unable to speak over the lump clogging her throat. "He doesn't know. It wasn't part of the plan. But it happened and there's nothing I can do about it."

Mother and daughter gazed at each other for a long moment. Then Gemma Granville pulled her daughter in her arms and held her as if she were a five-year-old who'd scraped her knee.

"Come on, let's make some tea," her mother said. "You can tell me all about it, starting at the beginning."

Two days later, Adam couldn't remember the details that followed the conversation with his mother and Teddy's. What was burned into his visual memory was that Teddy had asked who Chloe was and the question went unanswered.

Adam had told her about Veronica, told her he'd been married to Chelsea, but never had he mentioned that he'd been about to marry a second time. Teddy was honest with him, but he'd held back. The reason didn't matter. He was no longer hurt by Chloe. Just as Veronica was old news, Chloe had found her place in the far reaches of his mind. Her betrayal no longer stung. He had no feelings for her, yet he'd kept her a secret. Everyone did, except Quinn. Quinn would mention Chloe's name, but the rest of his family took their cues from Adam and never mentioned her. They all knew how hurt he'd been by her that they'd agreed to his unasked request to never mention her.

Sitting in his family room, he could see Teddy everywhere he looked, even on his phone. The image of her in the wedding gown at the fashion show came up when he selected her number. She smiled from the small screen, innocent of the news that would change her opinion of him forty-eight hours after that photo was snapped.

In his hand was the engagement ring he'd bought her. Despite what people said about diamonds being cold, he could feel the warmth, Teddy's warmth. He felt like a heel, an idiot, a jerk. Putting the ring on the table, he lifted his coffee mug and took a drink.

He told her he'd call. But he hadn't. It had been two days since he talked to her. Adam had opened his phone a hundred times and gone to her number, her photo, but he couldn't bring himself to press the call button. What could he say? Would she understand? Could he make her understand?

Staring at her photo, his heart ached. He never wanted to hurt Teddy, yet somehow he had. He'd broken her trust. It didn't matter that their relationship wasn't real. It didn't matter that they weren't really engaged or getting married. They had a deal. They'd made a pact and he'd held out on her.

Adam jumped as the phone in his hand rang. He expected Teddy's photo to disappear and the caller ID photo to show up, but it remained on the screen. It was *her*. Adam swallowed hard. He wanted to talk to

Teddy, but he wasn't ready. The phone rang a second time and a third. If he didn't answer now it would go to voice mail.

He pressed the answer button and said hello.

"Hi," Teddy said. Adam sat forward in the chair, pressing the phone closer to his ear. His heart was beating so fast he could hardly hear her. Yet the sound of her voice lifted his spirits.

"How are you?" he asked.

"I'd like to talk to you."

"I think that's a good idea. Should I come over?"

"No," she said.

"No?"

"I'm outside. Can I come in?"

Adam was at the window of his condo in a second. He looked down on the parking lot. Teddy looked up at him, holding her phone to her ear. He signaled for her to come up and immediately went to open the door.

When she entered the town house, he forced himself not to rush to her and gather her in his arms. She came inside and Adam took her coat, throwing it over the hall banister before leading her into the family room. The sun was setting and the room had become dark.

Teddy looked around. "The fire's dying," she said.

Adam didn't remember making a fire. He went to the hearth and added more of the liquid that burned the crystals. Sparks flew up but died quickly.

"I talked to my mother," Teddy said when he turned around. She was sitting on the sofa where he'd been only a few moments ago. "We're back to being friends. I told her everything." Teddy paused. Time stretched between them as if they were ex-lovers who hadn't seen each other in years and were at a loss for what to say after "hello." Teddy lifted his glass and took a sip of his coffee.

"I talked to mine, too. We're walking on eggshells."

"Do you think you'll work it out?"

"I'm going to try."

She smiled and he knew she approved. Teddy picked up the ring he'd left next to his coffee mug.

"I see you didn't return it," she said.

Adam shook his head.

"Why not?"

"No reason. I haven't been back to the store."

"But you are taking it back?" Teddy questioned.

Sitting down next to her, he said, "I've gotten us into a fine mess."

She nodded with a smile. "It's too bad we didn't just fall in love and make everything real."

Adam stared at her. He wanted to tell her that he had fallen in love with her, but her statement told him the love was one-sided.

"That would have solved all our problems." He paused a moment and took a drink. "But that didn't happen."

"No, it didn't."

He felt they were talking like two people who wanted to say something but were refusing to do so. He knew it was his turn to explain. Setting his mug on the table, he faced Teddy and took one of her hands.

"Chloe," he said, speaking only the one word.

Teddy waited.

"I should have told you about her."

"I understand that we didn't tell each other everything about our past. The point is moot now," she said. "Since the proverbial jig is up, I don't need to know."

Adam kept her hand in his. He ignored her comment. He wanted to tell her about Chloe. Other than Quinn, no one knew the whole story.

"It was a fairy-tale romance. We met at a picnic the year before I got out of college. Remember what that was like?"

Teddy nodded.

"Did you have a boyfriend that year?" he asked.

"Yes," she said, but didn't elaborate.

"I didn't have a girlfriend," Adam admitted. "I went out with many women, but there was no one special. Then there she was, sitting on the sand, all golden and brown. She was like honey to a bee and there was an entire hive of bees buzzing around her. I didn't think I had a chance. So I looked but didn't enter the fight for her attention."

"Before you knew it she was standing somewhere near you." Teddy completed the thought for him.

"Something like that," he said. "How did you know?"

"It's a woman thing." She left it at that.

"We didn't see each other after that. I met and married someone else. When that dissolved, I started my business. Getting it off the ground took all my time. One day Chloe came in with her aunt to talk about estate planning."

"You started seeing each other," Teddy stated.

Adam nodded. "I was working night and day, but she was there when I had free time. She was supportive, fun, easy to talk to. She even helped out just to be with me. I thought she was so different from Chelsea. She was interested in the business, interested in me."

"And so you fell in love," Teddy suggested.

"We did. And we were planning our wedding. We didn't have the white lace and orange blossoms. We were just going to go off one afternoon and get married."

"But that never happened?" Teddy questioned.

"We'd been dating a little over a year," Adam said.

He stopped and Teddy waited. Adam knew she thought there was more to the story. And there was.

"What happened?" she asked.

Even now, five years later he still found it hard to talk about. "Chloe was having an affair with another man. I found them together. We argued and she walked out on me."

Teddy gasped. "I am so sorry."

Adam didn't want to go on, but knew he had to. "When she left, we were both angry. She jumped in the car and took off. I thought she was alone but found out later she was with a guy. Less than a mile from our apartment, there was an accident. She'd driven too fast and lost control. It hit a telephone pole. Both of them died. The autopsy revealed she was pregnant. The child wasn't mine."

"Oh, my God," Teddy said. She reached for him, hugging him close and holding on, giving him the support he needed. "I can't imagine how you must have felt."

"It was hard for a time," he said. He kept his arms around her, took in the smell of her hair, the softness of her body. Teddy was nothing like Chloe. She was her own woman, with her own goals. She didn't attach herself to anyone like Chloe had done to him. Chloe had been content to hang on to his coattails, let him do the work and support her. She'd had little ambition and as soon as the ring was on her hand, she'd never come to the office again. Adam wondered if she'd ever loved him or if he just happened to be the one with the most potential.

He didn't look at Teddy. He knew he was in love with her, but she also scared him. Chloe had done a number on him and it wasn't Teddy's fault, but after his experience with his wife and then Chloe, could he trust another woman the way he'd trusted Chloe? When he'd taken his vows before God and their friends, he'd meant them. He fully expected to spend his life making Chelsea both rich and happy. That had changed. Then Chloe had come along and he felt as if this was real love. But that had collapsed, too. Veronica added to his vase of black roses. Like Chloe she'd betrayed him. But she didn't have her claws as deeply into him as his ex-fiancée had.

"I know what happened to you is hard to deal with," Teddy said. "And now I think I understand your mother better."

"My mother? How's that?"

"Chloe broke your trust. You were younger, less

experienced with the world. You grew up in that moment."

"I can't argue that," he said.

"You also decided to go it alone. Women weren't trustworthy. Even when you loved them, they would let you down."

Adam had never heard it put that way before. "That's not altogether true. I went out with plenty of women. I just never found the right one." He challenged Teddy's characterization.

"You didn't really want to. You used your job as a crutch to end a relationship. You used your past relationships as a reason to not risk your heart on another disappointment."

"I've been out with you more than any other woman," he said.

Teddy smiled. "Because I'm safe. We had an agreement from the beginning. There was no chance of us getting close to a relationship. No danger of me stepping across your line in the sand. No risk of me challenging your heart."

How wrong she was, Adam thought. She'd affected his heart more than any woman ever had. And that included Chloe. Adam couldn't say when it happened, but it had.

"You said something about my mother."

"Your mother's quest is to help you find someone to replace Chloe in your heart."

"I assure you, Chloe is no longer in my heart."

"Maybe," she said. "Maybe not."

"What about you?" Adam asked. "Is that guy still in your heart?"

"Chad? He was, but he's no longer part of my life. And he has no hold on me anymore."

He patted her hand. "We are a pair."

"But not a couple."

Chapter 10

Snow showed up for the holidays. It came down heavy, coating the ground and everything in its path. It was white and beautiful, but for Teddy it only added to her depression. By December 15, there were several layers on the ground and more coming.

She was in no mood for shopping, but staying home was worse. She opted for the shopping mall. She meandered through the stores, looking but not buying anything. Her mind wasn't on finding the perfect gift for loved ones. She'd had her gift. Had it and lost it. She looked at her naked hand. The engagement ring had been on her third finger only long enough for her to understand how much she'd miss it. While it had only been there a matter of hours, she now felt as if part of her hand had been removed.

Still, she had her love for Adam and there was nothing that could top that.

Nothing could change things, either. Picking up a purse, she opened it, thinking of her sister Sierra. Purses were Sierra's thing. A moment later Teddy shook her head and replaced it in the display. She had only ten days to finish her shopping, but she wasn't going to make any headway today.

Leaving the shopping mall, Teddy walked slowly to her car, unmindful of the falling snow. Her body was covered by the time she opened the door and slipped behind the wheel. As she pushed the ignition button, her phone rang. The radio panel lit up, indicating a call from Adam. Her heart jumped and she let out a small cry of delight when his name appeared on the screen.

What was wrong? she wondered. They had talked about things and parted. They were not a couple. Why was he calling? She pressed the screen, accepting the call.

"Yes," she said.

"Teddy?"

"Yes."

"Are you all right?"

Adam's voice caught her off guard, even though she knew he was calling. "I'm fine."

"Are you in your car?"

"Yes," she said.

"You're driving in this weather?"

She looked around the parking lot. Despite the snow, the lot was full. "Not yet. I just got in the car."

"Where are you?"

"At the mall. I went Christmas shopping." She didn't tell him she bought nothing. She didn't ask why he was calling. She only wanted to continue hearing his voice. "Where are you?"

"Home."

Teddy had nothing else to say. Time stretched between them.

"I'm calling about the invitation," Adam said.

"What invitation?"

"You've forgotten," he stated. "We were invited to Stephen and Erin's holiday party, the guy from my office. Is that still on?"

"You're right. I did forget."

"I know we're no longer pretending to be engaged, but we did accept the invitation. Do you think we should go or cancel?"

Her heart sang. She could spend another night with him. Maybe he'd look at her differently. She was no longer a means to an end. Maybe they could just go and enjoy themselves. Maybe they could begin again.

"Like a first date?" she teased, not knowing if her words would really sound that way through the wireless technology.

She heard him laugh. "We never did really have a first date, did we?"

"We'll go then?" she said.

"We'll go. I'll pick you up on Saturday at eight."

"I'll be ready," she said. They rang off. Teddy put the car in gear and drove to the offices of Weddings by Diana. She was suddenly grateful for all the December weddings. Grabbing her purse, she got out. Her feet practically flew through the snow.

She needed a new dress, and this was just where she could get it.

The suits Adam had chosen and discarded numbered six. Ralph Lauren, Hugo Boss, Gucci, Prada, Dolce & Gabbana, and Giorgio Armani lay on the bed, one or two having slipped to the floor. He held a Versace in his left hand and a Brioni in his right. Brioni won.

He wore excellent brands for client meetings, but tonight he wanted to look his best. It had been a while, a long while, since he dressed to impress. Yet he wanted to impress Teddy. Adam pulled the suit off the hanger and began dressing. He shrugged into a dress shirt and collected the cuff links Quinn had brought him back from Ireland three years ago.

Once he and Teddy's secret was out, things between them had fallen off track. He missed seeing her. They had been together for months, seen each other practically daily. He liked the way she laughed, how she seemed to pull life toward her and not complain about it. He liked that she embraced family. He liked that she coaxed him into remembering how happy a Christmas tree could make him. And their lovemaking was beyond describable. She was more than he expected and he wanted to keep seeing her. Maybe tonight they could compromise. Begin again. This time without the interference of parents. They could take it slowly. He was willing to go as slow as she wanted, *if* she wanted it at all.

The thought stopped him in his tracks.

He remembered their first night together. Neither wanted to go on a blind date, but even then he realized there was something about her that drew him. As time went by, seeing her more and more became the right thing to do. Then the revelation ripped them apart.

A pair, not a couple, she'd said. They were back to their normal lives. Only, for Adam, things were no longer normal. He wanted a new normal. He wanted to spend his days and nights with her. He wanted to go where life led them.

Tonight would be the first step.

By Saturday night Teddy had completely altered the designer gown. Standing in front of her bedroom mirror, she surveyed herself. The gown was chiffon. Christmas-green in color. The strapless bodice was completely made of green and white bugle beads. The skirt swished about her legs as if it wanted to dance. Her waist was defined by a wide red ribbon that formed a rose at the base of her back, its streamers falling to the floor in two sharp points.

She'd pulled her hair up on the sides and secured it with beaded combs that matched the gown. Curls cascaded down her back. Catching a wayward strand, she secured it and turned toward the door.

Adam was waiting for her downstairs. He looked up when he heard her footsteps. Words must have escaped him for his mouth dropped open and he stared at her as if he'd never seen her before.

"I'm sorry I kept you waiting," she said.

He came to her, taking her hand and looking her up and down. "It was well worth it."

Teddy heard a wealth of meaning in those few simple words. He leaned forward and touched her cheek with his.

"Clearly you'll be the best-looking woman at the party tonight."

"You think so?" she asked.

"I know so."

"Then undoubtedly we'll be the couple of the evening because you look good enough to eat."

The expression on his face darkened. She could see need flood his eyes. Teddy felt her own body begin to arouse.

"We'd better go," Adam said. "Although I would like nothing better than to skip the party and stay here."

Teddy wanted the same thing. "Would Stephen really mind if we didn't show up?"

Adam stared deeply into her eyes. "He'd consider it a snub. And I'm not sure what message it would send to the staff."

"Then we'd better go. We wouldn't want to start any rumors."

She reached for the coat she'd left lying over the sofa. Adam picked it up and held it for her. Teddy slipped her arms inside and Adam pulled it up onto her shoulders. His hands rested there for a moment. Teddy leaned back into him. Her eyes closed at the feel of his body. She remembered it, knew it, yearned for it. He encircled her upper arms and together they stood as one for a moment.

Teddy turned in his arms and lifted her head. She was about to tell Adam to let Stephen stew, when he stepped away.

The snow had stopped, but there was a layer still on the ground. The party was in full swing when they arrived. Adam introduced her to the hosts and they got a drink.

"These are the people you work with?" Teddy asked.

"A few are clients, but mainly it's the office personnel."

"So who's minding the store? I thought you ran a twenty-four-hour operation."

Taking a sip of his drink, he said, "There's a skeleton crew on duty. Things move slowly this time of year."

"Stephen has a beautiful home," she commented, looking around at the colonial. The decorations were beautiful and it appeared he had children. There were photographs on several of the tree ornaments.

"Shall we dance?" Adam interrupted her thoughts. She set her glass on a nearby tray and he took her into the room that had obviously been cleared for dancing. Couples were already on the floor and a DJ was handling the music.

In Adam's arms she floated away. Closing her eyes, she matched his steps. Just as she predicted, the dress danced. Teddy was only the medium who wore it, and she was the one feeling the security of being held by Adam. She took in the smell of his cologne, allowing the heady mixture to rekindle the sensations he brought out in her. Her mind wasn't thinking straight, but she had enough mental capacity left to let her know they were on a dance floor and not alone in her house or his condo.

When the music ended, she wished they could leave. She wanted to be alone with him, spend what little time they had left together, not in the midst of other people. Teddy noticed a woman looking at them. She smiled. The feeling that maybe the woman knew Adam suddenly made her jealous.

"Who is that?" she asked.

Adam looked in the direction Teddy indicated.

"She's a business associate. She works for the Princeton office of a large financial corporation. Why?"

"She's staring at us as if she knows a secret. Have you two dated?"

He smiled. "Jealous?"

The obvious hope in his voice wasn't lost on Teddy, however, she suspected it was laced with sarcasm. She reminded herself they were only here because of a previous agreement.

"You didn't answer my question."

"The answer is no. I never dated her."

Teddy looked back. The woman was gone. In her wake, she'd left a question in Teddy's mind. She put it aside and concentrated on Adam.

"Is this party an annual thing?"

Adam nodded. "Stephen and his wife have hosted it each year since he came to work for me. Even before then."

"Have you come each year?"

"Most of them. There were times when I was out of the country, but if I was in town, I was here."

A steady stream of people came over to talk to Adam. He introduced her each time. He was the owner so it was natural that people would seek his attention. Teddy was getting a bad feeling as the night wore on. She thought they were more interested in her than in talking to Adam. Yet she didn't feel that it was the kind of curiosity about who the boss was seeing. There was an undertone she couldn't define.

After several conversations, Adam asked her to dance again. She went easily into his arms. That was where she wanted to be. They danced the same as before, only this time Teddy kept her eyes open and checked the other dancers. She noticed several people turning to stare at them and then whispering. She wondered what was wrong.

Excusing herself, she went to the ladies' room to check her makeup. Before she turned the corner she'd been directed to, she heard two women talking. And then she knew the reason for all the stares.

"Did you see her?" someone whispered.

"I did. She's stunning. I can see why Adam has her on his arm," another woman spoke.

"I wish he'd put me on his arm," the first one replied.

"If you have to compare yourself with her, you'd lose every time. This flavor has all the others beat by a mile."

All the others, Teddy was appalled. Arm candy! They thought she was arm candy.

Teddy wanted to say something, confront the two women. She wanted to let them know that she had a brain and that she and Adam were not an item. But what could she say? She didn't really know Adam. They had exchanged things about each other, about their pasts, but they hadn't talked about common interests. She knew women fawned all over him, obviously staring at him even when she walked with him. She didn't know his past. Other than Chelsea, Chloe and Veronica—and Veronica was definitely eye candy—Teddy didn't know that he'd dated enough women that his employees considered them nothing but the current fruit of the season. This included her. And she didn't like it. She didn't want to be lumped together with an invisible class of women who were interested in nothing more than being seen with a good-looking man.

When she reentered the party, she ran into Stephen.

"Having a good time?" he asked.

"Wonderful," she lied, but her smile was in place. Calling on her customer service background, she didn't want to let him know how she really felt.

"Let me get you a drink."

They weren't far from a bar that had been set up for the night. "White wine," she said, and Stephen raised his finger indicating he'd like one, too.

"Adam says you have this party every year," she opened with the first thing that came to mind.

"We do. My wife says it reminds her of the parties she went to during this time when she was younger."

"We used to go to a lot of parties during this season, too," Teddy told him.

"Now we work all the time," Stephen said.

"Adam said his hours are erratic."

The bartender set their glasses on the bar and they took them, moving away so another couple could order drinks.

"His are. For the rest of us, he tries as much as possible to keep us on domestic accounts so we can go home at reasonable hours."

"Doesn't leave much time for a social life," she said under her breath, then realized he heard her.

"He does all right," Stephen said.

Teddy decided to change the subject. She didn't want any of her feelings coming through after what she'd heard earlier.

"You like working for Adam?"

He nodded. "It's the best job I ever had. And even though I have some late nights, it's worth it."

Teddy looked past Stephen to where Adam stood. He was in the middle of a crowd where a lively discussion was going on. She noticed the two women she'd heard earlier were part of the group around him. She wondered which one wanted to be the arm candy.

"You're a wedding consultant," Stephen stated.

She nodded, taking a sip of her wine.

"From what I can tell, you're doing very well."

"What does that mean?" she asked.

"We've done some research into the financials. You seem to be on solid ground."

"Did Adam order that?"

"Not directly. We keep track of many small businesses. 'Small' means under twenty million in assets.

Weddings by Diana crossed my desk. But since you aren't a client, we're limited to only public information."

Teddy threw another glance at Adam. The crowd had moved away and he was coming toward her. Stephen's wife reached them at the same time.

"Adam, congratulations. I just heard you two are engaged." She looked from him to Teddy and back. "I must admit, I didn't think anyone would get you."

Teddy looked at the floor, then back up.

"We're not engaged," Adam said.

"You're not, but I…"

"We're not," Teddy confirmed.

"I'm sure there's a stadium of women who'll be glad to hear that," Stephen said.

Teddy felt the color drain from her face. Stephen's wife poked him in the side.

"I apologize," he said. "I didn't mean that the way it sounded."

"It's a long story." Adam protected her from further comments about their engagement. She was obviously embarrassed. "One night after I've had too many drinks, I might tell it to you." He glanced at Teddy. "But right now, I'm going to dance with the most beautiful woman at the party." He smiled at Teddy. She returned it even though there was no humor behind the gesture.

Adam took her arm and they headed for the dance floor, leaving a surprised host and hostess behind them. As soon as he turned her into his embrace, he said, "You and Stephen were deep in conversation."

Teddy missed a step and her shoe ended up on his.

"Sorry," she said and resumed. She placed her head next to his so he couldn't see her face.

"What were you talking about?"

"Working conditions, financial research and you." She tightened her arms.

Adam probably felt the change in her. She was stiff and she clutched him too close.

"Are you all right?" he asked. His voice was right at her ear.

She shook her head as much as she could move it. "I want to go," Teddy said.

"Why? What happened?"

"Please, let's leave."

"Don't let what Stephen said upset you."

"It's not Stephen," she said.

Adam sighed. "I'll say our good-nights and get your coat."

The woman Adam helped into the car was a direct opposite of the one who'd gotten in three hours ago. Silently they drove back to her house. Teddy didn't wait for him to come around and help her out. She stepped into the snow, unmindful of her shoes or the care she'd taken for their first date.

"Are you going to tell me what happened?"

Teddy reached her door and opened it. Inside Adam closed it and waited for her to speak.

"Why don't we just forget everything. The engagement is over. The party is over. We've completed our commitments. Let's just say goodbye and forget this ever happened."

"No." His voice held a finality to it. He was not

going to be easily pushed aside. "You talked to Stephen and everything changed. What did he say?"

"Stephen said nothing out of the ordinary. He told me about his job, about researching Weddings by Diana."

"And that upset you?"

"It's not about Stephen!" she shouted.

"Then what? His wife was misinformed about the engagement and the comment about a stadium of women..."

"It was none of that." Teddy looked at Adam. "Good night," she said.

Adam stared at her as if he could force her to explain. Teddy opened the door and he walked out.

"Goodbye," she whispered after he'd gone.

The "Wedding March" began. The doors opened and the bride and her father stood there. The sound of approval flew up from the crowded church as the congregation stood and the bride began her procession down the aisle.

Teddy felt tears mist her eyes. She blinked them away. This was the second wedding this month and it was the second time since she and Diana began their business that Teddy found herself moved by the ceremony.

She was aware of every word spoken, every sound of the organ, every gasp of the audience. And for the first time Adam's comments came back to her while she watched the bride. *Not once have you ever imagined it would one day be your turn?*

She imagined it now. She wanted to be the bride, wanted to float down that aisle with her one and only waiting for her.

Adam was her one and only.

But for him, Chloe was The One. She was the reason Adam swore off relationships. He didn't even realize it, but Chloe had changed him. She'd taken away his ability to trust anyone except himself. And he didn't realize it. To him, Teddy was only arm candy.

Teddy had felt the same when Chad betrayed her. She hadn't sworn off relationships, but she was much more particular than she had been before. Then Adam walked into her life. Reluctantly at first, but he'd taken up a large amount of space in her heart and he was unaware of it.

How much easier it would be if Veronica had been her competition. Teddy wished she was. Veronica was alive. Chloe was a ghost. Trying to exorcise a ghost was nearly impossible. Chloe had a hold on Adam's mind, and she was unchanging. He probably went through scenarios regularly of what he could have done differently. Why did she take a lover? Why wasn't he enough for her? That was the hardest question. And it had no answer. He couldn't remove the outcome of their argument. She'd gotten into that car and driven too fast. And she would never be there to explain, to relieve him of the guilt he felt over her death.

It was up to Teddy to fill that role. And she was going to do it.

"Teddy?" Renee's voice came through her earpiece. "Are you there?"

Teddy didn't know how many times her consultant had called her name. She was lost in her own thoughts.

"I'm here."

"Is the photographer in place?"

Teddy looked down the long aisle. "He's near the front."

"Good. The bride wanted to make sure there were photos of the actual ceremony."

Teddy knew the photographer. She'd worked with him many times and recommended him whenever asked. "She has nothing to worry about."

"Is everything all right with you?"

"I was a little distracted, but everything is in order."

Teddy had been thinking of Adam. The church wasn't Saint Patrick's Cathedral, yet Teddy continually looked around for Adam. He'd surprised her by showing up for one of her weddings. She wondered, hoped, he would do it again. But the ceremony was practically over and he had not shown.

Skipping the reception, Teddy opted to pack up and drive home. She hoped Adam would be waiting for her. But her driveway was empty when she reached it. They no longer had a reason to meet each other. Their parents knew the engagement was a sham. Adam had a business to run. As did she. Their agreement had come to an end. It was time to move on.

Teddy had been at this crossroad many times. Never had it been a problem to throw herself into her designs. Her concentration might be off for a day, but she would forget and go on. She had a sinking feeling this was not the case today.

Entering the house, she felt an echo of emptiness. She and Adam hadn't been there together that often, but they'd had breakfast in her kitchen, made love in her bedroom, kissed in her living room. Suddenly, she didn't want to be there alone. She could call Diana. Scott was out of town. The two could go for a drink. Teddy shook her head, discarding the idea. She was in no mood to be with other people. Diana would immediately sense her mood and ply her with questions on her feelings for Adam.

Those feelings were in chaos.

She wondered where he was. Was he at his office? It wasn't that late, only a little past seven in the evening. The international markets were open. He could be working. Teddy didn't call any of the phone numbers she had for him. She decided to take a bath and go to bed early, but once she stepped out of the tub, she knew she wouldn't be able to sleep.

Adam was on her mind. Was he all right? Could he be feeling the way she was? The two of them had agreed to a plan and now that was over. So why did Teddy feel as if she'd lost a friend?

Chapter 11

"The Nokamara stock opened three dollars higher than yesterday's closing."

Adam looked up. Stephen Bryant stood in front of him. He hadn't heard anything the man had said. In fact, he didn't know how long he'd been standing there.

"You look sick," Stephen said. "Maybe you should go home. We can handle things here."

Adam sat at his desk. His mind wasn't on business and he wasn't ill. He was aware that his vice president could handle things. In the past few months while Adam spent all his time with Teddy, Stephen had held things down. But Adam was back now. Teddy was in the past. Their agreement was over. Yet he was having a hard time getting back into the swing of office routine.

"I'll be all right," Adam said. "Now, what did you say?"

"Nothing important," Stephen said. "I apologize for what I said at the party."

Stephen had apologized hundreds of time since the party, even though Adam told him he had not offended Teddy. Something had, but still he didn't know what it was.

"Think about going home," Stephen said.

He left and Adam did think about going home, but it no longer felt as if it belonged to him. Teddy's ghost lingered in the rooms. He could almost smell her unique fragrance when he sat on the sofa, hear the smile in her voice when she talked.

"I think you should call her."

This time Adam did hear the voice. He looked up to find Quinn standing in the doorway.

"What are you doing here?" he asked. "Don't you have a job to do?" Adam got up and rounded the desk to bear-hug his brother.

"If you'd look at the calendar, you'd know it's the week before Christmas. Many people take vacation at this time of year."

"And many take it after Christmas."

"But you work 365 days a year. At least you had before Teddy. But now…" He let the sentence linger.

"She and I are done. We were only together to thwart Mom. And we know how that ended."

Quinn whistled. "I'm amazed you're still able to walk around on this earth. Is Mom speaking to you yet?"

"Barely. We've had a few conversations. They were short and stilted."

"I'm sure she'll forgive you soon." He paused. "Especially if you call Teddy and get things back to the way they should be."

"Why would I do that?"

"Because you're miserable without Teddy. You can't concentrate. I bet you haven't really eaten in a while, you look haggard and you said you were in love with her."

"I never said that," Adam protested.

"Not in words, but it's obvious in everything you do and say."

Adam didn't want to hear the answer to the question that was on his mind. But Quinn went on.

"You've begun to lose weight."

Adam looked at himself and then at his brother.

"Only a pound or two, but the spiral has begun. You don't sleep. You look like a dead man walking. So why don't you do yourself a favor and go tell the woman you love her."

"I can't."

"Why not? It's only three little words."

"And it's not like I haven't said them before," Adam said.

Quinn frowned. "There's no reason to think Teddy will be anything like Veronica or Chloe."

"No indication, but there is one problem."

"What's that?" Quinn asked.

"She's not in love with me. She wouldn't even tell me what happened the night of Stephen's party. She said good-night, got out of the car, and I haven't talked to her since."

"You're sure about this? Because from what I saw of the two of you, there was no one else in the room when you were there. I could say the entire planet was inhabited by only the two of you."

Adam knew that was how he felt. When he was with her there was no other world except the one that enclosed them.

"You already bought the ring," Quinn reminded him. "Mom saw it. Even though she was angry, beyond angry—her words—she didn't miss a detail."

"I could talk to her if she isn't at a wedding. She had four of them this month," Adam said.

"And Christmas is coming. And the clocks will stop. And the world will end. Don't put obstacles in your way. It's not like you."

Adam questioned what he was like. Since meeting Teddy, much about him had changed. He supposed falling in love did that to a person. Could Quinn be right? Had Teddy fallen in love with him?

There was only one way to find out.

Adam practiced his speech in front of his bathroom mirror. He repeated it while he dressed in a suit and tie. In the living room, he went over it again while looking for the keys to his car. During the drive to her office, he had committed it to memory and was sure of what he wanted to say. Pulling into the parking lot, panic set in. He hadn't accounted for her replies. He should have a plan for what her responses could be.

But he was too late. Teddy appeared at the door and walked toward him. She smiled broadly and as Quinn had predicted, the world around them disappeared. He couldn't see her curves because of the coat she wore, but Adam knew them intimately, and as she walked into his arms, he encircled her waist and she kissed him on the cheek. He held her a moment longer than necessary, inhaling her perfume and wanting to press her to him until the world tilted back in place.

"Don't you look like a member of the wedding." She stepped back and looked him over.

He knew she was talking about the suit, but the comment affected him as if she'd gone straight for the heart.

"I was surprised to hear from you." He opened the car door and she got in. "But I needed to get out of the office for a while."

"The weddings?" he asked.

"It seems all the brides want to change something at the last minute." She glanced at him as he pulled the car out of the parking lot. "But I don't want to talk about weddings. How have you been?"

"I miss our *dates*," he said honestly. Adam couldn't look at her long enough to gauge the expression on her face.

"They were fun." She laughed. Sobering, she asked, "How are things with your mom?"

"We're talking."

He pulled into the parking lot of his condo.

"We're having lunch here?" Teddy asked in surprise.

"I want to talk to you and I don't want a lot of people around."

Silently they walked up the few steps to the condo's entry. Inside, he took her coat and led her to the dining room.

"Wow!" Teddy said.

The table was set for two with candles lit and the food hot and ready. A flower arrangement made of pine branches, Christmas holly and mistletoe sat in the center, replacing the silver bells that she'd set there. The napkins were folded into shapes that looked like white doves. Christmas music played softly in the background. Everything was as he'd ordered it.

"How did you do this?" She smiled, obviously pleased. She touched the silverware and bent to smell the pine in the centerpiece.

Adam smiled, too. Involuntarily, a lightning bolt went through him. Forcing himself to stand his ground, he remembered his speech, but it wasn't time yet. He wasn't comfortable. This was unchartered ground and he found it hard to relax. "I had it catered. Quinn was here to supervise. He ducked out the moment we pulled in the lot."

Teddy nodded her approval.

"This looks like a very special occasion."

"Sit down."

He helped her into the chair and took his seat next to her. She opened the cover on her plate. "Duck à l'orange," he supplied.

"This conversation must really be something important," she said, taking a bite of the food. Her eyes swept down, revealing her appreciation of the succulent meat. Adam loved the way she did that. He'd seen her in the throes of passion and this compared with that expression. The thought aroused him.

Tamp it down, he told himself.

"You like the food?" Adam said.

"I love duck à l'orange." Teddy took another bite. "And this is excellent. Who catered this?"

One hurdle reached, he thought. This was the opening. It was what he was waiting for, but every word he'd practiced disappeared as if it was in a foreign language. One he didn't speak.

"Adam," Teddy called him.

"I'm getting married," he blurted out.

She didn't choke, but she came close. "What!"

"I'm thinking of having this as an entrée at the reception."

"Reception?" Teddy dropped her fork. It clattered against the china before settling on the white tablecloth.

"I'm getting married again. I'd like to hire Weddings by Diana to plan the wedding."

She sat back in the chair. "I should have brought a pad for notes," she said flatly. "I suppose congratulations are in order." She stood up, taking her wineglass with her as she moved away from the table. She hadn't touched it since they sat down, but must have needed it now. Raising it, she toasted him. The drink she took was long. She drained the glass and set it down next to her uneaten food. Turning away from the table, she moved to the archway between the kitchen and dining room. "Shouldn't I talk to the bride about the services we provide?"

"I'm sure you know them well enough to choose."

"I don't understand."

Adam moved from his seat at one end of the table to come and stand in front of Teddy. Taking her hands, he pulled her close.

"I love you," he said. "Quinn says you're in love with me, too. Is it true?"

Her eyes widened. They were clear and he held them, waiting for her to say something.

"I thought you weren't looking for a wife, just someone to please your mother."

"That was true in the beginning."

"And now?"

The words were delivered slowly, but the weight they carried was immeasurable. "Now I know she chose the right woman for me," Adam said.

"Are you sure?" Teddy asked. "This isn't another one of your schemes to get back into good graces with your mother, is it?"

Instead of answering, Adam put his hands on both sides of her head and pulled her mouth to his. He felt her surrender almost immediately. Her arms went around his waist and he deepened the kiss. His tongue swept into her mouth, drinking in the taste of her.

He felt as if years had passed since the last time he had her in his arms, since he could take in the smell of her shampoo, since he could revel in the nectar that was uniquely hers. Frenzy overtook him and he devoured her mouth. He wanted to get closer to her, wanted to speak to her through his kisses, through the texture of her hair, the smoothness of her skin. He wanted all of her.

Raising his head, he mumbled against her mouth, "I love you. I think I have since the first night we met." His voice was breathy, forcing him to speak in staccato measures. He looked deeply into her eyes. "You were leaving the restaurant and I didn't want you to go. I couldn't let you walk away so quickly. Despite the setup by our mothers, I felt the spark."

He kissed her again. Quinn had to be right. There was no way she could kiss him like this and not feel something for him. No way she could look at him the way she did and not feel the same way he did.

This time she pushed him back. Dropping her head, she took a long breath, then looked directly in his eyes. "I love you, too," she said.

Adam thought his legs would give out. He'd longed to hear her say it, but he was unsure until this very moment.

"I thought you were against marriage," Teddy said. "You told me that the first night we met. Then there's Veronica and Chloe, women who broke your heart and made you mistrustful of women."

"I know." He remembered their conversations, yet his voice held a bit of humor. "They tainted my views for a while, but there comes a time when you have to take a chance. Risk whatever is necessary for the promise of happiness."

"You're willing to do that for me?"

"That and more," he said, dropping a kiss on her nose.

"I don't think there will be much risk," Teddy assured him. "I love you and nothing will change that."

"There's only one thing missing," Adam said.

"What?"

He released her for a moment and went to the table in the living room. Retrieving a small box from the drawer, he brought it back to her. Adam lifted the black velvet cover. The Varrick name was emblazoned on the inside lid.

"My ring," she said.

He removed it. "You will marry me." He stated it as a foregone conclusion.

"I will," Teddy said.

He slipped the heavy stone on her finger. This time it meant more to both of them than it had in the past. When they chose it, Teddy had protested. But this time their engagement was real and the ring was real.

They sealed the engagement with a kiss.

The bed wasn't just in disarray. It had been destroyed. The sheets were hanging off the sides or completely removed from the mattress.

Adam caught one of the linens and covered them with it. Teddy's heart was beating double time, her body was bathed in a sheen of sweat, but she was happier than she'd ever been.

Adam lay beside her, cradling her in his arms, one hand on her breast. She'd asked herself if their lovemaking would equal the first time. Then the second. Would it always be this intense, this thoroughly satisfying? She couldn't answer that, but she hoped it would.

"You know no one is going to believe us when we

tell them we're engaged," she told him. Her voice was deep with sexual satisfaction.

He nodded against her hair. "They'll think it's another trick."

Teddy stretched her hand out admiring the ring. "We can't even show them a different ring." She laughed. "Maybe they'll believe us on our tenth anniversary."

"Do you want a different ring?"

He pushed back and looked over her shoulder. "Absolutely not."

"Whether they believe it or not, we'll know," Adam said and pulled her back closer to his naked body. Teddy felt the rise in heat, the familiar burn that accompanied arousal.

She turned over. He brushed her hair from her face and gazed at her. She could see the need in his eyes, feel the desire in the strength of his body.

"Your hair is a complete mess," he whispered as he threaded his fingers through it. Over and over, he combed the strands as if they were gold. His mouth kissed her face, skipping from place to place.

"I have you to thank for my messy hair," Teddy said. "Thank you." Her murmur was low and sexy, conveying everything she felt, everything that he brought out in her.

Adam took a moment to stare at her. Tension built within her as he watched, held her with only his eyes for a thousand years. Teddy's mouth went dry. She licked her lips to wet them. He lowered his mouth, replacing her tongue. Their lips mated and clung. Arms and legs circled and entwined, bringing their bodies into alignment. Teddy ran her legs up and down against him, touching in the most intimate way. Fire sprang up like meteors hitting the ground. She ached for him, to have him close, inside her, to feel the presence of his body joined with hers. She wanted the unbottled elixir they created. It was around them, holding them together. It was not for sale and had a shelf life of less than an hour, but it generated feelings so strong and so passionate that Teddy could die from continued exposure. Yet she wanted the elixir, wanted to open it, relive its effect at any moment of the day or night.

She felt the joy of penetration when they joined, the beginning of a dance that would take her to places never before found by anyone except the two of them.

His body drove into hers and she met him with each deep and soulful thrust. Her hips lifted off the bed, slamming into him, taking him inside to the hilt of his sex, draining whatever pleasure he offered. She took and she gave. Together they determined their own rhythm. It started on an upbeat and went up from there, going from frenzied to wicked as they mounted the levels of hedonism.

The room filled with the electric snap of lovers mating. Waves of emotion thundered inside her, crashing and reforming with the velocity of tidal waves. The seas of a primitive dance swirled and burst into raining fountains. Hands raked her sides and gathered her behind as Adam guided her up and into the heights of mutual love.

Teddy gasped for air but refused to stop the raging storm rocketing through her body. And then a new feeling took over. She was aware of everything about herself, not only the overwhelming pleasure that she and Adam forged, but every blood vessel, every nerve, the feel of Adam's hands on her, the softness of the mattress beneath her, and the deluge of powerful emotions that assaulted her senses and crossed her over into a land of pure sensation. Her scream came loud and long as she reached the height of ecstasy.

Together they fell back to earth, coming down fast and hard. Breath shallow and panting, her heart throbbing, Teddy tried to calm herself. Adam's weight pressed her into the bed, kept her warm. She wanted his weight, triumphed in the compassionate nature of this one and only. His arms enclosed her, holding on to a nebulous thread that bonded them together. For a moment longer, she wanted to resist the slowing of the sensation that connected them.

Adam rolled off her, pulling her into his side. He faced her, his eyes drowsy and his mouth curved in a half smile.

"I love you," he said.

Epilogue

The gown Teddy designed for her own wedding was her best effort ever. She used Viennese lace and bolts of satin. The dress fitted to her waist, the skirt was straight in the front, but the back bustled out into a train that rivaled anything she'd seen anywhere. Pearls and crystals covered the entire dress and glittered in the candlelit church. Her veil draped down her back and extended several feet beyond the train.

The two mothers proved the rule by challenging everything. The bridesmaids' veils didn't match the dresses. Should they wear hats and not veils? It was a June wedding so the men should be dressed in a lighter color, not the traditional black with white tie and tails. They went on and on, and Teddy felt sorry for Lisa, the wedding consultant handling the arrangements. Often she or Adam were called on to provide the deciding vote or to placate the mothers. But when it came to the ceremony, they were there with smiles on.

Lisa had the privilege of dealing with the mother of the bride and the mother of the groom—a fate that certainly proved her worth.

The organ music began. Teddy heard it from the vestibule where she stood. Diana looked at her and smiled. Renee and Teddy's two sisters were her bridesmaids. They gave her a final nod and started down the aisle. Diana, as matron of honor, followed them.

"Well, honey, I promise not to cry, but you look wonderful," her mother said and hugged her. Normally, the mother of the bride began the ceremony by being escorted to her seat by a groomsman. Teddy's father had that honor. Teddy would walk down the aisle escorted by her mother. Teddy had asked her mother to divert from tradition and give her away. Gemma Granville happily cried at the honor.

The "Wedding March" began. Both women looked at each other. Mist was in her mother's eyes. Teddy had heard that music a hundred times at other weddings. Today it sounded for her. Her heartbeat quickened. On the other side of that door stood Adam waiting for her. She loved him more than she ever thought possible. Moments from now they would be husband and wife.

The church was full, adorned with fragrant flowers and lighted with candles. There was a rolled out white carpet strewn with long-stemmed red roses that led to the altar.

Gemma Granville's arm trembled as the two stepped on the carpet and began their walk.

Teddy and Adam pledged their troth and the groom kissed the bride.

* * * * *

OUT NOW!

Farrah Rochon Jules Bennett Carolyn Hector

3 BOOKS IN ONE

TEMPTED UNDER THE *Mistletoe*

Available at
millsandboon.co.uk

MILLS & BOON

LET'S TALK·

Romance

For exclusive extracts, competitions
and special offers, find us online:

- MillsandBoon
- @MillsandBoon
- @MillsandBoonUK
- @MillsandBoonUK

Get in touch on 01413 063 232

MILLS & BOON

THE HEART OF ROMANCE

A ROMANCE FOR EVERY READER

MODERN

Prepare to be swept off your feet by sophisticated, sexy and seductive heroes, in some of the world's most glamourous and romantic locations, where power and passion collide.

HISTORICAL

Escape with historical heroes from time gone by. Whether your passion is for wicked Regency Rakes, muscled Vikings or rugged Highlanders, awaken the romance of the past.

MEDICAL

Set your pulse racing with dedicated, delectable doctors in the high-pressure world of medicine, where emotions run high and passion, comfort and love are the best medicine.

True Love

Celebrate true love with tender stories of heartfelt romance, from the rush of falling in love to the joy a new baby can bring, and a focus on the emotional heart of a relationship.

Desire

Indulge in secrets and scandal, intense drama and sizzling hot action with heroes who have it all: wealth, status, good looks…everything but the right woman.

HEROES

The excitement of a gripping thriller, with intense romance at its heart. Resourceful, true-to-life women and strong, fearless men face danger and desire - a killer combination!

To see which titles are coming soon, please visit

millsandboon.co.uk/nextmonth

MILLS & BOON

MEDICAL

Pulse-Racing Passion

Set your pulse racing with dedicated, delectable doctors in the high-pressure world of medicine, where emotions run high and passion, comfort and love are the best medicine.

Six Medical stories published every month, find them all at:

millsandboon.co.uk

JOIN US ON SOCIAL MEDIA!

Stay up to date with our latest releases, author news and gossip, special offers and discounts, and all the behind-the-scenes action from Mills & Boon...

 @millsandboon

 @millsandboonuk

 facebook.com/millsandboon

 @millsandboonuk

It might just be true love...

GET YOUR ROMANCE FIX!

Get the latest romance news, exclusive author interviews, story extracts and much more!